STRICTLY PROFESSIONAL

KATHRYN NOLAN

That's What She Said Publishing,Inc.

Editing by Faith N. Erline
Cover by Kari March

ISBN: 978-1-945631-28-3 (ebook)
ISBN: 978-1-945631-29-0 (paperback)

011321

For Tom: thank you for possessing me.

1

EDWARD

"I'm terribly sorry," I said, cocking my head to the side. "I'm not sure I heard you correctly. Can you repeat what you said?"

Emily, my girlfriend of two years, looked like a living doll with her smooth, pale skin and striking cheekbones. She pursed her perfectly made-up lips and tucked a strand of golden hair back into its bun.

"We're terminating our relationship," she said. "Once this dinner is concluded, I'll call the movers who have been instructed to pack up the few things I had at your apartment and move them back into mine."

She carefully sliced a thin piece of fish on her plate, popped it into her mouth, and chewed prettily. As always, Emily was aware of who could be watching us. We sat in the middle of Le Bernardin, one of the most expensive restaurants in Manhattan, surrounded by couples having the kind of polite, stilted conversations that passed for intimacy in the world of the extremely wealthy. A bottle of five-hundred-dollar white wine sat on the table. Emily was wearing a set of rare black pearls I'd given her for her birthday last year.

And she was dumping me.

"Sweetheart," I started, tugging at a collar that suddenly felt too tight. "You'll have to forgive me. I had no idea we'd be *terminating* our relationship this evening. So I'm a bit taken aback, to be perfectly honest."

"Well we certainly can't go on like this, Edward, can we?"

I opened my mouth. Shut it. Because I wasn't sure what to say. Go on like what? From an outsider's perspective, Emily and I were a perfect match. Although, in the words of my parents, it was *unfortunate* that Emily was an American.

Of course, she exhibited none of the brash, cheeseburger-eating traits my parents associated with the residents of England's former colony. Plus, she came from a similar amount of wealth, the same blend of old money and new money that the Cavendish family took as a point of pride.

We both inherited money *and* earned it.

"May I ask what's caused this sudden change of heart?" I said.

She surreptitiously glanced at the other couples in the restaurant. "Well," she said, voice low, "there is the sticky issue that I've been sleeping with Stuart for the past six months."

I choked on my wine, coughing into my cloth napkin for thirty seconds before I could compose myself. When I looked up, the tips of her ears were pink, but the rest of her was as refined as always.

"Stuart... my mate, Stuart? Who I play tennis with every week, Stuart?"

"Yes," she said simply as if we were discussing which opera to attend. "That Stuart."

I felt a slow-rolling fury combined with a sickening dread. Because I was pissed at Emily. Bloody *pissed* at Stuart. But I wasn't sure if I was upset to be losing Emily or just anticipating the cold, calculated disappointment of my parents that this ideal relationship was coming to an end.

"*Emily*," I seethed. "You're telling me that for six *bloody* months, you've been..." I stumbled over the word *fucking*. "You've been... *with* Stuart. And you're just now telling me?"

Her eyebrow lifted almost imperceptibly. "Don't get upset, Edward. We're in public."

"*You* were the one who wanted to go out to dinner," I shot back.

The walls of the restaurant were slowly sliding in, trapping me.

"Yes. Because I thought if we were in public you wouldn't make such a scene. Clearly, I was wrong about that." She cut another slice of fish. Took another small bite.

I didn't get angry often. I wasn't *allowed* to feel something as passionate as anger. But I was getting a delicious thrill at the feeling simmering in my veins. I wanted to flip the table, break the wine bottle, yell at the top of my lungs.

"Remember," she said coolly. "We saw quite a few of your parents' acquaintances when we came in. I wouldn't want your outburst getting back to them."

And just like that, I deflated.

I took a deep breath. Pasted on a fake smile.

"You're right, sweetheart," I said, pouring us both another glass of wine. "I had a stressful day at work, and I think I'm just a bit on edge."

Over the years, I'd learned all the tricks to suppressing my emotions.

"That's understandable. And should we discuss the Met Gala next week? We're both supposed to be in attendance, but if we're no longer together, I'd quite like to take Stuart."

I smiled, imagining bludgeoning Stuart to bits with a tennis racket. "Oh, absolutely. You already have your gown and everything. And what shall I tell the Allsworths about their dinner party? Shall I beg off due to illness?"

"Oh no," she said, shaking your head. "Please attend. They are technically your friends, not mine."

"Well," I corrected. "They are technically *Stuart's* friends, so, by all means, why don't the two of you attend?"

Plus, that party was in two days' time, and I planned on still being thoroughly pissed on expensive liquor.

"That's lovely of you; thank you, Edward," she said.

"Right, so, shall we discuss logistics?" I asked, waving the waiter over for the check. Trying to understand how on Earth I'd gotten here, having my world quietly ended in the middle of Manhattan's swankiest restaurant. As Emily discussed the bland details of breaking up, I desperately searched my memories for even the smallest inkling that this was going to happen. Our relationship had never been of the fiery variety, more like two polite acquaintances who liked attending the same social functions. A relationship like the one my parents had.

A relationship that was *expected* of a Cavendish.

And a relationship my parents approved of.

Had Emily been more distant recently? Had I? Christ, we'd had sex just a few days ago, albeit rote and in the dark. Standard. Was she with Stuart afterward? Had she called him?

The fury was coming back, sharp and hot in my veins, and for the first time I wasn't sure I could suppress it for much longer. I nodded along with the conversation, signing the check with a flourish. I stood, holding my hand out to Emily, who took it primly.

"Why don't you take the car? I'd hate for you to keep the movers waiting."

"But how will you get home?" she asked as we stepped out into the wet January air. I took a deep breath of icy wind.

"Oh, don't worry about me," I said softly, taking one last, lingering look at the woman I'd shared my life with for two years. She looked like a complete stranger.

Had she always?

I kissed her cheek, and she patted me kindly on the shoulder.

"Good luck, Edward," she said.

"Same to you," I replied, watching her slide gracefully into the car, apparently unperturbed by the events of the evening.

I adjusted my cufflinks, brushed a stray piece of lint from my sleeve, straightened my tie.

Tomorrow, I'd need to inform my parents and bear their standard level of disappointment that I'd once again ruined my chance at continuing their legacy.

Tomorrow, I'd let myself fully comprehend what it meant that my girlfriend had been so utterly unhappy with me that she'd sought out the company of my friend.

Tomorrow, tomorrow.

But tonight?

I was off to get bloody trashed.

2

ROXY

*J*t was nearing midnight, and the slightly shabby tattoo parlor that I owned was dead yet again.

Outside, the new sign I'd installed six months ago flashed, cheerfully soldiering on even though half the bulbs were burned out. It was *supposed* to say 'Roxy's', but the mismatched bulbs made the sign look like ancient runes instead of letters.

We were dead, and that was a problem. The second problem was the chart I was staring at.

"Tell me what these squiggles mean," Mack said, sitting on a bar stool with a cup of chamomile tea. Mack, short for 'Machete,' was one of my oldest friends. He was a huge, white, bald man. Tattoos covered every spare inch of his body, including his face. He gave off a terrifying first impression, until you got to know him and he started talking to you about the importance of yoga and meditation.

"Well," I said with a sigh. "This squiggle is revenue. This one is profit. This one is expenses."

Mack rubbed his jaw thoughtfully and pointed to the 'profit' line. "Then shouldn't this squiggle be higher?"

I bit my lip. "Yes. Yes, it should."

My laptop sat on a large stack of papers and books – research to finish a paper I had due in two days. I was six months away from finishing my MBA, but so far the fifteen hours a week I spent in classes didn't seem to be helping the *actual* small business I owned.

"It'll grow, Roxy. You'll see. The only way out is through," Mack said, sipping his tea. Mack was the only person in my life who could spout that nonsense at me.

"What way is that?" I asked, smiling grimly and shutting my laptop. I rubbed my eyes, feeling the exhaustion of three tattoo clients, class, and hours of studying settle over my body.

"Oh, sorry. I was just reading the quote on my tea bag," Mack said, flipping it over so I could see.

I laughed, and Mack pulled me in for a hug. "Listen, I hate to run, but Rita expected me home hours ago. Is it okay if I...?"

I gave him a shove. "Go home to your beautiful wife and beautiful children. We're basically cleaned up. It'll take me an hour, tops."

Mack slid his leather jacket on, grabbed his motorcycle helmet. "And you feel okay, locking up on your own?"

I arched an eyebrow. "Of course. It's just me and the hipsters across the street."

Mack opened the door, giving me a mock salute before leaving. I could see a long line of people waiting for the new artisanal ice cream parlor that had opened across the street. Next to it was a new brunch spot and next to that was a pet store that specialized in organic treats.

Five years ago, this block of Washington Heights, a historically Dominican American neighborhood, was mostly older homes, families, and bodegas. But the neighborhood was growing more expensive by the day.

I let out another sigh. Before I'd purchased this parlor, it had been called 'Skull and Bones' and had been run by a real piece of shit named Arrow. It'd been around since the seventies, thriving during New York's seediest years, specializing in vintage sailor tattoos. I'd always admired it, and after finishing my tattoo apprenticeship, I'd applied to be an artist there. I'd been thrilled when Arrow hired me.

And that's when the problems began.

Because Arrow ran a bad shop. It was unclean. Managed poorly. And, worst of all, he treated his customers like shit. It was immediately obvious, within the first few weeks of working there, that 'Skull and Bones' was a sinking ship.

So I'd done something that I now feared was monumentally stupid: I bought it from him. It hadn't been worth much, but it still cost me a small business loan from the bank (and an interest-free loan from my parents). Arrow had been happy to have it off his hands, and now I understood why.

Beyond the utter awfulness of how he'd run his business, there was the cold, hard fact that our block was becoming exponentially trendier. We didn't have succulents in our windows or serve cappuccinos to our waiting customers. We didn't specialize in the hip, new tattoo styles, and we'd been so broke I hadn't been able to afford to change anything inside with the exception of reinstating levels of cleanliness that should have been standard practice for our industry.

But none of that mattered because we couldn't get any customers to come in. Customers were heading toward the newer, nicer shops. A small, rational part of my brain knew that owning a small business (with absolutely no expertise) would be an uphill battle. And I'd happily accepted the challenge.

I was Roxy Fucking Quinn. I ate uphill battles for breakfast. Stomped on problems with my combat boots while shaving my head for the hundredth time.

Except... that profit squiggle was declining. Sharply. Persistently.

And so I'd grimly enrolled in CUNY's Executive MBA program—one year, ten hours of classes a week—thinking it would magically fix all of my problems.

It hadn't.

I turned on an old Misfits album as I wiped down the black leather chairs and cleaned the tattoo guns. Confirmed a few appointments for tomorrow and straightened my desk. Swept the floors and double-checked our inventory of ink. Tried to quiet my anxious thoughts with repetitive motions and loud punk.

Because even with all its problems, I loved this little shop as shabby as it was. It wasn't as brightly lit or cheerful as the newer places, but once I took over I'd filled the walls with black-and-white photos of my favorite musicians and old snapshots of New York City. I hung my art on the walls next to Mack's and Scarlett's, my other artists. It was a hodge-podge of vintage sailor designs (my specialty), surreal landscapes, and intricate black-and-white portraits. It wasn't overly *inviting*... but we were friendly.

We just didn't look it.

And now I was up to my eyeballs in school debt and business debt, and even worse, I'd convinced Mack and Scarlett to come over from other shops. We'd been friends for years, and they trusted me to keep them safe. They relied on me for their paychecks, their reputation, their livelihood.

And I was squandering that trust away.

Exhausted, I hauled my books and papers into my bag and flipped off the music. I was just turning off the lights when the bell rang over the door.

"We're closed," I called over my shoulder although technically we were open for another hour. But I just wanted to kick off my combat boots and crawl into bed.

"Please don't be closed," the customer said, and I turned at the sound of his refined English accent. I narrowed my eyes at his appearance: three-piece, striped suit. Tie only slightly askew. Hair immaculate. Shoes a gleaming crimson.

"We're closed," I repeated. "And I think you've got the wrong place."

The man sighed. "I don't think that I do, actually."

I popped a hand on my hip, smirking. "Yeah, the bank is that way."

I muttered *corporate asshole* under my breath as I gathered the rest of my things and pondered pepper-spraying the man in the bespoke suit and shiny shoes.

"Interestingly, I'm not looking for a bank. I'm looking for a willing tattoo artist to place permanent ink on my body that will help me forget the fact that I was just spectacularly dumped. In public. By my girlfriend of two years."

I stopped in my tracks. Noticed that he was listing, just slightly, against the doorway. My eyes narrowed further, raking over his form. He was white, with piercing blue eyes and light-brown hair. Tall and almost graceful, his broad shoulders also hinted at powerful muscle beneath those fancy threads.

I dropped my bag.

"Huh," I said, sauntering towards him. I didn't miss the way his eyes snagged on my hips. "Let me guess. You're drunk?"

He blushed just slightly. "Let's just say I'm not *sober*. Five strong drinks in. Drunk enough to make a decision I'll regret the rest of my life. Not drunk enough to not want to do it. Does that make sense?"

His accent was doing things to me. Things I'd rather it not do.

"I don't ink drunk dudes," I said, crossing my arms over my chest. "Even if you're only not *not* drunk. This might look like a piece-of-shit establishment, but I take it seriously. This is my business."

The man held his palms up. "Not looking for a fight, um, ma'am? I'm sorry, are you a ma'am? Or a... a miss?" He wasn't joking, but he *was* adorable, and I bit my lip to keep from smiling.

He noticed.

I wondered what else he was noticing or judging: my heavily tattooed skin, bleached-white hair shaved on the sides, septum ring and nipple rings (not that he could see those). I looked like Trouble.

He looked like Wall Street.

A slightly flushed *English* Wall Street.

"Neither," I said. "I'm Roxy."

"Roxy?" His eyebrows arched.

"That's my name," I said. "Why, what's yours? Something dignified like Dilbert?"

He snorted, eyes crinkling at the sides, and my belly tightened. "Good one. I expected something crasser, but Dilbert is good. And no, it's Edward."

Edward. He looked like an Edward. Gentle and polite. Certainly not the kind of man I was typically attracted to—dirty in all the ways that counted. Hard and muscled and silent—the kind of man that liked fucking me in front of my mirror.

Edward looked like the kind of man who would break for tea halfway through.

He plopped down on one of the leather tattoo chairs. "And

you haven't asked me about my very recent break-up. Recent as in three hours before I came in here."

"And you haven't told me what kind of tattoo you thought would obliterate the pain of heartbreak," I said dryly since I'd seen it all before. Had tattooed hearts and names and then inked them over when things went south.

Edward shrugged, lips quirking up. He tried to catch my eye, but I turned away quickly. "I'll tell you my story if you recommend a tattoo."

"That I'm not giving you now, are we clear on that?" I asked.

"Yes... ma'am," he finally said with a slight rasp to his voice that had the fine hairs on the back of my neck prickle.

"Okay, then," I said, sitting primly in the chair next to him. I crossed my legs, and his eyes trailed up my torn fishnet stockings. "Hello?" I snapped, even though I kind of liked the feel of it—a polite perusal.

"I'm sorry," he said, looking genuinely apologetic. "What you should know is that while I *am* a corporate asshole, I'm quite a nice one."

I opened my mouth. Shut it.

"I have excellent hearing, Roxy," he said. My toes curled in my boots. I shifted in my chair, shaking the feeling away. "I come from a long line of corporate assholes. Actually, that's not entirely true. My family comes from old money in England. We own The Cartwright Hotel chain."

The air rushed out of my lungs.

"You're familiar?" he asked.

"You know I am," I drawled, trying to mentally guess how much he was worth. The Cartwright Hotel chain was famously lavish and exorbitantly priced, catering to the mega-wealthy all across the world.

"So, yes, we're both corporate assholes *and* old money. The very worst combination," he said, smiling now.

"Okay, I get it. Don't judge a book by its cover or whatever," I said.

He chuckled in appreciation. "Unfortunately, I do *not* own The Cartwright Hotel in Manhattan. My parents do. I have managed it for them for the past decade. My younger siblings both own their own Cartwrights in various locations."

"They own their own hotels, but you just manage yours?" I asked, catching his clarification.

"Yes," he said, cheeks flushing slightly. "A vital aspect of this rubbish story. My parents, like most people in their extremely privileged position, are only concerned with their *legacy*. Ownership of our own hotels is written into our private trust funds. And that ownership is contingent upon marriage to a suitable partner. Suitable meaning a partner they approve of. And of course, a partner with whom we will reproduce, thereby joyously continuing their legacy."

I snorted—I couldn't help it. "That sounds like a business arrangement, Dilbert. Not a family."

Edward opened his palms face-up with a look of gratitude. "Ah, you understand. It *is* a business arrangement, and as I love The Cartwright Hotel, I'm more than ready to marry an approved partner and receive ownership. Was ready to marry, for example, the woman who just terminated our relationship at Le Bernardin."

"That's a fancy place to have your heart smashed in. And a very *corporate* vision of marriage," I said.

"I am a Cavendish, after all," he sighed. "But I don't want it to seem like Emily and I, over these past two years, didn't... didn't *care* for each other. Even though, and I can admit this to myself now," he said, sliding a hand through his hair and mussing it slightly, "she was likely a she-devil parading around on this earth as a human woman."

"She-devil," I smirked. "Explain."

"Well, she bloody broke up with me at a restaurant and wouldn't even let me get bloody *angry* as she ripped my heart out and stomped on it." He let out a long exhale, and for the first time I saw pain, not levity, in his gaze. I turned around and fired up the coffee pot behind me, pulling out two mugs.

Edward's brow lifted.

"Is this one of those new-fangled tattoo machines?"

"Har har," I said. "It's a coffee pot. Because at some point, after you've bored me with this story of corporate asshole-ry, you're going to need to be sober enough to leave me alone." I nodded towards him. "So, please continue. You were getting to the good part."

He smirked again, rubbing his jaw with his hand. "You've got a real mouth on you, don't you, love?"

"Don't call me love," I said swiftly. "Not the type. And continue."

"Well," Edward said, reaching up to loosen his tie. A small patch of his smooth skin revealed itself, right at the base of his throat. "As I was saying, in retrospect, and granted, it's only been three hours, Emily and I were more like polite friends than a couple in love. And that's the way she treated our break-up. A mutual parting of the ways, although I was shocked to pieces."

"And the sex?" I asked.

His eyes met mine, steady. A cool blue. "Not... like it was. Not like I, I mean... there's a way I think I prefer, to be honest." That blush again.

"Oh... kay," I said, rolling my eyes to cover up the incessant beating of my heart. What kind of sex did he prefer?

I handed him a mug of steaming coffee, and he gave me a

brief look of appreciation. "If this sobers me up, can I have that tattoo?" he said.

"Nope," I said. "And continue."

Edward's fingers continued to loosen his tie. I was salivating a little. Even though he wasn't my type.

Not at all.

"She's always been a bit... cold. Distant. But I guess it's been getting worse, and I never really noticed. Although, I thought, well... I don't know, I thought we might *be* something. Two years is a long time. Especially when the assumption is that you're to be wed..." he trailed off, staring into his coffee.

My fingers itched with the desire to rip this girl's throat out. "And then what?" I asked but softly.

"For the past six months, she's hardly been around. We've attended the proper social functions, of course, and made sure to be featured in the society pages as expected, but we've been lacking a connection. And then, well," he lifted his mug in cheers to me, "tonight, at this very swanky, very elegant restaurant, she told me she'd been shagging my mate for six months."

I choked on my coffee, and he laughed sadly. "Oh, Roxy. I know we don't know each other well—"

"—or at all," I interjected. "And I mean that literally. It's been, what, twenty minutes since you walked in here?"

He laughed again, but it didn't sound as sad. "I like you, Roxy."

"And I think you're really fucking strange," I said, but there was mirth in my voice. Mirth I didn't realize I had for corporate assholes.

"As I was saying, my life feels like a cliché. My girlfriend sleeping with my friend. Who does that? And thus, I had drinks. And got the brilliant idea for a tattoo. Which now you won't even give me."

"Having integrity as a tattoo artist makes me a real monster," I said dryly. "Plus, doesn't this break-up fuck up your plan with your hotel?"

"Yes," he said mournfully. "Yes, it does. I will continue to be my father's puppet and never get to rightfully own the place I love the most."

I tilted my head, thinking. I wanted to tell Edward that the kind of parent that would withhold anything from their child for their 'legacy' sounded like a real fuck-wit. But then Edward shrugged out of his suit jacket and unsnapped his cuff links to shove the material past his forearms.

His sexy forearms.

"I was cheated on," I said and immediately wished I could shove the words back inside my mouth. It'd happened a *long* time ago, and I barely even thought about it anymore, and I wasn't in the habit of sharing intimate stories with strangers.

"Someone cheated on you?" he asked.

"Why do you seem so surprised?" I lifted my chin. "Bad stuff happens to good people all the time."

"Because you..." There was a strained silence as his eyes drifted back to my legs again. He swallowed roughly. "You look like the kind of woman who could cut a man's heart out. Willingly. Maybe feed it to him in a creative twist."

I hid my smile behind my coffee. "I don't know what you're talking about."

"Well, it could be the giant knives you have tattooed on your arms."

I twisted the limbs in question, grinning at the multiple knives inked there.

"Huh," I shrugged. "Well, all I'm saying is, it happens. And it sucks. But the flipside is now you *know* she was a she-devil and can move the fuck on."

Edward reached his mug forward, clinking it against mine. "I feel utterly pathetic, Roxy."

I almost said something cutting then decided against it. "We've all been there. Believe me." Our eyes met. "I know what rock bottom looks like."

"Do you?"

"Absolutely," I said firmly. "Only way out is up." I'd said something similar to my little sister, Fiona, after I'd found out Jimmy had been cheating on me: *I'm so fucking pathetic.*

Edward slid closer, but I didn't want a closer look at his refined, handsome face. The aquiline nose. Steel-blue eyes. I wanted to caress his forehead, shift the hair away.

"Maybe it's because I've been drinking and am filled with despair, but nothing looks up right now. Except permanently changing my body." Edward looked at my skin. "You did it. Why can't I?"

I shook my head. "You'll wake up tomorrow, still sad, but with a tattoo you didn't want. And they don't come off. The despair, though, will go away." I gave him a tiny smile. "Promise."

"Plus, I was going to get it on my arse," he said, and I spit my coffee out. All over his nice white shirt.

"Oh my God," I said. "I'm so sorry." I tried to stand, but he reached out, grasping his fingers around my wrist. Holding me for the merest of seconds.

"Don't," he said.

And I sat back down.

"It's fine, really. It'll be my memory of this lovely night we're having together."

I bit my lip. Was this lovely night really happening?

"Were you really going to get one on your ass?" I asked.

Edward shrugged with a smirk. "You'll never know, Roxy. And now you'll never have the sincere pleasure of seeing it."

3

EDWARD

*T*his wasn't how I envisioned this night going. If someone had told me this morning that Emily would dump me, I would become moderately hammered, and then end up in a tattoo parlor with the most fascinating woman I'd ever met, I would have never believed them.

Roxy was scowling at me. I'd never really been attracted to scowling women before. I *thought* I liked women like Emily—sweet and gentle. Proper. Someone I could take to Sunday brunch and who would enjoy linen shopping.

Although Emily had proven herself to be none of these things.

And now I was sitting on a tattoo chair across from a surly vixen who looked like she'd light a linen store on fire.

Then drag me into an alley and have her way with me.

Which I quite liked the sound of, if I was being honest. Sex with Emily had been quiet. Muted. Boring.

But Roxy was reminding me of my hidden desires. The ones I kept an incredibly tight leash on. Because secretly I'd always wanted wild, dirty, messy fucking. Bared teeth and pulled hair and bruises on my neck.

And Roxy looked like the kind of woman who felt the same way. She had pale white skin covered in intricate and colorful tattoos. Piercings decorated her ears and nose. And dark eyeliner made the green of her eyes even more dramatic.

She crossed her legs again, and I almost dropped my mug. Her fishnet stockings had rips and tears and I had the strangest urge to press my tongue to the gaps in the fabric.

Work open the tears.

Expose her.

"Stop staring," Roxy said, but there was a slight twinkle in her eye.

"Sorry," I said quickly. Was she flirting with me? Was I flirting back? "And I'm sorry I'm keeping you from your... boyfriend? Girlfriend? Husband? Life—"

"Shut up," she interrupted, grabbing my mug. The tips of our fingers grazed each other. "I'm getting you one more cup, and then you're out of here."

She busied herself with the coffee for a minute. "And it's no one. In case you were wondering. Which you were. *So* obviously."

I hid a smile. "How long have you owned this place? And I believe we're at a stalemate with the tattoo, by the way."

Roxy scowled at me again, and I wondered what she tasted like. Everywhere.

"About a year and a half. I bought it from the owner, Arrow, because he was an asshole of epic proportions and was running a shop that was unclean and awful. Would tattoo drunk people and underage people." Roxy shuddered, stirring cream into our mugs before passing mine back. "I didn't... I *don't* know anything about running a business, but I've been learning along the way." There was a proud tilt to her chin.

"When you see something, Roxy darling, you take it," I said, lifting my mug to her.

odded, grateful. "How did you get over when you were
d on? How did you get up from rock bottom?"

xy looked away, and my eyes tracked the graceful tilt of
ck. I felt a swift desire to lean forward and lick her
from collarbone to under her ear. Was that the most
ve spot on her body?

was there somewhere else, somewhere deeper, where
et me lick her?

o you want to know the truth?" she asked, taking off her
and laying it behind her. She was wearing some
g combination of lace and metal.

ease. All I'm working with right now is this horrible
l of anger and regret. Surely it can't be like this forev-
vondered, knowing that I was sliding face first into the
st-tipsy part of the evening.

," Roxy promised, full lips pursed around the word. "It
be. You're too... I mean, you'll move on. Some bland,
woman will sweep into your life and change it for
For the better. And Emily will become a distant
y."

hy does she have to be bland?" I asked. "Roxy, I feel like
judged me too harshly." I laid a palm on my chest and
r pleading eyes until her lips quirked up.

oland, rich banker who you can have bland, boring sex
r the rest of your life," she continued, and I wanted to
ase, no.' Wanted to tear off my restrictive suit and tie
e off into the night. Preferably with her.

ll," I said, pressing my knee against hers. She didn't
Until I meet this bland, rich, banking woman, how am
g on? You still haven't told me what you did."

y looked both ways as if ensuring we were totally
First of all, I can't believe I'm telling you this," she said.
condly, fucking."

"How many gross endearments are you going to try, *Dilbert*?" she asked, and my cock twitched.

"As many as I can... *beautiful*," I replied, and we were definitely flirting now. Which shouldn't have been possible with a break-up barely three hours behind me, but Emily's image was fading by the minute, replaced by Roxy's fire.

"I can see why Emily dumped you now," she said.

"Mean," I said. "And—can I point out—*too soon*."

Roxy sat back down, closer to me now, and I could smell her. Sandalwood, which I wouldn't have thought she'd wear.

"I'm not apologizing. It's past one in the morning, and you've hijacked my entire evening. And I'm not even going to make any money off you because I have integrity," she said.

I rolled my eyes. "Who needs integrity when a drunk Brit wants you to tattoo his arse?" Another small smile, and every time that happened, it made me feel like I'd won a gold medal at the Olympics. No, *two* gold medals. And a silver.

"What was your first tattoo?" I asked, feeling completely out of my element. Not a single member of my family had a tattoo. Or anything beyond an ear piercing.

"Can't show you," she said. "It's in a... private place."

"It's on your arse, isn't it," I deadpanned.

"I'll never tell," she said, coyly.

"Did Emily have tattoos?" she asked. The fury came roaring back. I allowed myself to welcome it.

"Emily? The woman who shagged my mate for months and just told me three hours ago?" I said. "Not that I'm bitter. And no, none at all. Wouldn't have been proper."

Roxy swallowed, and I watched her throat work. "Have you talked to your friend yet? The one she fucked?" she asked.

I shook my head. "I've been too busy with the drinks and the tattoo planning. And I probably won't, to be perfectly honest."

"Why not? Don't you want to confront him? He *fucked* your girlfriend," Roxy said, and I noticed again the sheer number of weapons tattooed on her body. Knives and guns and something that looked like a rocket launcher.

"Maybe I should have *you* confront him, love," I grinned. "Scare the pants right off him, wouldn't you?"

Another haughty tilt of her chin.

"I've been known to hold my own, yes," she said, sipping from her mug. She didn't flinch when I held her gaze. "And it sounds like you avoid conflict."

"I bloody well do," I said. "Have you *met* me?"

"I mean, not really," she said. "It's now been an hour. Not even. I know almost nothing about you. Still."

"Well, it's not the way my family handles things. And, if you must know, *yes,* they are like that family from Downton Abbey."

"Did you grow up under a staircase like in Harry Potter?" she asked, tilting her head.

"Cheeky," I said. "And *no.* Although my parents do own a castle."

Roxy lifted her chin, looking beautiful and deadly in equal measure.

"And we don't go around openly sharing our feelings or fighting like Americans do left and right. Or at least, that's what I've learned from watching *Real Housewives of Orange County.*"

That got me an honest-to-God laugh.

"Tattoo me, Roxy," I pleaded.

"No," she said. "It's not what you *really* want, and you'll only regret it. Plus, I'm still not convinced of your sobriety."

"Shall I walk a straight line for you?"

"No," she said, shaking her head and moving behind the large desk. Shuffling things, putting things away. Cleaning up,

about to send me out. And suddenly, th[...]
wanted more than her hands on me.

Even if they were permanently inking[...]
that I didn't really want.

"I was thinking a realistic heart, you kr[...]
a giant dagger stabbing through it. Maybe [...]
like '*Fuck You, Emily.*'"

Roxy was flipping off the coffee pot. "[...]
what you want, it'll take me a couple of h[...]
Two hours, at least, to actually tattoo it.[...]
corporate assholes in the room, I *worked* al[...]
school. And I'm exhausted."

I wanted to ask her about school but hel[...]

She flashed me a sweet smile I knew[...]
really want it, you'll still want it tomorrow."

"How else do I get over her?" I asked, hat[...]
my voice. The vulnerability. I was trying to[...]
and fun, but the thought of going out into th[...]
too much.

"Edward," she said before settling back[...]
touched mine, but I didn't move it away.

Neither did she.

"This can't possibly be your first break-up[...]

"No," I admitted. "But it is the first time [...]
on. First time I was this shocked. Control, you[...]
I grew up with, and every relationship I've e[...]
tightly *restrained.* My break-ups have been a[...]
ways. And this one was too," I said, think[...]
mature, quiet way we'd gently discussed the[...]
was also..."

"About a hundred different types of f[...]
finished.

My fingers tightened on my mug. "Fucking?"

Roxy shrugged nonchalantly and grinned at me. "Sex therapy. I took home every attractive, single man I met and had my way with him."

"I've not done that before," I said and wondered what other secrets I'd be admitting to tonight.

"Have a one-night stand?" she asked, eyebrow arched. I shook my head.

"Highly recommended for getting over cheating exes," she said, and it might have been my imagination, but she was definitely pressing her knee against mine now.

"Emily would hate that," I said. "She was very scandalized by people who took home perfect strangers. She thought sex should be a civilized act. And only after you've confirmed your partner's pedigree."

Roxy spit a word 'hypocrite' into her coffee.

I liked that she was on my side.

"I'll have to disagree with your Emily," she said.

"Not *my* Emily. Not anymore," I said. "So I guess I should, um, go out and pick up a stranger?" My coffee was one sip away from being done.

"That's my advice," she said. "And if you still want that tattoo? Come by tomorrow, take off those pants, and I'll permanently ink the words *'Fuck you, Emily'* right above your ass."

Before I could stop myself, my palm was on her knee, thumb landing on an inch of skin bared by a tear in her stocking. Roxy stilled, and my heart slammed into my throat.

I pulled back quickly.

"Sorry, um," I stumbled. "Still a bit drunk, I guess." Which was a lie. I'd never been more brilliantly clear-headed.

"It's okay," Roxy said. "Although I will knife you if you do it again."

"Got a thing for knives, love?"

"I do," she said, and I didn't miss the glimmer in her eyes. My brain snagged on a fantasy: a barely clothed Roxy pressing a knife to my throat, one hand wrapped around my cock, her lips bruising mine.

And where in the hell did that come from?

re in a punk rock band. The Hand Grenades. They
nd tour even though they're in their sixties."

d grinned broadly. "Well, that's bloody fantastic."

ned. "Growing up, I think they were a little disap-
 my goth phase. A bit too Morrissey. Not enough
ut I'm kind of a punk now, so they're much happier."

wn at my torn fishnets and leather jacket covered in

k you look lovely. Like some kind of dark angel,"
id softly.

y cheeks heat. "Something like that," I said, clearing
 "But I had a terrible boyfriend who had a friend
n amazing tattoo artist. We lied about my age, I told
 wanted, and the rest is history."

t?" Edward asked.

 motherfucker," I said, and his laughter was like a
f light after drizzling rain. "But I also liked it."
"

ain," I said, remembering how turned on I'd been,
y boyfriend to fuck me in the car afterward. The
essed, ever-so-gently, on the skin that throbbed
nk.

 off on it.

was something about Edward that was causing the
re—to press and push and feel for why I was so
 him.

d be that I had the distinct impression that his
ell-tailored suit covered up a man who was
o let loose his darker passions.

 wanted that accent muttering filthy phrases in

" Edward asked as my hand was suddenly moving

4

ROXY

I had a thing for knives and all kinds of sharp objects. I had a thing for pain and pleasure, edging and release.

Not that I was going to tell Edward that—he'd run out of my shop so fast he'd leave an Edward-shaped shadow in his wake.

Plus, he still didn't look the type.

"Do you need advice for a one-night stand?" I asked, and I couldn't *believe* I'd just told a perfect stranger I enjoyed 'sex therapy.' Not that I was ashamed—not at all—more that I was battling an intense urge to smash my mug to the floor, straddle Edward's hips, and fuck his sexy English brains out.

I had no idea why. And the sex talk wasn't helping.

Remember: stress, numbers, class, homework.

Pushed to my limit. It had to explain it.

Yet here I was pushing *him*.

"I guess I'm not sure what to say to a woman I'm interested in a one-night stand with," Edward said thoughtfully. He swiped his hand through his hair, and a lock of it hung over his forehead. "Is there something you've found to be successful? Do I say, 'hello, I find you quite alluring. Would you appreciate an intimate evening with me?'"

I snorted. "Not unless you want them to fall asleep halfway through that sentence, Dilbert."

"Ouch," he said with a fake wince. "So what do you usually say?"

"I don't do much talking usually," I said. "I know what I look for in casual sex, so I go out specifically to look for it. Once I've chosen my target—"

"—victim—" Edward interrupted, and I bared my teeth at him.

"Lucky winner," I finished, and his smile was illicit. "Once I've chosen the lucky winner, I make sure of a few things."

"Those are?"

I held out my hand, ticking on my fingers. "Make sure they're not in a relationship. Make sure they understand consent. Make sure they're clean and have been recently tested. Make sure they like the same things I like."

Edward nodded like he was taking notes. "What are the things you like? If I can be so bold."

I squirmed, his knee pressing against mine. The scrape of his thumb along my inner thigh had unleashed a fury of sensation, almost making me dizzy. But then he'd apologized politely and let go—instead of grasping my tights and tearing them asunder.

"So now the English gentleman is bold?" I teased.

"Very."

"I like sex to be intense. I like pain. Toys. Restraints. Spanking." I paused. "Dominance and submission..."

"Which do you like better? Dominance or submission?" Edward asked, and there was no mistaking the raw need in his voice.

"Both," I said and watched his knu[ckles]
play bedroom games with Emily?"

"Never. She liked it polite, quiet, an[d]

"And is that what you like?" I watc[hed] ter. Or blushing. Not his eyes locked only thing that existed in this entire u[niverse]

Like he was moments away from barking an order.

"I don't think so, no," he finally rassed to admit I have very limited why even though I'm a grown man a[nd] and every day manage millions of employees, I, well, I don't know how come home with me."

He said 'strange woman' the way

"Hit her with the accent. Chicks l[ove]

"How about a suit and tie? Is tha[t] he asked with exaggerated air quote[s] American accent.

I smirked. "Some chicks enjoy fully improper things you can do wi[th]

He swallowed. "I see." Edward l[ooked] more but instead tossed his head. "[Want] to show me that first tattoo, love?"

"No. But I was seventeen yea[rs] Climbing out of windows, tearing Making out with boys. I was always

"A goth girl?"

I pursed my lips. "Maybe." A [smile tugged] the way, which is funny because aware that I was now freely shari[ng]

"Oh, well, my parents are old punk[s]

"As in...?"

of its own volition, up his surprisingly muscled thigh. It clenched beneath my fingers.

"Yes?" I said, totally dazed. I couldn't remember the last time a man had turned me on so much—and he'd barely even touched me. Just talked and teased and made me laugh.

My fingers crept up his thigh but avoided his cock. A low, masculine sound escaped Edward's lips.

I liked it.

"What are you doing, love?"

"I don't know," I said, still dazed. "But you should ask me." My fingers tracked up the fine stitching of his white shirt. The soft silk of his tie.

"Ask you what?"

I leaned far over, barely six inches from his face. Up close he was oh-so-handsome. More handsome than I was expecting. It felt like I'd been punched in the gut, arousal hollowing me out.

"I'm a strange woman, aren't I?" I asked, slowly wrapping his tie around my fingers. I wrapped and wrapped and tugged Edward's face closer and closer.

"Ah," he finally said, attempting to kiss me, but I stopped him. His grin was devilish. "I find you quite alluring, Roxy. Would you appreciate an intimate evening with me?"

I tightened my hold on his tie but kept him an inch away. The air between our mouths was charged with hot electricity. A storm about to erupt.

"Are you in a relationship?" I asked.

"You know I'm not."

"Do you understand consent?" I asked, the most important question.

His eyes were clear. "I would never hurt you, Roxy. You can trust me. And yes, I understand."

I believed him.

"When was the last time you were tested?" I pulled him an inch closer. Our lips danced but didn't touch.

"A month ago. I was clean. And Emily and I still used condoms."

I sighed. The final question.

"Do you like the same things that I like?" I waited, and Edward seemed to gather his courage, brow furrowed. But then he leaned forward, running the tip of his nose along the side of my neck. I shivered. And then he closed his teeth around the tender skin of my throat and bit me.

So hard I almost climaxed.

"I think I do, love," he whispered against my ear. "But it would be my, uh, my first time. Like this. The way that you like it."

My eyes fluttered closed in happiness.

A virgin.

So to speak.

Except Edward was all coiled muscle and low growls next to me, and something told me he wasn't going to need much instruction.

"After tonight, Edward," I said, yanking his tie so hard he hissed. "You're not going to remember Emily's name. You're not even going to remember your own goddamn name."

In response, he reached forward—nothing tentative in his movements—and gripped the back of my head. Pulled the small hairs at the base of my neck between his fingers, trapping me.

"Roxy, darling," he said, brushing his lips against mine. "After tonight? I'll be the only name *you* remember."

more circles, my hips were thrusting forward
cord. "Are you, Roxy?"

itive," he said, leaning closer, nuzzling along
e tip of his tongue tracing the metal in my

I groaned. And then Edward stopped, and my

hell are you doing?" I was gripping his shoul-
y out of control. Ready to get on my knees and

you," he said, yanking me onto his lap, hard
ght against that piercing like it was made to be
went around Edward's hips, his arms wrapped
ly.

Edward proceeded to give me the most fervently
of my entire life.

lips and teeth and tongue and desperate,
s I rocked against him. His fingers threaded
and pulled hard. I ripped open the buttons of
registering the sound of them flying over the
made quick work of his tie, mouth still fused
ard spread my ass cheeks apart like he owned
ne harder against his lap—and I responded by
o his tongue.

ck, blood on his lip. His eyes were wild with
mussed. Shirt half off his body, exposing his
est and a fine dusting of hair.

arge here, Roxy?"

y hips quickly, dry-fucking his cock, and his
ound my throat.

ed, raking my nails down his chest. "Clearly."

5

ROXY

I always wanted sex.

I'd always loved it, and I found it easy to fall in and out of relationships. One-night stands. Brief, but hot, hook-ups. I loved dating as much as I loved being single and fucking strangers.

Because I didn't overthink it. If it felt good, and the person respected me, then I didn't see a reason to deny myself pleasure.

But the exquisite sexual chemistry I felt with Edward was fast, even for me. The slow, teasing conversation we'd been having all night had only heightened my arousal to something almost painful.

I *needed* to fuck Edward. Needed to push him to whatever self-imposed limit he had that kept him tethered and in control.

With a wicked grin, I shoved Edward back, letting go of his tie. His eyes flared in challenge.

"One more question Dilbert," I said, grasping the zipper of my top between my fingers. I tugged it down one inch then stopped. "In case anything happens that makes you, or me, uncomfortable, we should have a word we say. That stops the game."

"A... safe word?" he asked.

I nodded. "How about *suit*?"

A teasing smile. "I love it. And what's this?" he said, hands on his knees. I could just make out the hard outline of his cock, straining against his pants.

"It's called a striptease," I said, and his nostrils flared. I tugged that zipper down, down, down, exposing my hot pink bra. Edward's eyes tracked over every single inch of ink that I was exposing.

It was a lot.

I let my shirt fall to the ground, and Edward was as still as a statue.

"What are you thinking?" I asked, hooking my thumbs into my skirt. Flicking open the button.

"Dark things, love," he growled. "Very dark things."

"Mmmm," I said, sliding the material down, leaving me in fishnet thigh-high stockings and combat boots. "That's not very nice."

"I'm not sure I'm very nice," he said.

"That's not true," I chided. "You're a very polite English gentleman."

In a flash, Edward reached forward and grabbed the back of my knees, yanking me to him. His face was level with my lace-covered breasts.

"Take this off, Roxy," he said. I shook my head, teasing. With an arch of his eyebrow, he reached up, unclasped my bra with reverent fingers, and let it drop to the ground.

"Pierced?" he said, rubbing his hand over his mouth.

"Of course."

Edward nodded, and I was desperate for him to touch me. But he hadn't yet.

"Off," he said, lookin

I shook my head
Edward made me sinfu
he reached forward with
tore it clean in half.

"Roxy," he whispere
I've ever fucking seen."

My eyes fluttered clo

"I bloody well am," h

"What?"

"Use your fingers to

My first instinct was
were trailing between
spreading my pussy apar

His breathing grew r

"Of course," I repea
restrained animal. A wo
finally, finally placed the
Dragged it up oh so slo
skin, breathing together
against my clit piercing.
its way from my throat.

"Oh, Roxy," Edward s
almost buckled. "What a

Another slide, then
steadying myself as Edwa
ease.

"You've never... you'v
panted.

"In porn," he said,
circles, and my forehead
there. Thought about it
about... how sensitive a

groaned. With
on their own a

"What?"

"Extra ser
my breasts, t
nipple.

"Fuck yes
world went da

"What th
ders, comple
beg to come.

"Punishir
cock nudging
there. My leg
around me ti

And ther
passionate ki

We were
needy moan
through my
his shirt, ba
floor. My fin
to his, and E
them. Dragg
biting down

He pulle
sheer lust.
lean, muscle

"Who's i
I snapp
fingers close

"Me," I

His laughter was dark and husky. "That's your contention?"

I was so close to coming. *So close.* And not just any old orgasm I routinely gave myself.

No, this orgasm was going to rip me in half. As if reading my mind, Edward reached down and swiftly rubbed my clit. I cried out.

"That's right," he rasped. "Who controls your pleasure, Roxy?"

"Me," I bit back, and he smacked my ass so hard I almost cried.

"Who controls your pleasure, Roxy?" he asked again, twisting a nipple piercing between his fingers. So close. So close. I could see my orgasm coming, and I wasn't sure I'd survive it.

And as I started to crest, I heard the words '*you, you, you*' slip from my lips.

But then the bastard stopped. Pulled away. Shoved me to my knees. Immediately, my fingers started to finish the job he wouldn't, but Edward trapped them between his. Bit one, and I practically snarled.

Like a king, he dragged his zipper down. The sound echoed in the quiet of the tattoo parlor and the air was so charged I feared spontaneous human combustion.

"What do you want?" he asked quietly.

"Your cock, please," I said, licking my lips. I was desperate for it. Hungry. The drumbeat of arousal between my legs propelled me forward, trying to get a glimpse. He grasped my chin, stilling me, tilting my eyes up until I met his gaze.

A smirk tugged at his lips. "Looks like we need to re-evaluate who's in charge."

"How many gross endearments are you going to try, *Dilbert*?" she asked, and my cock twitched.

"As many as I can... *beautiful*," I replied, and we were definitely flirting now. Which shouldn't have been possible with a break-up barely three hours behind me, but Emily's image was fading by the minute, replaced by Roxy's fire.

"I can see why Emily dumped you now," she said.

"Mean," I said. "And—can I point out—*too soon*."

Roxy sat back down, closer to me now, and I could smell her. Sandalwood, which I wouldn't have thought she'd wear.

"I'm not apologizing. It's past one in the morning, and you've hijacked my entire evening. And I'm not even going to make any money off you because I have integrity," she said.

I rolled my eyes. "Who needs integrity when a drunk Brit wants you to tattoo his arse?" Another small smile, and every time that happened, it made me feel like I'd won a gold medal at the Olympics. No, *two* gold medals. And a silver.

"What was your first tattoo?" I asked, feeling completely out of my element. Not a single member of my family had a tattoo. Or anything beyond an ear piercing.

"Can't show you," she said. "It's in a... private place."

"It's on your arse, isn't it," I deadpanned.

"I'll never tell," she said, coyly.

"Did Emily have tattoos?" she asked. The fury came roaring back. I allowed myself to welcome it.

"Emily? The woman who shagged my mate for months and just told me three hours ago?" I said. "Not that I'm bitter. And no, none at all. Wouldn't have been proper."

Roxy swallowed, and I watched her throat work. "Have you talked to your friend yet? The one she fucked?" she asked.

I shook my head. "I've been too busy with the drinks and the tattoo planning. And I probably won't, to be perfectly honest."

"Why not? Don't you want to confront him? He *fucked* your girlfriend," Roxy said, and I noticed again the sheer number of weapons tattooed on her body. Knives and guns and something that looked like a rocket launcher.

"Maybe I should have *you* confront him, love," I grinned. "Scare the pants right off him, wouldn't you?"

Another haughty tilt of her chin.

"I've been known to hold my own, yes," she said, sipping from her mug. She didn't flinch when I held her gaze. "And it sounds like you avoid conflict."

"I bloody well do," I said. "Have you *met* me?"

"I mean, not really," she said. "It's now been an hour. Not even. I know almost nothing about you. Still."

"Well, it's not the way my family handles things. And, if you must know, *yes,* they are like that family from Downton Abbey."

"Did you grow up under a staircase like in Harry Potter?" she asked, tilting her head.

"Cheeky," I said. "And *no*. Although my parents do own a castle."

Roxy lifted her chin, looking beautiful and deadly in equal measure.

"And we don't go around openly sharing our feelings or fighting like Americans do left and right. Or at least, that's what I've learned from watching *Real Housewives of Orange County*."

That got me an honest-to-God laugh.

"Tattoo me, Roxy," I pleaded.

"No," she said. "It's not what you *really* want, and you'll only regret it. Plus, I'm still not convinced of your sobriety."

"Shall I walk a straight line for you?"

"No," she said, shaking her head and moving behind the large desk. Shuffling things, putting things away. Cleaning up, about to send me out. And suddenly, there was nothing I wanted more than her hands on me.

Even if they were permanently inking art onto my body that I didn't really want.

"I was thinking a realistic heart, you know the kind? With a giant dagger stabbing through it. Maybe a quote underneath like '*Fuck You, Emily*.'"

Roxy was flipping off the coffee pot. "First, if that's really what you want, it'll take me a couple of hours to draw it out. Two hours, at least, to actually tattoo it. And unlike some corporate assholes in the room, I *worked* all day. And went to school. And I'm exhausted."

I wanted to ask her about school but held off.

She flashed me a sweet smile I knew was fake. "If you really want it, you'll still want it tomorrow."

"How else do I get over her?" I asked, hating the honesty in my voice. The vulnerability. I was trying to keep things light and fun, but the thought of going out into the cold, alone, was too much.

"Edward," she said before settling back down. Her knee touched mine, but I didn't move it away.

Neither did she.

"This can't possibly be your first break-up, right?"

"No," I admitted. "But it is the first time I've been cheated on. First time I was this shocked. Control, you see. That's what I grew up with, and every relationship I've ever had has been tightly *restrained*. My break-ups have been a polite parting of ways. And this one was too," I said, thinking back to the mature, quiet way we'd gently discussed the logistics. "But it was also..."

"About a hundred different types of fucked up," she finished.

I nodded, grateful. "How did you get over when you were cheated on? How did you get up from rock bottom?"

Roxy looked away, and my eyes tracked the graceful tilt of her neck. I felt a swift desire to lean forward and lick her throat from collarbone to under her ear. Was that the most sensitive spot on her body?

Or was there somewhere else, somewhere deeper, where she'd let me lick her?

"Do you want to know the truth?" she asked, taking off her jacket and laying it behind her. She was wearing some alluring combination of lace and metal.

"Please. All I'm working with right now is this horrible cocktail of anger and regret. Surely it can't be like this forever?" I wondered, knowing that I was sliding face first into the sad, post-tipsy part of the evening.

"No," Roxy promised, full lips pursed around the word. "It won't be. You're too... I mean, you'll move on. Some bland, boring woman will sweep into your life and change it for good. For the better. And Emily will become a distant memory."

"Why does she have to be bland?" I asked. "Roxy, I feel like you've judged me too harshly." I laid a palm on my chest and gave her pleading eyes until her lips quirked up.

"A bland, rich banker who you can have bland, boring sex with for the rest of your life," she continued, and I wanted to say 'please, no.' Wanted to tear off my restrictive suit and tie and race off into the night. Preferably with her.

"Well," I said, pressing my knee against hers. She didn't move. "Until I meet this bland, rich, banking woman, how am I moving on? You still haven't told me what you did."

Roxy looked both ways as if ensuring we were totally alone. "First of all, I can't believe I'm telling you this," she said. "And secondly, fucking."

My fingers tightened on my mug. "Fucking?"

Roxy shrugged nonchalantly and grinned at me. "Sex therapy. I took home every attractive, single man I met and had my way with him."

"I've not done that before," I said and wondered what other secrets I'd be admitting to tonight.

"Have a one-night stand?" she asked, eyebrow arched. I shook my head.

"Highly recommended for getting over cheating exes," she said, and it might have been my imagination, but she was definitely pressing her knee against mine now.

"Emily would hate that," I said. "She was very scandalized by people who took home perfect strangers. She thought sex should be a civilized act. And only after you've confirmed your partner's pedigree."

Roxy spit a word 'hypocrite' into her coffee.

I liked that she was on my side.

"I'll have to disagree with your Emily," she said.

"Not *my* Emily. Not anymore," I said. "So I guess I should, um, go out and pick up a stranger?" My coffee was one sip away from being done.

"That's my advice," she said. "And if you still want that tattoo? Come by tomorrow, take off those pants, and I'll permanently ink the words '*Fuck you, Emily*' right above your ass."

Before I could stop myself, my palm was on her knee, thumb landing on an inch of skin bared by a tear in her stocking. Roxy stilled, and my heart slammed into my throat.

I pulled back quickly.

"Sorry, um," I stumbled. "Still a bit drunk, I guess." Which was a lie. I'd never been more brilliantly clear-headed.

"It's okay," Roxy said. "Although I will knife you if you do it again."

"Got a thing for knives, love?"

"I do," she said, and I didn't miss the glimmer in her eyes. My brain snagged on a fantasy: a barely clothed Roxy pressing a knife to my throat, one hand wrapped around my cock, her lips bruising mine.

And where in the hell did that come from?

4

ROXY

I had a thing for knives and all kinds of sharp objects. I had a thing for pain and pleasure, edging and release.

Not that I was going to tell Edward that—he'd run out of my shop so fast he'd leave an Edward-shaped shadow in his wake.

Plus, he still didn't look the type.

"Do you need advice for a one-night stand?" I asked, and I couldn't *believe* I'd just told a perfect stranger I enjoyed 'sex therapy.' Not that I was ashamed—not at all—more that I was battling an intense urge to smash my mug to the floor, straddle Edward's hips, and fuck his sexy English brains out.

I had no idea why. And the sex talk wasn't helping.

Remember: stress, numbers, class, homework.

Pushed to my limit. It had to explain it.

Yet here I was pushing *him*.

"I guess I'm not sure what to say to a woman I'm interested in a one-night stand with," Edward said thoughtfully. He swiped his hand through his hair, and a lock of it hung over his forehead. "Is there something you've found to be successful? Do I say, 'hello, I find you quite alluring. Would you appreciate an intimate evening with me?'"

I snorted. "Not unless you want them to fall asleep halfway through that sentence, Dilbert."

"Ouch," he said with a fake wince. "So what do you usually say?"

"I don't do much talking usually," I said. "I know what I look for in casual sex, so I go out specifically to look for it. Once I've chosen my target—"

"—victim—" Edward interrupted, and I bared my teeth at him.

"Lucky winner," I finished, and his smile was illicit. "Once I've chosen the lucky winner, I make sure of a few things."

"Those are?"

I held out my hand, ticking on my fingers. "Make sure they're not in a relationship. Make sure they understand consent. Make sure they're clean and have been recently tested. Make sure they like the same things I like."

Edward nodded like he was taking notes. "What are the things you like? If I can be so bold."

I squirmed, his knee pressing against mine. The scrape of his thumb along my inner thigh had unleashed a fury of sensation, almost making me dizzy. But then he'd apologized politely and let go—instead of grasping my tights and tearing them asunder.

"So now the English gentleman is bold?" I teased.

"Very."

"I like sex to be intense. I like pain. Toys. Restraints. Spanking." I paused. "Dominance and submission..."

"Which do you like better? Dominance or submission?" Edward asked, and there was no mistaking the raw need in his voice.

32

"Both," I said and watched his knuckles whiten. "Did you play bedroom games with Emily?"

"Never. She liked it polite, quiet, and always in the dark."

"And is that what you like?" I watched him, expecting fluster. Or blushing. Not his eyes locked on mine like I was the only thing that existed in this entire universe.

Like he was moments away from snapping his fingers and barking an order.

"I don't think so, no," he finally said. "I'm quite embarrassed to admit I have very limited sexual experience. Thus, why even though I'm a grown man and hold multiple degrees and every day manage millions of dollars and hundreds of employees, I, well, I don't know how to ask a strange woman to come home with me."

He said 'strange woman' the way he said 'Roxy.'

"Hit her with the accent. Chicks love that," I said.

"How about a suit and tie? Is that something 'chicks dig'?" he asked with exaggerated air quotes and a hilariously awful American accent.

I smirked. "Some chicks enjoy ties. And all the wonderfully improper things you can do with them."

He swallowed. "I see." Edward looked like he wanted to say more but instead tossed his head. "And you're definitely going to show me that first tattoo, love?"

"No. But I was seventeen years old. A real wild child. Climbing out of windows, tearing my jeans on wire fences. Making out with boys. I was always an artsy, dark little thing."

"A goth girl?"

I pursed my lips. "Maybe." A pause. "Okay, I was goth all the way, which is funny because my parents..." I stopped, aware that I was now freely sharing. Edward tipped his head. "Oh, well, my parents are old punks."

"As in...?"

"They're in a punk rock band. The Hand Grenades. They still play and tour even though they're in their sixties."

Edward grinned broadly. "Well, that's bloody fantastic."

I laughed. "Growing up, I think they were a little disappointed in my goth phase. A bit too Morrissey. Not enough Blondie. But I'm kind of a punk now, so they're much happier." I stared down at my torn fishnets and leather jacket covered in patches.

"I think you look lovely. Like some kind of dark angel," Edward said softly.

I felt my cheeks heat. "Something like that," I said, clearing my throat. "But I had a terrible boyfriend who had a friend who was an amazing tattoo artist. We lied about my age, I told him what I wanted, and the rest is history."

"It hurt?" Edward asked.

"Like a motherfucker," I said, and his laughter was like a sharp ray of light after drizzling rain. "But I also liked it."

"What?"

"The pain," I said, remembering how turned on I'd been, begging my boyfriend to fuck me in the car afterward. The way I'd pressed, ever-so-gently, on the skin that throbbed above my ink.

Getting off on it.

There was something about Edward that was causing the same desire—to press and push and feel for why I was so attracted to him.

It could be that I had the distinct impression that his dapper, well-tailored suit covered up a man who was desperate to let loose his darker passions.

And I wanted that accent muttering filthy phrases in my ear.

"Roxy?" Edward asked as my hand was suddenly moving

34

of its own volition, up his surprisingly muscled thigh. It clenched beneath my fingers.

"Yes?" I said, totally dazed. I couldn't remember the last time a man had turned me on so much—and he'd barely even touched me. Just talked and teased and made me laugh.

My fingers crept up his thigh but avoided his cock. A low, masculine sound escaped Edward's lips.

I liked it.

"What are you doing, love?"

"I don't know," I said, still dazed. "But you should ask me." My fingers tracked up the fine stitching of his white shirt. The soft silk of his tie.

"Ask you what?"

I leaned far over, barely six inches from his face. Up close he was oh-so-handsome. More handsome than I was expecting. It felt like I'd been punched in the gut, arousal hollowing me out.

"I'm a strange woman, aren't I?" I asked, slowly wrapping his tie around my fingers. I wrapped and wrapped and tugged Edward's face closer and closer.

"Ah," he finally said, attempting to kiss me, but I stopped him. His grin was devilish. "I find you quite alluring, Roxy. Would you appreciate an intimate evening with me?"

I tightened my hold on his tie but kept him an inch away. The air between our mouths was charged with hot electricity. A storm about to erupt.

"Are you in a relationship?" I asked.

"You know I'm not."

"Do you understand consent?" I asked, the most important question.

His eyes were clear. "I would never hurt you, Roxy. You can trust me. And yes, I understand."

I believed him.

"When was the last time you were tested?" I pulled him an inch closer. Our lips danced but didn't touch.

"A month ago. I was clean. And Emily and I still used condoms."

I sighed. The final question.

"Do you like the same things that I like?" I waited, and Edward seemed to gather his courage, brow furrowed. But then he leaned forward, running the tip of his nose along the side of my neck. I shivered. And then he closed his teeth around the tender skin of my throat and bit me.

So hard I almost climaxed.

"I think I do, love," he whispered against my ear. "But it would be my, uh, my first time. Like this. The way that you like it."

My eyes fluttered closed in happiness.

A virgin.

So to speak.

Except Edward was all coiled muscle and low growls next to me, and something told me he wasn't going to need much instruction.

"After tonight, Edward," I said, yanking his tie so hard he hissed. "You're not going to remember Emily's name. You're not even going to remember your own goddamn name."

In response, he reached forward—nothing tentative in his movements—and gripped the back of my head. Pulled the small hairs at the base of my neck between his fingers, trapping me.

"Roxy, darling," he said, brushing his lips against mine. "After tonight? I'll be the only name *you* remember."

ROXY

I always wanted sex.

I'd always loved it, and I found it easy to fall in and out of relationships. One-night stands. Brief, but hot, hook-ups. I loved dating as much as I loved being single and fucking strangers.

Because I didn't overthink it. If it felt good, and the person respected me, then I didn't see a reason to deny myself pleasure.

But the exquisite sexual chemistry I felt with Edward was fast, even for me. The slow, teasing conversation we'd been having all night had only heightened my arousal to something almost painful.

I *needed* to fuck Edward. Needed to push him to whatever self-imposed limit he had that kept him tethered and in control.

With a wicked grin, I shoved Edward back, letting go of his tie. His eyes flared in challenge.

"One more question Dilbert," I said, grasping the zipper of my top between my fingers. I tugged it down one inch then stopped. "In case anything happens that makes you, or me, uncomfortable, we should have a word we say. That stops the game."

"A... safe word?" he asked.

I nodded. "How about *suit*?"

A teasing smile. "I love it. And what's this?" he said, hands on his knees. I could just make out the hard outline of his cock, straining against his pants.

"It's called a striptease," I said, and his nostrils flared. I tugged that zipper down, down, down, exposing my hot pink bra. Edward's eyes tracked over every single inch of ink that I was exposing.

It was a lot.

I let my shirt fall to the ground, and Edward was as still as a statue.

"What are you thinking?" I asked, hooking my thumbs into my skirt. Flicking open the button.

"Dark things, love," he growled. "Very dark things."

"Mmmm," I said, sliding the material down, leaving me in fishnet thigh-high stockings and combat boots. "That's not very nice."

"I'm not sure I'm very nice," he said.

"That's not true," I chided. "You're a very polite English gentleman."

In a flash, Edward reached forward and grabbed the back of my knees, yanking me to him. His face was level with my lace-covered breasts.

"Take this off, Roxy," he said. I shook my head, teasing. With an arch of his eyebrow, he reached up, unclasped my bra with reverent fingers, and let it drop to the ground.

"Pierced?" he said, rubbing his hand over his mouth.

"Of course."

Edward nodded, and I was desperate for him to touch me. But he hadn't yet.

"Off," he said, looking at my underwear.

I shook my head again, still teasing. Something about Edward made me sinfully defiant. He kept his eyes on me as he reached forward with two hands, grasped the material, and tore it clean in half.

"Roxy," he whispered. "This is the most beautiful pussy I've ever fucking seen."

My eyes fluttered closed. "You're lucky."

"I bloody well am," he said. "Show me."

"What?"

"Use your fingers to pull those pretty lips back. Show me."

My first instinct was to defy again, but instead my fingers were trailing between my breasts, down my stomach, and spreading my pussy apart for Edward's greedy eyes.

His breathing grew rough. "Is that a clit piercing?"

"Of course," I repeated, and Edward was like a barely restrained animal. A wolf forced to sit before its master. He finally, finally placed the tip of his finger just inside my knee. Dragged it up oh so slowly. We watched it travel along my skin, breathing together. Hot. Panting. And then he slid it against my clit piercing. A strangled, pleasured sound clawed its way from my throat.

"Oh, Roxy," Edward said, sliding his finger again. My knees almost buckled. "What am I going to do with you, love?"

Another slide, then another. I grabbed his shoulders, steadying myself as Edward strummed my clit with practiced ease.

"You've never... you've never seen a pierced clit before?" I panted.

"In porn," he said, switching his movements to small circles, and my forehead fell against his. "I... I quite liked it there. Thought about it when I'd touch myself. Thought about... how sensitive a woman would be. With this," he groaned. With more circles, my hips were thrusting forward on their own accord. "Are you, Roxy?"

"What?"

"Extra sensitive," he said, leaning closer, nuzzling along my breasts, the tip of his tongue tracing the metal in my nipple.

"Fuck yes," I groaned. And then Edward stopped, and my world went dark.

"What the hell are you doing?" I was gripping his shoulders, completely out of control. Ready to get on my knees and beg to come.

"Punishing you," he said, yanking me onto his lap, hard cock nudging right against that piercing like it was made to be there. My legs went around Edward's hips, his arms wrapped around me tightly.

And then Edward proceeded to give me the most fervently passionate kiss of my entire life.

We were all lips and teeth and tongue and desperate, needy moans as I rocked against him. His fingers threaded through my hair and pulled hard. I ripped open the buttons of his shirt, barely registering the sound of them flying over the floor. My fingers made quick work of his tie, mouth still fused to his, and Edward spread my ass cheeks apart like he owned them. Dragged me harder against his lap—and I responded by biting down onto his tongue.

He pulled back, blood on his lip. His eyes were wild with sheer lust. Hair mussed. Shirt half off his body, exposing his lean, muscled chest and a fine dusting of hair.

"Who's in charge here, Roxy?"

I snapped my hips quickly, dry-fucking his cock, and his fingers closed around my throat.

"Me," I groaned, raking my nails down his chest. "Clearly."

the floor. Then I bent down and lifted Roxy in one fluid movement, her legs wrapping around my waist, my cock nudging at her soaking wet entrance.

"I don't owe you a goddamn thing," I growled before slamming her against the nearest wall. Something fell and shattered, but her nipples were in my mouth, and Roxy was screaming with pleasure. I loved the way the metal felt between my teeth, and when I tugged gently, Roxy let out a string of curse words I'd never even heard before.

"Just don't stop," she begged.

I walked her over to the glass desk that held the cash register. Knocked off a collection of papers and books and files. Dropped her onto it.

"I was going to tell you to spread your legs," I said, wrenching her knees as wide as they would go. She hissed, and her fingers tightened on the edge of the desk. "But I knew you'd disobey me. Try to keep this perfect cunt away from my tongue." I leaned down, hooking her legs over my shoulders, secretly thrilled at the way *cunt* sounded—my first time saying the word. It felt dirty and wrong and *right*.

And then, with one long swipe of my tongue, Roxy was coming, riding my face and wailing my name.

But it was only the first orgasm I'd give her.

I hooked my fingers inside of her, using long strokes as the sensations rippled through her body. Kept her nipples in my mouth until she was sighing and panting again. I placed my hand between her breasts and gently pushed her down until she was laid out in front of me like a glorious feast.

Roxy propped herself up on her elbows, heaps of wild blonde hair around her face, grinning. I brought her hand to my lips, turning it over to press a kiss to her wrist.

"Is this okay?" I asked, sensing a natural break in the game we were playing. Sensing that this was important.

"Very, very, very okay," she said.

I nodded, pressing her back down. Stroking her internal walls with my fingers deliberately, enjoying her shudder.

"Good to hear, love," I said simply. "And it's time for you to come again."

7

ROXY

This was shaping up to be the sexiest night of my life. Because I was totally, completely, utterly wrong about Edward. He wasn't some shy, tentative lover who wanted me with the lights off. He wasn't *really* a virgin to pain and dominance—in fact, he didn't need to be shown the way at all.

No. This polite English gentleman was nothing like I expected. Because from the very first moment we touched, we were like two planets, exploding in the atmosphere—violent bursts of light and a furious volley of sharp movements. Fingers that burned and surges of pleasure so intense I felt like I was floating through space. Untethered. Filled with sensation.

Edward had me spread and vulnerable on my desk, half on top of the cash register, and his tongue was magic, magic, *magic*.

I was one orgasm down, and the second was already approaching rapidly. Except Edward was teasing me: light, rapid flicks of his tongue followed by long, even strokes of his fingers inside of me. But never at the same time, only enough to build me to the precipice without flinging me off.

"You're a monster," I said through clenched teeth, panting as he flicked my clit and pinched my nipples in that same irritating, incessant rhythm. His blue eyes latched onto mine, barest hint of a smirk on his lips. I grabbed his hair and yanked hard; thrust against his tongue just the way I liked it. Edward slapped the back of my thighs with his palm—*slap, slap, slap*—and my world shuddered and darkened as pleasure crested and crested.

"And I think I've got you figured out, love," he murmured. All at once, he pinched my nipple, bit the inside of my thigh, and circled his fingers against my g-spot. Pain and pleasure twisted deep in my belly.

"I fucking hate you so much right now," I gasped, but it was almost a wail. Edward removed his fingers and replaced them with his tongue.

"Goddammit, Roxy," he groaned. "You were hiding this sweet pussy from me all night." His tongue slid inside almost reverently, eyes closed in sheer happiness, and now he was moaning louder than I was. The wave of sensations was replaced with something gentle but powerful—like rapids before a waterfall.

"That's because it's a privilege to taste me," I finally said, but really I was saying '*oh God, oh God, oh God*' because it was that good. His tongue licked deeper, and stars twinkled across my vision. One hand left my nipples and slid down the crack of my ass. A thumb, pressing.

Edward pulled away, and I sobbed at the loss. "Please, don't..." I started, but he hushed me.

"Can I have this?" he asked gently, pressing his thumb again at the tight muscle. There was finally a shy hesitation to his movement, and I wondered if he'd done it before.

I wanted to give it to him—desperately.

"Yes," I said. "*Please.*" Edward's eyes lit up, both of us

watching as he slicked his thumb, pressing slowly inside. My toes curled.

"You're going to be the death of me, Roxy. You know that right?" he whispered, looking almost in pain. Like he couldn't believe this night was happening.

And I couldn't either.

And then he proceeded to fuck me with his tongue, and fuck me with his thumb, and he nudged his fingers against my clit so perfectly a tsunami-sized orgasm swept me away. I screamed for so long I went hoarse, thrusting and shaking. I almost pulled Edward's head off, but he stayed with me through it all, groaning and sighing and swallowing the juices that ran down my leg.

When he finally stood up, he was a dirty, filthy wreck. Jaw wet. Lips swollen. Scratches down his chest and hair askew. He was sweating, arm muscles bunched, bitten and flushed.

He looked like a fucking animal.

I jerked my head at my bag, dangling from the chair.

"Condom," I said, thanking the sex gods that I'd tossed a few in there last week. When he returned, he was already rolling it on. Then he yanked me to the edge of the desk. Grabbed my neck and pulled me flush against him. Kissed me like a soldier about to go to war. And I was pressing that perfect cock right where I wanted it.

"Roxy, darling," Edward whispered, sliding his lips against my temple then pinning me with a steely gaze, "I'm not sure we can go back after this."

"I don't want to," I said honestly, swept up in the chaos, this chance meeting, this whirlwind night. "I don't want to."

And then Edward thrust every sweet inch of his cock inside of me.

And we both screamed.

8

ROXY

*F*ucking.

I'd done it before. Dozens of times, in fact, and my experiences ran the gamut of skill and talent. I'd taken home plenty of sloppy men; inconsiderate men. Men who swore up and down they knew how to fuck me right and then failed miserably.

Those men, I sent packing.

But I'd also had my fair share of men who *did* fuck me right—made me scream to the high heavens. Sexy, rough bad boys.

Just my type.

All of this ran through my mind as Edward fucked me. Sweet, mild-mannered Edward, whose expensive suit was in tatters on the floor, was annihilating every other sexual experience in my mind.

There were no other men.

No other one-night stands. No other lovers.

Because Edward had a magic cock.

Big but not too big. Thick but not too thick. Curved just right and *smooth*. But it was more than that. I was still on the counter, legs wrapped around Edward's trim waist, my hands on his ass. His hands were everywhere, gripping my hair, squeezing my throat, palming my breasts.

It was Edward's *rhythm* that was pushing me past whatever ledge of sanity I still clung to. Because he was fucking me so goddamn slowly I could feel, every time, the glide of his cock through my pussy lips. The arch, the nudging against my g-spot. The sparking of my nerve endings. Slow but steady, and it was driving me mad.

"Watch with me," he said, grabbing the back of my neck and pressing our foreheads together. He was panting, voice hoarse, and together the two of us watched as he fucked into me. The sound so wet, so filthy, like watching the hottest porn except I was the star.

"So wet for me. So tight," he groaned, and I'd been right— I *did* need that refined English accent muttering dirty phrases in my ear.

"Faster," I said through gritted teeth.

Edward bit my throat, slowing down even further. I whimpered until he let go. But as soon as he did, I reached down and gave him a sharp slap on the ass. He hissed and wrapped my hair around his fingers, yanking my head back. He licked and bit up my exposed throat, so I fisted his chest hair and gave it a fierce tug.

"*Fuck fuck fuck*," he groaned, and his pace picked up.

"You like that?" I teased, slapping his ass again.

"Oh God, I think I do," he responded, lowering his head to take my nipples in his mouth again. I seemed forever balanced on the edge of orgasm with Edward—one ending and another beginning, some delicious limbo I never wanted to leave. He had me trapped there now, sucking my piercings between his teeth as he pulled on my hair. Tears stung my eyes. I raked my fingernails down his ribcage, and he shuddered.

And still *so slowly*. Cock gliding in and out. Like the two of us were fucking on a picnic blanket on a Sunday afternoon in the park. It was infuriating and hot, and I'd never been with a man who had such much skill and patience.

I yanked his handsome face closer until it was an inch from my own.

"Fuck. Me. Faster," I demanded against his mouth, and then the two of us were kissing angrily, tongues clashing, and at one point I was pretty sure he bit my lip so hard I was bleeding.

"No," he said with a smirk. "I'll take my sweet time with this pussy. Because it's mine now."

"Shut the fuck up," I hissed, but I was moaning and sighing at the possession—because it got me off, and he knew that. Edward seemed to know everything that got me off, and as he wrapped his fingers around my throat, keeping me still, we watched as his cock moved between my legs.

It was possibly the most erotic moment of my life until Edward's thumb slid over my clit. I tried to look away, but his fingers were still around my throat.

"Look at me, love," he said, pinning me with a heated gaze. "I want to watch this time."

"Watch... watch what?" I panted because the sweet orgasm that had been simmering beneath my nerve endings had woken.

"Want to watch you come with my cock buried inside of you," he said. He sped up his movements—a little. I let out a strangled cry.

"I want to watch you come with my fingers around your throat," he said, mouth against my lips. We were sharing the same breath, groaning together, eyes locked.

This orgasm was softer, gentler, but it still robbed me of my ability to be upright. I collapsed against his hard chest, and he rubbed my back and stroked my hair, cock still moving.

He was kissing me like I was the most precious thing in the world.

"Edward," I said. "That was... fuck, that was..." but I didn't even really have words.

He stood up with me still wrapped around his body. I felt suffused with light.

"I'm glad you enjoyed that," he said, chuckling softly.

He turned in front of the wall-to-wall mirror in the back. Slid out of me and placed me gently on the floor. Wrapped me in his arms and kissed me until I was actually *swooning*.

I was not a woman who swooned.

"Roxy?" he whispered.

"Yes?" I asked. He was so sweet and handsome.

Until his face changed, expression growing savage.

"Put your palms on that goddamn mirror."

9

EDWARD

$\mathcal{I}$t was a curious thing when your deepest, most private sexual fantasies finally came true.

Thanks to years of stiff-lipped upbringing, I knew how to repress my desires. How to bend to the expectations of Being A Cavendish, which involved a whole host of things—but definitely not embarking on a night of kinky fucking with an absolute stranger in a tattoo parlor.

But now, here I was, with Roxy bent over at the waist in front of me.

Roxy was my dream woman. I remembered I'd been dating someone not hours before this moment, but I really, truly couldn't fathom a time when I wasn't buried between Roxy's legs.

"What are you waiting for?" Roxy smirked, palms on the mirror. I scooped up my belt from the floor and cracked her against the ass with it. She yelped and gasped, and I did it again.

The sound of leather against skin was the most erotic sound I'd ever heard.

"Still so mouthy," I sighed, sliding my fingers between her

legs to find her soaking wet. Our eyes met in the mirror, and I flashed her a grin. She bit her lip, pushing back onto my hand. My palm moved up her back, between her shoulder blades, up her neck. Fingers threading in her long hair.

"Roxy," I said softly, twisting her hair between my fingers.

"Edward," she replied.

"How much can you take, love?" I pulled slowly, watching in rapt fascination as the upper half of her body arched back.

"I can take it all," she said. "Give it to me."

Our eyes met again. And I proceeded to fuck Roxy like the barbarian I'd always been deep down. Fast and rough, with none of the technique of earlier. And maybe the sound of leather against skin wasn't the most erotic sound I'd ever heard. Maybe it was the sound of my hips snapping against her thighs, the wet sound of our skin meeting, Roxy's endless throaty moans and her palm slapping against the mirror. Our eyes stayed locked, and the harder I pulled on her hair, the more crazed she became.

Another yank and I hovered my mouth over her ear as I fucked her.

"Was this your plan the whole time?" I murmured, pinching her nipples roughly. "As soon as I walked in here, did you know you were going to fucking destroy me?"

Roxy's sly smile was too much; I spanked her until she stopped.

"Roxy," I growled, speeding up the pace. I grabbed her chin, tilting her mouth towards mine, and took her lips angrily. She bit my tongue, and the pain shot down my spine. Our lips crashed against each other as I fucked her.

"I'll never tell," she finally said when I pulled back. There was that smile again. I bit the side of her neck and slid two fingers over her clit. A shudder rocked her body.

"Fuck, I can't believe I'm going to come again," she panted, and the thrill of owning this vixen's pleasure almost sent me rocketing over the edge.

"That's because I know just what you need, love," I said. "Isn't that right?"

She shook her head, the little minx, and then I let go of her hair, grabbed her hips, and thrust so hard she almost broke the mirror. And then she was only screaming *yes* as she climaxed.

I didn't come so much as I had an out-of-body experience. The most intense orgasm of my entire life raced through my body and blackened my vision. I roared with pleasure, feeling it from the top of my head to the bottom of my feet.

And then we collapsed to the floor.

10

ROXY

*T*he floor was freezing, but I barely noticed. I was floating in that peaceful, happy place that exists after four earth-shattering orgasms. I wondered briefly what time it was, if people on the street had seen us.

They definitely had heard us.

"Roxy?" Edward asked. His voice was hoarse.

"Hmmmm," I murmured, stroking his hair with my fingers. I'd never been particularly cuddly, but Edward had the kind of hair that begged to be stroked.

"I guess you did end up having the sincere pleasure of seeing my arse."

I snorted, giving his hair a soft yank "And I never even wanted to see it in the first place."

"Liar," he teased. "But I'm sober now."

"Point being?"

"You can give me that tattoo. Right on my arse. Like I want-ed," he said, sitting up to look at me. He smiled, brushing my wild hair back from my face, scratching along the shaved side of my head. I wanted to purr.

"I'm not giving you that tattoo," I said, fighting the urge to curl up on his lap. I was no stranger to this kind of hook-up, and it was approaching the time when he needed to leave. "You'll have to find someone else to tattoo *'fuck you, Emily'* on your butt cheek."

I sat up, attempting a coolly aloof straight face, but ended up giggling when I fully took in how wrecked the parlor was. How wrecked *Edward* was.

"Did you just *giggle*?" Edward's eyebrows shot up. "What on God's green earth was that? Has the apocalypse begun? Did the four horsemen gallop by while we were fucking?"

"Oh, shut up," I said. "I'm a woman who occasionally has reason to giggle."

"Before or after you cut a man's heart out?" Edward asked.

"During."

Edward laughed, leaning in to give me a sloppy kiss that I returned. He stood up, and I allowed myself the briefest moment to admire his fully naked body. He was lean and chiseled everywhere—except for the round globes of his ass.

I bit my lip as I remembered spanking them.

"Do you want to know my new tattoo idea?" he asked, finding his underwear and suit pants. Sliding them on. There was a bite mark blooming on his chest.

"Sure."

He shrugged into his crisp, white shirt. Kept his eyes on me as he slowly hooked the remaining buttons on his shirt.

"My new idea is a tattoo that says *'all hail Queen Roxy.'*"

Edward looked down at me with the lightest blush on his cheeks. Cinched his cuff-links, brushed back his hair. He'd transformed back into a dignified Brit.

My heart was beating so loudly in my chest I was positive he could hear it.

"I was that good, huh?" I finally said. I stood up on shaky legs with tender muscles. I slipped on my shirt. Pulled up my

62

skirt. I didn't want to send this stranger into the night—or dawn—while naked.

Edward walked over and kissed me. Hard. "Bloody fantastic, love," he said. And kissed me again. He tilted my chin up, examining my ravaged neck. Winced. "I'm sorry if I—"

I shook my head. "No need. I actually wanted to ask you if that was... okay? You weren't uncomfortable?"

"More than okay," he promised. "Epic. Life-altering."

"Was it like your secret fantasies?"

He ran his hand through his hair. "Better, in a lot of ways. The pain and dominance made me feel... free. Weightless."

"Floaty," I added, and he nodded.

"Was I... to your expectations?" he asked. "I wasn't too clumsy or strange?"

"Those are not words I would use to describe you, Edward," I said. "In fact, if you hadn't said anything before, I would have thought you were quite the expert."

He gave me a shy smile. "I thought I'd be more nervous but... that wasn't the case."

I thought about Edward's strong fingers, twisting in my hair. His palm on my ass. Spreading my legs and fucking me with finesse.

"It's always okay to be nervous," I said. "But you didn't feel that way. To me."

Outside, the sun was starting to peek over the horizon, and *shit,* I had to finish that paper, inject coffee straight into my vein, and somehow make it to class before opening the shop later that night.

And I wanted more of Edward, but that wasn't going to happen.

He was fully dressed now, looking as refined as he'd been when he'd stumbled in. A wealthy, upper-class hotelier from England. We couldn't *be* more opposite. And like every other person like him I'd met in my life—and there were a good deal getting their MBA with me right now—I was no more than an exotic oddity to him.

"Well..." I started, feeling more awkward than I usually did when I indulged in hot stranger-sex.

"Can I ask you another question?" he interrupted.

"Sure," I said.

"May I take you to breakfast? There's a diner right down the street." He wasn't looking right at me because he was cleaning up the giant mess we'd made. Righting the tossed papers and fallen photos.

"I forgot to tell you," I said, keeping my voice light. "You don't usually take strange women to breakfast after a one-night stand, Dilbert. That's not the point."

I looked down at the words on my wrist: *Never Again*.

I thought he would laugh, but instead, he looked up at me. Stalked over until we were a foot apart. I cocked my hip, propped my hand there.

"I disagree with this concept, love," he said. "Let me buy you breakfast. A proper date."

"Edward," I said, "what happened tonight, between us, was unexpected and amazing. Truly." He leaned in for a kiss, and I stopped him with a palm to the chest. "But it was a night of casual sex. With a stranger. After a bad break-up." A flash of hurt through his eyes, but then it disappeared.

"Sex therapy," he said with a small smile, straightening his tie.

"Exactly." I shifted on my feet, feeling the dull ache between my legs that I knew would be there for days. Courtesy of Edward's phenomenal cock. "Go out. Find some new women to experiment with." My stomach twisted, but I soldiered on. "You'll get over Emily. I promise."

"But it's not Emily I'm thinking about now," he said softly.

We stared at each other for a long moment. I'd fucked guys and tossed them into the night a *dozen* times before.

It never felt like this.

And I knew it was only *breakfast*, but Edward had walked into this tattoo parlor barely four hours ago and in that time had charmed me, seduced me. Gave me the fuck of my goddamn life.

Breakfast with Edward would probably lead to a handful of dates—and a few weeks of enthusiastic, dirty sex—and then a bruised heart. Because there wasn't a single universe where a man like Edward and a woman like me could mean anything more to each other than fucking.

"Things will be different tomorrow morning. Once you've slept and truly sobered up. A new start, I promise."

Edward held my gaze for a second longer and then finally looked away. "Yes, well, all right, then. This is goodbye, I guess?"

"I'll see you around," I said with an arch of my eyebrow. Attempting to affect my typical demeanor.

"Will we though, Roxy?" he asked.

I cleared my throat. "Remember: sex therapy. It'll help. And for what it's worth—" I kept my eyes on the ground. "—You deserve better than Emily."

When I looked back up, Edward was smiling at me. "Thank you for that. For... everything." He slid his arm around my waist, pressed a soft kiss against my cheek.

"Goodbye, love," he whispered against my ear, and even after four orgasms I felt my body respond to him.

"Goodbye, Dilbert," I said.

11

EDWARD

Three months later

 My parents, Edward and Rebecca Cavendish, looked slightly disappointed at the restaurant I'd chosen to bring them to. I'd miscalculated, taking them to a newer restaurant that, while still appropriately swanky, was also the barest shade of *hip*.

"I didn't realize mason jars were an absolute necessity to Americans," my mother said, staring at the glass like a botanist in the field, scrutinizing leaves beneath a microscope.

"Ah, well," I shrugged. "Who bloody knows what they're into these days?"

I did, of course, having lived in New York for more than a decade. And while I sometimes missed England so badly it was a physical pain, I felt comfortable here.

My parents did not.

They were here for their annual spring trip to the States, which coincided with the three months leading up to a charity ball for the Kenley Collection, an art museum in the city that my parents had been patrons of for over twenty years. They both sat on the Board of Directors, and The Cartwright was always both the presenting sponsor *and* the venue.

Like The Cartwright, the ball was high-class, ridiculously expensive, and quite elegant. A charity event that allowed people in our social circle to see and be *seen*.

And every year they flew to New York City and stayed in The Cartwright's penthouse suite for three months, allowing them intimate access to plan the event at our hotel, endlessly criticize every single one of my decisions, and meddle in every detail of my life—including my romantic one.

"The Board is looking forward to seeing you tomorrow. I'll do the presentation first on the quarter one figures. And then you can speak about—"

"—how the Manhattan Cartwright is faring with regard to the other properties. Some trends your siblings are seeing at their properties. Things to be aware of," my father interjected.

I swallowed and then took a generous sip of my martini. My two younger siblings, like my parents, barely paid attention to the hotel properties they oversaw. They were *stewards* of their wealth, but when I moved here—or rather, was sent—to manage the failing Cartwright in Manhattan, I didn't do so in name only.

And yet my siblings and parents were continually lecturing me on "trends" that I'd known about for years.

"Good to hear," I said, smiling stiffly. "This is an exciting time for The Cartwright. And the ball will be wonderful to showcase some of our new features. I'm actually in plans to develop the rooftop—"

"—and how are the quarter one figures?" my mother asked, raising one single finger to beckon the waitstaff. They hurried over as if the restaurant was on fire.

You didn't keep a Cavendish waiting.

"Robust," I said. "And five percent higher than last year."

I'd learned over the years how to keep the desperation from my voice.

My parents both nodded, the Cavendish equivalent of a hug and a pat on the back. We shared the same color hair and blue eyes, but the matching frowns on their faces were distinctly their own.

I finished my martini in one gulp. I blinked, and a fresh one was placed in front of me. I shot the waitress an apologetic smile.

"Thank you," I said. "Please tell the chef the food is delicious."

She smiled. "She'll be happy to hear that."

But the waitress wasn't even out of earshot before my father sighed his disapproval. "Is every restaurant in this city becoming more and more mediocre?"

I smiled through it. "When would you like to begin meetings to discuss the ball? It's scheduled for the end of May, correct?"

"Yes," my mother said. "And we'd like to begin meeting immediately. As often as possible. Your father and I were both shocked at the disappointing lack of effort on your part for this event thus far."

I wondered if the vodka in my martini could be fed to me intravenously.

"Ah, yes," I said, clearing my throat. "I'm looking forward to it."

My father put down his utensils and pushed his plate away, filled with a half-eaten dinner. "Edward, your mother and I would like to talk about something serious."

"Well, all right," I said. "Is something wrong?"

"Edward," my mother said. "Are you and Emily going to reconcile? It's been more than three months since the separation."

My stomach twisted at the mention of Emily's name. Although when I thought about Emily, I thought about the night we broke up. Which means I thought about—

"I'm sorry, mother, but we are not," I said firmly. "Within a few hours of our conversation, she had already had her things removed from the apartment. And she might even be dating Stuart. A friend of mine."

"Was he the man who..." my father trailed off at the appropriate time.

"Yes," I answered, feeling the familiar anger sifting through my veins. Although it was much softer now, the pain feeling less like an open wound.

"Right, then," my mother continued. "Then it's clear that Emily was not the proper fit for our family or the values we would expect from your spouse. It's time for us to move on and find you a suitable wife."

I looked down at my plate, hiding a grimace. I should have anticipated this was going to happen, but I thought they'd wait a bit longer before hunting for spouses.

"Edward, you are thirty-five years old. Both of your younger siblings have married and had children. It's time that you fulfill the same responsibilities of carrying on the Cavendish legacy. You *do* want to own this hotel, correct?"

More than anything—which was a hard pill to swallow. Over the past decade, I'd come to love The Cartwright Hotel intensely. Loved the business, the guests, my staff. Hospitality suited my nature, and now that Emily and I were *not* getting married, I resented the marriage stipulations in my trust even more.

I wanted to own that bloody hotel.

"Absolutely," I said. "I'm more than ready to assume my legacy. So you're right. Is there anyone you have in mind?" And even as I said it, there was a twinge of regret. Because, for the past three months, my thoughts had been consumed by only one woman.

"We do, yes," my father said. "Do you remember the Bartlett family?"

"Of course," I lied. I'd spent my entire childhood and adolescence forced to mingle with England's wealthiest families. After a while, they all blurred together.

"Their daughter, Phoebe, is a few years younger than you and recently moved to New York. They're not as..." my mother dropped her voice to a whisper, "*well off* as we are, but they've done quite well for themselves. And Phoebe is managing a foundation in her grandfather's name, right here in Manhattan."

I tilted my head. She worked an honest job. More than that, a job that *helped* people. "That's lovely." I smiled. "Truly. Is she interested in meeting with me?"

"Yes, dear," my mother said, patting my hand. A rare display of affection, although she had polished off four martinis during dinner. "Her parents have spoken with us, and we quite support your union."

"Delightful," I replied, feeling my spirits lift slightly. Phoebe, at least, didn't sound as boring as cardboard—which was the usual standard my parents worked toward. Both of my siblings, Gregory and Jane, had married painfully dull people, although they seemed happy. Not *in love*, of course, but content.

And maybe that was the goal in life.

Wasn't it?

Except as dinner waned on, and my parents discussed news from home, I kept glancing toward the door, praying for a blonde vixen with a sexy scowl and a leather jacket to swoop in, grab me by the arm, and pull me out of this restaurant.

Roxy.

I thought about her in the morning, drinking coffee on my balcony and watching the sun rise over the city skyline. I thought about her in the middle of meetings and during phone calls. In the banal tasks of answering emails, scrawling messages on post-it notes. On long runs, I'd sometimes run past her shop, hoping for a glimpse.

I never saw her. But even though she hadn't wanted to see me again, I was comforted by the fact that I knew where she worked. Could blaze in there months from now, and she'd be there.

And maybe she would even have changed her mind.

But nights were the worst. Before Roxy, it was the only time in my day I'd gently pry open the sexual fantasies I kept under lock and key.

After Roxy, they were flesh-and-blood *real*. I knew intimately, now, the feel of my palm against the smooth skin of her ass. The way she craved pain and pleasure in a beautiful dance. Her submission, which was as erotic to me as her defiance. The way she'd wrenched back control, over and over.

All the secret ways I craved to hand it over to her now. In fact, moments like these—of high stress—I longed for Roxy. Longed to be placed on my knees in front of her spread legs and commanded to serve.

"Edward?" My father said sharply, snapping me from my reverie. The check was in front of me.

"Ah, of course," I said, smiling weakly. "Dinner's on me."

12

ROXY

iona and I were standing outside The Red Room, one of New York City's oldest punk rock clubs. Bundled up against the wet March weather, we were huddled in the alley, attempting to find a quiet place to talk.

It was well past midnight, but our parents hadn't finished their set yet.

"I've often wondered if it's wrong that our sixty-year-old parents have always been able to stay up later than us," Fiona said on a yawn, leaning against me for warmth. She looked about as out of place here as you could get—suit by Armani, jacket by Dolce, diamonds in her ear, her honey-blonde hair tucked back into a delicate bun. She was Grace Kelly, standing in a sea of dirty punk rockers.

"I've always wondered if it's wrong that our sixty-year-old parents have face tattoos," I grinned. Fiona was the only member of our family *not* covered in ink, although I'd promised to design something beautiful for her: floral. Elegant, just like her.

But she always said no.

"Set was good though," I said, nodding along to the music

we could still hear, even outside. "I'm digging their new stuff."

Another yawn from Fiona. "Me too. I just wish they played at a respectable hour. Like 6:30. Some of us have clients in the morning. Persnickety ones."

I turned to my little sister. "Do tell. Who are these persnickety clients?" My sister was a lawyer in estate planning. My parents didn't understand the law. In fact, they'd spent much of their life actively circumventing it whenever possible. They were anarchists to the core—although they'd both cried tears of joy at my sister's graduation from law school. To which they had worn leather jackets that said *Subvert the System.*

I'd tried to point out the irony, but they didn't see it.

"The usual," Fiona shrugged. "It's not the client. She's fabulous. An older socialite who wants to dedicate her entire estate to three different charities after a lifetime of, according to her, 'hoarding it to herself.'" My sister smiled. "Which is wonderful and exactly what I can help her with. But it's her children."

"Brats, huh?"

"Fucking assholes," she said. She might adhere to that Grace Kelly aesthetic, but she was still raised in a household where the f-word was encouraged as an act of rebellion against the state.

"And don't you have class tomorrow?"

"Class and work, but tomorrow is the first day of my final Capstone Project for my MBA," I said. "Like a thesis, only this program at CUNY was designed specifically to be a mentoring opportunity. Working with actual business owners who will take a look at the shop and tell me how to fix it."

Fiona frowned in sympathy. "You think it'll help?" She knew my financial woes, having listened to me come up with any number of rescue plans if the shop stopped being sustainable.

"God, I hope so," I sighed. "I chose this program because of the Capstone Project. I wanted something that wasn't theoretical, but practical. You know, tell me what's wrong so I can make it successful."

Even though I had a feeling what was *wrong* with the shop was that I was the one in charge of it.

"Just three more months, probably mentoring with some bad-ass chick who owns, I don't know, an indie record store or something. Get some hands-on experience. And then I'm done with these corporate fuckers," I said.

Fiona smirked.

"No offense," I teased.

"Oh, none taken," she grinned. "And speaking of *hands-on experience*, did you ever hear from that guy again? You know, the one in the suit? The sexy English guy?"

I narrowed my eyes at my younger sister, the perpetual mind reader. "No. It was a one-night thing. I told you that."

"Yeah, but you think about him all the time though."

"It was three months ago," I pointed out.

She tilted her head, lawyer brain activating. "Evading the question."

"I *don't* think about him, Fi," I lied through my teeth. She knew it too. Since the night Edward had strode into my shop and rocked my goddamn world, I'd been perpetually horny— but unable to take any other strangers home to dull the ache. Instead, I got myself off every night to memories of his cock, his tongue. That sexy grin. Those filthy words in his sophisticated accent.

The feeling I'd gotten that he'd shown a part of himself to me that he'd never shown anyone before.

But it was right to send him on his way. The fact that I was kind of *pining* for him now only proved my point.

Edward led to heartbreak. I could *feel* it.

"We're going to talk about this later," Fiona said, pinching my arm.

"Hey, *ow*," I said before turning around to spot my parents, flushed and happy, spilling out from the club. Lou and Sandy Quinn beamed before wrapping us in a giant bear hug—no easy feat when their outfits were *spiked*.

"There's our girls," our mom said, looking, as usual, much younger than her sixty-four years. Pants still leather. Combat boots steel-toed. Except she'd let her hair gray and did much less eye makeup now ("I prefer more of the natural look now that I'm older," she'd once told me, only applying *one* layer of black eye-liner, instead of her usual three).

"Great set, guys," I said, patting my dad on the back. He flashed me a wink, waving to people as they milled out from the beloved concert venue. In the seventies and eighties, The Red Room had been famous for its underground punk rock scene: Patti Smith, The Clash, The Sex Pistols. And of course, as many times as they could, my parents' band, The Hand Grenades. They'd never seen any real meteoric rise or chart-topping success, but they had a loyal group of fans who followed them wherever they toured.

Fiona and I were the only kids in our school who had terrifying anarchist punks at our graduation parties. Except those terrifying punks were also our godparents Tom and Judy.

"Yeah, your mom was really rocking on those drums," my dad said.

My mom beamed up at him. "Well, your father screamed those vocals like a champ. I could have sworn it was Joe Strummer up there."

My sister and I *awwwed* since, in our family, being compared to the infamous lead singer of The Clash was like being compared to Mother Teresa.

"Are you back on the road for a bit?" I asked, but they shook their heads.

"Nope," Dad said. "We wanted to make sure we were around for your graduation. We've got a huge party planned. *Huge.*"

"It's three months away," I grumbled. "And I don't need a party."

"Of course you need a party," my mom exclaimed. "You are a smart, brilliant businesswoman—and now the second person in this family to get an advanced degree. Look at your father and I! We barely made it through the first year of college before dropping out."

"That's because you and dad didn't believe in the education system," Fiona said, rolling her eyes.

"So true," dad conceded. "So true. But your mother and I have always wanted what's best for our brilliant, talented daughters. And if being a... a—"

"Lawyer," Fiona filled in.

"Yes, lawyer! If being a lawyer or a renowned business-woman is what our daughters want to be, then fuck yes, we're having a fucking party!" My dad held his fist in the air, giving a roar, and behind him went up an answering chorus.

Fiona and I glanced at each other, amused. It was *always* a party in our family.

"Well, that would be wonderful," I finally said. "But you know you don't have to."

"Oh we definitely have to. We're planning it. You're going, no excuses," my mom said, squeezing my shoulders. "And did you get that paper back? The one you were so worried about?"

I'd had a huge final essay due in my Marketing class that I'd fretted over for weeks. Marketing wasn't my strong suit. I figured if you wanted to get a tattoo, you looked up a tattoo parlor.

Done and done.

But this paper was about strategies and improving the "stickiness of your brand." I didn't really give a shit about things like that.

So I was still fretting about it.

"I get it back tomorrow," I said, half-laughing when my parents held up their hands with every finger crossed.

"You can't see, but I'm crossing my toes," Dad said.

"Alright alright," I said, shoving off from the wall. "I get it. You love and support me." I leaned in for dual sets of hugs, opening up for Fiona to join in. "But your straight-laced lawyer daughter and failing business school daughter both need to get home so we can wake up at dawn."

"Thank you for coming out," Mom said, finally letting us go. "It's always nice to see you, moshing about."

I gave them a silly half-bow. "My pleasure. Walk you to your car, Fi?"

She nodded, linking our arms, and we left our parents to play music for another few hours.

We were a strange family. But a good one.

"I know you're worried, but you're going to do great. And you're not going to fail," Fiona said, shivering in the wind.

"Thank you," I replied. "And... yeah. I think it'll be fine. I'll meet my mentor. They'll have some kind of life-changing advice for me throughout the next few months. I'll save the shop. And meet a man who wants to spend his nights giving me multiple orgasms. And is into spanking."

"Oh, like the guy in the suit?" Fiona asked with mock innocence.

"*Not* like that guy," I grinned. "Someone else. Someone more my type."

"Hmmm," Fiona said, pinning me with a look that made me fidget. But she didn't say anything else. And neither did I.

13

EDWARD

"*A*nd so, as you can... um, see... well, yes, it's right in front of you, isn't it? Right? Right," I stumbled.

I could feel a drop of sweat rolling down my back. To my left sat my father, looking dapper as always, although his expression was one of mild embarrassment. This had quickly become the Board meeting from hell—although they always were for me. I did a lot of things spectacularly well in my life.

Public speaking wasn't one of them.

"The gist of it is, well, we ended quarter four up three percent over projections," I said, attempting a smile since this was bloody good news. Especially in light of our failing sister hotel upstate. "And quarter one, ah... let me... let me see..."

In the far, back I heard a muffled laugh, some whispering. Carter and Ian, two of our newest Board members who insisted on sniveling like public school boys during every meeting.

"Are we done, Edward?" my father asked, shifting in his chair and then standing, effectively ending my failed presentation.

"Of course, fath—um, *sir*," I finally managed, taking a seat and then a generous gulp of water.

The Board members were nonplussed by my stuttering as they'd witnessed this for years. But it'd been made worse by my father's presence. Every year during their spring trip, he sat in on regular Board meetings.

And every year I failed miserably.

My father pulled up a graph of recent trends in the hospitality business—a graph I'd actually already shown them six months ago when I put the plans in motion to expand the hotel. But the Board members were always in awe of my father, and so they politely nodded their heads at this delivery of old information.

I sat and stewed, tracing lines on my report, barely paying attention. I knew, at the end, he'd give a recommendation that we bring on additional amenities to the hotel—amenities I'd already brought on. And we'd say 'aye,' and they'd congratulate him, and he'd continue to overshadow me. This was the endless, vicious cycle of managing this hotel instead of owning it. My parents rarely intervened on the decisions that George and Jane made when it came to their properties, but that was not the case for me.

What I'd been *trying* to say, before his interruption, was that ever since I'd taken over this hotel, our revenue had been steadily increasing every single quarter, even during the recession. Even as other hotels in the industry had closed down or continued to do poorly, The Cartwright Hotel in Manhattan had thrived.

But he'd never mention it. Never would. And I couldn't quite help but feel ten years old again, attempting to impress my parents with my high marks.

When you were a Cavendish, perfection was *expected*. So when you provided perfection, what was there to praise?

I was never sure if it was like this for my two younger siblings, who'd toed the line—and performed their duties—with aplomb. Gregory still lived in England, and Jane lived here in the States. But we were never close, and I constantly wondered if I was the only one who desperately sought our parents' approval.

And ever since Roxy had shown me a few hours of heady, liberating freedom, I struggled in a different way entirely.

"So I want to see new ideas from this Board and the manager," my father said, looking at me, "within two weeks. We need to start moving on capital improvements if we expect to see *any* financial gains within the next two years. And with the Kenley Collection charity ball set here at the end of Spring, it's as fine a time as any to showcase those improvements."

The Board members were nodding although I'd said the exact same thing. But I nodded as well, giving my father a grim smile, and then he sat back down.

"Well then, if there isn't any more, um, business... we shall adjourn," I said, letting out a long, low exhale.

Fucking hell, I hated this part of my job.

It was the reason why I conducted almost all of my meetings one-on-one or in very small groups. It never bothered me then. But make me stand up in front of an audience?

I was a goner.

And it annoyed the daylights out of my father.

I shook hands and made idle small talk before gathering my papers and preparing to leave with my father.

"Great job in there, sir," I said. "Really rallied them to make some important changes."

"Yes," he replied idly. "Someone had to be the voice of authority in there, Edward. It didn't help the way you were blithering on."

I swallowed, wondering if Elliott was around to become immediately drunk with me. "Ah yes, father. Right you are. I'll be sure to work on it."

"Gregory never gets nervous in front of his meetings."

This was new, pitting the siblings against each other. I wanted, desperately, to rise to the bait. To tell him that Gregory routinely sought advice from me for his failing hotel in London, and I gave it. That his last three great ideas were my own. And that Gregory was an absolute wanker but I still helped him because he was my brother.

"I've always looked up to Gregory," I said through gritted teeth. "Thank you for that reminder."

My father didn't say a word but merely walked down the hallway toward the penthouse suite he'd be staying in for another... *fuck,* three months. This happened every year, and every year I somehow allowed myself to be surprised at the way they made me feel.

I took out my mobile phone, calling Elliott. Elliott St. James had been my best friend since I moved here a decade ago. He also hailed from a wealthy family in London, and he ran The Logan, a luxury hotel just a few blocks from here.

"Who is this, and how did you get my number?" Elliott said as he picked up.

"Listen, mate, how soon can you meet me for a drink tonight? I'm talking emergency-level beer at the pub."

"Let me guess. Edward and Rebecca are in town," Elliott replied.

"For their annual trip."

"*Shit*. We'll need shots," he said.

I laughed, looking at my watch. "I knew I could count on you. Listen, what about 8:30? That work?"

"For sure. And aren't you late for your thing?" he asked.

I furrowed my brow, glancing at my watch again. Then at my calendar.

"Bloody hell, I am."

14

ROXY

I stared at the "C-" on my marketing paper and grimaced. This wasn't good—especially since this paper was 20% of my grade in that class. I thought I'd done *well*. Not an "A," but at least a solid "B."

I mentally tried to figure out if this was going to make me fail that class. My stomach twisted since I really couldn't afford to delay graduation by taking it again.

I sighed, letting my head fall onto my desk. I was sitting in the room for my Capstone Project, and as usual I stood out like a sore thumb. I'd felt out of place for the majority of my Executive MBA experience, and if I was being honest with myself, it wasn't just that they didn't *look* like me.

Although they didn't. And men outnumbered women three-to-one.

But I also got the impression they didn't need this program. They all seemed *pulled together* in a way I didn't feel. Between taking on ownership of the business, maintaining my list of clients, managing two employees *and* enrolling in this program, I felt as stretched thin as I'd ever had. Running in four different directions, constantly anxious. Afraid of the bills that piled up at the shop. Afraid to look at my grades. I was the owner of a failing tattoo parlor in a neighborhood that was becoming too trendy.

My classmates, on the other hand, appeared to have their life together in a way I was deeply envious of.

"Welcome everyone," Professor Stevens smiled, leaning on her desk. She was an older white woman with short red hair and square-rimmed glasses. "This is your Capstone Project, the final thesis you must complete in order to attain your master's degree. This project is a hands-on mentorship program which will take place over the next three months." Other people were beginning to file in behind her, giving us small, nervous smiles.

"This is an excellent volunteer opportunity for local business leaders, and we paired their applications most closely with your business, your career goals, and your current challenges. The hope is that over three months of shadowing and meeting with each other, you will come away with real-life experience and a broader understanding of what *you* need to succeed."

My heart raced, just slightly, and I sat up taller in my seat. I didn't know what I needed, but I was putting my bright, shiny hopes in the hands of this person.

"Mentors, please go take your seats next to your mentees. I'll call out the names so you can find each other," Professor Stevens said, slowly reading down the list. When she reached my name, she frowned slightly, looking around.

"Roxy, I'm sorry, but your mentor appears to be running late. Shouldn't be an issue," she said, smiling kindly. I swallowed, smiling back, looking around at everyone else. Paired up and chatting.

Professor Stevens went back to the presentation, outlining expectations, and I tried not to read into their lateness. They were probably held up in traffic or coming from a meeting. It couldn't be that they read my application and looked at my business and decided it was a complete and total waste of effort.

Right?

Fifteen minutes crawled by, and instead of watching the door like a hawk, I tossed my hair, crossed my legs, attempted as much nonchalance about my missing mentor as possible. This was only the *very single reason* why I'd chosen to get this degree. It wasn't *that* big of a deal.

Another ten minutes, and I was jiggling my feet under the table. Professor Stevens was outlining how often we needed to meet with our mentor—at least once a week, shadowing each other, brainstorming. It was intimate, and I'd hoped that I'd get matched with someone like me. Someone I could learn from. Offer me guidance on things that were out of my control, like our changing neighborhood. The constant fear I felt when I ran our numbers. The intense, gut-churning guilt I got when I thought about having to fire Mack or Scarlett.

How was I ever going to be able to balance it all: the day-to-day tasks combined with the all-consuming *pressure*?

And now I was going to be paired up with this asshole who was almost *thirty minutes* late.

So I tuned out, opening up a blank page in my notebook and lightly starting to sketch the tattoo I was scheduled to do tomorrow. My specialty was vintage sailor tattoos, and my client wanted an anchor inked on her ribcage—except instead of intertwining rope, she envisioned roses. For a few precious minutes I was able to lose myself in lines of black ink.

Until there was a burst of sound from the front door.

"Oh, Mr. Cavendish, you made it," Professor Stevens said, and I glanced up on instinct to see Edward, *the* Edward, looking dashing in a dark suit while smoothing down his tie with a slightly sheepish grin.

"So sorry I'm late, Professor," he said in his clipped accent. "I don't want to interrupt, I think the name of my student is..." he pulled out a slip of paper.

I watched his brow furrow. He looked up, and our eyes locked.

"Roxy?" he asked, and it was a question directed right at me.

The world stopped.

I remembered my fingers, wrapping around his silk tie and pulling his face in for a kiss. The sound of utter gratification he'd made when he'd fucked me with his tongue. His look of euphoria when he'd taken me against the mirror.

The multiple orgasms.

"Hey," I managed as Professor Stevens led Edward to the chair right next to mine. He sat down gingerly, barely concealing the look of shock on his face. "I'm Roxy."

I held out my hand, and when his palm met mine, there was a shower of sparks.

"Roxy, this is Edward Cavendish, your mentor." The professor smiled at us before heading back to the front.

And in the quiet darkness, Edward squeezed my hand. "Pleasure to meet you, love."

15

EDWARD

I wanted to stand on top of this desk and dance a bloody jig.

Roxy was my mentee.

I'd been so distracted since my parents arrived, I hadn't once glanced at the email from Professor Stevens—only to put the time down on my calendar and note which room I needed to be in. I'd been mentoring in this program for the past five years. Always made time for it, even though it *always* coincided with my parents' arrival. But it was important to me—a way of giving back that was more personal than volunteering for an hour or sending a check.

My parents had sent me to the States at twenty-five with barely a chat about what it meant to run a luxury hotel in downtown Manhattan, and for the first few years, I'd had to work through paralyzing fear and anxiety.

If I'd had something like this, I would have grabbed onto it like a drowning man grasping a life preserver.

"Now this is a strictly professional relationship," Professor Stevens continued, "and I've had many mentees and mentors tell me they continue professionally supporting each other for years following this experience. If it's a good match, and I hope it will be, think of this relationship as a long-term investment. In your career, your business, your life."

I chanced a glance at Roxy and tried to picture thinking of her in strictly professional terms. Her eyes were boring into the presentation at the front of the class, completely avoiding mine, but I'd heard her slight intake of breath when our hands touched. Wondered if she was replaying our night together since I surely was. Wondered if she had thought about it every single day for the past three months because I surely had.

Even now, her mere presence had me aching to haul her into my lap. Let her grind her way to orgasm in the middle of this classroom

She was an electrifying punk-rock goddess. Half of her head was shaved; the other half was still that white-blonde hair coasting down her back. Thick black eyeliner and a nose ring. A tank-top with Debbie Harry's face plastered across the front. Ripped jeans and deadly looking boots.

Had I always dreamed of a woman like Roxy?

"You'll meet at least once a week to discuss the mentee's goals for themselves as outlined in their initial proposals. But this mentorship also requires a fair amount of job shadowing. Watching and assessing each other and providing feedback on strengths, weaknesses, and things they can improve upon," Professor Stevens said.

I fidgeted in my seat since I'd spent a fair amount of time with my past five mentees, and we *did* continue to talk and support each other even years later.

The thought of having Roxy, sitting in my office, semi-scowling as I told her how I'd learned to become a first-class hotelier was... arousing.

Strictly professional.

I shook my head, glancing down at Roxy's application and

reading it thoroughly for the first time. I'd had no idea she was getting her MBA, and it said here that Roxy Quinn was the owner of a tattoo parlor in Washington Heights.

The questionnaire listed some recent struggles: dwindling revenue. A changing neighborhood landscape. Challenges with marketing and finding the right target audience. I grimaced when I saw her most recent profit and loss statement which she'd included in the packet. Looked back up at her with sympathy since I understood that feeling well: the sheer chaos of numbers. Being held hostage by the ebb and flow of money predicating not just your future but the future of the employees who relied on you.

"At the end of the three months, the mentee will prepare a presentation on what they learned, the feedback they received, and any goals moving forward. The presentation, and participation in the project, is a requirement of graduation from the CUNY Executive MBA program." Professor Stevens beamed. "Any questions?"

There was a short silence, and then she flipped on the lights. I blinked, rubbing my eyes, but Roxy and I were still sitting here, knees almost touching, in a small classroom. About to be paired up for three months.

I wasn't dreaming.

"Then why don't you start by getting to know each other a little bit," Professor Stevens said, turning off the projector. "And please don't hesitate to come to me with questions."

The room filled with a low murmur, and I turned to face Roxy. Cleared my throat awkwardly, and she finally set those dark eyes on mine.

"What are you doing here?" she asked in her midnight voice. Her expression was a combination of shock and betrayal.

"I do this every year actually," I said gently. "It's really important to me, to give back to other small business owners. To be a support since I know what it's like to be all on your own." I paused for a second. "To take on that pressure. I know how hard it is, love."

"Don't call me 'love,'" she said firmly. She was all scowls and high walls now, arms crossed over her chest.

"I'm sorry," I admitted. "And the truth is, no one showed me how to run a hotel when I arrived in Manhattan ten years ago. I was twenty-five and terrified. I knew no one. Had no friends. And suddenly hundreds of employees were relying on me to get it right. We all have our challenges, even a Cavendish."

She swallowed, taking my words into consideration. I noticed her notebook was filled with a gorgeous design—an anchor blossoming with brightly colored roses.

When she looked away, I leaned closer. "Roxy. Do you want me to request a new student? Is this making you uncomfortable? What... what happened between us? Because I completely understan—"

"No," she said quickly. *Very* quickly. "No, I mean, I trust you, Edward. Because of what we did." The lightest blush appeared on her cheeks.

"Oh... right, of course," I said nervously. "That makes a certain kind of sense."

Roxy nodded, biting her lip. A dent in that brash confidence. "I guess, why rock the boat? Everyone's already been paired up, so might as well. And this is professional. The two of us. Right?"

"Absolutely," I said, wanting to get on my knees and weep with gratitude.

Because if I'd had any doubt that my electric attraction to Roxy was a one-time thing, seeing her now was blowing that theory to smithereens.

I wanted her. Desperately.

"Then I think it's... fine," she said with a careless shrug.

All around us, students and their mentors were standing and leaving, and I didn't want the temptation of being in this room alone with Roxy.

"If you think it's fine, then I do too," I said, standing and indicating the door. "So why don't I walk you to your subway stop?"

I stood outside the entry to the subway, nodding at the stack of papers Edward was holding. It was my application, exposing all the dirty, intimate details of what was happening at the tattoo parlor where he'd given me the most spectacular fuck of my life.

"I really need this mentoring, Edward," I said, meeting his gaze. "It's the entire reason I chose this program. And you'll see what I mean when you go through the paperwork. Any advice or guidance you could give me would mean everything to the shop and the people who work for me."

"It's a lot of anxiety, being the one in charge," he said softly, and my throat tightened.

"Not the same as running a world-class hotel, right?"

"Ah," he said, letting a smile linger on his lips. "That's the first thing you'll have to stop doing, love—I mean, Roxy." He coughed awkwardly.

"What?" I asked.

"Comparing your business to others. Judging. It only causes more misery, believe me."

I turned that sentiment over in my head, trying to find its

95

weak points. "You'll tell me more about that at a later date, I assume?"

"I'll tell you anything you'd like," he said. I gave him a tiny smile. He returned it. "But honestly, Roxy, this is what I'm here for. And I can continue to mentor you for as long as you feel it's appropriate." He lifted his palms. "No hidden agenda, just happy to help. I truly enjoy it."

I nodded, kicking a rock with my boots. Took a deep breath. "And we'll keep things professional, like Professor Stevens said."

"Of course," he said, voice rough around the edges. "We'll pretend that... that thing that happened, between us—"

"The hot fucking—" I interjected.

"Yes, that," he grinned, and my fingers itched to reach forward. Tug him closer.

"We'll pretend the *hot fucking* never happened," I said. There was a short, charged silence. "Can I ask you a personal question before the professionalism begins?"

"Of course," he said.

"How are you? After Emily?" I'd thought about him experiencing the same pain I'd felt when Jimmy had cheated. The rage, but also the embarrassment.

"I'm doing alright," he promised. "You were right. With time, it feels better. Plus, my parents are already working to marry me off with Emily Two. Although I'm not sure if she's the bland, boring banker you had originally suggested."

The thought of Edward with anyone else, no matter how boring, caused a hot spike of jealousy I couldn't ignore. "And did you do what I said? Sex therapy?"

I wasn't sure what answer I wanted.

But Edward looked startled and then a slightly sheepish. "Oh... Roxy, no. I haven't... well, there hasn't *been* anyone. Not since you."

I was speechless for a moment. "Oh... well. Okay." I kicked my boots against the gravel again, letting the silence linger. Wanting to say more but knowing I shouldn't. So instead, I crossed my arms across my chest. Straightened my spine. "What time would you like to set up our first meeting?"

Edward rubbed a hand down his smooth jaw. "How about I bring you coffee tomorrow? Meet you at the shop? We can discuss your goals, next steps. Set up some shadowing appointments. Sound about right?"

I nodded. "And you know where..."

"I remember," he said quickly with a slight blush.

Professionalism sucked.

"So I'll see you then," he said, starting to turn to leave, giving me a small wave.

"I'll see you then. And good night," I replied, turning rigidly toward the stairs.

When did I get *so awkward?*

But I chanced one last glance over my shoulder, watching him walk through the parking lot, admiring the long lines of his body in his expensive suit.

This was not good.

From my bedroom window I could see the blinking lights of 'Roxy's', the handful of missing bulbs glaring at me. I'd thought it was a good idea to move one block away from work when I took over the business, but now it felt like I could never escape it.

I sat on my bed, surrounded by the copies of the papers and reports that Edward had received. Attempted to study them again as, per the usual, all three of my animals were fighting to be both *on* the bed and *on* my body.

Apple, an old, sleepy cat, had been in the animal shelter for years and was probably close to a million years old. But she was the first animal I'd ever adopted, and even though they told me she probably wouldn't live long, the thought of her dying without a forever home was too much for me.

Plus, that was five years ago, and even though she was basically deaf, she was still going strong. Cucumber was a spry three-year-old tabby cat, who loved Apple with all of his heart and spent most of his day attempting to sit next to her (she sometimes allowed it).

And then there was Busy Bee, my three-legged pit bull, who was laying all 75 pounds of his weight across my lap, trying to eat my recent profit and loss statements. When I met Bee, he'd just had his leg amputated after surviving a car crash. A persistent stray, they weren't sure of his pedigree or his background, only that for the months he'd lived in the shelter he could only lay, mournfully in the corner, refusing to get up. The shelter staff had taken me right to him, at this point *well* aware of my secretly tender heart, and when he'd looked up at me with those big, sad eyes, I'd said, "That's my dog."

He was not only the sweetest animal on the planet but also needed to cuddle with every living thing around him at all times, including Apple and Cucumber who never failed to cast me bemused feline expressions as he tried to sit on them.

The Manhattan Island Animal Shelter called constantly, knowing that I'd adopt every single animal if I could. But my tiny, one-bedroom apartment was already maxed out as it was with three animals and one scowling human with a large assortment of sex toys.

I still took their calls though.

"If you eat my financial statements, I'll *never* achieve greatness, Bee," I half-scolded, kissing the top of his head. "Also if *you* can tell me what all of this means, that'd be great."

He could only sigh, laying his head in my lap, and I peeked again at the shop sign blinking hot pink in the dark.

I had a Cavendish for a mentor.

It'd been bad enough when I'd only *fucked* a Cavendish. And I didn't usually give a flying fuck about the wealthy families that showed up in the gossip rags. But everyone in Manhattan knew that family because everyone in Manhattan stared, in awe, at the rising, elegant skyscraper that was The Cartwright Hotel. It dominated the skyline—you couldn't *not* see it. The most lavishly elite hotel in the entire city run by a family famous for their elite, first-class properties.

I felt a strange combination of dread and elation. If Edward could help me bring even an *ounce* of that Cartwright success to the tattoo parlor, I'd be sleeping on a bed of money every fucking night.

But it also meant admitting that I was terrified and drifting in a sea of anxiety. Showing him my past two years of fuck-ups and mistakes.

I stroked Busy Bee's fur, feeling my heart thud in my chest when I thought about our coffee date tomorrow.

No, not a date. Our coffee *meeting.* A meeting of two business professionals, working to support each other. Professionally.

Except the dirty secret I hadn't told Edward was that I also hadn't slept with anyone since that night.

Three long months without sex. No strangers. No friends-with-benefits. No old hook-ups. I couldn't seem to work up the energy to be *attracted* to anyone else.

Except Edward. Who I never thought I'd see again.

17

EDWARD

*T*he pub was called The Crown and Elliott and I had been coming here to soothe our mutual homesickness for ten years.

It was dark, and quiet, and the owner was an old, grumpy Brit named Lewis who knew just what kind of beer to stock to make two ex-pats feel at home. It had a bit of a reputation in Manhattan and attracted its fair share of people like Elliott and me. It also attracted tourists and Americans, but on certain nights—like tonight—if I closed my eyes and *listened*, it sounded like any corner pub in the middle of London.

"Another, right, mate?" Elliott asked, flagging over Lewis, who automatically slid two pints our way with a grunt.

"Bless you, my friend," I smiled, feeling a little tipsy and more than a little maudlin. Elliott tipped his pint back, laughing, eyes flicking up to watch the telly, where Lewis only ever showed the Manchester United games.

Elliott and I had met at a hotelier conference ten years ago when I was new and nervous and desperate for a friend in this huge, terrifying city that was *nothing* like London.

"Technically, we're rivals," he'd said, the first day we'd met, "and if you ever stole any trade secrets from me, I'd beat you up. Probably."

"Duly noted," I'd replied, surprised at his bluntness. But liking it. "Same goes for you."

Then he'd flashed me that famous St. James grin, held out his hand, and shook mine tightly. "It should also be noted that I think the rivals thing is a bunch of bollocks. So why don't we be friends instead?"

We talked shop sometimes, and it was wonderful to have a friend who understood the pressures of our job. But really, Elliott and I connected over our shared pasts: wealthy, tight-lipped families where affection was hard to come by—but you were presented with the pressure and burden of continuing a family "legacy" from birth.

"How'd the Board meeting go?" he asked, knocking his pint against mine before taking a generous gulp. Elliott was Black, with a shaved head and a million-dollar smile. A handful of women at the other end of the bar were attempting to get his attention, but he ignored them.

"Bloody awful," I said. "I was all nerves, as usual, and then my dad stood up, spouted a bunch of nonsense, and they fell all over themselves for his approval."

"Right, right," he nodded. "Par for the course. And Emily?"

I grimaced. "At first, my parents asked if we were going to reconcile."

"Terrible idea," Elliott admitted.

Elliott had never *really* been fond of Emily, and even though he understood the complex pressures of maintaining a certain "appearance," his goal was always *authenticity*. Operating in this world was something he *could* do, and did, but he was continually on the quest for real people, buried beneath the fur and pearls. *Real* conversation and friendship. The only reason why Elliott hadn't pushed me harder to break up with Emily two years ago was because he thought I might *love* her.

Something I thought as well.

When I'd called him the morning after, I'd said something like "Emily's dumped me for Stuart, who she's been shagging for six months now. And I had life-altering sex with a complete stranger in a tattoo parlor."

He'd barely said a word, completely unlike him, but not thirty minutes later, he'd been at my door with food and liquor.

"Whiskey," he'd said. "For the absolute and utter awfulness that comes from a piece of shit like Emily cheating on you, mate." He pulled out champagne next. "Mimosas because it's morning, and we're at least somewhat elegant. And we need to celebrate your first successful one-night stand." I'd laughed, and he'd walked all the way into my condo. Laid out ingredients for a hearty English breakfast. "Coffee with two shots of espresso because you look like death warmed over. And breakfast because someone who's just been cheated on deserves a home-cooked meal."

And Elliott was the only person in my life who knew I still thought about Roxy. A lot.

"Couldn't agree more," I said, tuning back to the conversation. "But then they mentioned a new woman, Phoebe Bartlett." Elliott tilted his head. "Do you know her?"

"Doesn't ring a bell," he said. "She seem like a decent human being?"

"Actually, yes," I said slowly, shifting on my bar stool. "Which was surprising to me. And I guess we have a date next week?" I'd gotten the email from my mother—crisp, no superlatives —formally setting it up.

Elliott gave me the side eye. "Interesting."

Elliott understood the marriage clause of my trust—

understood that in order to achieve the career greatness I'd longed for more than a decade, I needed a wife. And not any wife—one that came parentally approved.

We drank in silence for a moment as I mulled something over. Something I'd been thinking about quite a bit.

"Elliott," I asked. "Do you think your parents are in love?"

He almost spit out his drink. "*My* parents? Absolutely not, mate. How could they be? It's like a business arrangement. A partnership. Not love."

"I think it's the same for mine," I said. "No, I take that back. I'm damn well sure of it. Does it ever bother you?"

Elliott rubbed his jaw. "I don't know. It's their life. Their choices. It seems to work for them. They have goals; they want to make money. They want to be splashed all over the society pages in England. Being married to each other accomplishes those goals so..." he trailed off, shrugging. "I don't think they're in love. But I don't think that bothers them. Which is why they keep begging me to go on these horrible dates."

"And who have they been sending you this time?"

He grinned. "Some woman; I don't know. As soon as I see it's the wrong gender, I don't even read the email. I keep *telling* them I fuck men, but they keep sending these women my way to set up my own personal business arrangement with. Or 'marriage' as we call it."

"You say it like that, yeah?" I teased.

"Well, no, not exactly. But I do politely decline, citing my romantic preference for men. Which they continue to ignore. And the vicious cycle continues."

"But what happens when you fall in love with someone, and you want to marry him?" I asked. "What then?"

Elliott shrugged, avoiding my gaze in favor of the game on TV. "Not their life. So it's not going to be their problem." He clenched his jaw, and both of us knew the unspoken tension—

as brashly authentic as Elliott was, it was still hard to throw off decades of pressure and societal conditioning. Like me, Elliot's two older sisters had married people his parents had approved of. And it worked for them because they adored being London socialites, getting their pictures taken at charity galas, and enjoying a life of luxury.

But Elliott, like me, was different. And as we both neared turning thirty-five this year, I knew the pressure from our parents would be cranked up to astronomical levels. We both despised it while at the same time struggled to shrug it off fully.

"How was your thing, though?" he asked, smoothly changing the subject. "At CUNY. You meet your mentee?"

I rubbed my hands down my face. "I did. And you'll never believe who it is."

"What?" he grinned. "Is it someone awful? Do you hate them already?"

"No, no, the exact opposite, actually." I signaled for another pint. "It's Roxy. The woman from the tattoo parlor."

Elliott's jaw dropped open. "The woman who you had, and I quote, '*life-altering sex*' with?"

"The one and only."

Elliott stared at me, jaw open. "Stop joking, yeah?"

"I am not joking, sir."

Then he punched me in the shoulder. Hard. "So for the next three months, you have to *intimately work with* a woman who fucked your absolute brains out?"

I bristled. "*I* did a lot of the fucking, too, you know."

But Elliott was laughing and shaking his head. "Oh, Edward. You're bloody well *fucked,* aren't you?"

18

ROXY

I stretched my aching neck, flexing my fingers, and looked up to see my client, Gina, grinning at me.

"It looks really good, doesn't it?" she asked, trying to see in the mirror. I'd just completed the anchor with roses I'd been working on the other night, and it did look stunning against her tan skin. She'd wanted it placed between her breasts with a few of the roses cascading further down her stomach.

I smiled, using a disinfectant wipe to swipe over the design, cleaning off the blood and extra ink. This was one of my favorite parts of the whole job: the reveal.

"It looks kick-ass," I said. "Although don't be trying to have any weird kinky sex for a few days. It'll hurt like a motherfucker."

Gina grinned. "But what if that's the kind of sex I like?"

Behind me, Scarlett hooted, and Mack, standing to my left, blushed. "A woman after my own heart," I winked, helping her gingerly sit up and face the mirror. She'd removed her shirt, and I'd placed privacy bandages over her breasts, but she didn't seem concerned at all, sitting essentially topless in the middle of my shop.

Mack busied himself pulling together a packet of supplies for her aftercare while Gina stared at her new design in the mirror. She gasped, her face brightening. "Oh, Roxy," she said, laying a hand on my arm. "You've outdone yourself this time, kid."

My throat tightened. Gina had been one of my first clients, years ago, and had dutifully followed me to this shop even though it had a shit reputation.

"Well, thank you," I said, admiring my handiwork. "You know that means a lot to me."

Gina tilted her head. "And how are things going with the shop? You guys doing okay?"

"Oh, yeah," I said, aware of my employees listening in. "Things are going great."

The bell over the door chimed, and all of us looked up to see Edward come in, wearing a dark gray suit and carrying two coffees. I remembered the night we'd met when he'd been half-drunk and leaning against the door frame in similar attire. How quickly I'd written him off.

And then how quickly I'd wanted his cock in my mouth.

"Hey," I called out, motioning over. "I'm finishing up with a client. Give me five?"

"Of course," he smiled, eyes widening when he saw Mack's hulking frame. "I'll just be uh... right here."

"Who in the hell is *that?*" Gina asked. "He's a sexy little piece of Englishman, isn't he?"

I scoffed, applying anti-bacterial cream to her skin to help the healing process. "Edward is my mentor for this class I'm taking."

"Huh," she said, craning her neck. "Hey, sweetheart, you wanna see my new ink?"

"*Gina,*" I hissed since she was still topless and *very*

exposed. But she only winked at me and shimmied her shoulders.

"Um... oh, alright," Edward replied, ever the gentleman. He glided over, hands in his pockets, and flashed me a brief, bemused look that I couldn't help but return.

"It's right here," she said, pointing. "Between my breasts."

I bit my lip as Edward turned pink. But he very dutifully leaned down, eyes glinting with good humor.

"Roxy did that?" he asked. Gina nodded.

"You're brilliant," he said, turning to me, and I shrugged, fighting a smile.

"All in a day's work," I said, putting my supplies away. "Plus, Gina sat like a stone. Didn't move an inch."

"You know I once tried to get Roxy to give me a tattoo, but she wouldn't," he said to Gina, gently teasing.

"I'd have liked to have seen that. She's a real stubborn bitch, this one."

We both laughed, and I gave her a quick squeeze of the shoulders. "Well, this stubborn bitch knows you don't need the aftercare speech, but just keep it clean and don't scratch it when it itches, okay?"

Gina slid her shirt gingerly over her head. "You got it, Roc."

I smiled. "Mack will see you're taken care of at the register. And don't forget to call when you have that idea for the piece on your leg. I'll design whatever you want."

She pinched my cheek. "You got it, sugar." She gave Edward a lingering perusal. "And it was very nice to meet you, Edward."

"Same here," he smiled.

Gina left us alone, and I pulled off my gloves, feeling nervous and unsettled now that he was finally here.

"You made it," I said, accepting the coffee he held out with grateful hands. "And thanks for this."

"Absolutely," he said. "It was nice to see your work. That was gorgeous, what you designed for her."

I tossed my hair. "Well, thank you. Tattooing I can do. It's running a business that I'm failing at miserably."

I took a sip of coffee so I wouldn't say anything else and ignored the look of sympathy that flashed across his face. "Let me introduce you to everyone before we get started."

I walked over to the cash register and felt Edward tense beside me. Knew we were both remembering, in graphic detail, how many times he'd made me come on that surface.

"So this is Mack," I said and watched again as Edward sized up my giant, hulking friend. "Short for Machete, of course."

Edward sputtered.

"It's true, man. My parents were *real* weird. But I haven't gone by that in years. Also, my wife hates it. But my youngest son calls me Mack the Knife, so that's cool."

Edward's polite smile turned into a sincere grin. "Pleasure to meet you, mate. I like your, uh, face tattoos."

Mack ran a hand over his bald head. I had designed, and tattooed, a screaming skull on his head with flames shooting out of his eyes. "I like 'em too. As soon as my kids turn eighteen, I'm taking them here to get them their first face tattoos."

Edward paled, but Mack laughed harder. "Only kidding."

But he flashed me a secret wink.

"And then this beauty is Scarlett," I said, introducing Edward to my bad-ass, roller-derby-playing colleague.

"It's nice to meet you, Edward," Scarlett said, brushing her dark curly hair from her eyes. Scarlett was Dominican American and her family had lived in Washington Heights for generations. "Welcome to our weird little family."

My heart squeezed painfully as it did every time when I

remembered that these wonderful people now relied on *me* for their paychecks.

"I can see why Roxy cares so much," Edward said, holding up my application. "She spoke so highly of both of you, of the family you had become. It's an honor to be part of this, even for a few months."

Mack and Scarlett turned to look at me, and I crossed my arms and looked away. "Yeah yeah, listen, we best get to mentoring so..." I said, grabbing Edward's shoulders and turning him toward the private back room. "You guys holler if you need anything."

"Aye, aye, captain," Scarlett said with a snicker. I wasn't one for a lot of *open affection,* and I knew they'd be teasing me about it later.

"So, uh, this is the back room, and I figured we could meet here," I said, looking in dismay at the tiny space—the crowded, old rickety table and mismatched chairs. I wondered what shadowing at The Cartwright would look like and inwardly cringed.

"Perfect," Edward said smoothly, sinking into one of the chairs. "We just need a quiet space to talk. Oh, also, did you know one of the bulbs in your sign was out?"

I sat down, tossing my hair. "I did. It's been out for ages, but I haven't fixed it yet. I think it gives it a bit of charm, don't you think?"

Edward tilted his head, flipping open a notebook. "But how can customers find you if your sign is broken?"

It was a simple question, and a good one, but it only served to poke at the tender part of my ego. "You've been in my shop for five minutes, and you're immediately critical?"

Edward looked up sharply, brow furrowed. "I didn't mean it to come off that way. I just... well, this is what I'm here for, Roxy. To talk to you about the strengths and weaknesses of your business. Your plan. Your financials. I know a burnt-out bulb seems silly, but it's really not."

"How many weaknesses did you find in there?" I said, tapping my finger on the stack of papers he'd brought.

He grimaced. "Weaknesses isn't the right word. I meant more *challenges*. No one gets this 'running a business' thing perfectly, especially in the beginning. It's a learning process."

I bit my tongue, feeling suddenly irritated. "What do you want to talk about first?"

Edward opened the file, pulling out some papers. "First, let's talk about what your goals are, as a businesswoman, and then we can create a plan from there. Especially around advertising and marketing since you said that was a critical need, and when I did a little research, I'd have to agree. You're going to have to double your investment in advertising if you want to compete with some of the other tattoo shops within a five-mile vicinity. If you look at this—"

"I'm not even entirely sure we need that much marketing, to be honest," I said.

"But you said that was your most critical need in your application," he said. "Am I misreading something?"

I shrugged. "No. I did put that. But now I think that 'Roxy's' can rely on word of mouth. It's a tattoo parlor; we rely on word-of-mouth. Like Gina, who you just met. She's not going to change her behavior as a consumer just because I do a flashy ad campaign. She's going to come in because she knows us. I'm not sure what advertising other customers would respond to."

Edward cleared his throat nervously. "Sure. I understand where you're coming from. But Roxy... you have no one in your tattoo shop right now. No walk-ins. No wait-list. Yet the two new tattoo parlors just down the street from you have clients waiting in chairs and no open appointments for months. Are you even carrying a wait-list right now?"

"No," I snapped. "And we don't need one."

"I disagree," he said, voice like steel now. "Your competition down the street has ads in the local paper. A pretty active social media presence. They're at conventions. You need an integrated marketing campaign that hits your potential customers at every single level of engagement."

"And what information are you basing this conclusion on?" I asked, eyebrow arched in challenge.

"Oh, just a decade of business experience running one of the most financially successful hotels along the east coast," he said dryly.

We stared at each other for a minute, nostrils flaring.

Then he placed his palms on the table, posture relaxing. "Listen, we're getting off to the wrong start. What I *wanted* to do was start with what your goals and expectations are of this mentorship. Of where you're looking to grow. Because you'll need to if you want to save this business."

All the wind was knocked out of me, and I fought sagging against the table in defeat. It was one thing to silently wonder to myself if I was failing this business. Failing my employees and disappointing everyone around me.

But Edward *was* a professional with a decade of experience, and if he saw the same thing...

Then I was really fucked.

"So funny story, I actually forgot that I have a client right now," I said, standing quickly and opening the door. "Can we reschedule this for a later time?" I put as much ice in my voice as I could muster.

"Are you sure?" he asked, a look of astonishment on his face. "I just got here."

"Yeah, well, you need to leave now," I said. "My client will be here any minute."

I stood swiftly, but Edward reached out, wrapping his fingers around my wrist. His thumb landed on my pulse.

"Roxy," he said softly, and I turned on instinct. "I'm just trying to help, love." I watched as his thumb stroked gently across my wrist. Only once, but it was enough to send heat rippling through every inch of my body.

For a moment, I wanted to crawl into his lap.

"I told you. I don't do nicknames," I finally bit out, and his gaze darkened with lust.

Then he let go. Stood up stiffly, smoothing down his tie and re-buttoning his jacket. Gathered his things. I could feel how pissed he was, but I refused to feel sorry.

"I guess I'll email you later. Find a different time," he said, walking past me.

"Sure," I said, ignoring Mack's quizzical look from the cash register. "That's fine."

We were reduced, again, to two stiff, awkward adults. *Professional.*

Edward said goodbye to my staff and then, with barely a glance behind him, walked right out the door.

I commemorated the occasion by slamming around the shop for almost an hour, aware that I had too much school-work and too much *actual* work to waste an hour feeling anxious and angry. But I did it anyway with Mack and Scarlett rightly avoiding me.

19

EDWARD

"So tell me again what your ideas are for the actual space itself?" I asked wearily, leaning back in my chair. My parents had been in my office for over an hour now, working through their list of tasks I personally needed to accomplish in order for the Kenley Collection Charity Ball to go off without a hitch.

Even though I'd been helping them plan this ball for eight years and knew just what needed to be done.

"Chandeliers, of course," my mother said, staring at her list. "But I want small ones, suspended on wires over each table."

"But the ceilings in that room are thirty-five feet tall," I said.

"Right, so you'll suspend them down twenty-five feet, so they dangle more intimately," my mother replied. I thought of the intricate work my staff would have to do to coordinate—and dangle—two hundred and fifty separate chandeliers over two hundred and fifty tables. I inwardly groaned.

Outwardly, I smiled. "Smashing idea."

"The only issue in that room, then, is the skylights," my father said. "Can you remove them? The light is just horrid."

"Remove the skylights?" I asked. "But we just... I just had those installed six months ago. Part of the new tenant improvements we just got approved by the Board. And we can't... I mean, you want me to take them *out*?"

"I don't remember approving those at all," he sniffed, crossing his legs. Of course, what he really meant was that he was pissed he hadn't thought of the idea first, months ago, and was now subtly punishing me for it.

"Well it was quite expensive to put them in..." I started.

"And whoever did it did an awful job," my mother said. "Honestly, they did, Edward. We can't have our Charity Ball guests mingling in a room that doesn't feel completely *elegant*."

"Skylights are elegant," I snapped. "And I'm not sure it's worth the financial capital to remove something so expensive for one *bloody* evening."

The heads of both of my parents jerked up, surprised at my outburst. I was always careful to maintain a neutral, respectful tone around them, but ever since my argument with Roxy yesterday, I'd been unsettled and on edge. And now I was displaying strong emotions to two people who'd never respond to them.

"I'm sorry," I said, quietly leashing my frustration. "Can't say I slept that much last night. Tell me again how you'd like the room to look."

They continued on for another hour before leaving, spouting a hodge-podge of subtle criticisms and disappointment, and I wondered, for the fiftieth time, why I allowed them to stay in this hotel. My relationship with them was either growing worse, or I was finally losing my ability to smile like a robot.

I was almost thirty-five years old and didn't want to be so affected by their unending criticism. Didn't want to *want* their approval of my business management so much. Feedback was a part of running a business, and opening yourself up to criticism was the only way you could grow. I'd done it, and it had been painful, and when it wasn't coming from my parents, I usually received it pretty well.

I usually gave feedback pretty well too, I thought, remembering the sudden hurt look that had come over Roxy's face when I'd mentioned the things she'd been doing wrong. The frustrating thing was that there were so many amazing things she was also doing *right*—things I was surprised by, given that she was such a new business owner. But she had a natural eye for it, a talent that just needed some gentle guidance and direction. Someone to tell her...

"Oh fuck," I said out loud, calling my assistant and having him reschedule my next appointment.

I knew what I'd done wrong.

An hour later, I was holding an apology-coffee for Roxy and watching her feed a hoard of skinny, stray cats with matted hair. I'd been coming up to the shop when I noticed her in the alley—a rare moment of March sunshine setting her hair aflame. There was a look of absolute devotion on her face as she crouched down, doling out tuna fish and bowls of water for these mewling strays.

She was also calling to them, sweetly, petting the rare few that let her get close. The alley was lined with old cans and bowls, and I wondered just how long Roxy Quinn had been feeding stray cats.

"See?" I said, stepping into the alley. "You're not as scary as you think you are."

Roxy looked up, and all the professionalism in the world couldn't stop the smile that lit up her face when she saw me. She shielded it quickly, but I'd seen it.

"Tell no one," she said, standing up and walking toward me. The cats scattered as she tossed her hair and reached for the coffee. "And what's this?"

"Coffee. Black. Like your heart."

She bit her lip, fighting a smile. "I guess you can come in. And thanks for this."

I followed her and was immediately hit with the sights and sounds of this tattoo parlor I was starting to enjoy. I was guessing that Mack had put Bob Marley on the stereo, and both Mack and Scarlett were bent over in concentration, tattooing clients and chatting amiably. On the wall hung black-and-white photos of seventies-era New York City, interspersed with pieces of art I imagined were created by Roxy.

"Edward, hey, man," Mack said, coming around to shake my hand warmly. "Wasn't sure if we'd see you again."

Roxy flushed slightly, but I shrugged. "I had an appointment I couldn't miss, but I'm here now," I said, eyes landing on Roxy's. "And I have a free few hours."

"So we're heading in the back, Mack," Roxy said, nodding her head toward the room. "Just let me know if we have any walk-ins?" There was a hopeful edge to her voice.

I followed Roxy into the small back room where she closed the door, crossed her arms, and cleared her throat awkwardly.

"Listen, Edward," she started, but I cut in.

"I'm sorry I was a bit of an arse yesterday," I said, sitting down and looking up at her. Which I quite liked, if I was being honest. "I had a whole list of things I wanted to commend you on, all the incredible hard work you've been doing, but I got off track. Went with criticism first, and, well..." I laughed nervously. "I know what that's like, and it's awful."

Roxy sank into the chair across from me, her knee briefly touching mine. "You shouldn't be apologizing. *I* should. I'm just so overwhelmed right now, I'm more sensitive than usual." She bit her lip, black fingernails tapping on the table. "You'd said something yesterday, about me needing help to save my business, and I *know* deep down that's true. That we're floundering out there. But hearing you say it..." her eyes fell to the floor. Before I could stop myself, I reached forward, tilting her chin until her gaze met mine.

"Sometimes hearing it from another person makes it too real," I said. "I've been there before. It's terrifying. All of this is."

Her gorgeous green eyes softened, something earnest and kind hanging between us.

"I'm sorry for yesterday," she said.

"I'm sorry for yesterday," I repeated, grinning until she gave me a tiny smile. "Now can I tell you all the things you're bloody brilliant at?"

Roxy tossed her hair, crossing one long leg over the other. "Please."

"Your online reviews are stunning. You're right, you have truly loyal customers who will continue coming back to you for every tattoo. And creating customer loyalty is the hardest step, and you've already figured that one out. Plus, it's obvious to me you've retained two employees who are highly talented and highly motivated. They're loyal to *you* Roxy, and that's another huge step."

"Thank you," she said sincerely, leaning closer across the table. For the first time, I felt that natural *ease* we'd had with each other the night we met start to slowly return. "Really, that means a lot coming from you. But I just feel like I spend all my free time worried sick I'm going to have to fire those amazingly talented and loyal employees, who are like my *family,* because I can't seem to get this thing right. All of this," she said, pointing around her.

"I know I'm a Cavendish," I started. "And my family is well-known, but I'm not them, Roxy. I have no idea if my parents were scared when they opened their first hotel. Because we would never talk about something as crass as our feelings."

"So you're scared too?" she asked, disbelief in her voice.

"All the time," I said on a long exhale. "My first week at The Cartwright, my assistant brought me checks to sign—the paychecks of the hundreds of people that worked for me now. And I'd already met the lot of them, knew what they did, how long they'd worked there. Knew that this job was critical to their livelihood. Knew that this piece of paper, for so many of them, was the difference between paying rent and not."

Roxy's knee brushed against mine again, and I couldn't contain the surge of arousal it sent straight to my cock. I refocused: *professional.*

"I get it, I do," I promised. "And one thing we can talk about during our mentorship is how you can start to handle that pressure. It never goes away. Ever." Roxy shifted, pursing her lips. "But we can work on it. Does that sound... okay?"

Roxy nodded. "Yes. In so many ways. I want this, Edward. I do. You make it look so easy. How the hell do you sleep at night?"

I smiled. "Well, when your hotel is doing well, it makes it easier for sure. So let's start with all the ways we can get this brilliant place back on track because I believe that we can."

Like she had in the alley, Roxy gave me a beautifully sincere smile, one that lit up her wonderful face.

"You do?"

"I really do."

Roxy winced. "You know I convinced Mack and Scarlett to come here. Stole them from two other tattoo parlors. We'd known each other for years, had been colleagues off and on. I love them. Very much. And I told them... I told them we'd turn this place into the tattoo parlor we'd always wanted. Right the sinking ship."

"You feel guilty," I said. "Guilty for bringing them over here."

"Because we're still sinking."

"Not for long, love," I said, the endearment slipping easily from my lips. "We'll fix it. Now what else are you looking for?" I took out my notebook, pen poised. Every person I'd mentored had a different list of expectations, and I never wanted to presume to know what they desired.

Roxy tensed up again, jiggling her leg under the table. "Ideas for... ideas for... how to change." She bit out the word *change* like it was something thoroughly offensive to her.

I smoothed down my tie, shifting in my chair. "You're sure?"

"Yeah, I'm sure," she said miserably, avoiding my gaze.

"So if that's the case, you might have to actually listen to me."

Roxy rolled her eyes. "Try not to be a dick about it, and I will."

"Ah, I make no promises," I smiled, and when she joined me, I knew I had won a tiny victory in the war for Roxy's affections.

Her *professional* affections.

20

ROXY

"What do you think? Can you touch it up?" my dad asked, twisting his arm to show me the older tattoo he had there: lyrics from a song by The Clash he'd gotten years ago. But the lines were fading and less crisp than they used to be.

"Oh yeah," I shrugged, passing him the plate of chocolate chip waffles my mom had cooked up. "Come in anytime. And if I'm not there, Mack will take care of you."

"I'd prefer if it was my brilliantly talented daughter, though," he said. "I only wish you'd been old enough to do this one when I got it."

"I was *seven*," I said.

"Old enough to hold a tattoo gun, if you ask me," he said, smiling at my mom as she handed us huge mugs of hot coffee. I was at my parents' house for our weekly Friday morning breakfasts, which you could only get out of if you were deathly ill.

And Fiona was late, which she often was.

Our childhood home was in Queens, a full hour on the

subway from Manhattan, and she had usually had early appointments she needed to make.

But this was the *one* thing my parents were strict about: quality time.

Our Queens house was a slightly run-down, ramshackle Victorian that while growing up was filled with a rotating mix of punk rock musicians, artists, and family members wanting to visit New York City and needing a place to stay. My parents never said no, and even if it meant Fiona and I were sleeping on the floor in the kitchen, we made room for everyone. They bought the house because of the large garage in the backyard, where we grew up listening to The Hand Grenades practice their set most nights.

Or sometimes just my parents, crooning to each other.

"Did you get an A on that paper?" my mom asked, sitting down next to me. She'd recently dyed her short gray hair hot purple.

"I did not get an A," I admitted. "I got a C-."

Her eyes widened. "How dare they."

"It's not a big deal," I said, sounding like a defensive teenager. "It's just a paper." I'd checked my other grades and would be passing this class by the skin of my teeth. "Plus, the most important thing now is completing the Capstone Project."

"The mentoring program, right?" my dad asked.

"Yeah," I said, thinking, of course, about Edward. "I'm all set up with my mentor, so now the real work begins. I'll be shadowing his work in a couple days, but mostly, the focus will be on the tattoo shop, our business model, our advertising strategies."

Fiona came rushing through the front door, letting loose a string of curses that would make a sailor faint. "Morning, morning, *I'm sorry, don't give me that look,*" she sputtered, crashing into a chair and grabbing the mug of coffee my dad held out with a bemused expression. "And I have to leave in, like, twenty fucking minutes."

It wasn't like Fiona to look mussed, but her delicate bun was slightly askew, and she was out of breath. "What happened to you?" I exclaimed.

"Nightmare client," she huffed, tucking into her waffle with enthusiasm. "And this is amazing, mom."

My mom reached forward, patting us both on the shoulders. "Anything for my beautiful family. Also Fi, do you need your dad or I to scare the living daylights out of this client?"

Fiona shook her head. "Not this time," she said with a wry smile. "I'm saving you guys for some *real* asshole. And what were you saying about your mentor, Roc?"

"Oh, well, it's Edward," I said calmly, immediately filling my mouth with waffles and chocolate chips.

Fiona looked up slowly, eyes wide.

"Who's Edward?" my dad asked. "You knew him already?"

"I did," I said lightly, fiddling with the syrup holder. "He and I had a... a..."

"Brief sexual encounter," Fiona finished for me. "Right?"

My parents turned red. As loud and loose and *wild* as they were, they still tiptoed lightly around my and Fiona's sex lives. They weren't *opposed* to us having sex, but they were always briefly taken aback. And oddly conservative about it in some ways—every boyfriend Fiona and I had brought home to meet them had to sleep in a separate bedroom.

"Oh," my mom said, clearing her throat. "How nice."

Fiona smirked my way because she knew our "brief sexual encounter" had been anything but *nice*.

"So you're going to spend three months with Edward then?" Fiona asked. "And that'll be... okay?"

I shrugged my shoulders, attempting to slow the racing of

my reckless heart. "Yep. No problems here." I looked at my parents. "He's not my type. *Extremely* wealthy. He owns The Cartwright, you know the one?"

"Of course," my dad said, surprised. "And *that's* your mentor?"

"It's not a big deal," I said. "I'm already counting down the days until I don't have to see his smug, rich face anymore, you know?" I forced a laugh then immediately became *very* interested in swirling the syrup around on my plate. I *knew* Fiona was staring at me, and if I made eye contact with her, I was going to lose it.

"Well, what an exciting development," my mom said with a smile. Her ability to cheerfully support us no matter what never waned. "Smug face or not, he probably has some good advice for helping you out at the shop, right?"

"Mhmm," I mumbled. "He sure does."

Just like the night we'd slept together, Edward was already *pushing* me, and I didn't quite know what to do about it. I did want things to be better. I wanted a thriving, flourishing business I could be proud of. But his initial criticisms had hurt more than I'd expected, so I'd done what I usually did: said something snarky and then shut down.

But after our talk yesterday, when we'd apologized to each other, I'd promised him I'd try. And I planned to.

Even if receiving critical feedback was ultimately making me want to smash a table in half.

"As much as I want to stay here and chat all day," Fiona said, taking her dish to the sink and rinsing it. "I have to run." She kissed both of my parents on the cheek then pinned me with a very sisterly look. "Maybe Roxy can walk me out?"

"I'm fine here," I said, but then she hauled me up off my seat, like a good younger sister, dragging me into the hallway.

"Fiona," my dad called back. "Leaving early from weekly

breakfast means you have to come to our show next week. The Red Room. Ten p.m."

We rolled our eyes. "Of course, dad!" she called back, before pulling me onto the porch.

"Shit, at least let me get a jacket," I grumbled, wrapping my arms around myself. "And you don't have to say—"

"Your mentor is *Edward?*" she half-screeched. "*The Edward*. Of the multiple orgasms and the spanking and the filthy dirty talk?"

I shifted back and forth on my feet, regretting the amount of graphic detail I'd shared with my sister. "Yes, he is, and it's really not a big deal. We already talked it over, and we're going to remain professional. It's *not* going to be an issue. I need this class to graduate, and it's only three months. I'm pretty sure we can keep our hands off each other for that length of time."

Fiona narrowed her eyes at me, crossing her arms. Letting me stew in my heaping pile of lies. But I *would* keep my hands off Edward.

Even though last night, all I could think about was his thumb, stroking down the tender side of my wrist. His knee, brushing against mine under the table. That delicious smirk of his that made me want to lean over the small table and kiss him—kiss and kiss until we were starved for each other.

I'd touched myself last night—twice—both orgasms spiraling through me as I replayed Edward's voice, ragged with need, against my ear.

Was that your plan all along, love? As soon as I walked in here, did you know you were going to fucking destroy me?

"What, you don't believe me?" I asked, mirroring her pose.

"Nope," she replied, buttoning up her jacket and picking up her messenger bag. "I do not believe you. Because I think you actually have a tiny crush."

I shook my head because it didn't seem possible. "Fi,

you've seen the guys I usually date. Edward's not one of them. He was an unexpectedly hot one-night stand, and that's it. I'll meet some beefy, tattooed biker any day now."

"Oh, you mean like Jimmy? The Cheating Asshole?" she asked, reaching forward to tap the tattoo on my inner wrist. *Never Again.*

"That was years ago. And I don't think I'm as angry about it as you still are."

Fiona glanced behind me, staring at her reflection in the window. With deft skill, she fixed her hair, brushing the strands back into place. "Of course I'm still angry. You're my *sister,* and that dick cheated on you for an entire year."

There was a brief pinch of pain at the memory, although I found it interesting how my heart had healed with time. The anger and embarrassment had faded like an old bruise.

"Jimmy does not represent the entire community of tattooed, punk rock bikers in this city," I said firmly, pulling her in for a hug. "And have a good day at work."

"You too," she smiled, walking down the steps. Our childhood street was waking up: neighbors off to work, kids riding their bikes to school, car radios blaring and dogs barking. For a moment, I flashed to a memory of Fiona and I sitting on these same steps as children, eating ice cream on a hot summer's day.

"Oh, and Roxy?" she called back just as I was turning to leave.

"Yeah?"

"Edward doesn't represent the entire community of smug, rich businessmen either."

21

EDWARD

"You know," Elliott panted, slightly out of breath as we ran through Central Park. "March in New York always briefly cures my homesickness for London."

I nodded, dodging two couples, strolling down the path. "This American obsession with sunshine will boggle me for the rest of my days."

"Exactly mate," Elliott said. "Give me a gray, dreary, London drizzle, and *that* right there is a beautiful day."

I laughed, increasing our speed just a bit. Elliott and I ran together in the park once a week, followed by a hearty English breakfast at the pub. "Just a dash of soot..."

"You're making it worse, yeah?" he said, shoving me slightly.

"Just trying to get your mind off of what you have to do today," I said, my body relaxing into the pace. "And it's going to be fine."

"I know it will be," he said. "I've fired people countless times. Unfortunately. But it never gets any bloody better, does it?"

"No," I agreed. "You could do what all the big hotels do and hire an HR firm that just fires people. Keeps you out of it."

But Elliott just shook his head, casting me a wry look. "You know I'd never do that. I'm not a total arsehole."

"True," I agreed. "And I'd never do it either."

"Plus, it was my decision, so I'd feel even worse. Having someone do it."

"You think he expects it?" I asked. Elliott was firing his Assistant Vice President of Marketing today who he'd spent the last few months attempting to coach and train, even as the man continued to not do his job. He wasn't the right fit, and their sales were starting to be affected by it.

"I don't think he'll be surprised. But I'm not sure anyone really expects it when they come in on a random, normal Tuesday," he grimaced. "This being in charge thing is awful sometimes."

"I had the exact same conversation with Roxy this week," I said. "She wanted to know if it was normal to feel anxious about the responsibility you have to your employees. If it was normal to stay up at night, worrying about it."

"Has she considered alcohol?" Elliott grinned.

"I told her you never stop worrying but that it does get easier. The pressure. Don't you think?"

"I do, although it's a different pressure than what we feel from our parents. They are connected, unfortunately," he said.

"I'd pay good money to see my parents' faces, or *your* parents faces, if I came home to England one day and said, 'Don't worry, but I'm leaving The Cartwright, and I've decided to become a public-school teacher. Oh, and please kindly fuck off,'" I said.

Elliott grinned at me. "Please can I have that gift for Christmas, mate?"

"I'll do it if you bring a guy home for the holidays."

"I just might. I mean, really, what's stopping me? I'd bet good money there are several St. James family members who are just as gay as I am. Maybe I'd start a trend," he mused.

If anyone would do it, it'd be Elliott.

"I support this wholeheartedly. And if your family disowns you, you can always come stay with me. Besides, life's too short, right?"

I sped up the pace again, and Elliott wheezed just slightly. "That's a nice mantra, Edward, but you and I both know it's easier said than done. And I'm going to guess there's a reason you have us sprinting through Central Park right now."

I ignored him for a full minute since the reason was sheer, pent-up sexual tension.

"Remind me to send Roxy a thank you note for helping me beat my personal best today," he said.

"Don't be daft. And just so you know, she'd probably light that thank you note on fire."

"Sounds like my kind of girl," he panted, matching my new, accelerated pace. "And you didn't really answer my question. Which was, essentially, are you pining for the beautiful Roxy?"

"Of course I am," I admitted. "I've never been so drawn to a woman in my entire life. I thought it was just the memories of... that night. But now that we're forced together all the time, it's even worse. An infatuation, really. One that I need to ignore."

"Counterpoint: you date Roxy. Fall in love and have tons of babies with her. And you continue to tell your parents to fuck off."

"I won't do that," I said grimly, hating the feelings that scenario evoked. "You know why."

Which was that my parents would *never* approve of me marrying a woman like Roxy, someone they'd deem so beneath our "station." And without that, how could I ever get out from under their thumb and finally *own* what was rightly mine?

"I do. You know I do," Elliott said, flashing me a brief look of understanding.

"Although I'd love for my parents to approve of just *one* of my decisions, just once in my life. But I'm thirty-five, and I honestly fear that approval will never come." We ran around a woman, walking six dogs, who were all barking. "Yet I continue to hope for it." I looked at Elliott. "What do you think that means?"

"I think it means that, like most human beings, you'd appreciate an outward display of love from your parents. And for the Cavendish family, they show their love through approval. Same as mine. That's the family we were born into."

"Yeah," I said, suddenly a bit miserable. "And maybe I'll like Phoebe."

"The woman your parents are setting you up with?"

"Our date is tomorrow," I said.

We reached the end of the park, and I stopped, bending over at the waist to catch my breath. Instead of obliterating the pent-up arousal, it only seemed to course stronger through my veins. I wanted to run to Roxy's shop, drag her into that back room. Drop to my knees and worship her gorgeous pussy for hours.

"Edward," Elliott said in a kind voice, clapping me on the back. "It's going to be okay. You'll figure it out. And who knows, maybe Phoebe's the one for you."

"Stranger things have happened," I said, looking up at the slate gray clouds that were so much like a London sky I felt that twisting nostalgia right in my gut. "Do you still have time for me to buy you breakfast?"

"Always," Elliott said, briefly squeezing my shoulders. "But only if you want to listen to me go on and on about *my* date last night."

"Who with?" I teased.

"The very sexy Vincent," Elliott said as we walked toward our cars, sweating and out of breath. "Who I will probably never bring home for a holiday, but I will seriously consider a passionate fling with."

"Lucky you," I grinned.

"Lucky me?" he said. "Lucky *Vincent*."

22

EDWARD

*A*n hour into my date with Phoebe, and I was struggling to muster up enthusiasm. We were at Per Se, and Phoebe was truly lovely. She was white with dark brown curls and expressive eyes, and had been educated at Oxford before moving to the States. She was in charge of her family's foundation, which I thought would be a great start to a first-date conversation.

Except she didn't have much to say about her job, even though I pestered her with questions. I liked that she had a vocation that gave back to people, thinking maybe it might mean she was less vapid and self-centered as the rest of the people my family tended to keep in their inner circle.

But Phoebe was less self-centered and more just... flat.

"So, do you enjoy what you do, Edward?" she asked politely as she finished her dinner. I'd barely touched mine, finding my appetite lacking.

"I do, actually," I said. "It appears that hospitality is in my blood, just like my father's."

"I've stayed at The Cartwright a few times, actually," she said. "It was quite elegant."

I smiled. "Indeed. And I love my job, although I'm not sure it's as rewarding as yours."

I paused, waiting for her to interject, but she only nodded and smiled.

"One thing I'm also passionate about, actually, is this mentoring program I've done for the past five years. Through CUNY. Have you ever done it before?"

"No, not at all," she said, sipping her wine.

"It's brilliant, really," I said. "They pair you up with students finishing up their MBA. Give them hands-on mentoring and feedback, help them get their sea legs a bit before going out into the real world of business. My current mentee, Roxy, owns a tattoo parlor that's struggling, so I'll be helping her draft a business plan, execute a marketing strategy, that kind of thing."

"A tattoo parlor?" she asked, crinkling her nose in subtle judgement.

"It's incredible there," I said, with a hint of pride in my voice. "She's a massively talented artist."

Phoebe smiled politely, a pretty smile, but I couldn't help but think about Roxy's scowling snarkiness the first night we'd met. The illicit way we had danced around each other.

"Do you have any tattoos?" I asked with a flirtatious grin.

Maybe she just needed me to push us there a bit.

"Me?" she asked, astounded. "No, of course not. You don't, right?"

I shrugged. "I almost got one a few months ago. I was feeling fairly distraught and just thought it would help. This was about three months ago after I'd just found out that my girlfriend, Emily, had been cheating on me for six months."

I didn't know where the hell that brutal honesty came from—not usually the way of a Cavendish—but my body surged with a spike of exhilaration. The truth! It had slipped out so easily, and really what was the point of hiding it? My parents would be disappointed in me after tonight either way.

I was still smiling at Phoebe, hoping, for a mere moment, that she would toss off the polite niceties and tell me something *real*.

But instead, her cheeks flushed pink, and she looked around frantically. "I know Emily," she half-hissed, half-whispered. "And she's dating a very lovely man named Stuart."

And that hurt, truly, like a knife right to the gut. Because I thought she'd at least take a little time between the two of us out of mutual respect at least.

Except it had been three months, and really, Emily was free to do as she pleased.

"Emily and I have spoken about this several times," Phoebe continued, "and she knows it's rather gauche to be seen with Stuart, especially since rumors have spread so rapidly. But they're truly in love and can't help it." Phoebe sat back, and I had to say I rather enjoyed her outburst. It was at least *passionate*.

"I see," I said, clearing my throat. "I didn't realize you were friends."

Of course they were. There was a very small circle of people my parents would deem "respectable" for me to marry, and they all bloody well knew each other.

"I thought your parents might have told you," she said, looking even more embarrassed now.

"It's fine. Really," I said, reaching forward and touching her hand. No spark. "You don't need to feel badly. It's better I know, right?" I smiled, and she finally returned it. And I felt the strangest sensation, sitting there with a woman my parents intended me to probably marry, who I felt about as much connection to as a cardboard box. Because even though Emily had lied to my face for months, and utterly fucked my life, there she was, gently pushing at these rigid boundaries. A few years ago, if a person in our "circle" had cheated on another, you wouldn't have shown your face for a year until we had all moved on to the next bit of gossip or outrage. And you *certainly* wouldn't have shown your face with the man you'd been cheating with.

Yet Phoebe had said they were in love.

Interesting.

"Let's get the check, shall we?" I said, motioning over our waiter. Phoebe sat quietly as I paid an exorbitant amount for our dinner, and then I led her outside to a waiting taxi. We didn't say much, but as the taxi pulled up, I was surprised when she turned to me, offering her cheek. I kissed it, feeling nothing again, and she said, "Let's do this again, Edward."

I fought to keep my expression neutral. "Absolutely. I'll call you," I replied, wondering if I would or if I was just being polite. She smiled and got into the cab. Undoubtedly, even with the intensity of our conversation towards the end, Phoebe thought that was a fine date. Because my evenings with Emily had been just like that, and I thought that was fine as well. A fine time. A fine dinner. A fine evening.

But what if I didn't want that anymore?"

Thoughts tangled and racing, I decided to walk home. Except I wasn't going in the right direction, something I knew subconsciously but chose to ignore. It was a chilly, London-like evening, and I tried to lose myself in the crisp wind, watching the couples walking down the street. Tried to remind myself that, per our Cavendish upbringing, love was not the goal in this world. Or, it was a nice *addition*, but there was also business, success, family, legacy. For the past ten years, I'd excelled at all of it, even though my family made me want to tear my hair out, and our "legacy" often felt like an albatross around my neck.

But I liked our business. I *was* successful.

Could love—real love, *true love*—be part of my life too?

After about a mile, I ducked down into the subway, and about thirty minutes later, I re-surfaced, facing the sign. And when I saw it, I knew I'd meant to end up here all along. Her application had listed her address, and I wasn't surprised she'd chosen to live right near the shop. She had a keen sense of this business; she just didn't believe it yet.

So I turned down her block, found her address, and looked up at a brownstone that was slightly worse for wear but appeared well-loved. Straightened my tie. Took out my phone and called Roxy.

23

ROXY

*I*t was a tea-pajamas-sketching kind of night, which I'd been having more and more of recently. Even a year ago, I'd spend at least a few nights at some of my favorite bars. Drinking with friends. Usually taking home some sexy stranger to play with for the evening. But as I sat curled up on my massive armchair with Busy Bee at my feet, I realized I hadn't done that in...

Three months.

Since Edward.

I shook my head fiercely, dislodging my thoughts, and focused on the sketch in front of me. Maria was a recent breast cancer survivor and wanted to commemorate her journey with a huge piece down her arm, a wild floral design that worked with the natural curves of her body. I'd only ever done one small piece for her, an anchor on her foot, but like Edward had said, customer loyalty didn't seem to be a problem for us. Once we got them *to* the shop, they tended to come back. A lot.

It was new customers that we couldn't seem to get.

Stomach churning, I tried to soothe my anxiety with lines

and shadow. Maria loved lilies, a trickier floral design to capture, and I was lost in concentration, awash in delicate petals, when my phone rang.

Edward.

I answered it, surprised. "Isn't this late to be calling about business matters?" I said and heard the soft rasp of his laughter in my ear. Goosebumps broke out over my skin.

"Look out your window, love," he said.

I did as I was told, sliding it open and leaning halfway out, to see Edward standing on the street, looking up at my third-story bedroom window.

He looked dapper as fuck. Black suit, crisp white shirt, black tie. One hand in his pocket, the other holding the phone to his ear.

"Fancy meeting you here," I said, and I could just make out his sly grin.

"Peeked at your application," he said. "You really shouldn't list your address. Just about anyone can find you, you know."

I smiled. "What are you doing here, Edward?"

A long sigh. "I'm coming home from a date. A date that didn't go well. And I thought I'd swing by and see what my lovely mentee was up to."

My body was warming at Edward's nearness, even down on the street. "Well, your lovely mentee is in her pajamas, sketching out floral designs for a client."

"Can I see it later?"

"Of course," I promised. "Tell me about this date." I felt the stirrings of jealousy, but he'd also come *here* afterward, which made me feel something else entirely.

"Ah, well, you called it months ago," he said. "She was sweet. And lovely. Definitely someone my parents would approve of me marrying."

"But?" I asked.

"But she was bloody boring, and we had zero chemistry, and she also told me that Emily and Stuart, the bloke she shagged while we were together, are now publicly a couple and completely in love."

I sighed, leaning down on my elbows. "I'm sorry. That fucking sucks."

"It certainly does," he replied.

"Are you still in love with her?" I asked, attempting to keep my tone neutral.

"No," he said, so quickly I knew it to be the truth. "I'm... angry. Did you feel this way after... what happened to you?"

"Jimmy," I said. "And we were together for a year. And he cheated the entire time. Not one person, like Emily. He needed to fuck every single thing that moved. And I was young, twenty-three, and hopelessly infatuated with him. He was older, and I thought he was a total rebel. A free spirit in a motorcycle jacket." Edward tilted his head, listening. "When you're twenty-three, and your older boyfriend is sleeping on the floor of his friend's house and never has any money and constantly smells like old cigarette smoke, you think he's the man of your dreams. So *rebellious*. So anti-establishment," I said, laughing a little. "But really, he was an immature asshole who didn't have his shit together."

"How'd you find out?" Edward asked.

Clouds shifted, and suddenly the moon was exposed, bright above Edward's head. He looked like an actor in a classic black-and-white film.

"One of the women he was sleeping with told me. He never said he had a girlfriend, but she'd seen a text I sent him. She felt bad, thought I should know." I shrugged. "And yeah, it's the anger that you hold on to. I actually confused that feeling with love for a long, long time. Was pissed because I thought I was *pining* for that asshole. But it was just another strong emotion. Fury, not love."

Edward nodded. "That's it exactly. I want to let *go*, and I thought I had, but when Phoebe told me about Emily and Stuart..." he trailed off.

"I think that's only natural, Edward," I said. "Give yourself time."

"And sex therapy," he said lightly, but I felt the electric charge even three stories up.

"It's not a bad idea," I replied as arousal began to pulse between my legs.

A heady pause, and all I could think about was the rough, masculine sounds Edward had made when he came in my mouth that night. I shut my eyes tightly, willing the image away.

"Roxy?" Edward asked, and there was so much yearning in his voice I almost invited him up right then. To kiss away his hurt and pain.

And then Busy Bee poked his giant, box-like head through the window and barked.

"Jesus Christ, what *is* that?" Edward asked, taking a step back, almost dropping the phone at his ear.

I laughed. "He's not gonna hurt you," I promised. "At least not from up here. And this is Busy Bee, my pit bull. He only has three legs. But three times as much heart."

"Ah," Edward said. "Roxy the softie."

"I don't know what you're talking about," I sniffed, kissing Bee on the head. "And you can't see them, but I also have two cats, Apple and Cucumber."

"You've got three animals up there?" he asked.

"I'd have more if I had the space, but these three have already taken over my entire apartment."

Edward was smiling broadly, looking handsome in the

moonlight, and as another tense pause lengthened between us, I let myself get swept up in the romanticism of this moment. A man, a *handsome man*, that I definitely had a tiny crush on, showing up outside my window.

Had any of my previous lovers *ever* done something so sweet?

"Do you want to—" I started to say just as Edward said, "Well, I guess I better call it a night."

We paused then laughed awkwardly. "Sorry, what?" Edward asked.

"Oh nothing," I said. "Just... thanks for coming by. I'm sorry about your boring-ass date."

"Thanks for letting me bother you at this ungodly hour," he said. "And... well, I have to say it. If I ever met this Jimmy, I'd beat his bloody face in."

"I'd be right there with you," I said, and Edward looked down, chuckling, before looking back up again. Pinned me with a gaze of quiet hunger. "Goodnight, Edward."

"Goodnight, Roxy."

24

EDWARD

*R*oxy stood out in the lobby of The Cartwright Hotel like a sore thumb, and I loved it. She was sitting on one of the chairs near the massive fireplace, wearing fishnet tights, combat boots, and a short leather skirt. Her shirt had David Bowie's face on it, but she *was* wearing a blazer.

And then she turned around and I caught the back of it.

"Nice, um, *blazer*," I grinned, hands in my pockets as I looked down at my mentee. She looked up and flashed me a cheeky smile. I'd barely slept, wound up and exhilarated from my chat with Roxy last night. She'd looked softer from the window—hair still wet from a shower and in an old, giant t-shirt. It made me want to climb into her bed, undress her slowly. Rock inside her until she clutched at my shoulders, gasping.

"I can get dressed up," she said, chin tilted.

"It says 'eat the rich' on the back, love," I said.

But she only shrugged and looked around at the lobby where supremely wealthy tourists were mingling. "Seems appropriate," she said, standing up.

I fought the urge to touch her in greeting, kiss her cheek, or drag her against my chest.

"It's good to see you," I said.

"It's good to be seen," she replied. "Now what kind of corporate mind-games are you putting me through today?"

"Have you ever seen *A Clockwork Orange*?" I asked, and her burst of laughter rang out. I smiled with her, leading her into an elevator that was luckily filled with people. "And actually, I thought we'd start with some coffee in my office, talk about some of the struggles The Cartwright has had that might mirror the struggles you're currently facing. Then on to a couple meetings—one with the head of Marketing. One with the Assistant Vice President."

Before Roxy could respond, one of our frequent guests, Shirley, tapped my shoulder. "Edward, dear, it's so nice to be back in The Cartwright."

"Ah, Miss Shirley," I said, turning to face her in the cramped quarters. "We're so happy to have you and your family back. Did you bring me biscuits?"

She flashed me a pretty flirtatious smile for a person pushing eighty years old. "Of course. Right from our favorite shop."

Shirley hailed from outside of London, and over the years, we'd discovered a penchant for the same biscuits from Fortnum and Mason. Every time she came to the States, she brought me some.

Shirley opened her bag, pulled them out. "For you and your pretty girlfriend too."

Roxy flashed me a bemused look. "Oh, I'm not his girl-friend, ma'am. He's teaching me how to run a business."

The elevator reached Shirley's destination, doors sliding open as she walked out. "Enjoy the biscuits, Edward. And young lady, I'd reconsider making this fine gentleman your boyfriend." With a wink and a wave, she walked down the lush, luxurious hallway that held some of our penthouse suites.

"Um..." Roxy said as we kept moving up toward my offices.

"Shirley Benedict. Been a regular guest of The Cartwright for years, even before I arrived. She's daft as a loon and one of my favorite people in the world."

The elevator doors slid open, and I was greeted with the busy sounds of our upper floor offices. A few people tossed "good mornings" our way. Staff darted around us, clutching stacks of files and cups of coffee. Roxy looked slightly dazed and maybe even *impressed*.

"This floor is mostly executive level staff, including our Vice President, marketing, and financial team," I said, as we strolled through the chaos I'd gotten used to and, to be honest, thrived upon. "And this is my office."

"Holy shit," she said, standing in my suite. Wall-to-wall windows, letting in the entirety of the New York City skyline. I'd had everything designed as sleek but still comforting—I had frequent meetings in this office with all different levels of staff, and I tried hard not to intimidate *that* much.

But based on Roxy's expression, she might have felt that way.

"Have a seat," I told her as one of my assistants brought us lattes and a tray of pastries.

Roxy quirked her brow.

"I *am* the manager you know. That means they bring me things," I said.

"I can see that," she said, settling in. "And what did you want to start with today?"

I pulled out an old file and laid the contents out on the table, fanning them like an accordion. "I wanted to start with a few of the struggles The Cartwright has faced over the years.

Struggles that you mentioned, in your application, you felt that the shop was currently facing." I kept my tone light, remembering her defensiveness the other day.

Roxy leaned forward, tapping her finger on an image from the turn of the century. "I didn't realize how old this hotel chain was."

"Very old," I said, pleased when Roxy took out a notebook and a pen. "My father inherited the Cartwright empire when he was twenty years old after his parents passed away in a plane crash."

"How awful," Roxy said.

I shrugged. "I feel the same way, but to talk to my father, you didn't wail about and grieve in his family. You buttoned up your suit jacket, brushed off your hat, and went to work continuing your parents' legacy."

"And you all work for the empire?" she asked.

"Yes," I said. "My younger siblings both own their own hotels, which they inherited after they were married. My parents oversee everything, which is what they're currently doing here in the States. That and we work together every year to plan this charity ball event happening in May."

"They need to make sure the empire is strong," she said, picking up one of the photos. It was a photo of young women wearing 1920s-era bathing costumes on a poster that said: "The Cartwright: luxury for all seasons."

"Exactly," I said. *And making my life hell.*

"Do you and your siblings help each other? Like, share tips and secrets?" she asked. "I can't believe what it would be like to all have the same career. If Fiona also ran a tattoo parlor—which, if you knew my sister, would be hysterical—I'd be calling that girl all day, every day."

"Is Fiona much different than you?"

"She's an estate lawyer, so we're as different as they come," she said. "And you unsuccessfully dodged my question."

I tapped my pen on the desk. "No. We don't help each other, which is a shame. In the English upper class, there's work, and then there's *work*. My parents both come from old money, but they've also capitalized on The Cartwright chain and are now happily reveling in their new money as well. So they do work hard. As do my siblings. But..." I thought about how best to talk about something so culturally ingrained in me. "They don't like to get their hands dirty. It isn't 'becoming' of our station in life. So there's always been a disconnect there since my siblings each have a sitting Vice President who essentially acts as the President in all aspects of the day-to-day management."

Roxy narrowed her eyes. "But they 'oversee' the business of the hotel?"

"Yes," I said. "And from a far distance, they are involved in the decisions and management as the owners of the property. Which is what my parents expected. Hire someone you trust, ensure they do their job brilliantly, and our reputation and empire will be sustained."

Roxy pointed her pen at me. "Except that's not what you do, though."

"Absolutely not," I said, running my fingers down my tie. "When I was sent here to manage this hotel at twenty-five, I knew what my parents were asking me to do. There is an expectation ingrained in you as a member of the upper-class. But I did that for the first few months and was so bloody *bored* I thought I was losing my mind. And the Board was making some decisions I didn't feel comfortable with. But I didn't feel comfortable telling them what to do without getting involved with the rest."

Roxy looked at me for a moment. "You've got a lot of layers, Edward."

"Is that your way of saying you may have judged me too harshly?" I asked and couldn't help the flirtatious edge to my voice.

Those dark eyes narrowed again. "Jury's still out, I'm afraid," she said.

"Well, let's stop chatting about the entrenched problems of the Cavendish family and move onto branding," I said, indicating the photos. "I pulled out some of our more well-done ad campaigns since the turn of the century so you could see how they've subtly changed over the years."

"And what would you call the signature elements of your brand?" Roxy asked.

"A quiet elegance," I said automatically as I'd done in meetings for over a decade. "Not flashy or over-the-top." I pulled out some of our newer campaigns, which I'd spent months working with our marketing team on. "These are our most recent ads, and even though we've slightly tweaked our logo over the years, it's still recognizable."

Roxy furrowed her brow, tapping on the photo. It was our restaurant, which was dark and lovely with four large gas fireplaces and exposed brick. I'd overseen the redesign a few years ago. A couple was close together, having an intimate conversation, and while their dress indicated wealth, they were also younger than previous ads had featured.

"This woman looks like me," she said. "She has tattoos."

"She does," I replied. "I hired a marketing team that focused on diversity because I wanted these ads to reflect New York City and the many different types of people who live here. Different races, ethnicities, cultures. People have expectations and assumptions about who stays in a hotel like this, and I wanted us to be different."

"But you haven't changed your logo?" she asked. She was standing up, leaning over the pictures, comparing our logos over the years. It was the artist in her, captivated by the nuanced shifting of lines.

"We have; it's just subtle. You want to continually stay up-to-date without losing client recognition," I said. "Something to think about for the branding you'll develop for Roxy's."

She sat back down, avoiding my gaze. "But I don't understand why you'd invest branding and marketing dollars when you run the most recognizable luxury hotel chain in the entire world? What's there to market? Everyone *knows* you."

I shook my head. "Rookie mistake, love," I said. "And one I've made before. I said the same thing at about twenty-seven. Woke up in the middle of the night, thinking I'd figured everything out. Why spend crucial dollars on something we didn't really need?"

"And?" she asked.

"And our first quarter absolutely tanked that year. Second quarter didn't do great either. I had to work my arse off to get us back to steady by the end of that year. You can never *ever* not invest in advertising and marketing. Because your customers may love you, but they don't go about their day thinking of you. They're busy, thinking of their kids, or work, or something stressful, and when it comes time to book a hotel, they're waiting for a taxi and see one of our quietly elegant bus ads—"

"—and they book with you," Roxy finished.

"So then," I said, leaning over the desk. "What is *your* brand?"

Roxy thought for a minute. "Come to Roxy's. It *looks* like you might get stabbed here, but we promise it won't happen."

"So mouthy, even in a business meeting," I said, unable to keep from smiling.

"I'm pretty sure you like my mouth, Edward," she replied.

I almost fell out of my chair. By the widening of her eyes and the slight flush in her cheeks, she'd surprised herself.

"I think my opinions on your mouth are well documented," I somehow managed to say, "and I also think your tagline could use a bit of shortening."

She tapped her lips. "Roxy's: No Stabbing Here."

I laughed, shaking my head. "You're a natural business-woman. And now you're avoiding *my* questions."

She was scribbling something down on her notepad, and I angled my head to try and see.

"Am I impressing you that much, love?" I asked, smugly.

"Oh, this?" she said. "I've just been drawing dicks this whole time."

"There's that mouth again," I said, and I couldn't keep the raw edge out of my voice this time.

She stilled, uncrossing her legs slowly, flashing me a *hint* of what was underneath, before crossing them again. I swallowed roughly, fingers tightening on the desk.

And that's when my father walked in.

25

ROXY

*T*he shift in Edward's body language wasn't even subtle when his father walked in to his office. His back went ramrod straight, expression neutral, eyes down.

"Good morning, father," he said politely, nodding at the man who looked like a much older Edward—if Edward was in a constant state of disappointment. Distinguished gray hair, a bespoke suit. "How nice of you to drop by unannounced. This is Roxy, my mentee for the CUNY MBA program. She owns a tattoo parlor here in Manhattan."

"Nice to meet you," I said automatically, even though I could already tell this giant douche of a man couldn't care less about me.

He muttered a "yes" under his breath as he avoided glancing my way, effectively ignoring my existence then strode over to Edward's desk, staring at the photos we'd been looking at of past ad campaigns.

There was an awkward silence, Edward and I sitting neatly as if I hadn't just *purposefully* flashed him my underwear.

"You know," Edward said, clearing his throat. "Roxy is a supremely talented tattoo artist. Well-known in this area for her vintage designs. Trained with one of the most famous female tattoo artists here in the States." I felt myself flush, surprised Edward had done research on me. I gave him a small smile of gratitude, and he returned it. "This one's also a right smart businesswoman."

I grinned, holding up my notebook page, where I'd hastily scrawled a crude doodle of a dick for his benefit. His father couldn't see, but Edward could, and he choked on his coffee, stifling a laugh.

But Edward's father wouldn't have cared, ignoring the two of us as if we were furniture.

"Two things," his father said, and Edward's brief moment of levity was replaced with that straight spine again. "First, I noticed several errors in the reports you gave me." He handed him sheets of papers, stacked a foot deep. "I'm assuming they were yours?"

"Oh, probably," he said with the most forced smile I'd ever seen. "You know me. Mistakes are basically my middle name."

I bristled on Edward's behalf but kept my mouth shut.

"Yes, and how was your engagement last night?" he asked, backlit by the skyline before him. He looked like a shipping magnate from the turn of the century. "Your mother asked me to ask you."

Edward flicked his eyes toward me then back to his father. "Phoebe was a lovely woman, thank you. We had a fine evening."

I shifted in my seat. Not that it would *ever* happen, but what the fuck would this man have to say if Edward had gone on an engagement with *me*?

"She is excellent marriage material, Edward. You'd be smart to remember that," his father continued. "I will be in touch with her parents to continue your contact with her."

"Ah," Edward started, and I thought about what he'd said last night. "That would be quite nice, thank you."

"Right," he replied, brushing imaginary lint from his cuff sleeve. "Well, I'll be off then."

"You know, sir," I interjected. "Your son Edward is *the* most sought-after mentor in my entire program. My professors couldn't stop talking about all the innovative things he's done for the hotel industry here in Manhattan. His work is quite impressive."

His father turned slowly, finally acknowledging my existence, and pinned me with a stare I'm sure was meant to intimidate.

I fucking gave it right back to him. His jaw tightened. But I'd stared down drunk punks who were more threatening than this Mr. Monopoly-looking fuckhead.

Then his father turned and left the room as if I'd never even spoken.

When I looked back at Edward, he was staring at me with such utter gratitude it made my heart beat wildly against my rib cage. I fully understood that people had parents that were giant pieces of shit, but I'd grown up with a father who would have given me every single thing in the world if I'd asked for it.

Edward glanced at his watch, standing up. "We should head to our meeting with the marketing team," he said, striding around the desk to stand in front of me. "And that was bloody brilliant, love. Thank you."

"No big deal," I said, a little breathlessly. His gaze was filled with a potent blend of yearning *and* submission. I wanted to command him to his knees and order him to eat me out on this classy desk, surrounded by all of New York City.

"It is a big deal. He can be... very hard for me to manage," he said, and I sensed deep, painful layers to that sentiment.

"So your parents fly here, make you plan this event for

them, and spend the entire time criticizing all of your decisions?" I asked.

"Something like that," he sighed. "My father was particularly hard on all of us growing up, but my siblings now can do no wrong in his eyes, even though they give about one-tenth to this legacy that I do. This is my blood, sweat, and tears. And each spring they come and stomp all over it."

Pure poetic instinct took over, and before I could stop myself, I leaned in to his warm, hard body and kissed his cheek. I allowed myself one extra second, to inhale his woodsy scent, before stepping back and untangling from him. Just a kiss, a chaste one, but my knees were trembling.

Edward touched his fingers to his cheek, eyes bright. "What was that for?"

I attempted nonchalance. "Because your dad's a dick."

Another grateful grin. "Am I really the most sought-after mentor in your school?"

"How should I know?" I teased. "But probably. I think they must have a system where they give the best, most accomplished mentors to the students whose businesses are doing the worst."

But Edward shook his head. "That's not true at all. I think they give the best, most accomplished mentors to the students whose businesses show the most *promise*."

I hid my smile at his compliment, shrugging on my inappropriate blazer. "Well, don't we have a meeting to get to or something?"

We did—several—and for the next two hours, I practically *hummed* with happiness.

I sat next to Edward as he introduced me to some of his key staff. We chatted advertising and marketing and tapping into the target customer base. I took notes obsessively, fingers cramping, oscillating between giving into my crush on Edward and feeling so anxious I could hardly breathe. Edward was cautious not to dump all over *my* mistakes, so we didn't talk marketing for 'Roxy's' exactly, although we danced around the topic enough for me to fully understand that he was right about what I needed to do. And his team was kind and generous, and at the end, I promised to give all of them free tattoos.

They'd laughed. But I knew at least some of them would take me up on it.

26

EDWARD

I had the cab driver drop me further down the street from Roxy's store, wanting to take in the neighborhood a bit. We'd just started to dance around this issue—fitting in with your environment—but every time we broached the subject, Roxy's hackles went up.

It was a crucial business tactic, though, and she was blatantly ignoring it.

Redevelopment had spread through a few blocks around Roxy's shop, located at the edge of Washington Heights in north Manhattan. It had always been a working-class neighborhood and was now one of the few affordable places left in the notoriously overly priced borough. Amid family houses and playgrounds, trendy bars were popping up. There were open-air farmers markets and coffee shops with string lights now. It was cute and hip, and she should have been capitalizing on it. Instead, as I walked toward her blinking, broken sign, her shop looked utterly uninviting.

"Sir Edward," Mack said as I walked in, giving me a bow. I grinned, returning the gesture. Today, Mack had Bach playing on the speakers, and the shop was half-full of customers. Roxy was in the back, setting up her chair.

It was good—a busy day. I knew she needed it.

As she snapped on her black gloves, Roxy looked up, meeting my gaze. Flashed me a tiny, private smile. Her white-blonde hair was pulled over one shoulder, green eyes ringed with black liner, lips bright red. She was wearing a short dress covered with black-and-white polka dots, ripped tights, and those ever-present combat boots. She looked like a punk-rock pin-up model, and all I could think about were her lips, pressed sweetly to my cheek. The way she'd stood up for me to my father—a man who rightly intimidated people when he walked into the room, with the confidence that clings to those with endless piles of money.

Roxy had known the man for less than ten minutes and had succeeded in flustering him. She couldn't tell because he'd walked out of the room so quickly, but my father had been *flustered* by her.

"The tables have turned," Roxy said, beckoning me toward her chair. "Now it's your turn to shadow *me*."

I held up my notebook. "I brought this just to draw penises," I said, and she smirked. "Poorly, that is. I don't have your artistic talent."

"I'd like to see your attempts, though," she said, waving to a client. "And what's this part like? The part where you come to my place of business?"

I sank into a chair, straightened my tie. "Well, the point is two-fold. When you shadow the mentor, you're meant to see some of the aspects of a successfully functioning business. But for the reverse, it's kind of like... a performance evaluation." I kept my tone light, but still, I saw her muscles stiffen.

"You'll be criticizing me?" she asked.

"No," I said. "Not at all. But you've got a list of goals here a mile long, and the only way I can start to help you work on those is seeing the day-to-day operations of your business. Which, I've got to say, it's nice to see this place busy."

Roxy relaxed, nodding her head. "Over the past six months, that source of income has really dwindled. But if I'm being honest, it'd been dwindling when I bought the place from Arrow. It should have been a red-flag, but I was so... I was so *excited* to own a place of my own. To make it something beautiful. I figured things would pick back up on their own."

"Walk-in appointments are pretty steady at other parlors, yeah?" I asked, taking notes.

She nodded. "Ideally, you've got a steady waitlist to match the walk-ins. New customers and loyal ones, blended together. Those two new shops down the street really fucked us."

"True," I conceded. "They are your competition. But maybe we can get at *why* potential customers are walking past your shop and not walking in. What did Arrow do for advertising or branding before you bought the shop?"

Roxy huffed out a breath. "Nothing. Which now, after a year of school and working with you, I'm discovering didn't really set this place up for success."

"And he was kind of like a dodgy wanker, right?"

A delicious smirk. "You could say that. A true piece of shit. So the reputation of this space was pretty shot when I bought it."

I scribbled more notes, and when I looked up, Roxy had me pinned with a desperate expression. "Before I bought it, I watched Arrow all the time, and it never seemed *hard* to him. He never seemed as worked up as I feel all the time now." She was bent over her table, prepping the ink, but I could sense the tension rippling between her shoulder blades.

I fought an overwhelming desire to wrap my arms around

her waist and lay my cheek between those shoulder blades. I knew these anxieties as intimately as my own skin.

But then her face shifted into a smile, eyes landing on something behind me. "Maria, come on back. I'm just getting prepped."

I turned to see an older woman with brown skin and dark hair, wearing more leather than I'd ever seen on a person. As if she'd caught me staring, Maria smiled kindly. "My bike's outside. Leather's in case I wipe out."

"Ah," I said politely. "That's good to know. I'm Edward by the way."

She shook my hand. "Maria Pérez. Nice to meet you."

"Are you uncomfortable with me being here during your tattoo? I'm helping Roxy with a project for her master's degree."

Maria looked impressed. "Oh la la, Roxy's gettin' *fancy*," she said, settling onto the black chair and shedding her layers. "And I don't mind you here at all."

"I'll never be fancy," Roxy said, pulling out a design and holding it up. "What do you think, lady? Is that what you had in mind?"

Roxy had drawn a complicated floral design with lilies and tulips that wound round each other. It absolutely took my breath away.

"I don't know how you do that," I said softly, mostly to myself, but Roxy heard. And blushed.

"I agree," Maria said, shaking her head. "She's a true artist. And that's exactly what I had in mind. How you do that every time..."

Roxy shrugged. "It's my job to make art for you. And you're still thinking upper arm, correct?" Maria nodded, and Roxy laid the stencil against her skin, checking it over and over for placement. It was an intense few moments, and I was content

to watch Roxy with her client, the ease with which she oper-
ated in this space. I'd seen this kind of thing happen at The
Cartwright when I'd promoted people to managers because
they'd loved their jobs—were good at them—but it didn't
necessarily mean they were good *managers*, dealing with all
the extra stress and commitment. Roxy had all the makings of
a smart, strategic business owner, but I could feel her yearning
for the simpler days when her singular task was creating art.

"I've been cancer free for a year now," Maria said, laying
back and getting comfortable.

"I'm so glad to hear that," I said. "Is this tattoo in honor of
that?"

"Yes," she smiled. "Because it fucking sucked. Don't ever
let anyone tell you otherwise. But I finally am feeling more
like myself again. My body feels more like mine. And I just
wanted to add something beautiful to it, if that makes sense."

"Of course," I said, watching as Roxy smoothed her gloved
hands over the stencil, ensuring it stuck perfectly. "Is Roxy
your favorite tattoo artist?"

Roxy flicked her eyes at me, and I shot her a wink.

"Roxy is one of my favorite damn people in the whole
world," Maria replied. "She's done every single piece of ink on
my body. I came in on a whim, a few years ago. Well, it was a
dare from my boyfriend at the time. Didn't think I'd go
through with it, but I showed that piece of shit."

Roxy laughed softly. "I've dated a few pieces of shit in my
lifetime."

"See? She knows," Maria said, wincing as the tattoo gun
landed on her skin. "But I've been coming to Roxy ever since.
I'd never go anywhere else."

A few tiny lightbulbs were going off in my brain. "Why is
that, Maria?"

Maria thought for a second. Roxy's face was locked in

concentration, looking so beautiful my chest ached. "Huh. Well, she's my favorite artist."

"Right," I said, sliding open my notebook. "But tattoo parlors are a dime a dozen in this city. You could literally go *anywhere* for a tattoo. Especially to some of the newer, friendlier looking ones."

Roxy pulled back, tattoo gun in hand. "What's with the third degree, *Dilbert*?"

"I thought your name was Edward," Maria said, confused.

"It is. She just calls me that when she's feeling feisty," I grinned, half-expecting a swift kick from Roxy's boot. But she ignored me, focusing back on the task at hand. "And I'm only asking because I'm curious to see what draws customers like you to this place of business. It might help Roxy get even more."

Maria tilted her head, tapping her chin with one finger. "I'm an old-fashioned woman, Edward, except I prefer a bike between my legs instead of a man, if you know what I mean."

I coughed into my hand. "Um... yes. I see the appeal."

"And I've lived in Washington Heights my entire life. Grew up here. Parents grew up here. All the new, fancy stores don't *fit*. Especially not a tattoo parlor. I don't want a latte while I wait to have a fiery skull tattooed above my ass."

"My thoughts exactly," Roxy agreed, wiping away ink. "It's about atmosphere."

"But some customers would say they want a nicer atmosphere. A boutique experience. They *are* getting permanent ink tattooed on their bodies. Wouldn't you want a space that was clean and well-lit?"

"This space *is* clean and well-lit," Roxy said. "It's just not decorated or designed the same way as the other parlors. Instead of succulents hanging everywhere, we have old photos. And punk albums. And designs by our artists. It's *real,* not some fake trendy bullshit."

I was writing notes down furiously because I felt like we were tapping into something. Roxy's brand as much as she'd hate the sound of that.

"Instead of blending in, you stand out," I mused.

"That's it exactly," Maria said.

"Which, I'd like to point out, is exactly what I've been saying this entire time," Roxy said smugly.

"Hmmm," I said, noncommittal, sketching some ideas out. I wasn't going to press her in front of her client, but she and I were going to probably fight over this tooth-and-nail for the next two months. Because Roxy, deep down, still didn't think she needed to change.

I watched Roxy work with Maria: the intense focus and concentration. The delicate way her design worked with the shapes and curves of Maria's body, like she'd been born with flowers there.

"How do you get the ink into her skin just right?" I asked, enthralled by the process and the rhythmic movement of her tattoo gun.

"Saturation," she smiled, head still down. "Every artist has to find the unique balance between their hand and the tattoo gun. Push too hard and you'll flood the skin with ink. Too softly and you won't break through."

"Interesting," I said. "So you just... keep trying?"

Roxy looked up, green eyes bright with contentment. "It's a balance. Like two people dancing together. With time, you find the perfect rhythm."

"That's beautiful," I said. She gave me another long look before ducking her head back down. Roxy was a joy to behold, and I'd be daft to deny the thought that going toe-to-toe with Roxy had my cock hardening, right there in the shop.

An hour went by, and I watched Mack with customers. Noted their busy times. Strolled out into the street and examined the foot traffic. Trying to put together pieces of this puzzle. Roxy walked Maria through the aftercare procedures, and for as hard of an image she tried to convey, Roxy's soft spots were peeking through. She was warm, making Maria laugh, and I fully understood why people kept coming back to her.

Roxy made people feel safe.

"She's a good woman," Maria reminded me as she got up to leave, patting my arm gently.

"That she is," I said, eyes pinned on Roxy's lithe form as she cleaned. "Your tattoo is beautiful. Thank you for letting me be a part of it."

"Well, we need as many people on this journey as we can get," she said. "Not just with cancer but with life, right?"

I nodded, throat suddenly tight. "That's true."

Maria waved to the staff before getting on one of the biggest, most terrifying motorcycles I'd ever seen. Shaking my head, I walked back toward Roxy, who was so obviously trying to read my notebook.

"See any penises you like?" I asked.

Roxy flashed me the middle finger.

I chuckled. "Stop trying to peek. I was only taking notes for our next meeting. Maria had some good points."

"I just want it to be known, again, I've been saying those things this entire time," she said, rolling her eyes.

"But you don't advertise, love, and that's a problem."

She crossed her arms, scowling. "I know, I *know*, but... I have no idea what to do. We don't have a big marketing team like you do. Everyone's ideas yesterday were great, but I have no idea how to implement them. What do I do, put an ad in the paper?"

I fought back a smirk. "Sure, but first can I recommend smoke signals?"

Behind me, Scarlett and Mack were chanting "*fight, fight, fight.*"

Roxy relented first, waving them away. "Okay, I'm being a snarky bitch. I'm sorry. We can talk advertising at our next meeting," she admitted, sinking into one of the black leather chairs. "I never felt this exhausted at the end of the day, but now, with everything on my mind..."

"Can I suggest alcohol?" I teased, and she gave me the finger again—but with a grin this time. I sat next to her, our hips just touching. "Do you have a friend you can talk to who's going through something similar?"

She thought for a minute, and I gazed at the gorgeous ink dancing across her collarbone, was tempted to taste her there.

"Not really," she finally said. She dropped her voice. "I used to be able to talk to Scarlett and Mack, but I'm their boss now, so it feels different."

"It is different," I affirmed. "You have to set that boundary."

She nodded. "My parents are beyond supportive, so's Fiona, but none of them have run businesses, so it's hard for me to explain. Does that make sense?"

"My best friend, Elliott, runs another luxury hotel," I said. "He just... gets it. And it's *very* helpful to have a friend like that."

Roxy shifted, brushing her hip against mine again. "I guess you're my friend who I can talk to." Her dark eyes flicked up to mine. "Right?"

"We're professional mentors, I'm afraid. Not friends," I said.

Her face fell.

"I'm joking, Roxy," I said quickly, even though I really hadn't been. It was only natural to *want* to be friends, but the program had professional boundaries for a reason. Friendship made things messy. But the look on Roxy's face devastated me.

"Oh, okay," she said, smiling awkwardly. "I appreciate being able to talk to you about it. As friends too."

We shared a brief smile, and I didn't want to leave. I liked it here—liked Roxy's presence, the endlessly revolving clients with unique stories. The music and the staff.

"You two lovebirds coming to the show tonight?" Mack asked.

"Not lovebirds," Roxy scowled. "And of course. My parents didn't have a lot of rules growing up, but missing one of their shows got you in a fuckton of trouble." Roxy yawned, rubbing her face. "Even though I really just want to crawl into bed."

"What show?" I asked, curious.

"My parents' band, The Hand Grenades. They're playing a show at The Red Room."

"Oh that's right, I remember you telling me when..." I trailed off, aware of Mack's presence since I had been about to say, "when we fucked each other's brains out five feet from here."

"Want to come, Ed?" Mack asked. "Not sure if it's your scene, but you're invited."

I covered my smile since Roxy didn't know that it *had* indeed been my scene. "I've been known to hit up a few punk shows in my day."

Roxy turned fully, eyebrows raised. "Did your servants drive you from the castle?"

I ignored her, jabbing my thumb in her direction. "She's got a real mouth," I said to Mack, who just shrugged.

"Means she likes you," he said, ducking and laughing as Roxy chucked her pen at him. "And I'm going home to shower, and then I'll meet you guys there. Sound good?"

"Yeah, yeah," Roxy scoffed. "Make sure you say hi to my

parents or they'll be disappointed." Mack gave her a salute, before walking out.

I stood, sensing it was time to exit. "So..." I started.

"If you want to come or whatever, it's not a big deal, but you could," Roxy said quickly, the words spilling out like a swift rain. "Or like... whatever."

Roxy was messy.

Too fucking messy, and in the span of five minutes, I felt myself vacillate wildly. Friends-colleagues-mentors-lovers. Then back through the whole bloody cycle again. I reached forward, brushing a strand of hair from her shoulders, completely unable to stop myself.

"I'd like that," I said. "A three-piece suit is within the dress code, I'm assuming?"

Roxy smiled. "Oh, Dilbert. You're trying to get your ass kicked, aren't you?"

27

ROXY

he Red Room was a heaving, breathing entity of swaying bodies. I stood outside on the street with Fiona, waiting for Edward, and I could feel the heat emanating from the doorway. When we were little, my parents would sneak us in to see some of their favorite punk and new wave bands—often calling us out sick for school the next day and letting us stay in our pajamas, eating chocolate-chip pancakes.

I grinned at the memory, looking down the street for the millionth time to see if I could spot Edward.

"Girl, you've got it *bad*," Fiona said next to me, still dressed impeccably from work.

"I just don't want him to get lost is all," I said. "There's a lot of people here."

Fiona glanced at her watch. "Speaking of. Mom and Dad go on in twenty minutes, and if they don't see us out there, we'll be in some deep shit."

"They'll make us watch that Joe Strummer documentary with them another ten times," I said, rolling my eyes.

"You know, other people's parents grounded them. Or took

away their video games," Fiona pointed out, and we both chuckled in the blustery March air. I huddled closer to her, legs freezing. "And can I ask why you're wearing your super sexy, super short dress on a freezing cold night?" she said slyly.

I glanced down, liking the way my legs looked in my ripped fishnet stockings. "It gets hot in there."

"Sure," she said knowingly. "And it has nothing to do with a certain smug, rich businessman who's meeting you here tonight for a date?"

"Not a date," I corrected sharply.

Fiona turned. "I repeat. Girl, you got it *bad*."

"We're keeping our hands off each other, just so you know," I said, flushing with the lie. Thinking about my lips on Edward's cheek. His fingers, brushing a strand of hair from my shoulder.

"Right, but for how much longer? It's not even been a month, and you're already inviting him to shows."

"We're *friends*, Fiona. And really, it was Mack that invited him," I said.

"Mhmm," she hummed. "And are you supposed to be friends with your mentor?"

I opened my mouth, prepared to make one of my typical snarky comebacks.

But then I spotted Edward strolling my way, and I knew without a doubt that Fiona was right.

"Ladies," he said, deep voice rippling with his refined accent. "I'm guessing this is your lovely sister, Fiona?" he asked me, turning to shake Fiona's hand.

Who was fucking speechless.

"Fi," I whispered, jostling her back to Earth. "Shake the strange man's hand."

"Sorry," she said, with a secret smile. "You just don't look as dapper as Roxy had described you."

"Not that I've ever described you," I cut in quickly. "And I do have to commend your ability to fit in."

Edward was out of his suit for the first time since I'd met him, dressed in dark jeans and a leather jacket. He held it open, and beneath peeked out a worn, clearly loved Sex Pistols t-shirt.

"Impressive," Fiona said. "Did you have to order that shirt in?"

Edward laughed, eyes twinkling. "I should have expected to get the third degree from *both* Quinn sisters."

Fiona and I shrugged in unison. "Our reputation precedes us," I said, admiring the broad lines of Edward's shoulders. "And the question still stands. Where did you get that shirt?"

Edward's eyes landed on mine. "I'm from England, love. I grew up on punk rock."

I swallowed, another layer of Edward revealing itself brilliantly. "Oh," I managed, scouring my brain for something witty and coming up empty.

"Roxy talks about you all the time," Fiona teased.

I elbowed her side. "*Shut up*," I hissed. "And that's not even remotely true."

"And how's our Roxy doing? Is she slaying her mentorship with her usual brand of scowling wit?" Fiona continued.

Edward slid his hands into his pockets, face brightening. "Roxy is incredible. Truly. We need more businesspeople like her in this world."

Fiona's fingers found mine and gave them a quick, enthusiastic squeeze. "That sounds about right. And you're quite the charmer, aren't you?"

"Ah, it seems like *my* reputation has preceded me," he said, lips quirking up. "Although Roxy once told me it's only because, and I quote, 'chicks dig the accent.'"

I'd told him that the night we met. The night we fucked. And from the light blush of his cheeks, I knew he was thinking the same thing.

But Fiona was laughing, squeezing my fingers in a sisterly Morse code. "We do like it."

"Want to tell me why I'm showing up to a punk show involving your *parents*? What's their story? Roxy's told me a little, here and there. Breadcrumbs, really," he smiled, switching tracks.

Fiona and I shared a look, but it was her turn to tell the story.

"Our parents met in college, their freshman year, and then promptly dropped out," Fiona said. "It wasn't their style anyway, being cooped up in classrooms and taking orders from 'the authority.'"

"They're more 'damn the man' than anything else," I said, "and had already both been threatened with expulsion a few times. Mostly for trespassing, vandalism, noise complaints."

Edward's eyebrows shot up. "They got in trouble for *all* of those things?"

I grinned. "Yeah. They're our heroes. When they met, they both were in separate bands that were kind of fizzling out. They fell in love, started singing together, and that's how The Hand Grenades were born."

"They played CBGB a few times, have had about five albums released. Plenty of tours. They don't make a ton of money, but they love being on the road with their band," Fiona finished. "Suffice it to say, Roxy and I had a slightly non-traditional childhood."

"Except it was traditional in that our parents are *obsessed with us*," I said.

"It's true," Fiona said, shaking her head. "One second they'd be lecturing us about Big Banks and their continual war on poor people. The next, telling all of their friends about our good grades. Or showing up to every single one of our school events—"

"—concerts, art shows, debate team, you name it," I continued. "And there, in the front row, in their full Hand Grenades attire, would be our parents, filming us with their old video camera for posterity."

A brief look of pure *yearning* flashed over Edward's face before he gave us a broad grin. "I can't wait to meet them," he said. "And it sounds like they love you both very much."

Fiona glanced behind us, noted the changing sets. "That they do. And if we don't get in there to watch them, they'll be pissed as hell."

～

EDWARD WADED through the crowd in front of us, seemingly unperturbed by the seething mass of bodies and sound. We were heading toward the back, a darker corner, and every nerve ending thrilled at the idea.

"Roxy," Fiona said, grabbing my wrist. I turned toward her shit-eating grin. "He's hot. Like *really* hot."

"I know," I said. "That's why I fucked him in the first place."

"No but you two, together," she continued, "it's like... it's like watching a lightning storm."

"Hardly," I said, fighting the pleasure I had at her assessment.

"Hardly, my *ass*," she replied. "I'll repeat: you've got it bad. And I'm just going to say, as your sister, I think you should go for it." And with that she gave me a quick, squeezing hug, and then disappeared into the crowd. Even dressed to the nines and perfectly coifed, my little sister could rage at the front with the best of them.

I watched her go and turned to look at Edward leaning against the bar and ensnaring me with a look of quiet longing. I moved gracefully through the crowd, my eyes drinking up his lean form. Edward held out a beer, the glass cold against my palm, and leaned close.

"I spotted a slightly quieter alcove further in the back," he said, breath feathering beneath my ear. "Care to join me?"

I nodded, briefly speechless, following Edward toward the alcove—an alcove I'd had my fair share of hot make-outs with strangers in. We squeezed into it, still able to watch the show but with just a bit of a barrier.

"So," I started, facing him. "Tell me about your misspent youth going to punk shows."

Edward grinned, sipping his whiskey. "Ah, love, I don't think my youth was as misspent as yours, sounds like."

"It was pretty misspent," I agreed. "Although so many of the 'bad kid' things that I did were somewhat sanctioned by my parents, so it didn't feel as rebellious. They were supportive of tattoos and sneaking out and wearing all black and acting like a surly teen. But they also expected Fiona and I to get good grades, be kind people, and essentially live a truthful, authentic life."

"Did you fight often?" Edward asked, and I shook my head.

"Not really," I said. "There were a few times, of course. But really the most bewildered I'd ever seen my parents was when Fiona declared she wanted to become a lawyer and started studying for the LSAT."

"Most parents would be proud," Edward mused.

"Oh, they are," I said, laughing. "They tell all of their friends about their brilliantly talented daughters. The difference being they understand what I do. And have no clue what Fiona does."

"Too straight-laced for them," Edward grinned, leaning a bit closer to me. "What would they think of me?"

"I already told them my mentor was a smug, rich hotelier from England," I said. "And they were pretty impressed, actually."

"I am quite impressive," Edward said.

"You are," I said, remembering his tongue dancing across my clit with expert precision. "And you dodged my question, Dilbert."

He chuckled softly as The Hand Grenades started another song, the sound ricocheting through the small concert space. "When I was growing up, music like this was something all the bad kids listened to," Edward said, voice low against my ear. "Especially if you were from the wealthier classes like my family was. We all went to boarding school, and we'd sneak out after hours. Eventually we started sneaking out to go to shows, riding our bikes to the train station that would take us to London."

"You were a *bad kid*," I teased, completely taken aback by this story of Edward's slightly rebellious youth. Thinking about a group of teenagers biking through the night alive with youth and a thrilling sense of freedom.

"Just a little bad," he said. "And only when it came to music. And girls. I was a little bad when it came to girls."

I was intrigued, but he didn't elaborate.

"But I was so bloody frightened that my parents would find out, that they wouldn't approve, I stopped going eventually."

I pulled away so I could see his face. "Do you regret that?"

"Yes," he said softly. "Yes, I do." He looked sad for a moment, so I reached forward, rubbing my fingers against the

179

soft material of his shirt. "Did you ever see The Sex Pistols live?"

He shook his head. "Never. Although I did see The Distillers perform the night before my graduation from Cambridge. A sudden spur-of-the-moment show, and even though I'd been fraught with worry all day and stressed about what my parents were going to think, I snuck out at midnight to go see them." A knowing smile. "Show of my fucking lifetime."

"Being wild pays off sometimes," I said. "And I wish I had been there. With you. That would have been my senior year in high school, and The Distillers were a favorite."

"I wish you had been with me too, love," Edward said, eyes slowly assessing my body. I fought the urge to preen, instead taking a long sip of beer. Waiting. "All of my mates would have been right jealous of my punk rock queen."

"All Hail Queen Roxy," I said without thinking, a reference to our night together. Edward's tattoo. And the slow, seductive grin that slid across his face let me know he was remembering the exact same thing.

"You look good here," I said, hoping he couldn't see me blush. "I mean, you look comfortable. More so than I thought you would." And he did—leaned against the wall, jacket off now, the soft material of his shirt beckoning my fingers.

"Ah yes, it's not just the boardroom I enjoy; although, to be honest, I don't always feel quite comfortable there either."

"Why not?"

Edward looked at me for a moment and then said: "Fear of public speaking. Massive, I'm afraid. As soon as I stand up in front of a group of more than two or three people..." he trailed off, laughing. "I'd hate to have you see me like that."

"But I'm shadowing one of your Board meetings next week," I said, surprised at his admission. "And I'm sure it's not as bad as you think. I always pictured you dominating in a space like that. Making your employees weep with fear."

He chuckled again, shaking his head. "Not quite like that. And I would never make my employees weep. At least not purposefully."

"Should I be writing this down?" I asked, and the brief memory of our mentorship seemed to dampen his spirits for a moment. But only for a moment.

"You should write down everything I say because I am a magnificent businessman," he replied with a wink, and a steady pulse beat between my legs. "And I think I feel happier here because it reminds me of what it was like, before The Cartwright. Before I left England. My parents are not like yours, Roxy. You met my father. And although they've always been like that, constantly criticizing without any affection, it was easier to deal with before I was tasked with continuing their legacy. And all the strings that come attached to it."

My heart dropped. I remembered the "strings" he spoke about the night we'd met: marriage.

Edward turned toward the stage, smiling at my parents who were really hamming it up. He seemed looser, more himself. "It's nice to remember my misspent youth, as you call it. Nights like this, although without the company of a pretty girl."

I mock-scowled, looking around us. "I don't see any of those."

Edward brushed the hair from my neck again, lighting up my nerve endings with a shower of electric sparks. Leaned in, hovered his soft lips against the shell of my ear. "I'm sorry, love," he whispered. "'Pretty' is too dull of a word for a woman like you. I meant to say 'absolutely stunning.'"

I'd read about women who swooned and always considered myself not the type. Because I'd had big, sexy men talk dirty to me before. Sing the praises of my mouth or my cunt. Even tell me I was "pretty."

But I realized my fatal mistake: none of those men were Edward. Because just the dance of his lips below my ear, the lust-filled rasp of his voice, the notion that someone would find my tattooed, bad-girl, shaved-head aesthetic *stunning* was, well...

Swoon-worthy.

"Another drink, love?" he asked, leaning back with a devilish smile that told me he was *well* aware of my trembling knees.

"Sure," I managed, sighing as he walked through the crowd. Knowing that Fiona was right, yet again. Because I never should have brought him here, to this warm, friendly place that meant so much to me.

To this dark, hidden alcove where no one would see us do illicit things.

28

EDWARD

*W*hen I'd mentioned to Elliott—as casually as I could—that I was going to the show with Roxy, he'd laughed uproariously and said, "Good fucking luck, mate."

I'd scoffed, shrugging it off, even though deep down I knew he was right. And then knew, as soon as Roxy and I had paired off in that dark corner, that I was only adding fuel to a banked fire, dousing until it burst into a brilliant flame.

And I loved it.

"So tell me," I said, passing Roxy another drink. "How many men have you dragged back here to have your way with?"

Roxy bit her lip. Eyebrow arched. "Wouldn't you like to know."

"Little minx," I teased. I drank her in: she was wearing blood-red lipstick and some black sheath dress that barely covered her ass. I wanted desperately to slide my palm up her smooth thigh, slip my fingers between her legs. "Is that your relationship of preference? One-night stands?"

"I've done it all, truthfully," she replied. "Jimmy was a year-long relationship."

"The guy who cheated?" I asked.

"Yep," she said. "And I definitely fucked my way around for a while after that. Sex therapy, as you know."

I swallowed. "I'm aware."

"But I also had longer term relationships too. Good men, who I cared for, but we just never seemed to... I don't know. It's hard to put my finger on it. I guess I just see this beautiful relationship that my parents have, and they've been together since they were nineteen years old. They don't seem bored with each other. Nothing about their relationship seems lackluster."

As if on cue, we turned to watch them sing to each other, dancing on stage like they were college kids all over again. "But with the guys I dated long-term, I just kept thinking '*this* might be the person I spend the rest of my life with?'"

"And then what?" I asked.

"And then I'd realize that when I pictured my future, they weren't in it. At all. Not because they weren't great but because I was already bored." Roxy tilted her head. "Did you feel that way with Emily?"

I grimaced. "To be honest, ever since we've broken up, I've spent way too much time analyzing every single relationship I've ever had."

"Because she cheated?"

Because I met you, I wanted to say but stopped myself. "Being in love is not a requirement for marriage in my family's social circle. It's not like I was ever modeled this wild, passionate love before. Emily was safe. We had nice chats. Enjoyed similar things. If we had to spend the rest of our lives together, it would have been... fine."

Roxy was shaking her head. "That's it, though; don't you

see? For the rest of your *life*, which means she would be your partner during some of your worst, lowest moments. If you got sick, she'd care for you. When your parents died, she'd comfort you. If you had children together, you'd be *parents* together."

"Your point, love?" I asked, even though I could guess.

"I think that person should be *everything* to you. The air you breathe. More important than anything else, more *vital* to your life. I think every moment with this person should be so fucking fraught with passion you can barely be in the same room without tearing each other's clothes off." She grinned and took a long sip of beer, her eyes on me.

"Roxy the *romantic*?" I mused. "I never would have guessed. You seemed like the kind of woman to fuck and run."

"I *do* fuck and run. Quite often. Because it's fun, and I haven't met that person yet, so why not enjoy myself?"

I leaned in closer, hand next to her head. "What if you've already fucked that person, that *stranger*, and they *were* your person?"

"I'm pretty sure I'd know, Edward," she finally replied. "I wouldn't send that person back out into the night." But there was the slightest glint of regret in her gaze. The rest of the world felt utterly far away as if we only existed in this bar, in this corner, in this dark, private place.

I reached forward, twisting her wrist upright, the words *Never Again* in block letters printed there.

"But what about this? The tattoo you got the night you found out Jimmy was cheating? To me, it reads like, well, like the kind of thing a person would get when they didn't believe in love anymore."

Roxy looked down where our hands were joined. "Cheating, to me, is about disrespect. The other person, even if they feel like their reasons for cheating are *just*, doesn't respect you, your time, your heart, your emotions. They're a thief, really, stealing your choices. Take Emily, for example."

I thought about that dinner, the way she'd primly taken a bite of her fish and declared we were over.

"You might have broken up organically six months from now. Fallen out of love or realized you weren't right for each other in some key way. But instead, she cheated and made the choice for you. She stole it. This," she said, holding up her wrist, "is my reminder. Not that I'd never again fall in love or believe in love. But I'd never again let a man disrespect me. Because I'm worth *more* than that."

I ached to take her then, against this wall, pressed together in our tiny alcove. Take her and show her—show how much she was worth to *me*.

"Couldn't agree more," I finally said. "I'm pretty sure you're worth all the riches in the world—and then some."

"It's true," she said. "And you are too. Emily never should have made the decision for you."

The music changed, some guitar riff driving through the room, pushing the edges of my restraint.

"So sex therapy, for you, wasn't because you don't ultimately want to be in a committed relationship?" I asked.

Roxy shook her head, red lips quirking up. "You should know that I want to be married as fuck."

"I'm having a hard time picturing you in a white dress," I admitted.

"That's because I wouldn't be caught dead in a white dress," she said. "And before I'm married, before I find The One, I just think it's fun to fuck strangers, Dilbert."

"Well, I've only really done it once," I said, aware that I was willingly smashing through whatever semblance of a professional boundary we'd constructed between us. Smashing through it gleefully. "With you."

Her pupils darkened... but she didn't shove me away. "Did you not like it?"

I shook my head, leaning closer. "That wasn't the problem, Roxy. I liked it *too* much." A pause as we locked eyes. "Haven't been able to replicate it with anyone else." I placed the edge of my finger right beneath her chin. Tilting it up, just slightly. "Tell me what's fun about fucking strangers. Because wouldn't it be risky? You could take someone home who you have no chemistry with." I slowly stroked my finger down her throat, landing at her rapidly beating pulse. "Who's terrible in bed."

"True," she said, breathlessly. "Although I think you know enough about me to know I can command a man to do what I want." My finger slid down her chest then up along the swell of her breast. Stroking. Teasing.

"Is that what you do, love? Take home someone you can play with? Who you can make do your bidding?" Back and forth roamed my finger, almost sliding beneath the fabric of her dress but then pulling away.

"It's not hard," she said. "In fact, usually once I take my clothes off, men are like putty in my hands. Free for me to bend to my will." I swallowed a growl at the memory, retaliated by sliding the tip of my finger over her hardening nipple. Swiping across it slowly. Roxy's entire body curved off the wall, and I slid my other hand around her back, holding her against me.

"They'd do anything you'd say, wouldn't they?" I replaced my finger with my entire palm, cupping her breast roughly, and she hissed in a breath.

"All Hail Queen Roxy," she said, eyes briefly fluttering closed. "It's a privilege to fuck me, Edward. You know that."

"I bloody well do, love," I said, rocking between her legs. Just a reminder of what my cock could do. "It's why I haven't been able to fuck any other woman since that night. It's been four fucking months now, and all I ever think about is *you*."

I'd barely gotten the words out before I was being forcibly dragged through the crowd of bodies, everything a blur except for Roxy's hand in mine, the delicious sway of her hips in that tight dress. I blinked, and we were suddenly in the brisk March air, and Roxy was dragging me into the even-darker alley.

I had Roxy's back against the wall and mouth on mine a second later, crashing our lips together in a hot, hungry kiss. My hands gripped her face, trapping her there, and the tiny whimpers she made had me snarling like a wild animal. Her tongue slid against mine before she nipped my lip, deepening the kiss until an entire galaxy of stars swayed across my vision. One hand trailed down my chest, my stomach, landing on my cock. Cupping it and dragging her fingers up and down, and I just about lost my damn mind.

"Not *yet*," I snapped, grabbing both of her wrists and hoisting them roughly over her head. She practically lunged at me, teeth grazing my jaw, and all I could do was laugh darkly.

"You're going to make me work for this, aren't you, love?" I taunted, ripping down the top of her dress and taking as much of her breast in my mouth as I could, tongue lavishing the metal around her nipple. I took long, hungry pulls, eyes closed in ecstasy, as Roxy writhed above me.

"Spread your legs," I commanded.

She complied with a bratty smirk. Still keeping her hands above her head, I slid my other palm between her legs, my forehead landing against hers when I realized she wasn't wearing underwear.

"I can't stop thinking about you," I groaned, thumb sliding

against the piercing in her clit. "Can't stop thinking about the way you came for me. Your glorious pleasure, such a *gift*."

I slid one, and then two, fingers inside of her, sheathed in her pussy, wet and warm just for me. Roxy kissed me, moaning and shuddering against my mouth as I slowly fucked her, pausing to grind my palm right where she wanted it.

"Please don't ever stop," she begged, hooking her leg around my waist and pulling me closer. We made one hell of an erotic sight, backed against this wall with just my hand, working beneath her dress. Roxy's breathy moans and arms held above her head.

"That's the problem, Roxy," I admitted, licking up her throat. "I told myself I could do this."

"Wh—what?" she asked, panting as I found her nipple again. An almost-shriek tumbled from her lips, a guttural, gasping sound. I circled the pads of my fingers on her g-spot, deep inside her.

"Keep my hands off you, and I can't. Why is that?" I demanded, speeding up my fingers, needing to wrench an orgasm from her in the middle of this goddamn alley. "At night, when I close my eyes, all I see is you. Spread on that desk, naked and so fucking beautiful, and all it takes is one stroke, Roxy. *One stroke,* and I come."

"Oh God you... *fuck,* tell me you touch yourself and think about me," she panted.

I loved that this woman was seconds from climax and still making demands of me. I lowered my lips toward hers. Slowed the motions of my fingers dramatically.

"Only if you admit the same thing," I said against her mouth.

She responded with a bite. I curled my fingers even deeper inside of her, index finger working that sweet spot, and her entire body started to shake.

"Every night," she said. "Every night I fuck myself and think about you. About *us,* together. I can't stop, and I wish that I could, but I *can't.*"

Roxy kissed me then with so much desperate yearning I knew there was no going back now, no going back to the way things were. I let my beautiful vixen come then, finger-fucking her in the rhythm I remembered her loving, grinding my palm against her clit, watching in wonder as she climaxed. I kissed her, a futile attempt to quiet her screams of pleasure, and she'd barely come down before I had my cock out, nudged right at her entrance.

With her hands free, she wrapped both hands around my cock and stroked, the dual sensations almost too much. With my last shred of coherence, I pulled a condom from my pocket, opening it with fingers that trembled.

"Roxy, darling, I'm not going to—" I tried to say, but she quieted me with the sweetest kiss as her hands did the filthiest things. Rolled the condom down my length, preparing us.

"I'm always thinking about you," she said. "I just need you to know that. Not just at night, but all the damn time, Edward."

"*God*, me too," I groaned. "Me too."

"Good," she said simply. "Now fuck me." I lifted her against the wall, and she wrapped her legs around me.

We didn't talk anymore—couldn't—because I fucked Roxy with a coarse precision that had us both gasping and groaning, clutching at each other helplessly. I yanked her top back down with my teeth, licked her nipples as Roxy held my head in place, back arching off the wall. We kissed and kissed, her mouth so fucking *sweet*, teeth leaving marks on my jaw, my throat, marking me for all to see. I was close, so *bloody close*, but my hands were full with Roxy's perfect ass, and I knew she needed more.

"Touch yourself for me," I said.

I couldn't stop grinning when she complied, so turned on at the sight in front of me: Roxy filled with my cock as she rubbed her clit. I tore myself away from watching to drag my teeth against her nipple piercing, and then she climaxed, her pussy squeezing me so tightly I fell right over the edge with her—flew, really, my orgasm lingering for longer than I thought possible.

I lowered her to the ground gingerly, both of us out of breath. Brushed the wild strands of hair from her face. Roxy was looking up at me with an expression I couldn't decipher, but it gave me a happy, song-like quality in my chest—like birds at sunrise, bright and hopeful.

I cupped her cheek, swiped my thumb across her bottom lip.

"You *are* impressive," she said with a sly grin.

"I told you," I replied, and of all the many millions of ways we could have ended the encounter, I never would have imagined the beautiful reality: Roxy, laying her head on my chest. Wrapping her arms around my waist. Holding me like she never wanted to let go.

"Are you all right, love?" I asked, stroking her hair. Kissing her temple.

"More than all right," she replied softly. "I'm perfect."

29

ROXY

*B*usy Bee watched me hungrily as I laid the strips of bacon on the frying pan, grease sizzling and popping.

"Not for dogs," I admonished, before breaking off the tiniest piece of bacon and tossing it to him.

"You're a bad influence on your animals," Fiona said blearily, slumping onto a barstool in my cozy kitchen. It was an unusually warm morning for the end of March, and I'd opened up the door in my apartment that led to my tiny fire escape, which was filled with plants and a small birdfeeder (I told myself it was for Apple and Cucumber's enjoyment, but I found myself watching birds more than I liked to admit).

"And that's kind of snarky to direct at the big sister who's making you a breakfast that'll cure your hangover," I said, passing Fiona a Gatorade, two Advil, and a large mug of coffee. She downed all three quietly while I flipped her eggs.

"I'm not hungover," Fiona rasped. "I have to meet a client in two hours to go over their will, and being hungover for something like that would be *very* unprofessional."

"Mm-hm," I mused. "Want to use my shower and makeup

when you're done?"

"Fucking yes, *please*," she said, with her head on the table.

I slid her a plate of breakfast, which she eyed warily. "Eat, you'll feel better," I commanded. "And when did you turn into a twenty-year-old sorority girl?"

Fiona winced. "I made some... bad decisions last night."

"With who?" I teased, crossing my arms and glancing at my watch. I needed to open the shop at noon, do some paperwork, and then meet Edward for another shadow day at his office.

The thought had butterflies taking flight in my belly.

"After mom and dad's set, I ended up at the bar, flirting with this cute guy..."

"Name?"

Another wince. "I have no idea."

"What did you guys do?"

She flushed a little. "He was *so* not my type. He didn't *say* he was in a biker gang? But if later I found out he was, I wouldn't be surprised. And also we did some shots." A pause as she chewed on her bacon, Bee at her feet. "And we did some kissing. A *lot* of kissing. Like beneath-the-bleachers-at-homecoming type of kissing."

I laughed. "Fiona Quinn, Esquire, big-time lawyer, getting drunk in a dive bar and making out with a punk-rock dirtbag." I shook my head mockingly. "What am I going to do with you?"

"Ugh," she groaned. "I feel like shit, and I have literally a million things to do today. Why did I do that, Roxy?"

I shrugged since it was no secret Fiona was pretty all-work-no-play. She had been since she was in high school: driven, ambitious, hard-working. "Maybe you just wanted to let loose. Do something *fun* for once."

"Don't start," she warned, but it lacked any threat. Apple

and Cucumber both jumped up onto the table, watching her eat. "Also, do you not feed your animals or something?"

"They are *very* food motivated. And I feed them constantly," I said.

I poured myself another cup of coffee, leaning against the counter. I wanted to tell Fiona about last night, about Edward, but I wasn't sure how. She'd gotten home hours later than I did and was pretty wasted. As she snored in bed next to me, I laid awake, my body suffused with the deepest satisfaction. For three months, I'd pined for Edward—even if I still didn't really want to admit it to myself. And if I had any doubts in my mind that our connection that night in the shop was a *fluke,* last night had smashed that theory to pieces.

Edward, yet again, gave me the best fuck of my life.

"I fucked Edward in an alley last night," I said simply, and Fiona spit her coffee across the table and directly into the faces of my cats.

"Oh my God, *what*?" she said, mopping it up quickly as Apple and Cucumber gave me a look of dignified horror.

"We were talking, and kind of flirting, and then we were *really* flirting. And I swear, Fi, I know it sounds like complete nonsense, but I've never been so attracted to someone before in my entire life."

"Lightning storm," she smirked. "Told you. And it's not nonsense."

I rolled my eyes. "Yeah, yeah. So what do we do now, though?"

"Fuck each other some more."

I threw a piece of bacon at her, and Busy Bee leaped in the air and snatched it.

"You're lucky," I said. "I'm serious though. I need this class to graduate. I truly *need* Edward's mentoring wisdom because the store is—"

"The store is what, Roc?" she asked.

I looked out the window. "Well it's not exactly *thriving,* and I need all the help I can get. But I also think you were... you were..."

"Say it."

"*Right*. You were right about me and Edward." I scowled at her smug little-sister expression.

"Can't keep your hands off each other," she said.

I blushed, thinking of Edward growling the same thing against my ear last night. "So do you think Edward's the kind of person to shirk his professional duties as your mentor just because you guys are also fucking each other's brains out?"

I bit my lip. "No. He's actually very honorable."

"And do you think you can both keep it a secret from your professor? I'm guessing she *shouldn't* know about this."

"It wouldn't be good. For my reputation. For Edward's. For the program's."

Fiona stood, rubbing her face. For a second, she looked nothing like my hotshot lawyer sister, and everything like the six-year-old girl who'd climb into bed with me when she had a nightmare. "The sex, between you and English McFancyPants, what was it like? As good as the first time?"

My hands tightened on the mug, heart fluttering. "It was *epic.*"

Fiona walked over, gave me a quick hug, then strode into my bathroom, looking less hungover than she had an hour ago. "Keep the epic sex a secret from the professor, and you're good to go. Just don't, you know, break up before you graduate. Because that would make it *really* awkward."

"Well, that couldn't happen because we're not together," I said.

Fiona only quirked an eyebrow knowingly. "Just keep telling yourself that."

30

EDWARD

J rubbed my hand down my jaw, staring at the email on my screen.

CUNY Capstone Project: One Month Progress Report

Bloody hell, I'd forgotten I needed to fill out progress reports on Roxy—it was part of the overall evaluation process.

What progress or breakthroughs have you seen from your mentee this past month?

The truth was, I *had* seen Roxy have small breakthroughs, moments when I saw a lightbulb go on and she'd scribble something down furiously—and not just penises. Actual notes and words of advice. She was still quick to defend, and stumbling when it came to some key areas, but for the first month, *objectively,* she was right on track compared to past mentees I'd worked with.

But I couldn't seem to type the words. Because all I could think about was that goddamn alley and the filthy, *un*-professional things we'd done to each other there.

I woke up this morning expecting to feel regret, some

sense that what we'd done was *wrong* or would make things more complicated. And maybe it was wrong, and maybe it *would* complicate things, but I couldn't find an ounce of remorse.

Not a single one.

Except I did need to find time today to write this progress report and actually *focus*. Not on the feel of her legs around my waist or her panting, breathy moans. Not on the sweetness of her lips or tight clenching of her pussy around my cock as I fucked us into oblivion. *Certainly* not the way her nipples—

"Dilbert," Roxy said. I looked up to see my punk-rock queen, leaning against the doorway with a smile on her face.

"Roxy, darling," I said, beckoning her inside. I was aware of my staff buzzing about, the complete inappropriateness of what I wanted to do to her in my office, but I couldn't help myself. I crooked my finger, and she came around my desk. Obedient. "You're a little early."

I reached forward, threading our fingers together, letting my thumb stroke her palm.

"I know," she said, biting her lip. "I was excited."

"To see me?"

"Maybe," she said, smirking. "Or maybe I was just excited to steal more of your office supplies."

I brought her wrist to my lips. Kissed it, noted the way her breathing hitched. "How were you this morning? After…?"

"Wonderful," she said.

"Me too," I replied, reluctantly letting her hand drop. I cleared my throat, standing. "So shall we get to our meetings? I see you're dressed in slightly appropriate business attire today."

Roxy gave me a twirl, and indeed her black blazer had not a single adornment on it. "I thought I'd step up my game. Wanted to impress my mentor after all."

"I'm afraid he's already impressed, love," I said with a wink.

Her answering smile lit up the room.

~

"Roxy, this is Crystal, the head of our janitorial and maintenance department," I said, introducing the two of them before we settled into Crystal's office on the first floor. "Roxy is my mentee through the CUNY mentoring project, and she's here to shadow me for the day."

"Pleasure to meet you," Crystal said, pulling out her notebook. "And please forgive me as we lay into Edward about how fucking annoying his father is."

"Crystal and I have worked together for more than a decade, and I'm afraid there's no love lost between her and... um, several members of the Cavendish family," I explained. "Especially around the Charity Ball."

"Come in here every spring, tear this place to pieces, and poke their heads into things that don't concern them," Crystal said.

"Luckily, my father's been at the Atlantic City property for a couple days, so there's been a bit of a breather," I said to Roxy by way of explanation, "but what's been going on before that?"

"Those heaters on the roof top deck," Crystal explained. "Wants them installed now and wants the ones that are especially complicated and expensive."

"It's the Cavendish way, I'm afraid," I sighed, writing down some notes. "And talk to me about the Charity Ball. Is everything going to be okay with those bloody chandeliers?"

Crystal rolled her eyes then launched into a diatribe. We chatted pipes and venue maintenance and the myriad of things my staff worked to keep on top of every day as Roxy watched me with an intent expression. There was some simmering extra sense that existed between us—a recognition of what happened last night. A quiet happiness.

"Thank you, as usual, for putting up with Edward and Rebecca's endless demands," I said apologetically, leaning forward on my knees. "I know they feel the need to weasel into everyone's business in the most infuriating manner."

"Yeah but they don't do any of the actual work *themselves*," Crystal smirked, and I joined in.

"Truer words have never been spoken, I'm afraid," I agreed. "Natalie doing okay? How's the leg?"

"She's doing okay," she said, pulling out a picture to show Roxy. "My daughter, Natalie, broke her leg during her soccer tournament three weeks ago, but it's healing nicely."

Roxy glanced at the photo with a tiny smile. "Your daughter looks like a badass."

"Roxy and I can't stay, I'm afraid," I said, glancing at my watch. "I've got a Director's meeting in half an hour."

"Good luck," Crystal said knowingly, and I grimaced.

"Ah, maybe Roxy will be my good luck charm," I said, leading her out of the room. "And call me if my father is pissing you off too much."

Her laughter followed us down the hallway, and Roxy gave me a secretive smile as we walked through the lobby of the hotel. She still stuck out here but in the best way possible.

Roxy Quinn was not a woman who blended into the background.

"You really care about your staff," Roxy said, shoulder brushing against mine.

"You're surprised?" I asked.

"I guess you don't fit the stereotype I have in my head about, you know, managers of powerful companies or fancy, rich-people hotels. I wouldn't think you would make time to check in with your janitorial staff. Don't you have, you know—"

"—someone to do that for me?" I filled in, expecting the question. "And yes, I do. And they often check in if my schedule is too busy, but the majority of my time during the week is spent doing that. Making sure my staff is happy and heard, even if I can't comply with the requests they're making. But the people who work for you need to feel that you care about them regardless of where they are in the chain of command."

Roxy nodded, biting her lip. "Is that a particular value of the Cavendish family?"

"Absolutely not," I scoffed, showing her into the elevator. "With the exception of their yearly trip to criticize every fiber of my being, the Cavendish family essentially invented the concept of *delegating*."

Roxy grinned. "Not you, though."

I glanced at her. "Would it surprise you to hear that I had to learn this lesson the hard way?" We strode down the hallway toward my office, settling into leather chairs. "When I started, besides eliminating the entirety of our advertising department, I also refused to check in personally with my staff. For the same reasons you just mentioned: this hotel employs over three-hundred people, and I *do* have managers and middle managers to do that work for me. But what happened instead was that I developed a horrible reputation for being a snobby arse."

"But they loved you," Roxy said. "You were so at ease with them. There's been a level of mutual respect between you and the people who work here the entire time," she said, looking flustered.

"And you pictured me as a snobby arse?" I asked.

"Well... fuck it, okay, yes. The night we met," she said, cheeks coloring. "I just assumed..."

I shook my head, letting her off the hook. "Not a wrong assumption since I literally *was* that for my first two years here. And Roxy, I've spent the last eight years rebuilding bridges that I burnt to the ground. It's taken a long time, but you, as the leader, need to know where your staff stands with you. It's vital."

Roxy sank back against her chair, avoiding my gaze. "Edward."

"Yes?"

"What if I have to fire them? If we can't get our profit back up? The truth is I've kind of ignored Mack and Scarlett the past few months. Mostly because if they asked me how things were going, I wouldn't know what to say. And the more I ignore them, the more worried I get that if I 'check in,' they're going to say they hate me."

I leaned forward, squeezing her knee. "You wouldn't be the first boss that was hated, love. You'd get used to it," I said. "But having witnessed your interactions between your staff quite a few times, I don't sense any animosity there at all. I actually sense a great deal of camaraderie. Strength. You inspire loyalty."

Roxy blushed adorably, my punk-rock vixen letting her guard down. "You ever fire someone?"

"Yes," I said honestly. "And it's horrible every time. Can't sugar coat that one for you. And I think you need to bite the bullet and ask your staff how they're actually doing."

"Maybe I will," she said.

"Have you followed any of my advice so far?"

"Of course not," she said. I reached forward with both hands and gripped the edge of the chair. Pulled her close until our legs were flush.

"Roxy," I said quietly. She responded to me; I heard her breath hitching. "Are you going to be mouthy this entire day?"

She shrugged lazily but tossed her hair, exposing her throat. "Why? Do you like it?"

"You know I do. And I think you like the idea of sending me into my next meeting with a cock that's hard for you. Isn't that right?"

A sharp knock on the door, and we both jumped. It was Mario, one of my assistants.

"Sorry to interrupt," he said. "But you know the Board chairs are waiting for you in the conference room."

I sighed, nodded my thanks. "Tell them I'll be there in five. And where do you keep the Scotch again?"

Mario laughed. "You'll do great. Don't think about it."

"The infamous Board meeting. I'm intrigued," Roxy smirked as I stood up, buttoning my jacket.

"Roxy, darling, you're about to witness my least favorite hour of every month."

31

ROXY

"*A*re you going to pass out?" I asked, watching Edward with concern. He looked paler than normal, slightly shaky. I'd just watched him be charming and sincere with his janitorial and maintenance staff, but now the chairs of his Board were filing into the room, and he looked moments away from fainting.

"As you know, public speaking makes me want to simultaneously puke everywhere and run away to Mexico," he muttered quietly. "What's worse is that my father *loves* it, and every time he comes he takes every bloody opportunity to stand up in front of people and 'show me how it's done' as he calls it. This meeting is even worse—it's not the general Board but just the top brass. The people who make the decisions."

I narrowed my eyes at the buttoned-up, conservative-looking assholes walking into the room. "If you hate this part so much, why did you invite me to witness your misery?"

Edward gave me a nervous smile. "I thought some of your overall bad-assery would rub off on me. Thought maybe you'd give me some courage, love."

Edward was constantly doing this—saying something

sweet that stole the words right from my mouth. I'd never struggled so much in my life to retrieve my never-ending supply of snarky come-backs. But Edward had me beat.

"Okay," I said. "I can give you some of my bad-assery. Would picturing me crawling under this table and sucking your cock while you give your presentation put some steel in your spine?"

Edward broke the pencil he'd been holding in half.

"Yes. Yes it does," he said then turned his attention to the crowd. "Gentleman, ladies. Let's get started. I know we have a packed agenda today."

The room was darkened and hushed for Edward's presentation. I sat in the very back, impressed with the way Edward stood at the head of this sleek, mahogany table, looking dashing in his navy-blue suit. He was surrounded by wall-to-wall windows, the New York skyline a veritable presence in this room, pressing in on all sides. I'd never considered myself to be a woman attracted to sheer power, but in that moment, if Edward had snapped his fingers and demanded I crawl on my hands and knees down that table, in front of everyone, I would have fucking done it.

And then Edward's presentation started, and he immediately began to flail. Nervous mumbling. Nervous laughter. All the confidence of his body draining away as he presented updates on recent tenant improvements. He wasn't *bad*, but he lacked a certain charisma that commanded the room. Which was strange since his actual charisma fairly radiated off his body the few times I'd been here—staff scrambling to do his bidding with joy, hotel guests flirting with him in the elevators.

It was like a light had been switched off in his body.

There were two men about my age sitting next to me, and no truer archetype of Wall Street Bro had ever existed. Both men were white, with styled blond hair and pricey-looking suits. They were whispering to each other and laughing as they ignored Edward's presentation. One scrawled something on his notebook and showed it to his friend who barely concealed his laughter. Taking my eyes off Edward for a moment, I glanced down at what he'd written.

What a fucking nerd.

I clenched my jaw. So juvenile. And at a Board meeting. In the countless times during my experience of getting my MBA, I'd felt dismissed by people just like them—because I didn't dress like them or look like them. My business was trashy while their business "added value to the community." And I always thought, deep down, that it meant they were *serious* about their lives. Why else scoff at my very existence if you weren't at least going to behave professionally in every context?

But no. I was slowly learning that it didn't matter what you dressed like. You could look rich as fuck and still be an asshole.

As casually as I could, I leaned over, flashing them a disingenuous smile. They returned it, assuming we were on the same team, watching as I scrawled something beneath their message about Edward.

Why don't you shut the fuck up and pay attention?

Their eyes lingered on the large knives I had tattooed on my arms, Asshole #2 looking wary. I sat back, crossed my arms over my chest. Gave them a distinctly predatory look.

And then they turned around and kept talking.

A few minutes passed in which Edward struggled while the assholes chatted, and my fingers clutched angrily at the table. I felt a surge of protectiveness toward Edward—so strongly I wanted to grab the vase of roses on the table and clobber the assholes over the head with it.

But I raised my hand instead.

"Um... Roxy?" Edward said.

"Sorry to interrupt," I said, glaring at the assholes, "but I can't quite hear over the conversation being held right next to me."

Both men narrowed their eyes at me, so I bared my teeth.

"Why don't you mind your own business?" one of them whispered.

"And why don't you please shut the *fuck* up?" I said with false sweetness. The corners of Edward's lips twitched as the heads of his Board swiveled my way.

"We were just—" Asshole #2 began.

"Gentlemen," Edward interjected, voice harsher than expected. "You can either leave the room to continue your discussion, or you can stay and respect this meeting. But you can't do both." He slid his hands into his pockets, face stern, and I couldn't help but shiver at his show of dominance.

"We'll stay," Asshole #1 mumbled, turning toward the front of the room.

Edward nodded in response, continuing his speech. He didn't experience some miraculous surge in confidence, but he did become less nervous and a little more focused. His face stayed slightly stern, and I fucking *liked* it.

And the men next to me didn't say a damn word.

~

"WELL, if there aren't any other questions..." Edward asked an hour later, trailing off as he looked around the room. The board members were already shuffling their papers, eager to leave. I counted my blessings that tattoo parlors didn't have to answer to a higher body of stiff assholes.

"When's your father back?" someone in the front asked,

and there went that shift again. Like just the mere mention of his father made Edward *smaller* somehow.

"Next week, I believe," he said with a fake smile. "He's looking forward to updating you all on the things he's learned." There was a murmur of assent, and then people began slowly to leave. I stretched like a cat, giving the two Wall Street Bros another sharp look.

They both flinched.

"Gentlemen," Edward said as they walked past him.

I smiled smugly as the room emptied, and then Edward turned toward me.

"Can I see you in my office please?" he asked, face neutral.

"Of course," I said then followed him back through the busy hallways, nerves on edge.

Had I angered Edward?

We stopped for a moment while he told Mario to hold his calls and re-schedule his next meeting. Then he held the door to his office open.

"Roxy?"

I strode through, chin lifted. Edward followed, gently shutting his door.

Locking it.

Slowly, he tilted on his heels until he faced me in his giant, elegant office, hands in his pockets.

"That was an interesting way of gaining the respect of the Board," he said.

"Yeah, well, those guys were giant douche-turds," I replied, crossing my arms.

He laughed darkly. "I concur with your analysis." Then he walked behind his long, sleek desk. Sat down in the chair and leaned back, looking like royalty. "Up on my desk, love."

"*What*?" I asked, looking around. We were alone, of course, the only windows facing the city skyline.

"Crawl up onto the table," he said, "and don't make me repeat myself again."

The night we met, I'd teased and taunted the dominant side of Edward that he'd suppressed his entire life—poked and prodded until he'd snapped, twisting his fingers in my hair and forcing me to my knees.

This was the side of Edward I'd craved these past months. He'd appeared last night, fucking me against that alley wall like his life depended on it. And now here he was again, although I was wary.

Unsure of what punishment I was facing.

Edward looked down at his watch. Then back up at me.

"Yes, sir," I said, crawling up onto his desk, mimicking the fantasy I'd had in the beginning of this meeting.

I was on my hands and knees, eyes locked on Edward's. He gave me a cool assessment, approving. Nodded, then crooked a finger at me. "Come."

I came. Crawling like a supplicant to the edge of his desk. Some part of me understood this as a pivotal moment between us—a changing. And the longer I was on my hands and knees, the hungrier I became.

And Edward, leaning back, considering me with a neutral expression. Although the tic in his jaw gave him away.

That and his erection, visibly pressing against his suit pants.

"Sit," he said, patting the space in front of him. I slid my legs around until they dangled over the edge. Legs closed like a good girl. He laid his palms on my knees, squeezing.

"Did I make you upset?" I asked, surprised when I heard my voice shaking.

Edward's expression broke for the merest of seconds before hardening again. "Quite the opposite, Roxy darling. Quite the opposite." He peeled my knees open, slow as molasses, letting the cool air caress my inner thighs. "You know those two Board members have been a thorn in my side for months now. Total fuckheads, as you saw. And you, my love," he said, pausing to press a reverent kiss on the inside of my thigh, "frightened them into silence."

"I'm sorry," I said, and he stilled. Eyes on mine as his mouth hovered near my skin.

"You're *sorry*?" he growled, yanking me closer. My ass hit the edge of the table. "Sorry for what? Sorry for roaring into my life like a fucking hurricane? Sorry for up-ending everything I thought I knew I wanted? Sorry for standing up for me all the times I needed you to?" His fingers climbed higher, curling into my underwear and pulling it down my legs. I felt suspended in time, a moment so vitally *alive* it couldn't possibly be real. Edward leaned forward, head beneath my skirt, and gave my clit a long, broad lick.

"Oh my God," I sighed, smile breaking across my face.

"Don't you ever apologize for being who you are," Edward growled again. "It doesn't fit you."

"That's true," I said, twisting my fingers in Edward's hair. Pulling him back into my pussy. "All hail."

"You want to use me, love?" Edward hissed, fingers coming around to bruise my ass. Spreading me further. "Because I think I could be quite happy being your fuck toy."

I smiled languidly, loving the push-pull of Edward's sexuality. Such a dual desire to submit and dominate at the same time. It was addictive, letting myself be both with him.

"I thought I was being punished," I said, stroking his cheek. One of his long fingers was teasing against my pussy, dipping in and out. His thumb was pressing against my ass. Tempting.

"While the thought of punishing you is quite captivating,

love," he said, breaching both openings in my body at the same time, "my intent was to reward you."

His finger curled; his thumb pushed, and then his tongue landed on my clit again. I squealed, attempting to close my legs against his head, but he snarled a warning against my skin, and I stopped. Spread my legs further.

"Then don't stop until I come," I commanded softly, our eyes connected for one blazing second before he dived between my legs. Filling me everywhere, a blurred dance of tongue and fingers and thumb. His tongue twisted and lapped, taking me right to the edge and back again. Kept me suspended in limbo, balanced between orgasm and relief. I moaned against my own hand, aware of an entire hotel filled with staff and guests scurrying outside, the threat of getting caught sending the most delicious thrill up my spine.

And even sexier than the scenery, the table, my spread legs was the sounds Edward made against my wet cunt—this delicate, incessant *groaning* like he was moments from coming himself.

"Edward," I whimpered, back arching off the table. Tears in my eyes. "Edward, I can't... I think... *God* please..." because I was moments away from shattering into a million pieces, and there was no way I wasn't going to scream this hotel down. Let every single person in this fucking place know that Edward Cavendish III was tonguing me to a glorious climax.

But then he stopped, two seconds before I broke apart, and I didn't even have a chance to growl at him. Because he stood, yanked me off the ledge, flipped me around. I heard the sounds of a condom, a zipper, and then he lifted up my skirt and thrust every perfect inch of his cock inside me.

Edward slapped a hand over my mouth, lowered his lips to my ear, and the masculine sound of sheer pleasure he made had me clenching and shuddering around him. Like last night, and like our first night, I felt some sense that Edward's cock was made just for me—solely for my pleasure. That the way he fucked me was unique to *me*, that someone had given him a manual on my body, and he'd memorized it ruthlessly before we'd met.

"You can let go now, darling," he rasped. "I've got you. I promise. Let yourself feel it. *Everything*."

Edward tilted his hips, stroked some bundle of nerves deep inside me, and set off an electric current of unending climax, dual orgasms that had me clutching the back of his neck, head thrown back against his shoulder, a guttural wail against his palm. As I came, he kissed my cheek tenderly, licked down my jaw, pressed a palm against my clit and brought me down through the aftershocks. Stopped for a second to let me catch my breath.

"Are you okay, love?" he asked, stroking my hair, cock like steel inside me. He removed his palm, and I gave him a passionate kiss.

"I should attend your Board meetings all the time," I laughed softly, shivering as he rocked his cock against me. I felt his fingers shift up my back, my neck, the base of my spine. Finding a chunk of my long hair and twisting it. I shivered at the bite of pain.

"You should let me eat your pussy every goddamn second of the day," he replied. "How does that sound?" He was thrusting harder now and how he was able to converse, I had no fucking idea.

"Sounds like a life fit for a queen."

He growled at that, teeth closing around my throat—just like our first night when he'd told me he was going to fuck me until the only name I'd remember was his.

And he was right.

"Forgive me if I've counted wrong, but did you come

twice?" he said, twisting tighter.

"Mhmmm," I sighed, his cock stirring the remnants of my pleasure, sending me back to the edge again. Gentle, languorous kisses along my neck, and I couldn't help but arch against him, let him play my body like an instrument. Edward tilted my lips toward his, claimed my mouth. A possessive kiss, every moment of it screaming *mine mine mine,* and there went that sensation again, something shifting in my heart.

Things were changing between us.

"Two orgasms seem a bit dull, don't you think?" he asked, and then I was being lowered to the table, cheek pressed against the cool surface. Edward's fingers closed around the back of my neck, holding me in place.

"What did you have in mind?" I purred.

Edward snapped his hips roughly, the new angle hitting a spot deep and sinful. A tortured sound clawed its way up my throat.

"Oh *fuck.*"

"Stay quiet darling," he said, stroking the back of my neck. Another thrust, and I covered my own mouth again. "Because I don't want people to hear us as I fuck two more orgasms out of you." His palm curved around my hip, slid between my legs, setting off a riot of tingling pleasure.

"I think that seems a bit..." I panted as his index finger landed on my clit, "a bit presumptuous."

"Except your body is hungry for it," I heard Edward growl above me. "And I know just what you need."

The defiant side of me wanted to push back at his smugness, snap back a snarky comeback and maybe get myself spanked in the process.

But then Edward let himself loose on my body, and I lost the ability to form coherent thoughts. Could only do what Edward demanded of me: let my hungry body climax.

It was the delicious angle and Edward's perfect cock and his insatiable rhythm and his fingers, circling my clit intricately. My third orgasm was fast and brutal, my body shaking uncontrollably on the table as Edward stroked my hair sweetly.

And the fourth...

In a post-orgasm haze, I felt my body flip over on the table and get yanked to the edge. Lifted until I was wrapped around Edward's waist like last night, face-to-face. And through deep, passionate kisses timed perfectly with his thrusts, Edward and I came together. Gasping into each other's mouths, clutching and trembling, my name on his lips. An orgasm that sent tears to my eyes and rolling down my cheeks.

"What's this, Roxy?" Edward asked as he caught a tear with his finger. He was out of breath and rakishly handsome, tie half-torn off, hair a mess.

"Happiness," I said simply, at a total loss for words. My body felt wrung out and completely sated, my heart hammering between Edward's stern domination and gentle sweetness.

Edward's smile was big and bright and completely sincere. "I meant what I said, Roxy. Everything in my life before I met you was stable. Set." A twist of his lips. "Boring."

"And now what?" I asked.

"Fireworks," he said. "A hurricane. A total destruction of everything I've ever held dear."

"That's a good thing?" My voice shook. This man had me turned inside out.

"That's a great thing," he replied.

"The night I met you, you'd always wanted to have sex like that," I said. "To be liberated. Let yourself be who you'd always wanted to be."

"What's that?" A teasing smile.

"A sex freak," I said.

He laughed and stroked my hair tenderly. "Yes, but it's not that. Or it's not *just* that," he said, pressing his hand to my heart. "It's the two of us together. More than sex. Do you feel it?"

I swallowed roughly. "I don't think this is the strictly professional relationship CUNY had in mind when they devised their mentoring program."

"I could give a fuck about that, Roxy," Edward growled, yanking me roughly back against his body. Against a cock already hardening between my legs. Our need was shameless. "And do you feel it?"

I thought about the shop. My MBA. Graduation requirements and falling profit margins. Anxiety and fear. The words I'd said to Edward just last night, about stumbling upon my soulmate.

I'm pretty sure I'd know, Edward. I wouldn't send that person back into the night.

But I *had* done that. The night we'd met. Ignored that feeling in my gut that cautioned me to *wait*. Except Edward and I were too different, our worlds too separate, to make a relationship work.

Right?

Except against all odds he'd come back.

"I feel it," I said, laying my palm over Edward's heart, feeling it beat recklessly beneath my fingers. "And the next time we do this? We're in a bed." I gave him a quick kiss. "With actual pillows. And naked would be nice."

He grinned—a predatory grin, no more sweetness.

That shifting sensation clicked into place. Edward and I. Together.

"Roxy, darling, when I get you into a bed? It'll be days before I let you leave."

32

EDWARD

"*L*isten, mate, I don't want to say it," Elliott smirked, straightening his tie.

"So don't," I said cheerfully, closing my menu. "We haven't seen each other in a week and are about to embark on a lovely lunch—"

"I fucking told you so," Elliott said on a semi-yell. "I fucking *told you so*."

I rolled my eyes. "I can't seem to recall this conversation you're referring to."

"That's why I brought notes," Elliott said, pulling out a small notebook. "There was our run in the park two weeks ago. Our night at the pub, when you first mentioned that your mentee was the same woman that had literally re-arranged every cell in your body with her sex powers—"

"Roxy doesn't have *sex powers*," I said, although all it took was being in the same room with her, and I somehow had the ability to re-enact every secret sexual fantasy I'd ever had.

Maybe she *did* have sex powers.

"—and then the other night, before you went, you know,

on a *date* with her at some club, I wished you a *very* sarcastic 'good luck,' and what did you do that night, Edward?"

Elliott took a generous sip of martini, looking smug.

"We had a lovely evening talking about punk rock and our childhoods. We talked about falling in love and soul mates. And we fucked in an alley."

Elliott let out a booming laugh, and I finally grinned.

"Okay," I said, palms up. "I forfeit and am acquiescing to your demands. Which are...?"

"Set me up on a date with your hot new VP of Marketing. Dante."

"Done," I said, shaking his hand. "And how long are you going to be smug about this?"

Elliott shook his head. "Not smug, mate. Happy for you. Truly."

"Yeah?" I asked, distracted. In the back corner of the room, I thought I saw someone I recognized.

"Yeah," he said. "For the first time in your thirty-five years on this earth, you've *rebelled*. Shaken off the chains of your parents and decided to go after something *you* want. Not them."

I leaned back, letting myself think about what my feelings for Roxy actually meant. Until now, I'd just been acting on instinct, responding to what my body demanded of me.

But I liked Roxy. A lot. And she liked me too.

"I don't want to jump ahead. We're not *dating* each other. We're just... seeing where things go."

"Fair," Elliott said. "It's a long process, starting to live your life for *yourself* instead of for other people. Especially in the world we operate in. I mean, at some point, you're going to have to tell your family, right? And not that I'm trying to marry you off, but she knows about your situation, I'm assuming?"

Reality slammed into me. I'd been happily encased in my

all-consuming longing for Roxy. And my parents had been out of town, first in Atlantic City and now upstate, so I truly hadn't thought about them once.

"Um... right," I said, surprised that I stumbled. "Or we could date in secret forever and ever until we died. That's another option."

Elliott leaned forward across the table. "No jokes, mate. I'm being serious. I've never seen you so wrapped up in a woman before, not even Emily when you first met her. In fact, when you first met Emily, we discussed her like she was a business arrangement."

"She was," I said, relieved that I could at least embrace *that* truth.

"Exactly. A business arrangement. And yet here's this woman, this fierce, fiery, passionate woman who *does not belong* in our tiny, wealthy social circle, and you're mad over her."

I sighed. "I absolutely am. How I ever thought I was going to get through these months..." I trailed off at Elliott's smirk, and if we hadn't been in a five-star restaurant, I would have pitched my fork at his head. "I'm already setting you up with Dante, you don't have to rub it in."

"I do, though; I really do," he said, flipping over his phone and grimacing at an email on the screen. "And remind me again why we do these bloody awful jobs?"

"How'd it go with Gregory?" I asked.

Elliott let out a pained sigh. "Not great. Even with all the meetings we'd had and the number of times I'd said to him directly, 'if you do not improve I am firing you,' he was still surprised. Still didn't think it was actually going to happen. And now I'm stuck in hiring panels, and I just hate every single candidate. You ever want to change your name, quit your job, and move to an island?"

I smiled since Elliott said this at least once a week. "The stress is overwhelming sometimes, yes, but I love my job. Especially now. Ask me that question nine years ago, and I would have been halfway through changing my name before you'd finished the bloody sentence. But now?" I shrugged, eyes snagging on that familiar form in the back. "I'd do anything to own The Cartwright."

"Including marrying someone your parents approve of?" Elliott asked quietly.

I grimaced, the sticky-reality-feeling coming back. "Let me live in this bubble for a little bit," I pleaded, and he gave me a sympathetic nod.

"Okay I'll be less of an arse. And maybe the mention of parents is why I'm twitchy," he said, leaning back in his chair. As usual, I spied about four women staring at him in wonder. "My parents delivered a missive from London. They expect me to be at The Kenley Collection Charity Ball at your hotel. But they also not-so-delicately reminded me that they'd appreciate if I brought a date with me. A 'marriage candidate.'"

"Female?" I asked.

Elliott nodded. "I wanted to tell them to piss off."

"But you didn't," I said. "It's always easier in our heads."

"Maybe my stress levels are from the fact that I need to shag Dante senseless," Elliott said.

"Senseless shagging certainly keeps the cortisol levels down," I agreed.

Elliott laughed. So loudly the vaguely familiar figures in the back turned their heads. Locked eyes with me. And immediately hurried over.

It was the reality-freight-train.

"Ah, mother," I said as a flood of anxiety rushed through me. I stood, kissing her cheek. She looked almost royal with her large hat and overly dignified expression. "I didn't think you and Father were back from your trip yet."

"We are," she said, accepting a kiss from Elliott as well. "And hello dear. How are your parents?"

"Building their empire, ma'am," Elliott said, motioning the waiter over for another martini. "And who's this behind you?"

My mother stepped aside, revealing Phoebe, my date from the other night.

I attempted every facial expression in the book, but I looked astounded, and I knew it.

"Phoebe," I said, stepping forward to give her the same chaste kiss on her cheek. "I'm sorry I didn't see you standing there. You were, uh, having lunch with my mother?"

They smiled at each other, and it was obvious I'd been the topic of their conversation. "We've known Phoebe's family for some time, and now that we're in the States for a while, I thought it would be nice to get together. You know she's grown up to become such a fine young woman," my mother said, looking at both Elliott and me. As if she could care less *who* married Phoebe, just that she was married off properly.

Elliott and I smiled politely per years of ingrained training. "Well, this is my friend Elliott," I said as he shook Phoebe's hand. I hid a smile at her reaction since she didn't seem immune to his male model looks either. "Elliott, this is Phoebe Bartlett. We went for dinner the other night."

"And I was just telling your mother that you didn't call," she said, gently teasing, although my mother pinned me with a hawk-like look.

"And I'm so sorry about that," I said, sliding my hands in my pockets. "Work has been outrageously awful recently."

The lie came easily since I'd been lying to my parents and their friends since I was ten years old. But this particular one unleashed a new set of nerves.

Because work wasn't the reason. It was Roxy.

It's more than sex. It's the two of us, together. Don't you feel it?

"I think you should call her, Edward," my mother admonished. "Work can wait. What's keeping you?"

Next to me, Elliott coughed into his hand awkwardly.

"I think Phoebe and I can discuss this whenever I get a free moment this week," I said, already dreading this phone call. Wondering why I had to break up with a woman I'd only gone on one date with. Yet even agreeing to a date, in our circle, was practically an intent to marry.

Phoebe smiled sweetly at me, which made me feel like an arse. Wishing I *was* the kind of man she could marry.

But I was the kind of man who wanted to bury my head between the thighs of a mouthy vixen with sharp, brilliant edges.

Elliott gave me a look, and maybe it was the martini-lunch or a sudden infusion of bravery, but I wanted to tell the truth, something like, "You know, mother, I'm actually dating someone right now. I think. I hope. I'm not sure what having wild sex against a wall in an alley means to an American girl, but it means a whole hell of a lot to me."

Elliott narrowed his eyes, sensing my hesitation. "Anything you'd like to say, mate?"

My mother looked at me—never the maternal figure I'd yearned for but imposing and strict. I often wondered if she was the one who held my father's strings, making him dance. Or if they were both equally as power-hungry, equally able to view their children as money-makers and not their *children*.

But there wasn't a single reality in this brilliant universe where my parents would approve of Roxy. Not one. And to be confronted with the loss of that approval, of their version of *love*, released a sickening dread in the pit of my stomach.

"I don't, actually," I said, hating myself a little more. "I was just wondering what you both were up to next?"

"Shopping," my mother said. "And then Phoebe has to get back to work. But your father and I do have tickets to the Opera in a few weeks." A pause, and she gave me another brutally assessing look. "I expect I'll see you and Phoebe there."

Next to her, Phoebe brightened, and I fought to turn my grimace into a smile.

And Elliott guzzled martini number two.

33

ROXY

Summarize your first month of mentorship. What new ideas have you implemented? What challenges do you still face?

The cursor on my screen blinked maddeningly as I formulated my response.

Summarize your first month.

I sat back in my chair, crossing my arms over my chest. In the past month I'd pined, furiously, for my mentor. Attempted to deny my feelings for my mentor. Was fucked spectacularly against a wall in a dingy alley by my mentor. Got eaten out on a conference room table by my mentor.

And then my mentor and I confessed that we had feelings for each other.

It'd been two days since I'd walked out of Edward's hotel on unsteady legs, satisfied grin on my face and no fucking clue what Edward and I were going to do next. I'd thrown myself into work, completing a large back-piece for a client the previous day and trying not to count down the minutes to when we'd see each other again.

Which was today. In twenty minutes.

But in the past week, I'd horribly neglected my assignments for the Capstone Project. Every other class was done, but in my euphoria, I'd forgotten that the mentoring program came with assignments and papers and ultimately a giant presentation that would determine if I graduated or not.

What new ideas have you implemented? What challenges do you still face?

I pulled up the other tab on my computer where I'd been finishing up this month's financials, running payroll, and cutting checks. The QuickBooks screen made me vaguely nauseous, just like it had almost every month since I took over. We'd had a small reserve when I took over that helped close the gap when our expenses outpaced our income.

I was going to need to dip into it again, and in the next few months—if things didn't change—it'd be empty.

I tapped my pen against my paper, swallowing a rush of spiky nerves. Looked at the numbers over and over as if that would make them change. Income. Expenses. The red line on the bar graph taunted me, surging over our income. It wasn't that the tattoo parlor had gotten more expensive to run in any way. It was that a notable source of our previous income—walk-in appointments—were being cannibalized by the two other, trendier, shops down the street.

I flipped through my notes from my sessions with Edward. Being in Edward's hotel had been oddly thrilling; there was a whirling sense of movement and progress. Teams of people working on one single problem, and through it all, Edward charmed his way into his employees' hearts. His early ideas for how I could fix the shop were numerous—and creative—but every time I came in the back to get some work done and assess what I'd learned, a wall of defensiveness would rise in me.

1. Implement an aggressive ad campaign that accelerates your brand

2. Consider re-design of front of building

3. Re-decorate the interior

4. Affirm staff's loyalty and happiness in their jobs

5. Create business plan specifically for the walk-in revenue stream

The cursor blinked. *What new ideas have you implemented?*

The answer was none of them.

Because they took money, which we didn't have. And time, which I didn't have. And, deep down, I just didn't think traditional business ideologies were the right fit for a dingy tattoo parlor in a working-class neighborhood.

But I'd *told* Edward I wanted this from our mentorship. Ideas for how to change.

Why the fuck couldn't I do it?

There was a sharp knock, Mack's giant head appearing at the door.

"Hey boss? Sir Edward Cavendish III is here to see you." I heard Edward laughing behind him.

"I think I have time to meet with Sir Edward," I said, and as soon as he stepped into the room, my nerves evaporated. He stood in front of the door in the same gray suit from the first night we'd met, hands in his pockets, sly grin on his face.

"Roxy," he said. I kicked the chair out, and he sat down.

And I immediately crawled into his lap.

"Edward," I said, wrapping my arms around his neck and breathing in his scent. He rubbed big circles on my back, nuzzled my cheek.

"Are those monthly financials that you're looking at, love?" he asked with kind eyes. I blew out a breath.

"Yes. And my progress report for the Capstone. Did you write yours yet?"

"Ah," he said, laughing gently. Cheeks red. "I did, although I struggled at first. Kept starting the report talking about how breathtakingly beautiful you are." He pressed an open-mouth kiss to my neck and I shivered.

"Shut up," I teased, nipping his jaw. "You're supposed to tell them that I'm a brilliant businesswoman and you've never, not in all of your years, seen such progress in four weeks' time."

"I might have said something like that," he hedged. "And not to be *all* business, but since this is technically our shadow day, what's going on in here?" He tapped his finger against the screen, right against the rising red line.

"We didn't make enough money this month to cover payroll, so I have to use our reserve. Again. And it'll be empty soon, and I don't know what to do about that." I laid my head against his chest, feeling slightly miserable.

"This is a stressful time, Roxy," he said. "In the beginning. The first few years are a struggle, never knowing when you might go under."

"Oh good," I said sarcastically, and he chuckled.

"Not trying to be the Grim Reaper over here, just affirming that you're not the first businesswoman to stare at those bloody numbers and attempt to make them different through sheer force of will."

"That is true," I agreed. "I've attempted sheer force of will a *lot* these past months."

"Here's an idea," Edward said, reaching forward for my notebook. "You could start to work on an aggressive marketing campaign. Per my suggestions."

"Here's an idea," I mimicked, grabbing his face and turning it toward mine. "We could make out instead."

He smiled against my lips, but our kiss turned ravenous immediately. One second I was in control, and the next I was breathless and writhing on his lap. With deft skill, he turned my legs until I was straddling his waist, grabbed my ass, and pulled me snugly against an erection that felt like steel. Our tongues slid together, my hands gripped his face—our hunger for each other like an all-consuming wildfire, tearing through a forest.

"Um... boss?" Mack said from the doorway, and we sprung apart like horny teenagers.

"Oh, yes, Mack," I said, discreetly wiping my lips as Edward smirked. "How can I help you? Edward and I were having a professional business meeting."

"Right," Mack said dryly. "Well, we've got a group of friends who just walked in, all wanting matching tattoos. Can you help?"

Edward brightened considerably. "A group of walk-ins. That's good news, love."

"Damn right it is," I grinned.

34

EDWARD

I wanted to lose myself in Roxy, in the feel of her hair between my fingers. The space between her neck and her shoulder, where the edge of my teeth could send her rocketing towards bliss. The way she so easily smiled at me now, her sharp edges filling with softness and vulnerability—her complexity a beautiful discovery.

In so many ways, I'd rather be at this funky little tattoo shop than re-live the conversation I'd just had with my mother and Phoebe. Their presence had dampened my lunch with Elliott, and I knew he was ruminating on the same things. So instead, I shoved those feelings down deep inside my brain and focused on Roxy.

"So, spontaneous best friend tattoos..." I said to the four women in front of me: Emma, Maya, Liz and Kate. They looked to be in their early forties, close with each other and happy about it. It was 2:00 on a weekday, and they'd suddenly decided to do something they'd thought about since college. "Tell me about that. And do you mind if I take some notes?"

I felt like every single customer in this store contained a secret to Roxy's future success.

"Absolutely," said Emma. "Although there isn't much story to tell. We've been best friends for twenty-five years, and with kids and our families, we don't always see each other much."

"Twice a year, we all play hooky from work and kids and take a day off in the middle of the week and do absolutely ridiculous things. Spa, pedicures, fancy lunches," said Maya.

I glanced at Roxy. Her long hair was up in a high ponytail, exposing the shaved sides of her head, and she was dressed in black jeans more ripped than not and a cropped Nirvana shirt. I was entranced with her exposed skin right above her belly-button and right beneath her breasts. Brightly decorated with tattoos and begging me to worship it.

"And today, you decided tattoos," Roxy said, and they all nodded, laughing. "I mean, why the fuck not, right?"

"Let me ask you something," Maya said. "How many tattoos do you have, sweetheart?"

Roxy tapped her lip, thinking. "Too many to count. Why?"

"Do you regret any of them? Worry that they'll look gross and wrinkly when you get older?" Liz asked. I watched Roxy since I had the same question and wondered about the mindset of getting permanent ink placed on your body. Even though I'd been so sure of it the night we'd met, Roxy had been correct in her assessment; I hadn't really wanted it.

"I don't regret a single one," she said, twisting her arms to show off a glorious burst of patterns and designs. "I was never the kind of girl to choose art from the book. Some people like that kind of thing, but every tattoo I've ever gotten is meaningful to me and my life." She began pointing to certain things. "This is a portrait of my parents on their wedding day. This is my little sister Fiona's handwriting. Coordinates of our house growing up. Lyrics from my favorite song by The Clash..." she trailed off as the women leaned forward, admiring her many vibrant tributes. "I don't regret them

because they represent things that mean the world to me."
She shrugged. "And if I live to be old enough to be wrinkled, I
figure that's a privilege, right?"

"See? That's what I said," Emma laughed, nudging her
friend. "We've talked about getting these tattoos since we
were nineteen years old. Life's too short; why not live a
little?"

"Exactly," Roxy said, picking up the design they had in
mind—a tiny elephant—and asking them to hold out their
arms. One by one she laid the stencil on the inside of their left
wrists, assessing the size and shape. They were giggling with a
shared happiness, and the sun was streaming into the shop,
and Mack had turned on an old Van Morrison album, and for
a moment I just *got it*. The point of it all. The senseless
worrying about my parents and their attitudes and all the
million ways my life could go wrong.

Why not actually *live* a little?

"Oh, and this dashing man next to me is Edward, by the
way," Roxy said, pulling on her gloves. Mack ambled over to
help, giant and terrifying, but gave the women such a kind
smile they melted in his presence. "And this goon is Mack. He
looks scary, but I promise he's a practicing Buddhist."

"I don't bite. But I *do* meditate," he joked.

"Edward does bite, I'm afraid, but only when asked," Roxy
winked, and I widened my eyes at her. The women howled
with glee, although at least two of them gave me an appraising
look.

"And really, only when *Roxy* asks," I said, giving it right
back, and her cheeks turned bright red in the most adorable
way.

"This your boyfriend?" Maya asked.

Mack snorted. "If he's not, then I lost an office-wide bet. It's
like *Moonlighting* with these two all the time," Mack shrugged.

Roxy bit her lip, grinning at me as I flipped open my notebook, fighting a similar smile.

"Lingering sexual tension aside," I continued. "I *am* helping Roxy with a project to improve the success of this small business."

"He owns The Cartwright," Roxy interjected, and the women said "*ooooooooh.*" More appraising looks this time, but I waved it off.

"I am a famous, extremely handsome hotelier, yes, thank you," I teased, holding up my palms. "But *really,* I am here to help. And I wanted to ask the four of you: why spontaneous tattoos in *this* shop? Of all the tattoo parlors popping up in this neighborhood?"

Liz looked at her friends before shrugging her shoulders. "Well, it was after brunch and shopping, and we had just decided to get them. I searched for tattoo parlors in the area, and the reviews on this place were great. All five stars."

I nodded. Roxy was holding Maya's wrist, talking to her in soothing tones, making her feel comfortable. "That makes sense. Shop has three highly trained artists."

"And I guess, a lot of the reviews singled out *authentic*. We liked that. Nothing fancy. We just wanted to go to the kind of tattoo shop our parents would have gone to—"

"—if any of our parents had ever gotten tattoos," Emma said.

"I actually do my parents' tattoos for them," she said. "They're in a punk band. And this is *definitely* the kind of shop they would have gone to."

"See?" Liz continued. "That's the kind of experience we were looking for."

I was writing notes down, trying to get at the heart of what I was starting to recognize could be an advertising campaign for Roxy. Something cheeky and on-the-nose, playing up the slight grunginess of their shop but in a funny, appealing way.

"This is helpful ladies, thank you," I said, just as Maya shrieked, "*Holy fucking shit.*"

Startled, I looked down at Roxy, who was holding Maya's wrist tightly. "I know it hurts sweetheart," she crooned. "But this one is tiny. A few more minutes and you're done. Like a champion."

"Champion?" Maya whimpered.

"Oh yeah," Roxy continued, eyes on her skin. "Mack here cried like a baby when I tattooed his skull."

"Factually correct," he grinned, Emma's wrist looking tiny in his massive palm. "But every tattoo I've ever done for Roxy? Sat like a fucking stone."

Roxy smirked. "Well, I do have a lot of them. And I like the pain."

The women went "*ooooooooooh*" again, nudging each other as Mack laughed. My eyes were locked on the space between Roxy's shoulder blades as she bent over her work, but I could feel a piercing recognition between us. That night we'd first met, dancing around our secret, kinkiest desires. Bending her over the tattoo chair I was now sitting on and spanking the tender skin of her ass, the print of my palm dark on her decorated skin.

I cleared my throat, attempting to ignore the rush of blood to my cock. "This is helpful, ladies, thank you. Would you recommend other people get spontaneous tattoos here?"

"Absolutely," Maya said, wincing in pain. "Especially if a handsome Englishman in a suit came as part of the ambiance."

Roxy sat up on her stool, turned around to look at me. Flashed me a dazzling smile I knew was meant *just* for me to see. "I think we can make that happen."

I fought the desire to kiss her senseless right there, but my phone was buzzing in my pocket and when I glanced at the screen it was my father calling.

I held up a finger at Roxy, walked to the back corner of the parlor.

"Father," I said. "How was your trip?"

"Fine," he said. "I think I fixed the upstate New York location."

"Good to hear," I said through gritted teeth. Before they'd left, he'd had me create a plan for that location, all of my ideas for revitalization and how to get revenue back up to previous levels. I'd spent days on it, stayed up all night, and yet *he* had been the one to fix it.

I rubbed a hand down my face. "So what can I do for you?"

"Will your mother and I see you and Phoebe at the Opera in a few weeks? She told me you saw each other today and that Phoebe is quite besotted."

"Oh um..." I said, searching for some kind of lie or excuse. "Well, I'm not quite sure, to be perfectly honest. We've only been on one date, so 'besotted' seems a bit of an over-exaggeration—"

"We like her, Edward. After the disaster and embarrassment of Emily, you need a stable woman to be your wife."

"Yes sir," I said automatically and like a coward. I caught Roxy's gaze, and she gave me a saucy wink. "I'll see what, uh... what I can do."

"Right," he said briefly and then hung up.

My heart surged toward the woman in front of me, ablaze with a wild glory. There'd been not a single spark between Phoebe and I on our date, not a single spark when we met again.

A dull realization settled over my skin, rough as a wool blanket. Was this the chartered course of my life? Marrying a woman I had zero connection with—a woman my parents approved of—just to gain ownership of my hotel?

Why this endless, driving desire to make *them* happy? To choose their legacy over love?

But my internal response to their demands felt as natural as breathing—ingrained in my DNA, and I had no idea how to shake it off.

For a moment, I considered leaving. Leaving Roxy alone— for good—so she could settle down with a man who could give himself to her fully.

But Roxy's saucy wink turned into a beckoning finger, her red lips curved into a smile, and I was helpless against the electricity that had sparked between us from the very moment we met.

Roxy called, and I came.

35

ROXY

J wasn't entirely sure what Edward was talking about on the phone, but I knew it was his father because of the total shift in his body: slumped shoulders, sad expression, utter defeat radiating from him.

If Edward's mother was anything like his father, then both of his parents were complete assholes. Their love for him was contingent upon what he accomplished—how good he made them look in the eyes of high society—and not because he was, quite simply, their *son*. Made worse by their self-imposed bullshit of mandating who he married by dangling his career dreams in front of him like a prize.

All of this made my heart ache. Made me want to take him home and keep him in my bed, show him what true affection could be.

Even as a tiny voice in my head wondered if that meant Edward would ever consider marrying *me*.

A voice that was growing in volume.

But I shook that voice away because watching Edward had given me a remarkable idea.

"I'm so happy all four of you came in," I said to my four

best-friend-customers. "Meeting people like you is my favorite part of my job. Seeing your friendship, the love and care that you have for each other."

They beamed at me, holding up matching wrists swathed in plastic wrap and black tape. "Life's too short, and our friendship is too meaningful," Maya said, leaning against her friends. "Plus, now we have an amazing story to tell."

"And don't forget to mention the hot British guy," I winked, and they all turned around to admire Edward one last time. He stood out here, and while initially his refined, elegant look had startled me, it now seemed to turn me into a crazed sex monster.

"Oh, we won't," Liz promised as they walked out the door. Mack was cleaning up, and I sighed and stretched my neck, starting to straighten up the cash register. I tossed Edward a wink when our eyes met and crooked my finger. He strode right over.

"Business or family?" I asked lightly.

"Family, I'm afraid," he said with a grim smile. "Although in my case they're technically the same. Would you like to do something spontaneous?"

I arched an eyebrow his way, amused at his sudden change in tone. "Always. In fact, I kind of have an idea."

"Is it sexy?"

"No," I said.

"Kinky, darling?"

"Nope."

Edward started to roll up his sleeves. "You're finally going to give me that tattoo I've been begging for?"

"Absolutely not," I said. "Give me an hour to close up with Mack, and then I'm taking you somewhere special."

He grinned slyly, and I could just imagine the thoughts

running through his head: sex dungeons or lingerie shops. Public sex or erotic indecency.

But I had something even better in mind.

IT WAS LATE, but I'd called in a special favor from a friend. Our cab driver dropped us off, and as Edward stepped out his brow furrowed.

"The Manhattan Island Animal Shelter?" he said, giving me an incredulous look. As if they were suddenly aware of our presence, there was a chorus of barking dogs from inside the squat gray building.

"It's not much to look at, but Busy Bee, Apple, *and* Cucumber all came from here. They'd been abandoned, found as strays on the street. It's a no-kill shelter, so they get to stay until they meet their forever family."

The door opened, my friend Sasha grinning wildly under her spiked lime green hair.

"You coming in?" she asked.

I gave a small cheer, dragging Edward behind me.

"Roxy, what on Earth are we doing here tonight?"

"Isn't it obvious?" I teased, planting a kiss on his cheek. "We're getting you a dog, Dilbert."

36

ROXY

J wrapped Sasha in a big hug, avoiding the spikes of her halter top. "Thank you for doing this. I wouldn't have asked you if I didn't think Edward wasn't the right fit for her."

"Any time, babe," Sasha grinned back, peering behind me to catch a glimpse of the man in a bespoke suit behind me, looking nervous. She was white, quick to smile, and had a giant, animal-loving heart. "And how do you know this fella again?"

"He's my MBA mentor," I said. "And also my current... sex partner."

"Okay, right," she said as Edward chuckled softly. "All of the dogs and cats miss you around here, but you probably already know that."

I turned toward Edward. "I volunteer, sometimes, if I can handle it. It's hard not to adopt every single animal, so I limit myself to just a few times a year."

"You'd take them all home, wouldn't you, love?" he asked.

"In a heartbeat," I said. "So have you ever owned a dog? A cat? Pet hamster?"

He shook his head sheepishly. "Pets were seen as a frivolity in the Cavendish household."

"*Castle*, you mean."

"Technically, yes. And frivolity was frowned upon in general, which was why I had to sneak out of boarding school to go to punk shows."

We started to walk through the back of the shelter, passing countless dogs in cages. It was friendly and warm here, and the animals received endless love and care from the volunteers, but still—I kept my gaze focused on Edward's handsome face to fight the temptation to open their cages and put them in my car.

"What do you think about dogs in general?" I asked. "Say, for example, do you want one? And don't say no because you're adopting one tonight."

Edward laughed, linking our fingers together. "I guess you leave me no choice. Although I'm not sure my lifestyle is set up for a dog, quite frankly. Don't you have to do things for it? Like walk it and feed it and make it happy? Do they get sad when you leave for work?"

"Some dogs get sad when you leave for work," I said. "Which is why it's great that you're the manager of a hotel. You could institute a 'pets' policy for your employees. Boost morale."

He scoffed. "I highly doubt I'll be bringing dogs to work— oh, who's this?" He stood in front of Matilda's cage, which had been my plan all along. An extremely large white pit bull with a giant, boxy face lay curled in the corner.

"This is Matilda," Sasha said. "And she is the sweetest dog I've ever met. But she's older and looks scary, although she's actually great with other dogs and children."

"She looks quite lonely, doesn't she," he said, leaning closer. "How long has she been here?"

"Two years," I said. "I would have taken her if I had the room, but I don't. My pets are crowded enough as it is, and she's a pretty big girl. I bet if someone lived in, say, a giant penthouse, there'd be plenty of room for her to roam."

"I live in a giant penthouse," he said softly, eyes on her listless form. "Can I go in and see her?"

Sasha and I exchanged a glance—this was going even better than I'd hoped.

"Of course. Why don't you go sit? See if she responds to you." Sasha turned the key, and Matilda didn't even respond.

My throat tightened since it'd been devastating to see her decline these past few months. "Busy Bee was like that right before I adopted him. I got him into my car, and he laid down, head in my lap, and smiled the whole way home."

Edward squeezed my fingers. "You rescued him."

"Other way around, actually," I said, following Edward inside. I stood in the opposite corner as Edward, in his posh, Hugo Boss suit, sank to the floor, legs out in front of him.

"What should I do?" he asked.

"Just call to her," I said. "See what she does."

He nodded, loosened his tie, and cleared his throat. "Hey, Matilda. Hey there, girl," he said soothingly.

She looked up at him.

"Want to come over here?" he asked, patting his lap. "Hey girl, you can come over. I'm nice, I promise." Matilda's tail thumped hopefully on the ground, and then she slowly stood up.

"Christ, she's big," he said, looking slightly afraid.

"She's a sweetheart, though," I said. "You don't have to be afraid of her."

Matilda walked over toward Edward, and he held out his hand, letting her sniff it. Her big, boxy face looked uncertain.

"Hello, sweet girl," he crooned. "I'm Edward. It's nice to meet you."

Her tail wagged again—a good sign. And then she plopped herself right between Edward's legs, head level with his.

"Oh, um... What do I do?" he asked.

"Give her some love," Sasha said. "She likes to be hugged, so let that happen if she makes a move."

"Hugged?" he asked. "Isn't that like a thing that humans do?"

"Well dogs and humans are a lot alike," I replied. A dubious arch of his eyebrow, but I nodded in encouragement. Gently, Edward stroked her head, scratched along her back. Her tail wagged, and her mouth opened in a smile.

"Oh, she's, well, she's quite cute, isn't she?" he asked, smiling back. "I can't believe no one wants to adopt her."

"She's our favorite here at the shelter," Sasha said. "We've all been rooting for her to find her forever home."

"And what does that entail?" Edward asked, petting her with both hands now and grinning into her face. Her tail was wagging and then she took another step closer and laid her head on Edward's shoulder.

My heart squeezed, and my ovaries exploded.

"What does she want now?" he whispered.

"Give her a hug," I encouraged. "She likes it."

Gingerly, he wrapped his arms around her, continuing to croon and stroke her sides. She wiggled with happiness, mouth wide, tongue lolling out.

Edward laughed as she licked his face. "What a strange creature."

"You know Edward," Sasha started. "Roxy here can vouch for you, and that makes the process of becoming, say, Matilda's forever home easier. She could help you get set up, show you the ropes."

"You'd let me take her home?" he asked, incredulous. "But what... how do I care for her?"

"I can show you," I said. "Tonight. At your place. We'll swing by a pet store, get her some food and a bed. A leash and a collar. But really, all you've got to do is love her and show her affection."

I walked over, giving Matilda a kiss and patting her head. Gently sank down until my eyes were level with Edward's.

"Dogs are wonderful because they love you unconditional-ly," I said, thinking of his parents. His frantic quest for their approval. "You don't have to impress them. Or make them money. They just love you because you're *you*."

Edward swallowed hard. "And who am I?"

"Not a legacy. Not a pawn for your parents to move around as they see fit," I said. "You're a kind, loving, funny, charming *person* who deserves all the love in the world."

"Do you really believe that?" he asked roughly.

"I not only believe it. I know it," I said, reaching out to brush a strand of hair from his forehead. His eyes filled with an emotion so pure I felt bathed in it, as if it were an alpine spring, crystal-clear and shimmering in the daylight.

"Thank you," he said softly.

"No thanking required," I replied. "Plus, Matilda chose *you*, not the other way around."

Edward grinned crookedly. "To be perfectly honest, I never fancied myself a dog owner."

"I think you're a natural," I said. "And there isn't really another option now, is there?"

Matilda was fast asleep, giant body leaning on Edward as he supported her weight.

He grinned, delighted, before letting out a long sigh. "I'd just like the record to show that I blame you for this."

"Duly noted."

37

EDWARD

The paperwork I completed to become the owner and caretaker of a living creature—albeit an adorable one—seemed flimsy and thin. But Roxy and Sasha were beaming at me the entire time.

"So I just take her home? To live? What if she gets hurt?" I asked.

"You take her to a veterinarian," Roxy said. "And they'll make her better."

"What if she wants to eat everything in my home?" I asked even as a new voice in my head replied, '*let her eat whatever she wants.*'

"Well, you don't let her do that," Roxy said, arms crossed. "Although you're adopting an adult dog who's very well-behaved, not a puppy, so that shouldn't be too much of an issue."

"She will pee all over your house the first few days though," Sasha said, handing back my credit card. "Prepare yourself for that."

"Bloody hell," I said, eyes to the sky, wondering how on Earth I'd gotten here. But all I had to do was look at the tattooed vixen to the right of me, smiling like I was making her the happiest woman in the world.

And I knew.

Sasha headed to the back of the office, and I took our brief minute of privacy to yank Roxy flush against my body.

"That's a hell of a smile for someone who's usually so scowly, love," I said, running my nose along the edge of her jaw. I pressed a kiss beneath her ear, and she shivered.

"You adore my scowl," she said, fingers trailing up my spine. "And we're about to do my favorite part."

"What's that?" I asked as Sasha walked back up with a collar and leash.

"The part when Matilda realizes she gets to go home," Roxy said, grabbing the collar and leash from Sasha's hands and placing them in mine.

I swallowed against a strange lump in my throat, unnerved by the massive range of emotions I'd felt since we'd gotten here. The kind of spontaneous 'who gives a fuck' attitude of letting Roxy take me on an unplanned night of frivolity. Leading to her firm decision that I would, in fact, be adopting a *dog.*

Roxy's gentle recognition of my twisted desire for approval.

And then Matilda staring up at me like I was the person she'd been waiting for.

"Let's get on with it, then," I said as Roxy and Sasha practically shoved me down the hallway to Matilda's cage, and as soon as I opened the door again, she perked up, unlike last time. Came right over, big furry tail wagging, and as I squatted down in front of her, some missing piece of my life clicked into place.

"Let's go home, shall we?" I said, slipping on her collar and connecting the leash.

As soon as she felt the tug, Matilda jumped up, paws

landing on my shoulders, and knocked me to the ground, licking my face and vibrating with happiness.

I heard Roxy laughing and then scrambling in to help me, pulling Matilda's giant, excited form back so I could stand.

"I think she's happy," Roxy said, handing me the leash, and as we walked Matilda down the hallway, I wasn't sure I'd ever seen a more joyous animal—head lifted, tail wagging, glancing back continually to ensure I was still there. There was that lump again, a tightness, and I seriously worried I was going to cry in the middle of this animal shelter.

Sasha almost knocked me over herself with a hug, thanking me for rescuing Matilda.

"Don't thank me," I said, eyes on Roxy. "Thank this woman here."

"Yes, but Roxy has *excellent* judge of character. When she used to volunteer here, she'd help us match up humans to animals. And she was clearly right about you and Matilda."

Matilda was yanking me toward the car with all her strength, and I wondered for the millionth time what I'd gotten myself into.

"I think Roxy's right about a lot of things," I said as she and Sasha hugged each other.

"You sit in the back with Matilda, and I'll drive us around and get pet supplies," Roxy said, holding the door open for me. Matilda shot right into the back, curled up on the seat, and smiled at me expectantly, pink tongue lolling out of her mouth.

I went to join her, but then Roxy grabbed my tie, pulling me in for a sweet, lingering kiss.

"You know, when I'd suggested a spontaneous night, that was more what I had in mind," I said against her full lips.

"Well, the night is young, Dilbert," she said and then

shoved me in the backseat. As soon as I sat, Matilda climbed into my lap, head on my shoulder.

"Is she going to want me to hug her this entire time?" I asked.

"Probably," Roxy said. "Get used to never having personal space again."

I tried to be grumpy about it, upset that this woman had just talked me into a fairly large life-change within a few minutes' time. But as we drove away, Matilda gave me a big, slobbering kiss, and really, all I felt was pure joy.

TWO HOURS LATER, Roxy and I were riding the elevator to my penthouse apartment with a wiggling Matilda, a giant dog bed, and four bags' worth of toys.

"You know you didn't have to buy her every single toy in that aisle," Roxy mused.

"Well, but she seemed to like all of them," I said. "What's the harm?"

"No harm," she smiled. "Just interesting. I think she'll be very spoiled."

I scoffed. "Roxy, darling, Matilda is a *dog*. You can't spoil an animal."

Roxy smirked, giving a very pointed stare to the four bags, over-spilling with balls and bones and stuffed monkeys. So I kissed her instead.

"I'm right, though," she whispered. And then the doors to my suite opened, and her jaw dropped.

"Holy *shit,* this is where you live?" she asked as Matilda streaked past her to climb up onto my very expensive, *very* white couch. Curled up and almost immediately fell asleep— although not before giving me a look of sincere gratitude.

"Should she be up there?" I asked, depositing the bags onto my kitchen counters. "Or should I be sternly disciplining her?"

Roxy shrugged. "Won't work. Those are her couches now. And, to be honest, for the entire time I've known you, I kind of forgot the reality of how rich you are."

"I *am* very rich, thank you." I tried to see my home from Roxy's eyes—the skyline view. The elegant furnishings and high-end art. Really, the only bit of personality was the Union Jack flag stretched across one wall. A few photos of London. A couple of me and Elliott and those of some other friends.

It wasn't that my home *didn't* reflect my personality; it's just that Roxy's entire *life* emanated who she was. And for me, so much of my home was The Cartwright.

"You know," she said, trailing her finger along the edge of my wall. "You could fit a *lot* of animals in this place."

I laughed. "Let's just start with the one giant dog over there who's probably pissing all over my shoes."

Roxy wandered over to the wall-to-wall windows that lined most of the penthouse, illuminating a glittering Manhattan skyline. Lights winked at us from skyscrapers, more plentiful than any stars we could see. I'd opened one of the windows, and the room was filled with the endless white noise of a city that seemed to live and breathe on its own.

"You're an incredible woman, Roxy Quinn," I said, walking slowly toward her, admiring the graceful outline of her body backlit against the windows. I slid my hands around her waist, buried my nose in her hair. "That spiky exterior hides a very soft heart."

"People can be many things," Roxy said. "And this can be a cold, scary world. It's important to do good."

"Like adopt a dog that no one else wants?"

"Yes," she said.

"Or take over a failing tattoo parlor from a bloody awful man?"

Roxy swallowed. "Mack and Scarlett rely on their jobs. That's important too."

"Even though that decision has caused you countless sleepless nights?" I loved her hair up in this ponytail, leaving the entirety of her neck bare to me. I couldn't stop kissing it, and Roxy couldn't stop arching back into me.

"Soft heart, remember?" she said, smiling. "And you bear the burden of an intense family legacy you didn't really want just to make your parents happy. To make sure your employees are treated well and with respect within an industry that doesn't always allow for that."

I grimaced, thinking of my parents. Phoebe. Emily. Those suffocating feelings I couldn't seem to escape from even though I knew they were irrational. "I think that's a kinder assessment than I would give myself."

Roxy turned, looking brilliant in the moonlight, city glittering behind her. "You're different than I thought you'd be. The way I judged you to be."

She pressed an elegant finger against my lips. Turned and began a slow, sultry walk toward my bedroom, shedding items of clothing as she went. I followed obediently, and then there was a fully naked Roxy stretched out on my bed.

"Now you," she purred.

"Jesus Christ," I groaned, ripping the tie from my throat. Undoing the buttons of my shirt with fingers that trembled. We'd certainly seen each other in various states of undress, but a naked Roxy in my sheets was more than I could handle. White hair like flames around her head, skin vivid with art. I managed to get my clothes off without tripping and falling before crawling up the length of Roxy's colorful body like a starving man.

Slowly, luxuriously, without a destination in mind, just to *feel*. I lapped at her clit with long, even strokes. Kissed every inch of her stomach, teeth grazing her hipbones. Danced my tongue across her nipples as she writhed beneath me. When I reached her lips she grasped my face, kissing me for a long, long time. Endless, our lips and tongues dancing together. A gentle exploration, so different from our times before which had been fevered and furious. This was *passion*, electric and real, and as Roxy flipped me onto my back and lowered her mouth down the length of my cock, the only thing I could do was cry out. She hummed with appreciation, taking me deeply, eyes on mine the entire time.

"You're so beautiful," I said, hips thrusting, but then she sat up. Straddled me. Rocked her slick cunt along the head of my cock.

"I'm on the pill," she said. "And still clean. How about you?" Another rock of her hips, and I was about to lose my mind.

"Ye—God *yes*, and why?" I asked, hands full with her breasts. She placed the tip of my cock at her entrance and sank all the way down.

"Because I want to fuck you bare," she moaned, and fuck me she did. Hands on my chest, hair wild, face a mask of ecstasy, Roxy moved with a languorous grace. A leisurely, grinding rhythm that had me gasping. I sat up, wrapping her legs around my waist, and pulled her closer.

"I swear you have the most perfect cock," she moaned as I licked up her throat. I held her tightly against my body as we ground together, slid my thumb to her clit.

"Oh God *yes*," she sighed, hands in my hair.

My orgasm lingered at the base of my spine, and I knew it was going to shatter my world. I tipped her lips toward mine, kissed her sweet, gorgeous mouth, and rubbed my thumb in tight circles against her clit. Felt her clench and climax, screaming into the kiss. I had her on her back in seconds, one leg over my shoulder, and with a handful of hard, powerful thrusts I'd fucked her into a second orgasm. Let mine wash over me like waves in a storm, a pleasure so powerful I briefly lost my vision. Could only gasp against Roxy's ear at the inde-scribable ecstasy.

I stroked Roxy's hair for a long time, soothing my fingers down her spine. I was enraptured with her bare skin, the curve of her belly, the sharp angles of her hip bones. My fingers explored and caressed until they landed right above her left breast.

"I like your soft heart," I said, quiet in the darkness.

Her palm landed above my own heart—warm and steady. "And I like yours."

38

ROXY

I woke up in Edward's giant, fancy, incredibly warm bed, nestled between Egyptian cotton sheets. I pulled the covers all the way up, allowing myself one more minute to snuggle deeper. Edward wasn't there, but I sensed his presence somewhere in this giant penthouse. It was just past midnight, the city skyline twinkling through his open windows.

I thought coming here would have made me more uncomfortable, confronting the sheer truth of how *different* our worlds were. How different our upbringings and families were.

Plus, thanks to my parents, I'd spent a decent amount of time thinking people like Edward were the literal worst.

But if anything, Edward was gently pushing at those stereotypes. Showing me a man as complex as he was kind. The night we'd met, it'd been so easy to send him out into the night, assuming we'd never work. That we'd fuck a few times before he cast me off for a woman that was like Emily. A woman that *fit* this life.

Yet here we were. One month later, and I was falling for

Edward Christopher Cavendish III. My dirty, kinky English-man. My friend. My *mentor*.

Cocooned in this lovely evening, the complicated reality of our future felt the farthest away. Because Edward had worshiped my body with a reverence so pure I'd felt filled with bright, joyous light.

Maybe I could fit into his life after all.

I crawled out of the covers and pulled on one of Edward's shirts. Glanced in the mirror to see my hair a wild, snarled mess and my eyeliner smeared everywhere. I smiled at my reflection, because I looked truly *happy*.

And then I turned the corner to find Edward, bare-chested in running shorts, feeding Matilda dog treats.

"Are you a good girl?" he crooned. "I think you're the best girl, don't you?" And all Matilda could do was wiggle and dance and look up at him the way Busy Bee looked at me. Sheer gratitude.

"How many of those have you fed her?" I teased, enjoying the look of awe that came over Edward's face *every time* he saw me. He wrapped his arms around my waist, kissed my temple.

"Is it wrong to say 'all of them'?" he asked.

"Nope," I said, bending down to give Matilda a kiss. "And do you mind if I raid your kitchen?" I sauntered past him before he could answer, admiring what I figured was the most expensive oven I'd ever seen. Everything was sleek and dark and shiny, and I couldn't stop running my fingers over the gleaming surfaces.

Five minutes later, I'd made a bag of popcorn and cracked open a beer for us to share. Walked back out to the living area and popped myself up onto the counter. Handed Edward the beer as he came to stand between my legs, palms high on my thighs.

"You know, our kitchen in Queens had the best acoustics

when we were growing up," I said, tossing a piece of popcorn to Matilda. "So it wasn't strange to come down in the morning when we were kids and happen upon our parents doing vocal exercises while they made us breakfast."

Edward took a swig, passed it back to me. Even after all we'd just done, had *been* doing, I still got a thrill from placing my lips where his had been.

"What made your parents decide to have children?" he asked. "From the way you've described them, I would have thought they would have wanted a life on the road. Touring, playing shows. Not taking you and Fiona to spelling bees or soccer tournaments."

"Well, you at least pegged Fiona accurately," I said. "She was such a brainiac, loved studying, loved doing extra credit and staying up late to do homework."

"And you, love?" he asked.

"I loved sneaking out to kiss boys and being surly in my room. I was always drawing. Constantly. Would draw on napkins at restaurants and the backs of cereal boxes in our kitchen. Any blank surface called to me. I did okay in school but flourished once I got to college. And now..."

"Now what?" he asked.

I swallowed. "Well, now I'll have my master's in six weeks, and I never thought I'd accomplish something like that."

Edward smiled, brushed a strand of hair from my cheek. "Your parents must be very proud."

"My parents would be proud if I joined a commune and lived in a mud hut in the middle of the desert," I laughed. "They only ever encouraged Fiona and I to do what made us *happy*. Not to climb some bullshit career ladder just because." I grinned. "No offense."

"None taken," he said. "I'm quite happy up here at the top

of the ladder. But is it that they always wanted to be parents *and* be in a band?"

I thought for a second, tilting my head. "I don't think they ever saw those two desires as mutually exclusive. There's a... a *strength* to their decision-making. A sense of 'who says we can't'? Who says we can't have a radical, political punk band *and* be parents to two rambunctious daughters? Who says we can't raise them in this loud, raucous environment and have them grow up to be successful?"

Edward smoothed his palm down my leg, squeezed my knee. "There's no limit to what they think they can do."

"And no limit to what they think we can do. Or be. Fiona is a brilliant, ambitious, buttoned-up lawyer who curses like a sailor and loves a good mosh pit."

Edward laughed, handing me the beer. "And you?"

"What do you think?" I asked, lifting my chin.

Edward assessed me for a moment. "A bad-ass, punk artist who loves her family. Sharp edges but a soft heart. A kinky, sexually adventurous siren who also believes in true love and passionate marriages." A pause, as he pressed a kiss to my fingers. "A woman who I'm desperately falling for."

Matilda suddenly barked, breaking the moment, and Edward sank down and plied her with treats.

My heart was racing so fast I felt like I'd run a marathon.

"Were your parents different when you and your siblings were younger?" I asked, already guessing the answer.

Edward sighed, standing back up. "No," he said simply. "They were not. I wish I could say otherwise, but Jane, George, and I were expected to present a respectful, elegant, and most importantly *silent* image for my parents when we were around high society."

"Which was all the time, I'm guessing?"

"It was. *All* the bloody time. Once at a gathering, there

were a group of boys playing football across the street. My age, in fact. And I remember thinking that they must have all been orphans because who had parents that let you play?"

My heart broke a little. I reached forward, brushed the hair from his forehead. His smile was bashful as he stole the beer back. "Both of my parents inherited fortunes: my father, of course, inheriting the Cartwright empire. So it felt like twice as many people to impress. Around their families and other "old money" royalty, it was an image of stoic responsibility. Extreme politeness. Not a hair out of place."

"And the new money?"

A wry shrug. "That Jane, George, and I would be the bearers of that legacy. So even as children, we were to be aware of our role as future leaders. Which was a lot for a child to understand. I wished it had made us closer as siblings, the way you and Fiona are close. Or Elliott and his brothers—they connected over a shared misery. But it only served to keep us separate and suppress our happiness. And to instill a constant belief that I was disappointing people."

"Thank God they sent you to that boarding school," I said. "Where you could at least be around children your own age away from their prying eyes."

"Absolutely," he agreed. "I think it had the opposite effect of what my parents wanted. I'm still friends with some of those blokes, and in so many ways *they* became my siblings. I wouldn't have had a misspent youth otherwise. Or any bloody fun, if I'm being honest."

"Did you have kinky sex fantasies as a teenager? Or more as an adult?"

"I just fantasized about having *sex* as a teenager," he said with a bemused expression. "There was a girls' boarding school down the way, and when we were older, we all snuck out together. Flirted. Kissed." Head tilted. "Then more than kissed."

"Edward Cavendish, did you lose your virginity at *boarding school*?" I teased.

"Yes, yes, I did," he said. "And it was all very posh and restrained. I'm going to guess you lost yours someplace cool. Like... like the *mall*."

I laughed, head thrown back. "When I was a teenager I thought the mall was the coolest, but no. My parents were at band practice, and Fiona had a debate club meeting, and I snuck in my boyfriend at the time. Goth everything. *Very* Morrisey."

"Impressive," he said. "And how was it?"

"Quick and uneventful," I said. "It was only later, around the time that I got my first tattoo, that I thought about dirty, kinky things."

Edward nodded, placed my fingers against his lips. Lightly nipped with his teeth. "The pain and pleasure."

"Yes," I whispered, already breathless. "What about you?"

"About five years ago on my thirtieth birthday. Up until then, I'd dated women like Emily. Not unsuccessfully, but in hindsight, my feelings for them were fairly lukewarm. Never, well..." he blushed. "Never like it is with you. And our sex was also *fine*. But our intimacy always lacked a connection or a hunger. There was something so muted about it. And I'd have these fantasies that I couldn't quite discern. Couldn't quite *see* what my body was trying to tell me." He brushed the hair from my shoulders, locked his palm across the back of my neck. Holding me in place. Gentle but firm.

"So on my thirtieth birthday my best mate, Elliott, took me to a sex club because he thought it'd be hysterical. Of course, the wanker met a hot guy about five minutes in, and they went off to shag each other senseless." He grinned at the memory.

"You've not met Elliott yet, but he's got charm for days. And either way, *I* was left there, alone on my birthday. And I was nursing this whiskey in the back, kind of generally taking the whole thing in and wondering why I didn't feel more ashamed."

"Ashamed?"

"Like any other crusty, English upper-class family, sexuality is a private affair. Not out in the open for all to see like the performances at the club. People fucking on stage, dancing, stripping—a night of pure sensuality. But I wasn't ashamed. Didn't feel like I ought to be. Instead, I'd never felt more *alive*." Heat was pooling between my legs at the image—Edward, looking refined and handsome in his suit, while all around him people engaged in carnal pursuits. Cock hardening in his pants as he sipped an expensive, aged whiskey.

"Go on," I said, voice hoarse. "Did you see something that sparked your interest?"

"Two women," he said, fingers moving from the back of my neck to the base of my hair. Gripping. "One, a domme, in full leather get-up. Looking regal. Poised. Riding crop in her hand. I'd never seen such a thing in real life. Had clicked around it when I watched porn but really, *truly,* had never seen it before. And at her feet was this gorgeous woman. Submissive. On her knees and looking up at her with so much *passion*. Love and... and a tenderness. She kept stroking her face. But really, it was the woman on her knees that held the power."

"It's all a game," I said. "A dance. The power exchange is complicated, which is why it's so hot."

Edward's eyes roamed down my body with a sudden, sharp expression. "After that, I couldn't get enough," he said, twisting his fingers just *once*, and I dropped from the counter on my knees eagerly. My fingers reached for his straining cock, but his low growl stopped me. So I waited sweetly, mouth open.

"I watched whatever I could find," Edward said, staring down at me with that same tenderness. Slipped his heavy cock out from his shorts. Groaned when I ran my tongue up the length of it. "Became obsessed with the submissive on their knees. Man, woman, it didn't matter. I wanted to experience all of it."

"Because they're truly the ones in control," I purred, taking the length of Edward's cock to the back of my throat. Holding it there as his fingers tightened painfully. Loving the roar of heady ecstasy in my ears.

"Yes, they are love," he said, letting his head fall back in pleasure. "Yes, they fucking are."

"What the bloody hell is happening?" Edward mumbled, head pillowed between my breasts as I stroked his hair. He'd been asleep for a while, and I'd been content to doze peacefully, enjoying the moment. There was a delicious burn between my legs, a heat on my ass where Edward's palm had cracked against it. We'd fucked and played and teased each other for hours, but I wasn't tired yet.

And neither, apparently, was Matilda. Like a good dog, she'd hid in the bathroom as soon as my knees had hit the floor earlier, scurrying away and then avoiding the bedroom. But it'd been a bit since I'd last screamed myself to orgasm, and she clearly understood it to be *her time*.

"That is your new dog whining because she wants to sleep with you."

"I have a *dog?*" he groaned, squeezing me tightly. I tickled his rib cage as he chuckled. "Wait, when did that *happen*?"

"Like... six hours ago," I yawned. Maybe I was finally feeling a little tired. "And I'm pretty sure you adopted a sweet, dopey girl who's lived in a cage for two years and just wants to sleep with her new favorite human."

"Me?" he asked, turning on his side and giving me an adorable smile. I whistled, and Matilda bounded onto the bed directly between us.

"No, me," I said, wrapping my arms around her wiggling form. "Isn't that right, sweetheart?" Matilda responded by licking my face and whacking Edward in the balls with her giant tail.

"This feels like some kind of coup, if I'm being perfectly honest," he grimaced, cupping himself in pain. But then she rolled over onto her side and gave him a big, doggy smile. "Also, I really think she is the cutest dog in the world. Don't you think?"

"I do," I smiled, starting to drift off. "I really do."

39

EDWARD

"So," Professor Stevens said, dropping into her seat. "The two of you have officially reached the two-month mark. Just four weeks to go. How's it going?"

It'd been two weeks since Roxy took me to the shelter to adopt Matilda. Fourteen days of absolute bliss. I wanted to tell Roxy's professor that I'd picked her up from the tattoo parlor for this meeting and we'd spent the majority of the drive over here discussing the rough business plan she was working on with my guidance.

And then, since we had fifteen minutes to spare, I parked the car in a deserted alley and licked my mentee to two spectacular orgasms right there. Roxy laid back on the chair like a queen, legs spread on the console, holding my head as she ground against my tongue.

I rubbed my hand across my mouth, smelling Roxy's earthy, musky scent, and grinned. "I don't want to speak for my mentee, but we've made a real connection these past two months. Even though we had a bit of a bumpy start."

Roxy was sitting a few feet away from me; legs crossed, the barest hint of a smug expression on her face. "It's true," she conceded. "In the very beginning we were so different. I assumed he was, well..."

"Go on," the teacher said.

"A smug, corporate arsehole," I finished.

Professor Stevens laughed. "But I'm assuming that you've looked past those differences, since your progress reports have been very exciting." She glanced through my file, nodding her head. "Roxy, I know a small business can't see dramatic profit changes in such a short amount of time, but it seems like you and Mr. Cavendish have generated some decent ideas for how to breathe some life back into the shop. Is that accurate?"

"It is," she said, giving me a small smile. "In fact, we were just finishing up a draft of my business plan. And Edward's marketing team at The Cartwright have really helped me see some of the big-picture changes I can be implementing." She swallowed. "Like rebranding."

"I know it's hard," Professor Stevens said. "It's hard to take endless critical feedback for three months, and I know how strongly you feel about your business."

Roxy nodded, nervously clenching her fingers in her lap. "True. I'll be honest and say I'm struggling with it still, but Edward is a wonderful mentor. He's really guiding me down a path that I think will lead to success."

Two nights ago, we'd stayed up late in my office at the hotel, mildly arguing about her business plan—her pushing back, as usual, on some of the more dramatic changes I wanted her to do. I was trying to get her to see that success was within her reach, but I kept bumping up against her pride. I knew where it came from, had felt the same way as a young business owner a decade earlier. After hours of snarky, silly bickering, we finally came to a plan filled with compromises.

And then I'd bent her over my desk and fucked us both into oblivion.

"I'm actually taking Roxy to a tattoo convention that's happening downtown today. Assess the competition. See what trends she can begin incorporating into her work." I glanced over, smiling at Roxy's barely concealed glower. Suffice it to say, she did *not* care about things like "trends" or "competition." And I couldn't blame her—having to endlessly tweak and change The Cartwright over the years often left me weary.

But it was also *necessary*.

"I'm happy to hear that," Professor Stevens said. "Because that is something Roxy knows she needs to do." Professor Stevens gave her a firm look, and Roxy nodded like an obedient schoolgirl. But as soon as she turned her back for a moment, Roxy flashed me her middle finger.

In response, I gave her a wink and enjoyed her flush.

"Let's talk the next four weeks, shall we?" Professor Stevens said. "Roxy, you know you'll be delivering your presentation on May 30th, and I expect Mr. Cavendish to be in attendance as well."

"Absolutely," I said. "Wouldn't miss it."

"This is a requirement for you to graduate," Professor Stevens said, and Roxy's fingers twitched again. "And I'm happy to see the two of you are taking this so seriously." She stood, and we did too, shaking her hand. "I look forward to our next meeting and your progress reports."

Roxy gathered up her things, and I picked up her books, holding them like a besotted teenager. As soon as we were in the elevator, Roxy pressed against me.

"Am I taking our mentorship seriously enough for you, *Mr. Cavendish*?" she purred, sliding her hands down my chest. I trapped her fingers for a moment, stilling her.

"You're nervous, love," I said. "Talk to me."

"I'm not," she said. "That meeting went great. I really thought I was going to break. Just lean forward and tell her that in between studying my profit and loss reports, we fuck like animals. But I didn't." She gave me a coy smile, but her spine was rigid. I rubbed my fingers there, finding the knots, and she all but collapsed against me.

"Not that, Roxy," I chided. "You're not nervous about us. You're nervous about graduating. *Talk* to me."

The doors slid open, and I led us toward the subway stop. I wanted to pick up Matilda and take her to the tattoo convention. Conservatively, some might say I was *obsessed with my dog.*

And it was true.

"I just..." she started, blowing out a breath. "Everything is happening so fast. I bought out Arrow and immediately realized I'd taken on a sinking ship. Enrolled in this program thinking I'd be able to turn everything around in a year. And now I'm about to graduate, and you've given me so much guidance and wisdom, and I can't thank you enough, but still *what if I can't do it?*"

"Can't do what? Be an extraordinarily talented tattoo artist?"

"Edward," she sighed. "You know what I mean. Be a successful business owner. What if I have to close the shop? Let go of my staff?"

Roxy looked beyond beautiful in the waning sunlight. Magenta lips and big dark eyes, ears glittering with diamond piercings. She reminded me endlessly of a wild, rare bird discovered in the tropics somewhere by a lucky biologist.

"First, I don't think that's going to happen," I said. "And I really mean that. I've seen the dirty bits of your business, and there is nothing happening that can't be reversed. Fixed. Changed. All of that is possible, especially with someone like you at the head."

Her eyes softened, glowing with gratitude. "And secondly,

if that did happen. *If* for some extraordinary reason, you had to close the business, well, that's okay, too. Failure, unfortunately, is a part of life, and you would not be the first businessowner to fail. The important thing being..."

I chucked under her chin.

She rolled her eyes, laughing. "The important thing is I don't give up."

"That's my girl," I said, kissing her cheek.

"This feels like a segment on Sesame Street," she grumbled. "But also... thank you."

"For what?"

"You're an incredible mentor, Edward Christopher Cavendish III," she said, looking uncharacteristically shy. "And a really, really good boyfriend."

She stopped suddenly, eyes wide. And then she ducked down the stairs leading to the station, covering her face.

"I'm sorry, love," I said, following her. "I didn't quite hear that last part. What did you say?"

"You're a really good mentor," she said, refusing to look at me.

"No," I teased. "Not that part. The *other* part."

"Your cock is perfect."

"Okay, now you're just trying to distract me with compliments," I said. I grabbed her wrist, pulling her toward me. Gave her a long, lingering kiss, our tongues meeting. Lips sweet but passionate, my fingers threading through her hair.

"Say it again," I said.

"You're a really really good... boyfriend." Roxy bit her lip, looking unsure.

"Well, that's exciting news," I said. "And lucky for me that you're such a good girlfriend."

We hadn't said a *word* to each other about labels or dating or monogamy. Had just spent the past month laughing and

271

fucking and laughing some more. But I'd never felt more *right* saying a word in my life. And Roxy's answering smile—as brilliant as the sun outside—was something I wanted to hold on to forever.

"Since I'm your *girlfriend* now, does that mean we can skip the tattoo convention?" she asked, tossing her hair.

"Cheeky girl," I said, shaking my head. "And absolutely not. But first, do you want to go pick up our dogs?"

40

ROXY

*B*usy Bee and Matilda strutted ahead of us like dogs in a parade—heads high and tails wagging.

"Have you bought her more toys?" I asked Edward, our shoulders brushing together. The way he kept staring at her with pure tenderness had my heart beating like a hummingbird's.

My *boyfriend* was very sweet.

"I've only gone back three times, I'll have you know, and *only* because Matilda basically demanded me to."

"She can't talk, Edward," I pointed out.

"No, but she can look at me with that face, and I'd do anything," he mused, slipping his arm around my waist. "We've finally come to an agreement about sharing the bed. Which is that she can have all of it, and I take the edge."

"*Now* who's the soft-hearted one?" I teased, spying the open-air convention up ahead. It was a cool, sunny spring day, and I couldn't help but feel a little *hopeful*. "And tell me again what we're looking for today? I think Mack and Scarlett are set up somewhere in the back."

Arrow hadn't paid for booths at this convention for the last ten years, and even though the price was steep at a time when we didn't have much to burn, Edward had talked me into investing. Gaining new, loyal customers was the goal.

"Well, first, just having 'Roxy's' here is a great strategy to implement for next year, and you can find other conventions to add to the list. Maybe you make it a quarterly goal, to drum up new business while keeping a close eye on the competition."

I took a deep breath to clear my spiky defensiveness and turned to look at Edward's regal profile. He was smiling, arm around my waist, one hand idly patting Matilda's giant head.

I *trusted* this man.

"You're right," I said, and Edward turned to me in mock horror.

"I'm sorry, I was preparing for you to tell me to bugger off," he said. "As usual."

I shrugged. "You're my mentor. I appreciate your valuable wisdom."

"I've been your mentor for two months, Roxy darling."

"Yeah, well, you're also my boyfriend now, so it's different."

Edward tilted my head, running his thumb along my lower lip. "I like hearing you say that word," he said, eyes on my mouth.

I *liked* saying it—hadn't had a real, honest-to-God boyfriend in a long time, but this felt like the most natural next step to me. Like putting one foot in front of the other. Easy.

I closed my teeth around his thumb in a sharp bite. He growled softly. "The things I'm going to do to my girlfriend later..."

I smirked, dancing out of his reach. "Come on, *mentor*. Don't you have some wisdom you need to share with me?"

He laughed, meeting me down the aisle. I tuned into the

busy sounds of a tattoo convention—the dull roar of the guns, people talking and laughing, beautiful art *everywhere*. I suddenly itched to mindlessly sketch.

Then I reached an entire row of tables that represented, as Edward called it, our "competition." I stopped so suddenly Edward bumped into me, grabbing my waist again to keep me from falling.

"You okay?" he asked.

"So these booths are from 'Atwater Ink' and 'Inked In Stone.' The two parlors that opened up around the same time last year, all within a mile radius of my shop. The most *immediate* competition."

Usually at conventions, artists offered more affordable "flash art"—small pieces of pre-designed art at a flat price.

There were *long* lines streaming from their booths.

Edward stood next to me, arms crossed. "Yes. One of the first days I shadowed you, I walked down the blocks near your shop, saw those first two parlors. I feel pretty strongly they're the reason why you're getting less walk-ins, don't you agree?"

"I do," I said, feeling anxious and angry, even though—as an artist—I wanted them in this world. Wanted them to be doing their art and painting permanent pictures on people's bodies.

I just wanted them to do it not in my neighborhood.

"So, this is why we're here," Edward said kindly. "And this is how *I* usually do this when I'm conducting research on competition for The Cartwright."

"You don't actually have competition though, right?" I asked.

"All the bloody time," Edward said. "Unfortunately, it's the nasty side of business. But I like to think of it as an external reset. A grander performance evaluation that makes me continually strive for the best."

I glanced at Edward who once again stood out in his five-thousand-dollar suit, not a hair out of place. Clean-shaven, Rolex on his wrist, diamonds in his cufflinks.

"So, what does that mean for 'Roxy's'?"

"Well, first, let's look at what they're doing that's *different* than what you do," he said.

Busy Bee sat at my feet with a silly look, and I scratched under his chin.

"Aesthetic and style," I said. "I mean, like a lot of shops, they'll clearly give you whatever tattoo you want. But 'Atwater' specializes in grayscale portraits. 'Inked in Stone' specializes in watercolor and geometric style. And in the past few years, those specific styles are trendy and popular, especially for people younger than us."

"True," Edward said. "And their shops reflect that style. They offer lattes and tea, have outdoor seating areas and plants in the windows. And the design and layout of their shops reflect the tattoo designs they specialize in. It's a wrap-around experience for the client."

I nodded, looking at the people standing in line. "A lot of these people probably didn't grow up with tattooed parents or family members. It's new and trendy now, and they want shops that reflect that."

I glanced all the way at the end where Mack and Scarlett were doing vintage flash—anchors, skulls, roses, sparrows. Classic designs that still had huge numbers of fans but *not* what seemed to be attracting a younger generation.

Still, I was proud to see we had a decent little line going. A good sign.

"What we need to find out is not what makes 'Roxy's' different because I think we've got a pulse on that. But how to use that to attract new, younger customers that will stay loyal to you as they continue to modify their bodies. Being *different* is what makes you stand out from the rest. The customers I've talked to at your shop have all said something similar," Edward pointed out.

I tapped my finger on my lip, thinking, and for the first time felt a small jolt of anticipation, instead of fear, at the thought of implementing Edward's ideas.

We kept walking, and the tables seemed to grow trendier and trendier. People doing tattoos out of vintage Airstream trailers that traveled around the city, paired with food trucks. Tattoo artists with handle-bar mustaches and sweet, delicate designs on their bodies.

And then we got to our table, and Mack had cued music, and the people standing in line looked like bikers and punks, in heavy leather and with old, fading ink from their time in the service. Bearded and loud and certainly not looking for a tattoo that came with a taco truck.

"Oh hey, Roxy's here!" Scarlett called out, and the line went up in a cheer. Edward smiled at me, amused, as I waved.

"You guys hanging in there?" I asked, bending over to check out the rose design Scarlett was tracing on a customer's left hip.

"Oh yeah," she said, winking at the customer. "Met some regulars. Chatted with some new folks. I think Sir Edward had a pretty grand idea, don't you think?"

"Again, I'm *not* knighted, merely English," he said, tying the leashes of our dogs up to a post behind the table.

"Whatever you say, sire," Scarlett drawled. "And hey, you want to pop in? Do a few pieces of flash?"

"Maybe for your parents?" came my dad's voice right behind me. I jumped, turning around, and was swept into a massive bear hug. Behind me, Busy Bee barked excitedly.

"What are you guys doing here?" I said, laughing into their twin leather jackets.

"We saw the convention and thought why the hell not get some more ink?" my mom said. "And is this your mentor?"

I turned to a very surprised-looking Edward who was doing his best to straighten his tie and his cufflinks all at the same time.

"Oh... um, yeah. My mentor, Edward Cavendish the Third," I said, doing a slight-bow. "He manages The Cartwright Hotel."

"Just Edward is fine," he said, smooth accent always causing an immediate burst of butterflies. "And I saw you perform about a month back. I was incredibly impressed. Made me yearn for the days of my misspent youth in England."

My father gave him a firm handshake. "I'm Lou, and this is my wife, Sandy. Nice to meet you, Edward. And good man— American punks owe a lot to your forefathers."

I hid a smile because only my parents would be more impressed with Edward's punky youth than the fact that he managed the most prestigious hotel in New York City.

"Thank you, sir," Edward said. "And I think Roxy should absolutely tattoo you right this very moment. In fact, maybe I could ask you some questions while we do it?"

I groaned, covering my eyes. "Can I just tattoo my parents in peace?"

"Absolutely not," he said cheerfully. "Your parents are our ideal targeted customer base."

"It's true, honey," my mom whispered, and Edward winked at her. She blushed then gave me a conspiratorial look that said *you're in trouble*. At our weekly breakfasts, I *thought* I'd been managing to talk about Edward and my mentoring experience in general, non-romantic terms. But the expression on her face indicated otherwise.

"Tell me what you want, and I'll make it happen," I continued, pulling out one of the extra chairs as my dad leaned back on it. "You already know what you want?"

He shed his leather jacket, rolled up his sleeve. There was a bare section of skin on his forearm about six inches wide. The rest of his arm was almost entirely covered in ink.

"I like that skull-and-crossbones one," he said, tapping on it. Beneath, in vintage-style-lettering, it said *Sailor Beware.*

"A classic," I grinned, snapping on gloves and pulling up his arm. "And I think I can just fit it. Mom, you want the same one?"

She shrugged. "Sure, why not?"

Edward looked delighted. "How many times has Roxy tattooed the both of you?"

"Ever since she became a tattoo artist, she's the only one I allow to do it," my dad said. "I think she's the best artist in the entire city."

"Or the world," my mom finished, eyes bright.

"Yeah, yeah," I said, tossing my hair, barely fighting a smile "You just say that because we're related."

I prepped the stencil, laying it across my dad's forearm. It fit perfectly.

"So Edward, what did you want to talk to us about today?" my dad asked. "It's about Roxy's business?"

Edward leaned back, looking dapper with his arms crossed. At his side sat Matilda, pressed against his leg.

"I believe the core struggle that Roxy's business is facing is standing out in an industry that is suddenly booming. As I'm sure the two of you experienced in your lives, the art of tattoos used to be considered devious, trashy..."

"If you had tattoos, you were probably a dangerous low-life," my mom said.

"Exactly. But now, a lot of the stigma is gone, at least for the younger generation. And I feel like Roxy's shop taps into something..." he thought for a moment, head tilted. I glanced at him, tattoo gun in hand, waiting.

"Something dingy and poorly lit?" I teased.

"Classic," he said, and both of my parents made a sound of approval. "Classic. No frills. Nothing trendy that will go out of style. People looking for either a shop that will remind them of where they went when they got *their* first tattoo. Or new customers looking to tap into that same feeling."

"Like New York City in the seventies," my dad said, wincing at the first bite of the gun. My head was down, focusing, but I liked the fact that Edward and my parents were conversing so freely with each other.

"Dangerous, but there's a certain nostalgia for some of that time," my mom said. "And in fact, tattooing was illegal within city limits until 1997, so there was the added benefit of actual danger to what you were doing."

I pulled the gun back, wiped away ink and blood.

"Tattooing was even more discreet then," I said. "Hidden in plain sight, especially before the sixties."

"Are there official documents about the ban still floating around?" Edward asked. "Might be something you could frame, warning your customers that they put their very liberty at risk to enter your store."

"Huh," I said, tiny tendrils of inspiration starting to sprout in my brain. I leaned back over my dad's arm. "I'm not hating this."

"Well, there's a start," Edward said.

"You know what I've always loved?" my mom said. "Those old-timey signs outside of businesses, like the kind barber shops used to have. Or Route 66. Something that lights up. 'Tattoos Here.' A mix of vintage side-show and seventies appeal."

I knew exactly what she was talking about, and I was

warming to the idea.

"That's brilliant," Edward said. "If you were looking for a shop now, is that what would draw you in?"

"You know, the industry thought punk rock would be dead and gone by now," my dad said above my head. I let the comforting sound of my father's voice and the whir of the tattoo gun wash over me. "Would never last. Sound was too brash, too different. Too out of the mainstream. And yet, thirty years later, here we are. Our audience skews all over the place. Old punks like us. Young punks. People continue to discover this music and want to tap into it. *Not* the glitzy pop they hear on the radio that is constantly changing."

"Yes," Edward exclaimed. "Same with tattoo parlors. Some of these shops will ebb and flow as trends change. But the art that Roxy and her staff provides is classic. Meant to honor the tradition of the art form. It taps into a different type of customer, but one that I think will stay loyal over time."

"Who wouldn't want to stay loyal to Roxy?" my mom asked as I sat back up, stretching my neck.

Edward and I locked eyes. "I feel the same way," he said.

"What do you think, dad?" I finally managed, wiping away the final bit of ink. He looked down, flexing his arm.

"Fucking love it!" he cheered, patting me on the shoulder. "Is this girl the best artist or what?"

"It's 15-minute flash, dad," I said. "Any apprentice could do it."

My mom pushed my dad out of the chair. "That's not true, and you know it. Now do me."

I patted the chair and she slid in, removing her leather jacket. Her shirt said *Up With Trees. Down With Capitalism.*

"So how long have you two been dating?" my mom asked, and I gave her a wide-eyed look.

"*Mom*," I hissed, just like a teenager.

"You can't hide it," my dad said. "Plus, didn't Fiona tell us that before Edward was your mentor, you two... um..."

Both my parents went red in the face, and I prayed for a giant hole to come and suck me into the earth.

"Had a lovely evening together filled with mature, honest discussion," Edward filled in, and my parents and I gave a collective sigh.

"A very lovely evening," I agreed, giving him a private smile. "And we're together," I said, attempting to read Edward's expression. "Edward and I are together."

"She's my girlfriend," he smiled, and behind him, Mack and Scarlett both turned, tattoo guns in hand, and gave me the biggest shit-eating grins I'd ever seen.

"Don't you two have permanent ink to place on people's bodies?" I said.

"We're talking later," Scarlett said. "We are *talking*."

"If you ever see Professor Stevens out in public, don't, uh... don't mention this," I said. "And *definitely* don't mention it at the graduation ceremony. I don't think CUNY looks too kindly on mentors and mentees developing a non-professional relationship."

My parents made the same lock-and-key motion, zipping their lips. "We'll never tell," my dad said. "But why don't the two of you come over for dinner this week?"

I tried to give them another pleading look, but Edward surprised me instead.

"That sounds smashing," he said. "I'd love to. Shall I wear a suit or one of my punk shirts from my youth?"

"Oh, Edward," my mom said kindly. "We don't allow suits in our home."

"But can I bring my dog?"

"Of course," my dad said. "And Roxy, can I get another tattoo after your mother's done?"

41

EDWARD

"How often did you get dinner with Emily's parents?" Elliott asked over the phone as I stood outside of Roxy's parent's rambling green home in Queens. They'd hung a giant flag with the anarchy symbol on it, and it fluttered pleasantly in the light spring breeze.

"Often enough," I said. "They were nice people. Attended events with us on occasion."

"Did you like them?"

I thought about it. In so many ways, the time in my life *before* I'd stumbled into Roxy's tattoo parlor felt a million miles from here.

"They were very nice, just like Emily," I finally said. "They were just not as... *interesting* as Roxy's parents."

Elliott made an approving sound. "You're bloody heart-sick over this girl, yeah?"

I looked down at Matilda, who gave me a distinctly human look. *I told you so.*

"Well she did convince me to adopt a giant dog, which I recommend by the way."

"Noted," he said.

"And I've never laughed so much. Or been so challenged. Or happy. Oh, and we routinely engage in the best sex of my entire life."

"Edward," he said softly. "What have you told your parents?"

I glanced down at Matilda again, who nuzzled into my palm. Roxy had been right about being a dog-owner. Matilda seemed to have a canine intuition of when I needed comfort or silliness or just to lay on the couch and nap. And she had no judgments on the way I chose to live my life.

"Nothing," I finally said. "I've told them nothing. Which feels horrible. And I swear they've been *watching* me somehow. In my office all the time, endlessly criticizing. Always bringing up Phoebe and whether or not I've called her yet. They're leaving in a month after the charity ball, and I think they feel this extra intense urge to get me sorted out. Too quick for a proper marriage but at least dating a woman like Phoebe who I can safely become engaged to."

"Their final project. Their eldest son, Edward, who is currently shaming the family legacy by dating a woman with tattoos and a penchant for spanking."

I grinned because just the thought of Roxy made me feel better.

"Right now, I'm just enjoying this time and not thinking past... well, past anything really."

"Constant denial. Oh, I am *familiar*."

"I knew you'd get it," I said. "Do you think I'm doing a terrible thing? Keeping it from them?"

"No," he said. "I think you're doing self-preservation, which is important. But—" he said, and I *knew* it was coming. "Roxy doesn't seem like the kind of woman who enjoys being kept in the shadows. I mean, she'd bloody *hate* your parents.

But depending on what happens in your relationship, how serious things get, she's not going to be kept a secret."

"She's not a secret. She's an omission," I said defensively.

Because I knew he was right. And it was too soon, really, for Roxy and I to even *consider* marriage, but she knew, and I knew, and even fucking Elliott knew, that the daft marriage clause was an issue.

"Whatever you have to say to sleep at night, mate," Elliott said. "I'm not saying I live my life truthfully all the time. You know I struggle, fight the instinct to make *them* happy over myself all the damn time. It's a journey. But you're better off with honesty. Every time."

I exhaled loudly. "You're right, you're always right." Through the open curtains, I could see Roxy chatting with her parents, leaning against the cupboards, hands in motion. It looked domestic. Warm. Welcoming.

"What do you think it'd be like to have a family that loved you no matter what?" I asked Elliott.

"The hell if I know," he said. "But I'm guessing you're about to find out."

ROXY'S CHILDHOOD home was sheer chaos on the inside. Old band posters were interspersed with family photos and Roxy and Fiona's adorable childhood art projects. Black curtains, black couches, Patti Smith on the record player, and a continual banging of pots and pans in the kitchen.

"Edward, you made it!" her mother cheered, beckoning me into their kitchen. Her parents both hugged me, which I appreciated more than I realized. Matilda barked until Roxy's parents descended upon her with pets and cuddles, and then she curled up in the middle of the floor and fell asleep like she owned the place.

"I wasn't sure what to bring, to be quite honest," I said, holding out a bouquet of flowers. "Do you appreciate flowers? Or um... burn them?"

They both laughed, and behind them I caught Roxy, leaning back against the wall, legs out in front of her and arms crossed. Eyes filled with mirth and a sexy tilt to her mouth. She was wearing a simple black tank-top tucked into blood-red jeans that had small, metal spikes down the sides. Stiletto boots, blonde hair pulled to one shoulder, exposing the shaved side of her head.

"We love them," Sandy exclaimed, taking out a big cup and plopping them in some water. "I promise we're not nearly as destructive as we seem."

"We're pretty destructive though," Lou grinned. "Just not with company. Here, sit, sit." He practically shoved me into a small booth at the far edge of the kitchen, just big enough for a family of four. Roxy slid gracefully next to me.

"Hello, darling," I whispered, dropping a kiss to her shoulder.

"I'm surprised you came," she said, eyes scanning my body. "This is a pretty big step, Dilbert."

"Ready for it," I said and meant it. "How else am I ever going to see your embarrassing childhood photos?"

"We already prepped them," Sandy said, walking over with a giant salad and glasses filled with wine. "For after dinner. Roxy had a goth phase that was just so adorable we couldn't stand it."

"It felt like I spent years scrubbing black hair dye out of our towels," Lou said dryly. "But she wanted to look like the Angel of Death."

I burst out laughing as Roxy scowled. "I *wanted* to look like

Wednesday from *The Addams Family*. But I could never quite pull it off."

Lou slid into the booth across from us, bringing with him a giant bowl of pasta and a plate of garlic bread. "It's simple fare tonight, Sir Edward. Not as fancy as I'm sure you're used to, but I promise you we make a mean bowl of spaghetti."

I smiled, shaking my head. "I'm not as big of a snobby arse as Roxy would have people believe. That's more my family, not me."

Sandy began serving us giant helpings of food, and I felt like I could see an entire family history from this table: her parents writing song lyrics at midnight, Roxy and Fiona bickering as they did their homework, endless cups of coffee and glasses of wine. Whereas dinners in the Cavendish castle had been quiet and stoic, more of a report than a conversation.

What have you accomplished today to continue the Cavendish legacy?

"I've never called you a snobby asshole," Roxy said.

"You *literally* called me that yesterday," I said, and her parents chuckled.

Matilda wandered over, eyes hungry, and Roxy slipped her a piece of garlic bread, patting her head.

"Agree to disagree," she said, but underneath the table she squeezed my knee.

"What is your family like, Edward?" Sandy asked. "They must be very proud of The Cartwright and all that you've done."

I grimaced at their mention. "Well, not exactly. Or in their own special way they are," I said, although I wasn't sure what that was. "My parents come from very upper-class English families, and they were raised to believe that the love you have for your children stems from their accomplishments. And that is certainly how they raised me and my siblings. They sent me

287

here when I was twenty-five to take on The Cartwright, something I'd been told I would do since I was a little boy. That makes them happy, I believe." I paused. "I hope."

Lou tilted his head. "But does managing The Cartwright make *you* happy?"

"It does actually," I said. "Which is the surprising bit of it. I love running a hotel because it's fun and exhilarating and stressful and strange all at once. I'd resent my parents more if I didn't love The Cartwright so bloody much."

Or if I didn't have to be married off to own it.

Sandy and Lou looked at me as I twirled spaghetti round my fork. A look of compassion that caused an odd tightness in my chest. Next to me, Roxy openly stared. But I couldn't read her expression—I was keeping the marriage clause from my explanation, and she knew it.

"You know, people can certainly parent how they wish," Sandy said. "And it seems you've turned out to be quite the person, even though you are part of the bourgeois ruling upper class that Lou and I would like to see destroyed."

I threw my head back and laughed, and next to me Roxy chuckled.

"They're not joking though," she teased.

"Oh, I know," I said. "And I appreciate you allowing me into your home."

But Lou and Sandy continued to smile at me with so much kindness I forgot we were joking. "You're welcome," she said. "And please allow me just to say, as a parent, if you were our son, we'd be very proud of you. Regardless of what you've done. You know, Edward," she said, leaning forward on her elbows. "Lou and I learned early on that life's not about accomplishments. Climbing some ladder that doesn't mean anything. Building a career that could fall to pieces at any moment. It feels like that's all your parents care about."

I leaned back against the booth, surprised that this was the kind of "getting to know you" conversation that Roxy's parents engaged in. But I wasn't offended—rather, it was refreshing.

"You're not wrong," I admitted. "And well, I can't believe I'm about to defend my parents, but there's an enormous amount of pressure that comes from inheriting an exorbitant amount of wealth and reputation." My palms went up in surrender since I could *feel* their hackles raise. "And I'm not saying that to dismiss the fact that they are incredibly, incredibly privileged. Because they are—that's very true. But I think their lives have been one long fear that they will *lose* everything. Lose their power, lose their wealth; they are endlessly scrambling to stay ahead. To keep up and be better, wealthier than the other people in their lives. There isn't a lot of love there."

"What is it then?" Roxy asked softly.

"Comparison," I said. "Competition rather than love or friendship or enjoyment. I think, for them, life is nothing *but* accomplishments. Things you can brag about at social gatherings. Your children become bargaining chips and pawns rather than family. Your friends are nothing but a source of rabid jealousy instead of support or affirmation."

"Hmmm," Sandy said primly, eyebrow raised. "I don't think that's really an excuse for being a shitty parent though."

I smiled, looking down. "Ah, Sandy, I think you might be right," I said. "Things were different for Roxy and Fiona, yeah?"

"Oh God," Roxy groaned. "Try the *exact opposite*."

"Roxy and Fiona are the most perfect creatures in this entire universe, and it's a privilege to be their parents," Lou said, reaching forward to squeeze Roxy's hand. She flashed him an embarrassed, but grateful, smile.

"Thanks, Dad," she said. "Fi and I feel the same way." She

stood. "Now I'm getting more wine because you two spent the first part of this dinner grilling my boyfriend on why his parents fucking suck."

"They do fucking suck, dear," Sandy said sympathetically. "But sorry for grilling you."

"No apologies necessary," I said. "Truly. I've never really hid who my family is, especially not here in America. It's not like you'll end up at the Met Gala, whispering nasty secrets about them to some reporter."

"Of course not. I don't believe in galas," Sandy said.

"Can I ask you a question?" I said.

"Of course," Roxy's parents said, both at once.

"What is life about then, from your perspective? If it's not accomplishments or climbing the career ladder or... or gaining approval."

Roxy slid back next to me, glass of wine in hand. Beneath the table, our fingers interlaced.

"That's easy," Roxy answered. "They've been talking to Fiona and I about this since we were little girls. Life is about chasing joy and not giving a shit."

"Um... what?" I asked.

"Chasing joy," Roxy said. "Rushing headlong into happiness or sweetness or feeling. Never hesitating or waiting for it to come along again."

We locked eyes, and I thought about the night we first met. The walls I'd sent tumbling down—the restrictions I'd always placed on my actions and emotions. To just *feel* with a woman I barely knew.

"Take music, for example," Sandy said. "People told us we were weird, or freaks, or irresponsible, or bad parents—all because we continued to play music after we had children. But it gave us *joy*, and just because our family was non-traditional didn't mean we were a bad family."

"And it leads into the second rule: not giving a shit," Lou said with a shrug. "Because in this world, people will endlessly judge the things that give you joy or the ways that you express yourself. You're laughing too loud. Your hobby is too strange. Your marriage doesn't look like mine. Your life choices aren't 'right.'"

"Don't you want your daughter to be a heart surgeon instead of a tattoo artist?" Roxy smirked.

"And Fiona, our strange child, is a lawyer," Sandy said. "And she's *happy*. That little workaholic loves her life—not because she felt compelled to go to law school by some bull-shit idea of competing with her peers. But because it was her joy."

I swallowed tightly, and like clockwork I felt Matilda's big, craggy head pop up on my knee. She'd squeezed beneath the table and was now trying to climb onto the seat with me.

"Oh, sweetheart, I don't think—" I started to say, but Roxy whistled, and Matilda climbed fully up, seating herself in my lap.

"We allow dogs at the table in this household," she said.

"Because why not?" I finished.

"That's the spirit, Edward," Lou said, and that tightness came back. I smoothed my palm down Matilda's fur since she was a product of joy as well. Acting in the moment, chasing an instinct. Giving into the desire to live life without overly analyzing the outcomes.

That was Roxy's doing as well.

"You are essentially the antithesis of my family," I finally said. "And I have to say, I quite enjoy it."

Sandy leaned forward, patting my hand. "Come by any time. And do you want to see those photos now?"

42

EDWARD

"This is Roxy and Fiona when they were thirteen and fifteen. That summer, we took them on tour with us, and we drove through thirteen states. Everyone else on the tour bus, and her dad and I in our minivan with our daughters," Sandy said, showing me a picture of a scowling, punky Roxy and an equally scowling Fiona. They were standing in front of a sign for the Great Smoky Mountains National Park, reluctantly posing with their beaming parents.

"We loved that trip," Lou said. "And Roxy and Fiona were both in such *moods* the first month."

"We were very angry teenagers and had just wanted to stay at home and go to the mall and be morose with our friends," Roxy laughed. "But by the second month, Fiona and I were like total roadies. Carrying amps and doing sound check and moshing at these little punk clubs all across the country."

"It was pretty rad," Sandy said. "They've always been very brave, our daughters."

I looked at Roxy, at the photos spread around her. Her various ages and memories, the timeless moments her parents had captured. Our photos were staged and done by a professional, framed over mantles and fireplaces. These photos were old and silly and random—some were cute, others poorly lit or caught at a bad angle. Smudged or out of focus. But it was, to the Quinn family, a beautiful representation of who they were.

"The night I met Roxy, she looked just like that," I said, tapping the photo of her. "And I knew she was the one for me."

"Shut up," she said, rolling her eyes, but she was fighting a smile.

"That's our Roxy," Lou said. "Never afraid to be herself. Scowls and all."

I leaned forward, picking up a photo I at first thought was Fiona. A tiny blond wisp of a thing with a toothy grin and pink bows in her hair, twirling in a tutu.

"What's this?" I asked, tapping on the photo.

Roxy made a sound of semi-embarrassment.

"Roxy didn't tell you she wanted to be a ballerina until she was about ten years old," Sandy exclaimed, holding that photo up with bright, shining eyes. "We put her in ballet at three, and I have to say we always made a bit of a stir showing up to the recitals."

"Think my parents' burly, scary-looking bassist in the front row, cheering for me," Roxy grinned. "And then these two." She picked up a corresponding photo—her in the same tutu and bows, grinning between a very young-looking Sandy and Lou. They both had spiky blue hair and steel-toed combat boots on.

"I wish I could have been a fly on the wall, truly," I said. "Especially to see Miss Roxy in a tutu."

"Roxy was always the sweetest, kindest, most compassionate little girl," Lou said. "She wanted to be held, constantly. Even by perfect strangers. She'd walk right up to them in a restaurant, crawl into their laps, and immediately begin talking. Sandy and I were constantly running after her." He was shaking his head, and Roxy was all embarrassed smiles and pink cheeks next to me. The longer I knew Roxy, the more I understood her harder exterior was just one small part of the complicated tapestry of who she was.

But I couldn't help but look around at photos of a looser, more relaxed-looking Roxy and wonder just how much the stress of running this business was affecting her.

"It's hard for me to reconcile this girl in a tutu with the woman who yelled at two of my misbehaving Board members a few weeks ago," I said.

"Nicely done," Sandy grinned. "What were they doing?"

"Being dicks during Edward's presentation. Like really juvenile assholes," Roxy shrugged.

"I hate public speaking. Truly despise it—and I'm awful at it. Every month, those two sit in the back like sniveling schoolboys, and it only makes my nerves worse. But Roxy shut them right up." I winked at her. "I have so much respect for what you both do, getting on a stage like that in front of all those people. I could never, ever do it."

"I still get nervous sometimes, right before I go on," Sandy said. "Although it's mainly nerves that something in the set will go wrong because punk fans are pretty tough. Once, we had a *bad* set. Just awful. For no particular reason, just that our chemistry was off for the night."

"And halfway through they started chucking their beer glasses at us," Lou said, rolling up his sleeve and exposing a nasty scar. "This is from that night."

"Fucking rad," Roxy said.

"What a lot of wankers," I agreed. "And that gives me even more fear of it. At least, in my day to day, the only thing I face is embarrassment and wanting to desperately crawl into the corner. You literally take your lives into your hands."

They both shrugged. "All part of the job," Lou said. "And I'm taking you off the list for giving a speech at Roxy's graduation party. Since it'll be half old punks who won't take your mumbling lightly."

"*If* you want to come to my graduation party," Roxy said. "And *if* I pass my Capstone and actually graduate."

"I'll be at your graduation party with bloody bells on, love," I said. "And I'm pretty sure you'll pass your Capstone. And I'm honestly not saying that because I'm your boyfriend who also happens to be your mentor. I'm saying that objectively, I promise."

"What a great opening to the speech you'll give at the party," Sandy said with a wink. Tried to imagine myself standing up in front of a twitchy mob of bikers and family members and shuddered.

Next to me, Matilda yawned loudly, tail thumping, and I accidentally joined her. It was late, but I wasn't quite ready for the night to be over. I glanced at Roxy, tossing her a questioning look, but Sandy cut in before I could say anything.

"Edward, please spend the night if you'd like. It's a long trek from Queens to Manhattan, and we've got an extra bedroom out in the back garage in our practice space. We'll even cook you breakfast in the morning."

"Chocolate chip pancakes is their specialty," Roxy grinned, wrapping her mom in a side hug. "I'm not sure if Edward will take you up on your offer, but I will."

The thought of a sleepy, cuddly Roxy and pancakes was too tempting to pass up. "I'd love to stay actually; thank you so much for your kind hospitality."

"And you'll stay in separate bedrooms, of course," Lou said, standing up and clapping me on the back with a bit of extra strength. Next to me, Roxy's face reddened, and she gave her mom a pleading look.

"Roxy, you know the rules in this house," Sandy said. "No sharing rooms with whatever gender or person you are sexually attracted to. Edward, come with me; I'll show you the way."

Sandy smiled sweetly, leading me almost forcefully toward the garage, Matilda at my heels. I chanced a desperate look back at Roxy, who looked every bit the embarrassed, scowling teenager she'd been in those photos.

43

ROXY

 slid a bobby pin into the window latch, jiggling it just like Fiona had taught me. There was a *click,* and then it opened smoothly—a trick Fi had developed to sneak out without our old windows creaking to the high heavens and waking our parents. I'd waited an hour until I was pretty sure they were deeply asleep, and then I slid out the window and dropped from our low roof in one fluid movement, my body remembering the countless times I'd done this as a teenager.

I crept around the side of the house, the night shimmering with darkness, stars barely visible with the lights of all the houses in Queens crammed close together. I wiggled between our fence, eyes on the garage.

"Edward," I whispered, tapping softly on the side door. "Are you awake?" I pressed my ear to it, listening for sounds of movement.

"Edward?" I whispered again. I chanced a slightly harder knock this time, memories of doing something similar with one of my first boyfriends. I watched my parents' window like a hawk, but it was quiet, no flickering of bedroom lights. The night air was brisk and chilly, and I was shivering in the tiny pajama shorts I'd found in my old drawers.

"*Ed—*" I started to hiss, and then the door was opened, and I was yanked inside by a very handsome, basically naked, smug Englishman.

"Sneaking out, are we love?" he asked, tucking a strand of hair behind my ear. His body was warm and hard, and at our feet Matilda wiggled with happiness.

"Rules were made to be broken," I said, grabbing his hand and leading us to the back of the garage. It was a practice space for my parents, a semi-destroyed-looking garage filled with old instruments and microphones, band posters, and a tiny refrigerator always filled with beer. In the back, they'd built a lofted bedroom to house any number of musician friends who continually rolled through our house.

"What on Earth are you wearing?" he asked, breath on my shoulder, as we climbed back up the short ladder. Matilda whined below, unable to come up.

"Old pajamas of Fiona's that I found in my drawer," I said, lying back on the soft sheets. I crooked my finger, grinning, and Edward stretched his lean, muscled body next to mine. "Do you like them?"

"Well, this shirt declares you a *princess*, which doesn't quite fit, does it?" he said, finger sliding between my breasts, tapping on the glittered, hot pink lettering.

"You don't think it's possible that I could have royal blood?" I tilted my chin proudly.

Edward's eyes flashed with humor. "Ah, *princess*, I think you're a bit too filthy for that."

I curled into Edward's side, looping my leg over his waist. "Were my parents too much? I mean, did Emily's parents sit you down, force-feed you an enormous amount of spaghetti, and then tell you your loved ones are assholes?"

"Not quite," he mused. "Emily's parents thought *my* parents should have won an award for embodying dignity, success, and quiet power. That's what they always said about Rebecca and Edward the Second. Emily tried to model our relationship after theirs, in fact, something I didn't entirely pick up on until after we broke up and I had time to think about it more."

"Dignity and quiet power sounds boring," I said.

"Couldn't agree more," he said, stroking my cheek. "Although, before I met you, I had this inner sense that whole parts of my life were a fraud. Not *me*. So at times, while dating Emily, I would find myself acting just like my father. Even though, at the same time, I'd get drinks with Elliott, and I'd complain about them." His palm landed on his chest, right over his heart. "There's a bit of a war on in here, I'm afraid."

"I think that's pretty normal when you and your siblings were trained to believe parental love was something you earned through achievements. Rather than it being given to you unconditionally."

"That's probably it," he said. "I don't *want* to care what they think about me or say about me. I *want* to make decisions in my life that are my own. Through and through." He looked away, pensive, and I danced my fingers through his hair. "It's what drew me to you, initially. Your brazen authenticity. Like your parents said—"

"—chase joy, and don't give a shit," I said, laughing softly. "Easier said than done, but the home I was raised in was all about self-discovering and self-acceptance. Not labels or forcing yourself into little boxes. And I didn't have to earn my parents' love."

"Your parents seem to have an endless amount of love to give in this world," he said. "I was a bit surprised I'd gotten such a warm welcome, given who I represent."

"They're all bark and no bite," I said, holding up my wrist. *Never Again.* "After Jimmy cheated on me, they were a little bit overprotective for a while. Wary of any guy I brought around to meet them. But my bullshit detector became pretty sensitive after that, and as soon as I caught even a *whiff* of fuckery, I'd break it off. So after I brought around a fair amount of *nice* guys, they started to open themselves up again. Trust those relationships to be good and healthy."

"So you... told them I was to be trusted?" he asked hesitantly.

"Of course," I said, tapping my wrist again. "Edward, I wouldn't have dragged you out into that alley, the night at the club, if I'd thought you were going to break my heart."

"But we can still break each other's hearts, darling," he said. "You don't know that."

I shook my head. "I mean... break my heart on *purpose*. Not just the natural ending of a relationship that's run its course. Which is sad, and if that happens to us I'll be devastated, promise." I kissed his cheek. "But I don't think that Edward Christopher Cavendish the III is going to do that on purpose."

"Is that why you sent me out that night, the first time we met?" he asked. "When I asked you on a date and you smashed that idea to pieces?"

I covered my face for a second, groaning. "I know, I know," I said. "But I have an extremely sensitive bullshit detector, remember? And you were sexy and filthy, and I'd wanted to fuck you but..."

"What?"

"Edward, we're *very* different people who come from *very* different backgrounds. I thought you were a nice guy, but I also thought you'd just been dumped, I was a hot, kinky experience, and I wasn't going to let myself fall for you and then be dumped a few weeks later because you'd met another Emily. I figured I was just kind of a fetish to you. And I thought I'd cut it off before I fell in love with you."

Something rippled across Edward's face, an expression I couldn't quite read. "I told myself something similar in the months afterward. That it was for the best that you'd turned me down. We'd never work out."

"Because your parents would never approve of me," I said, the reality of that settling in my gut like a heavy stone, dropping through water. The topic we avoided like the third rail, rightfully afraid of its sparks. "Which means they'd never approve of *you*."

In the time that we'd been together, we'd charged full-steam ahead, never giving a moment's thought to what would come in the future. I'd thought the complicating factor of our relationship would be that his approval of my business expertise could make-or-break my graduation.

In actuality, it was Edward's desperate need to marry someone his parents approved of because it was wrapped up in a complicated, complex desire to finally receive their love no matter how distorted.

Edward's blue eyes were pained. "I want to own The Cartwright, for real, not just be my parent's puppet. For ten years, I've tried everything to impress them, worked myself half to death to make that hotel bloody succeed. And yet they won't give it to me on those merits alone."

"The marriage clause," I said. "They want you to be in a nice, neat package to continue their legacy. A sweet woman who you can have 2.5 children with and ensure no tarnishing comes to the Cavendish name."

"Yes," he said on a long sigh. "Yes, that's it exactly."

I hooked my leg around his waist, yanking him closer, craving his hands on my body.

Because I could never be that woman for Edward.

"What does that mean for us?" I asked, noticing my own internal struggle. Frantically clinging to this man I was falling head-over-combat-boots for.

And ready to push him right off this loft and into the night if he wasn't prepared to fight for a relationship that continued to surprise me in its intensity. Its *realness*.

"Roxy, darling," he said. "I'm not going to pretend that my relationship with my parents, *especially* because of the hotel, isn't a bloody complicated mess. Because it is. But I want..." He took a deep breath. "The past two months with you have been the happiest of my life. And I don't want my parents to be a deciding factor anymore. I want to be in control, truly, to live my life like, well, like you."

"I think we could make that happen," I said. "I can help you."

"Maybe you could yell at my parents too?" he asked, tapping his chin.

"Oh my God, a girl does that *one time*..." I teased, but Edward was kissing me. Sweetly at first, but we never truly did anything *sweet*. His lips stayed gentle, a delicate caress, but his rough palm slid down my back and cupped my ass possessively. Yanking me against his perfect cock.

"I can't believe your parents wouldn't let us stay in the same room," he finally said, pulling back as I struggled to plant my feet back on the ground. "They seemed like the kind of parents who would have welcomed pre-marital sex for their children."

"They do, kind of," I said. "They are very open and accepting about sexuality, loving your body. But at the end of the day, they're both a bit traditional. Thus this very strict rule that they'll probably hold Fiona and I to for the entirety of our lives."

"You know I've never had a girl sneak out to meet me,"

Edward said. "Although I snuck out of school quite frequently to meet *them*. But when you knocked on the glass earlier, I assumed you were a very polite murderer."

I snorted. "You say that, but I bet *all* the girls at boarding school had massive crushes on you. Such a *heart*breaker."

"Ah, Roxy darling, except the dashing, stupendously successful businessman you see before you was quite the late bloomer. Even at the end of high school, my voice still cracked, and I had this awful floppy hair, and I'm sure the first couple girls I slept with thought I was a total nerd."

"Not possible," I said, kissing his palm, the tips of his fingers. "I would have snuck out to meet you. Dragged you behind some tree and French-kissed you."

"French-kissing the bad girl?" he mused. "I like the sound of that." He palmed my ass again, harder this time, before sliding his long, delicate fingers down my bare thigh, stroking his thumb down my knee. "Does being here make you nostalgic?"

"A little," I said. "It's the start of May, and sun's coming up just a bit earlier, and the mornings are just the *slightest* bit balmier. Which means Fiona and I would have started our giant six-week countdown to the Last Day of School."

Edward grinned. "I bet the two of you got up into some trouble during those summer months."

"Maybe," I said. "Our block was filled with other families though, and until high school when all of our hormones exploded, we ran this street to death. Baseball, hockey, spy games, capture the flag, lemonade stands..." I trailed off. "But my absolute *favorite* day was the first one."

"Day one of vacation?"

I nodded. "Just remember, as a kid, how much summer vacation felt like some kind of beautiful paradise, but those last few weeks had this sense of dread to them. Almost back to school, the air shifting toward autumn. But the first day, Fiona and I would wake up, and my parents would be making blueberry waffles, probably dancing around to a Blondie album. We'd stuff our faces filled with waffles, go sit on our front stoop, and wait for the other neighborhood kids to come out. And in those few hours, as the morning was already hot and sticky, and we knew we'd be having Popsicles for dinner, and we'd play our first day of Capture the Flag, and you just *knew* you had another three months of this ahead of you." I shivered against Edward's chest. "*That's* what I feel nostalgic for whenever I'm home. Moments like that."

Edward smoothed the hair from my face, stroking the soft, shaved part, causing a different kind of shiver. "Unfortunately, *leaving* boarding school to come home was my least favorite time because it meant a dreary, boring summer while George, Jane, and I were stuffed into uncomfortable clothes and trotted out for events and dinners. No friends, no fun."

"Hmmm," I said. "Maybe I *will* stab your parents. Who ruins summer vacation for their children?"

"Ruining fun is the Cavendish way, love," he said. "Although I'm at your house for one night, and I've already let the bad girl sneak into my bed while her parents are sleeping." Those long fingers left my knee, slid back up to the edge of my shorts. "That's pretty naughty, wouldn't you say?"

44

EDWARD

*I*t was so easy, after a night of loving affirmation by Roxy's parents and unyielding support from my sexy vixen of a girlfriend, to cast off the chains of my family's legacy. Or, at the very least, to declare that I was my own person, regardless of their approval.

Cocooned in that loft bed, soft sounds of the neighborhood seeping in, with a gorgeous woman wrapped around my body, there was no way I couldn't seize the reins of my life.

I didn't know, exactly, what that meant for me, for The Cartwright, for anything.

But I'd bloody well figure it out.

"I got up to a lot of bad things in this loft bed," Roxy said, jolting me back to the present moment. "Kissed a lot of boys."

"Such a dirty girl," I admonished, fingers dipping beneath those shorts to find her pussy bare—and very, very wet. I slid the pad of my index finger around her clit, and she jumped. "Did you ever touch yourself in this bed? Think about a boy you had a crush on and get off on it?" There was a hard edge to my voice—less a question, more a command.

Roxy nodded, biting her lip.

"Why don't you show me, *princess*," I said, lifting her leg from my waist and pressing her back into the sheets. "Show the boyfriend you broke the rules to see exactly what you do when you fuck yourself."

Her dark eyes lit up in challenge. "Maybe. But what's in it for me?"

She was such a little brat.

"Take off those damn shorts," I snapped, and they were off in a second, flying across the bed, exposing her colorful legs and bare cunt. She finally gave me a look of true submission.

"How do you make yourself come when you're thinking of me?" I said, my palm gliding beneath her shirt to cup her breasts. Her nipples hardened against my palm as her back bowed off the bed.

"Like this," she whispered, index finger sliding between her legs and circling her clit. She moaned at the contact, eyes fluttering closed.

"That's right, love, show me." I kissed up her neck and under her ear, pinching her nipples roughly, just like she liked it. She was already panting as her finger flew against that bundle of nerves. "What are you thinking about?"

A tiny smile, fingers slowing. Her eyes opened, shining with mischief. "Do you remember fucking me in front of that mirror the first night?" I lifted her shirt up and sucked her left nipple between my lips. She cried out, back bowing off the bed.

"That entire night is burned into my memory forever," I said, letting the tip go, licking my way to the right one. "Why the mirror though?"

"Because..." she moaned, "because you fucked me like this... wild animal. Oh *God* it was so good."

"Yes it was, darling," I rasped, sliding a finger inside her pussy to find her soaking wet and clenching. "That's because you make me that way, do you understand?" I nudged against her g-spot, and curse words flew from her mouth like birds in flight. "You broke through, found the *real* me, and you'd known me for all of an hour."

Every secret button I had, Roxy Quinn pushed. Every secret, she uncovered. Every thought, she drew out of me and examined. I had never been more stripped bare in my entire existence.

I cupped her beautiful face, licking my tongue deep into her mouth. Grasped her wrist and pulled her fingers off her clit. Slowly slid from her pussy.

"Such an asshole," she smiled, groaning in frustration. I took her index finger, slid it between my teeth. The taste of her exploded across my tongue. I bit her finger, kind of hard, and she responded by scraping her nails down my chest. Pain and pleasure twinned together, and I shuddered, briefly closing my eyes. I heard her purr her approval, felt her do it again. Nails gliding around my waist before giving me a sharp, resounding spank.

"God, that feels amazing when you do that," I hissed, lowering my forehead to hers. "Again."

My little vixen complied, the pain radiating up my spine, my cock grinding against her clit.

"I could come this way," she sighed, gripping my ass and flexing against me. Spanking me when I slowed down.

"Just like in high school," I managed to tease, giving her a particularly long thrust that had her eyes rolling back. "Except, darling, we can do something even better."

"Is my boyfriend trying to have *sex* with me in my parent's garage?" she purred, giving me a particularly sharp slap that had me biting her shoulder to keep from yelling out.

"I can't promise I'll last long," I said as she chuckled softly. "And curl your fingers in that goddamn headboard."

Eyebrow arched, she reluctantly pulled her hands from my ass and lifted them overhead, twining them in the metal like a good girl.

"I find that hard to believe," she smirked as I flexed my hips and filled her. Roxy let out a delicious wail, and I clamped my palm across her lips.

"Shh, darling," I said, starting to thrust in the steady rhythm I knew drove her wild. "We don't want to get caught, do we?" I let her go, interlacing our fingers in the headboard and bringing every inch of my body in contact with hers. Her legs stayed wrapped around my waist and she met me thrust for thrust.

"I'll be in so much trouble if we do," she moaned, letting me lick her throat, taste every single inch of her gorgeous skin. "But it's worth it, isn't it?"

Her eyes held truth and not mischief—something vulnerable and real in her gaze that had me driving into her forcefully, needing to *show* her that this, her, all of it was worth it.

"You are the most beautiful thing in my life, Roxy Quinn," I whispered against her lips, and her answering kiss was all I needed. Besides, we'd reached the point where talking and coherent thought were no longer options—we were just feeling and sensation. Roxy's soft sighs, her eyes on mine. Our fingers together, the fluttering of her pussy as I fucked us closer and closer to a sweet climax.

It was a very strange thing to discover at thirty-five that you'd been living your life beneath a wall of water, separate from true sensation. Not just erotic sensation—because certainly Roxy had shown me that—but affection, feeling, acceptance. Joy and pain, happiness and struggle. Because there was so much trust in the depths of her gaze as I slid my thumb between us, giving her just what she needed to go off like a firework. Pressing my lips to hers, drinking in her pleasure, groaning with an intense climax just a few seconds later. Her name on my lips.

Always.

"I think I'm dead," I said, our limbs curling together on the bed.

"I've been known to slay a few men in my life," she replied, kissing my cheek, my temple. Fingers stroking through my hair. "And that was definitely the hottest sex I've ever had in this garage."

"Hotter than all your daft high school boyfriends?"

"Fuck yeah," she grinned. "You lasted *at least* a minute longer than all of them."

"Cheeky little *minx*," I teased, tickling her ribs as she pealed with laughter. "You know it was at least *two minutes*."

"Okay, okay, truce," she said, wiping tears from her eyes. "And, uh, I think Matilda is ready to come up now."

I sat bolt upright, looking down the low ladder at my adorable dog, tongue lolling and big eyes begging. She gave a soft bark, tail thumping against the ground.

"How am I going to get her up the ladder?" I asked, already pulling on my boxers.

"I have faith in these shoulders," Roxy said, patting the muscles in question. "You can do it. I'll help."

I quirked an eyebrow at her but dutifully slid down the ladder as Matilda collectively lost her little dog-mind. I scooped all sixty-five pounds of her up in my arms and half-pushed, half-slid us up the ladder. She caught on quickly, climbing it the best way she could, and two-thirds of the way up, Roxy leaned down and dragged her into the bed. We were both laughing hysterically, Matilda barking in excitement, and when I finally reached the top, Matilda was curled up on my pillow, licking Roxy's face.

"Oh, so I'll just sleep down here on the floor then," I said dryly, but Roxy patted the spot behind her.

"Just enough room for you here, Dilbert," she said, and there was. Just enough room for me to slide behind her, arm curling around her waist, lips pressed to her hair. She was relaxed and warm and cuddly, face scrubbed clean and in those ridiculous pajamas. This was Roxy-with-all-soft-edges; no eyeliner or combat boots to get in the way. And I was falling hard for both sides of her.

"There she is," Roxy's father boomed from the kitchen as he tossed chocolate chips into a sizzling pan. "Edward's been up and at it for an hour now. He's already helped us start the crossword puzzle *and* listened to a new song we've been kicking around."

I sat in the Quinns' tiny kitchen, Matilda at my feet, pencil in my hand, and gave Roxy a smug smile. "Good morning, beautiful. How'd you sleep last night?" At dawn, she'd snuck out of the garage to climb the tree that led to her window—but not before kissing me senseless.

"Oh fine. Just fine," she shrugged, cheeks pink, as she grabbed a mug of coffee and gave her mom a hug. "Did you make Edward do Sunday's? Because you know that's the hardest one."

"Except he's been flying through it just like the Oxford grad he is," her mother grinned, tossing a blueberry to Matilda. "We're stuck on a ten-letter word at the end."

"Plague, as in bubonic," I read, wrapping an arm around Roxy's shoulders as she slid into the booth next to me. "We've wracked our brains but even my prestigious Oxford education can't crack it."

"*Pestilence*," Roxy said, tapping her finger at the empty boxes. "A fatal disease, typically the bubonic plague. Also the name of a punk band Fiona and I started ever-so-briefly in high school."

"Oh, we *loved* Pestilence," her dad cheered. "Sandy and I tried to get them to give it a go, but they broke up pretty early on."

"Turns out Fiona and I received not a single genetic ability to sing, play, or read music from these two," Roxy said, crooking her thumb at her punky parents dancing around the kitchen. "But we did use it as an excuse to tear holes in all of our jeans."

"That's my girl," I winked, writing in the word as Roxy leaned her head against my shoulder, eventually stealing the pen from me and taking charge of the whole crossword operation.

Her parents laughed and made chocolate chip pancakes, and we talked favorite punk albums and the benefits of Maple syrup and finished an entire pot of coffee. And I had the strangest sensation that every single moment in my life had led me to getting drunk and stumbling into Roxy's tattoo parlor that night.

Because all of it had led me to this.

45

ROXY

I was trying to envision a five-year strategy for building the customer base of my tattoo parlor, but my mentor wouldn't stop nuzzling his lips along the skin right beneath my ear.

"If you don't stop, I'm going to fuck you in Central Park, and then we'll really be in trouble," I chided, laughing as I pulled away from Edward's wandering lips. It was a gorgeously warm spring day in New York City, and it felt like every single person was out in this park, strolling in the dappled sunshine. Busy Bee and Matilda sat dutifully at our feet, tongues lolling, tails thumping.

"What's the worst they can do—arrest us?" Edward asked with a dignified arch in his brow.

"Yes, and then everyone in New York City will shake their heads at the injustice of it all. That famous hotelier Edward Christopher Cavendish—"

"—the *Third*—" he interjected.

"—was led astray by overly sexed dirtbag Roxy Quinn."

Edward laughed. "If you're overly sexed, love, then put me in the same category." He kissed me full on the lips. "I actually think I need to start drinking protein shakes during my work day to adequately prepare for your natural rambunctiousness."

I shrugged, wry smile on my lips. It'd been a week since Edward had met my parents, and we'd spent it bickering mildly over my business plan, walking our dogs like an old married couple, and having wild, passionate sex on every surface we came in contact with.

I was happier than I'd ever been in my life. Even with the threat of our murky, ill-defined future hanging over my head. We didn't discuss his parents or their desire to marry him off to someone distinctly *not* like me or his pressures to conform. In fact, he seemed to never want to talk about those things anyway, so I let the topic lie, content to rile him up until he'd bend me over the nearest flat surface and fuck me into submission.

Or talk to him for hours as we laid in his giant bed at night

Or drink beers with him at the shop with Mack and Scarlett.

Or... or... or...

"This is my final assignment before I prep the presentation. *The* presentation, so I need these ideas to be actually executable. Do you think I could have a sign offering Mack to perform lap dances for waiting customers? Do you think that would drag those hipsters away from the trendy shops and into my grimy one?"

"Vertical integration," Edward mused. "I like it. Instead of coffee or tea, a terrifying-looking man will grind on you. But as they turn to run in fear, you welcome them into a tattoo chair where suddenly the thought of a giant needle puncturing their skin for an hour is more appealing than Mack on their lap. I think customers would love it."

I pretended to cross it off my list. "Okay, okay, I see your point."

Over the past two months, Edward and I had discovered that I was less defensive—and more open—to criticism and feedback if we spent the majority of the time joking about it. Because usually, as we teased each other, a golden idea would slide through all the bullshit and teasing.

Edward snapped his fingers, suddenly serious. "Did we write down for you to have a mini-grand opening in a few months?"

I checked my list. "We did. As a way to welcome new customers, show off our new 'look'—whatever that's going to be—and maybe do some sales."

"What if your parents performed? What if, since the weather's supposed to warm up soon, you turned it into a punk-rock street fair? Emphasis on vintage tattoos, vintage punk. Nothing fancy, very 'on brand,' *and* if you were nice about it, you'd invite the other parlors on your block to participate. You'd probably get more business that way, honestly."

"Hmmm," I said, writing the idea down. "I like that idea. Would be really fun, and we could do it every year. An annual thing—offer new flash, maybe bring down some guest artists to draw in new customers."

"Brilliant, darling," he grinned, giving me a sweet, sloppy kiss, and then I turned away for just the briefest of moments —five seconds, maybe—to scrawl down the words 'punk rock street fair,' feeling my future brighten, my store shift and change, my idea of myself as a businesswoman stretch just a bit closer to reality.

I felt it all—the sun on my face, the warmth of my boyfriend next to me—and when I turned to tell Edward this, he was no longer there.

Or, at least, the Edward I had come to know, and was definitely falling for, was no longer there.

No. Edward had frozen in place, smile gone, spine rigid, face pale as a ghost.

"Wha—" I started to say, but something was blocking the sun.

Edward's parents.

I'd recognized his dad from the time we'd briefly interacted in Edward's office. His mother appeared just as wealthy, wrapped in a dark fur and a haughty, scowling expression.

"Mother. Father," Edward stumbled, standing up somewhat sheepishly. He'd changed out of his suit after work and into work-out clothes, and he looked out of place and younger next to his sharply dressed parents.

I wondered if they'd ever seen him in running shorts before.

"I thought, um, you were visiting some more properties this week," he hedged, giving his mother a kiss on the cheek and his father a firm handshake.

"There's too much planning that still needs to happen for the Charity Ball," his father said in his clipped accent. "Which we need to talk about since you'll need to get your staff to overhaul the sound system in the ball room."

"Yes, of course," he said politely.

"And I also discovered, to my mortification, that you did *not* make plans with Phoebe to attend the Opera this week per our lengthy discussion. I just received a phone call from that girl's parents, who are rightly miffed, since I'd all but guaranteed them you two would be a match."

Edward flashed me an embarrassed, apologetic look, but I could only lift an eyebrow in response.

Of course he wasn't taking some woman to the Opera.

He was with *me*.

"Edward," I said, but he ignored me.

My stomach began twisting in fear.

"Yes, and I'm so sorry for the embarrassment I caused you and our family," he said, hand on his heart.

I waited for the second part of that sentence, something along the lines of: *You see, I'm actually dating someone. She's sitting literally right in front of you.* I knew about Phoebe—he had, after all, come to *my* window as soon as their first date had finished. But to my knowledge, he had no interest in her.

Why wasn't he saying that *now*?

"I would have thought," his mother said, dropping her voice to a hiss, "that you would have sorted yourself in the time since you and Emily parted ways." Her gaze slid my way, finally acknowledging the human being sitting one foot in front of her. And it was brimming over with contempt.

"Roxy Quinn," I said with false brightness. "What a pleasure it is to meet you, Mrs. Cavendish. And Mr. Cavendish, it's a pleasure to see you again."

Both ignored me.

Anger and nausea were now roiling in my gut.

And Edward, looking like he was praying for a giant sinkhole to suck him into the earth.

Yet my pity for him was *severely* limited in the moment.

"Who is this?" his mother asked, and Busy Bee let out a low growl. I shushed her since I was suddenly more interested in hearing Edward's answer than scaring the wits out of Edward's mother.

"My, um, my mentee. Roxy. She's the businessowner I've been telling you about," he said. Except in the past two months, whenever he'd said those words, they were filled with pride and sincerity.

Now he sounded apologetic.

"Your *mentee*?" I prodded.

"Y-yes," he said, voice growing stronger. "Yes. I mentor Roxy about once a week as she's completing her business degree. But it's ending soon."

Ice settled in my veins, pooled in my chest right above my heart.

"Oh, of course," Edward's mother nodded. "Your *charity* program."

"Yes," he said, cheeks flushed. His parents quickly assessed me, and there was embarrassment there. Not for themselves but for *me.*

Edward's mentee. His *charity.*

"Edward," I said, willing him to look at me. "Are there any other words you'd use to describe who I am to you?"

But he could only avoid my gaze like a coward. And I knew. I *knew* how complicated his feelings were for his parents. Knew he truly struggled with their approval, and over the past two months, I felt heartsick over the way he'd been raised. The denial of affection and the focus on legacy over love. I understood the many savage ways that could distort and twist your thoughts.

And I understood that by choosing to have a relationship with someone like me, he was choosing to let go of The Cartwright, which he loved dearly.

I knew all of this and still—

I expected Edward to stand up for me. To tell his parents who I really was to him.

The woman he loved.

But Edward only avoided my gaze and said nothing.

Not a single goddamn thing.

Anger fell away like rain from the sky, only to be replaced with the hot threat of tears. Which I would *not* fucking do right now.

Because wasn't this the reason I'd sent him away the first

time? Hadn't our destiny already been dictated by the circumstances of our birth, our upbringing?

I glanced down at my wrist.

Never Again.

My heart felt utterly crushed, and the tears fell anyway.

I grabbed Busy Bee's leash, shoved my papers in my messenger bag.

"Roxy," Edward said softly, and when our eyes finally met, his were filled with pain and yearning. Next to him, his parents looked shocked and anxious, already glancing around to see who might be noticing my behavior.

I shook my head at him. Because it was too fucking late.

He'd waited too long.

"You know, I might just be the owner of a failing tattoo parlor," I said, chin tilted in defiance. "I might just be some *charity* case, but at least I'm not *afraid*." I swallowed against a lump of tears, and I could feel them streaking down my cheeks. "At least I'm not afraid to be who I am. Who I *really* am. And to be honest about who I'm—" I stopped, and Edward looked on the verge of tears himself. "Who I *was* falling in love with."

And with as much quiet dignity as I could muster, I stomped through the Cavendishes with my dog and my books and my poor, poor broken heart.

46

EDWARD

I was such a blithering, fucking fool.

I stood absolutely still, and said not a thing, as my parents asked me to define exactly *who* Roxy Quinn was to me. As if some ancient witch had cast a spell, turning me entirely to stone, a statue frozen in helpless fury.

From the moment Emily had dumped me in that restaurant until now, I'd been taking these tiny steps toward taking control of my life—liberating myself from the tight control of my parents, their pressures and their legacy. Slowly, with Roxy's help, it hadn't really been hard at all to embrace the person I was, buried beneath years of denial.

Steps to bring me to this moment. This *bloody moment* to declare to the cold-hearted people who had raised me that the person I loved was none of their goddamn business.

That the person I loved was worth more than their warped expectations and clauses.

Because of course she was. Roxy Quinn was worth *everything* to me.

And I'd followed those steps dutifully, knowing this was

inevitable, ignoring Elliott's warnings, dodging Roxy's questions.

Followed them here, to this moment where despite every cell in my body screaming for me to tell the truth—for once—I did the same cowardly thing I'd done since I was a child.

"Edward?" my mother asked, hand to her chest, in shock at Roxy's beautiful declaration of authenticity and love for me.

Was falling in love.

I was a blithering, worthless piece-of-shit.

"Oh God," I said suddenly, sinking back down into the bench. Matilda was next to me in a second, head on my shoulder as I wrapped my arms around her for a much-needed canine hug. "I can't believe that just happened."

"And what on Earth is this?" my father asked, sniffing at Matilda like she was a piece of excrement on the bottom of his shoe.

"This is my dog, Matilda. She's a rescue, had been abandoned at the shelter for two years until Roxy—" My throat tightened. "—until Roxy helped me adopt her."

My eyes closed, burning with the image of Roxy stomping away. *Never Again.* How many times had she told me she was done with fuckwits? With men that didn't deserve her?

Now I got to join the ranks.

And to be honest about the person I was falling in love with.

And that, that was like an arrow right through my heart.

"Edward, who was that woman? She was not *just* your student mentor. There was nothing *professional* about that."

I looked up into the face of a man I dreaded seeing every spring. Who made my life miserable, criticized me, dismissed my thoughts and ideas, had turned my childhood from something carefree and joyous to something cold-hearted and lonely.

"Roxy is a woman I've been dating," I said, and even that

kernel of truth now felt like sand in my mouth. Because 'dating' couldn't describe the wild rollercoaster of being in her presence, the sheer force of my feelings for her.

"Then you'll break up with her immediately," my mother said without an ounce of sympathy in her eyes. "If The Cartwright is something you want, and continuing our legacy is something you care even an *iota* about, then you will date, and marry, a woman like Phoebe. A suitable woman. A woman who can uphold the Cavendish name. Now we are not like other families in England, Edward. We could have *arranged* something for you, completely privately, so you wouldn't have to worry about this marriage business. But we let George and Jane choose their partners, barring we had deemed them suitable, and were quite fine with letting you do the same. Of course, as usual, you can never do anything right."

I let go of Matilda, dropping my head into my hands, eyes pressed tightly closed. Seeing Roxy walking away from me, over and over again, like a film I could never turn off.

I never could do anything right.

47

ROXY

"**G**o away," I yelled at the knocker at my door, who I just *knew* was my nosy little sister. "You don't want to come in here. It's like a fucking—"

"Hey," Fiona said. She was standing in my doorway, a vision in a suit. Grace Kelly bun, tan business suit, red lips, slick heels. "You know it's really easy to break into your apartment."

"Only you could put yourself through law school and still remember that credit card trick Dad taught us in case we ever needed to take down The Man," I said, although it was more of a sigh and muffled since my face was mostly buried beneath a blanket, and every animal I owned was curled up on top of me.

"My skills know no limits," Fiona said, taking out a bag and dumping an obscene assortment of junk food and liquor on the bed. "Now move over and tell me what happened with Corporate Asshole McSpanky Pants."

I immediately started bawling.

"Oh... oh Roc..." she soothed, sliding beneath the blankets and pulling me in for a hug. "I'm sorry. I thought, well, usually

327

you're just in the anger phase the whole time, and we can sit around and come up with stupid nicknames for how small their dicks are."

"I know," I hiccupped. "And I thought 'Asshole McSpanky Pants' was really funny actually except... except..." and then I was bawling again. This had essentially been my state for the past three days ever since Edward had stomped all over my much-too-tender heart and I'd stomped out of his life. He'd called and texted me so many times I turned the damn phone off, uninterested in his apologies or excuses. Mack and Scarlett had graciously stepped in to cover for me at the shop, and I had two more weeks until my presentation was due to graduate.

Which my exhausted, overwrought mind couldn't even begin to fathom.

"Roc," Fiona said, stroking my hair. "Can you tell me what happened?"

"Easy. Edward's a stupid jerk, and I hate everything about him."

She chuckled softly, reaching over to open a bag of Cheetos and twist off a bottle of cheap red wine. Grabbed the remote and turned on my TV, flipping through channels until we came to some reality show I didn't understand with the word 'housewives' in it.

"Ugh, Fi, can I just wallow in peace and drink my weight in wine?" I asked, sitting partially up in bed to get a better view of the screen.

"Shhh," she said. "Let *The Real Housewives* wash you away."

~

FIVE HOURS LATER, and it was nearing midnight.

"I just don't understand what Shannon was thinking, you know?" I said, biting a Twizzler in half. "She knew that Heather was going to be at that party, and yet *she still came*." I shook my head. "She's just inconsiderate."

"Mhmm," Fiona grinned, stretching lazily on the bed next to me. "I agree. I hate Shannon too. Would you say you hate Shannon as much as you hate Edward?"

"No," I said quickly. "Because I could never truly hate Edward. I'm in love with him too much."

I stopped, fingers half-way to my mouth, as Fiona muted the beautiful, frosted *Housewives*.

"See? I knew *The Housewives* would help," she said smugly, sitting up and turning to me. "And now we're really going to talk, Roxy Ramone Quinn."

I rolled my eyes. "Okay, okay, what do you want to know?"

"Why did you and Edward break up?"

"I'm not sure we're even really broken up," I snapped and then softened when Fiona narrowed her eyes at me. "Sorry. I just mean, I walked away from him at Central Park, and I haven't returned his thousands of calls, and, quite frankly, I don't want to. Time to cut my losses."

"What'd he do?" She prodded my foot with her own. "Spill the beans."

I swallowed thickly. "We were at Central Park with the dogs when Edward's parents walked up. They're not Edward's biggest fans."

"His own parents?" Fiona asked.

"It's part of his upbringing. Both of his parents come from old money in England, and his father inherited this hotel empire, you know. The Cartwright. Edward is essentially his parents' puppet. He runs the hotel but doesn't own it."

"And he wants to own it?"

I nodded, unable to stop a small smile. "He loves it. Has

loved it for the past ten years, and all he wants is to be inde-
pendent from their clutches. Their reach. But in order for him
to be released from that, he needs to be married and on his
way to having little baby hoteliers who can continue the
Cavendish 'legacy.' When he was with *Emily*," I said, with
barely concealed spite, "it was pretty much assumed that after
their wedding The Cartwright would become his. After they
broke up..."

"Let me guess. His parents have been shopping for wives."

I rolled my eyes, biting into another Twizzler. "Yes, and it's
so gross, Fi. And it wasn't like Edward lied about it; we'd
talked about it but before we started dating. And falling for
each other."

My voice caught, and Fiona smoothed her palm down my
back. "And I was so *stupid* not to push the issue because I knew
it would be one. Because, spoiler alert, I am *not* what the
Cavendish family would consider a 'good match' for their
precious Edward. But we were so happy, and he seemed to no
longer *care* about them. Seemed to want something real and
authentic for once. And the real world, the reality of his life,
felt very far away."

Fiona nodded. "Especially in the beginning, it's easy to
ignore the problems until something like this happens and
you realize the tenuous ground you were walking on the entire
time."

I winced. "Yep. And that is exactly what happened. His
parents seemed kind of surprised to see us together, which
makes sense. They thought Edward was dating this woman
named Phoebe—"

Fiona looked suddenly murderous, but I shook my head.
"No, no, he *wasn't* dating her. But I don't think he necessarily
let them know that. Entirely. So then they come around and
see him kissing me. And they asked—" my face burned,

remembering the embarrassment. "They asked who I *was*. And he introduced me as his mentee."

"And then?" she asked.

"And I said, 'Is there any other word you'd use to describe who I am to you?' He said nothing. Just stared at the ground. For what felt like *years* but, in all seriousness, was probably only ten seconds. But it was enough. Enough to be..." I swiped away a traitorous tear, "dismissed like that. Like we hadn't woken up that morning in the same bed together. And fucked each other. And ate breakfast together and walked our dogs together. I know his parents are pieces of shit, and I get the complications of being with someone like me, but—" I trailed off.

Fiona stroked my hair, and for a few minutes, we both wordlessly watched the housewives shop for new shoes and gossip. It was such a shiny, shallow, stupid world, and I wanted to be whisked away to it. To a world where my boyfriend hadn't just denied my existence and my business wasn't days away from failing.

"Has he called you?" Fiona asked softly, and I nodded. Turned on my cell phone to show her the bevy of missed calls and desperate text messages.

"Hmmm," she said, tapping the screen. "You haven't spoken to him?"

"No, and I never will again," I said, even as I felt my heart break a little bit more at that thought. But I was so fucking *angry*.

"Hm."

I looked over at her. "Fiona."

"Yeah?"

"What are you hm-ing about over there?"

Fiona turned off the TV, and I gasped. "I need those housewives!"

But she grabbed my hands, forcing me to look at her. "A few things. After tonight, I'm going to need you to take a shower, open up all the windows, and go outside in the beautiful fresh air."

"Um, pass?" I said, horrified at her suggestions.

"*Roxy*," she warned.

"Okay, okay, *fine*," I said. "I have smelled better in my life."

"It'll make you feel better, I promise. And then I need you to consider talking to Edward."

"Nope," I said emphatically. "Not going to happen."

"Not immediately," she said, shaking her head. "But, like, a week from now. Let his cowardly ass stew for a while because he fucking deserves it. But I have to tell you something."

"What?"

"I like Edward," she smiled. "I know what he did was shitty and shady, and if you ever considered getting back together with him, you'd need to *trust* each other. But I've never seen you laugh more. Smile more. In a million years, I never saw you finding your soulmate in a smug, corporate businessman, but Roxy, sweetheart, I think you did."

I looked away, blinking away tears. "A *soulmate* wouldn't deny your existence."

"Soul mates are still human who make really stupid mistakes. A mistake I'm guessing Edward wishes he could take back. If he didn't want to *fix it*, then he would have just let you walk away." She picked up the phone, showing me Edward's messages.

Roxy, darling, can we please talk?

Matilda misses you. I miss you.

I've never felt this way about anyone before. Please.

"None of those are apologies," I pointed out.

"Right because he probably wants to do it in person because he's not *that* much of an asshole," Fiona replied smugly. "And I'm not saying you shouldn't put him through the goddamn wringer but think about Jimmy."

"What about him?" I asked.

"Can you even *compare* the feelings you had for Jimmy with the ones you have for Edward?"

I shifted, uncomfortable. "No," I finally said. "Jimmy was an asshole."

Fiona reached forward, touching my wrist. "I'm not sure if this mantra applies to McSpanky Pants."

I laughed, surprised. "I'm not sure I can believe you yet."

She wrapped me in a hug, kissing my cheek. "That's okay, sis. Just think about it. Shower, get some real food, go back to work. And let yourself slowly consider the possibility that Edward might deserve a second chance."

Fiona stayed another hour, letting me have more housewives before turning them off and leaving me to my obsessive, Edward-themed thoughts. And in the morning, I got up, showered, and took Busy Bee on a long walk in the cool spring air. Opened up the shop at noon to find Mack smiling and dancing to reggae as usual.

And Edward continued to call me, and I continued to ignore it.

But I did read his text messages.

48

EDWARD

One week later

$\mathcal{T}$he days were endless and gray.

I had a new routine now. Wake up, take Matilda for a walk, call Roxy, leave a voicemail. Go to work, where I could barely focus. Call Roxy, leave a voicemail. Attempt to avoid my parents and their dating suggestions at all costs. Call Roxy, leave a voicemail.

And at night, wallow in a depressing mix of guilt and shame. Playing those ten seconds over and over in my mind.

Are there any other words you'd use to describe me?

Screaming at the memory. Attempting to force open my mouth and say, "Oh, of course. Roxy is also my girlfriend. Isn't that great news?"

Because The Cartwright now felt empty and bleak without Roxy's snarky presence. And it was, after all, just a goddamn *building*.

A building I had sacrificed love for. A sacrifice I was quickly realizing wasn't at all worth it.

On day eight of my new routine, Elliott dragged me from my condo and took me to our favorite pub.

"Don't worry, mate. We're going to sit in a dark corner, and you're going to let me lecture your blue-blood ass for an hour," he'd said, shoving a baseball cap on my head.

"'kay," was all I could manage, and even when we got there, we sat silently for the first hour as I finished a pint and mindlessly watched football on the telly.

"This game is bloody awful," I finally said.

"And you're a bloody arsehole," Elliott replied, clapping me on the back so hard I winced. I'd called Elliott the day after the incident with my parents and had given him the gory details. He'd been silent on the other end, which I'd mistaken for supportive, but really he'd just been gathering fuel for his argument.

"You remember Dante?" he asked, and I turned, surprised at the subject change.

"My VP of Marketing?" I asked. "The one I set you up on a date with?"

Elliott nodded, handsome face breaking out in a wide grin. "Man of my dreams, Ed. I'm serious. We're in love, and I know it's only been a month, but it's different with him. Do you know what I mean?"

"Elliott that's... my God, that's brilliant news," I exclaimed, pulling him in for a hug. "Honestly, I couldn't be happier for you. Dante's quite the catch."

"I know it," he grinned. "And I've dated enough people to know this isn't some half-assed, temporary relationship. This is real."

I nodded, thinking of Roxy. Always thinking of Roxy.

"When you know, you know," I said, voice cracking. Elliott gave me a sympathetic look.

"So on to the part where you're an arse," he continued,

sympathy vanishing. "I realized something the other day. After I called my parents and told them about Dante."

"You *told* them?" I interjected.

"I did, mate," he said. "I told them about our relationship and our plans for the future. Marriage, babies, the whole fairy tale. I know it was a lot to expect from them, but I thought, deep down, if their son, their *child*, was in love—deeply in love —it wouldn't matter if it was a man or a woman or any other gender." Elliott swallowed, nodding his head. "I mean, right? Let's take away all the bullshit of our upbringing and goddamn legacies and wealth and keeping up appearances. Strip that all away, and they're my *parents*. We're a family. And when I told them I was in love, do you want to know what they said?"

I shook my head, a sick feeling in my stomach. Because he was speaking a truth the two of us had been tap-dancing around for years.

"They said it'd be fine if Dante and I wanted to keep our relationship a secret, but if I wasn't married to a woman within a year, they'd disown me." Elliott took a swig of beer, wincing. "Their legacy, their *money*, was and is more impor-tant to them than their own child. And I have spent the entirety of my life attempting to make them happy when real-ly..." the smile was back, "they're monsters. And newsflash, Ed: it's not their life."

A riot of emotion exploded in my chest. "They said that to you? Christ, Elliott, I'm so sorry."

He waved a hand between us. "I'm not. I'm sorry the two of us are still stupid enough to be *surprised* that they said that. Because I'm positive Edward and Rebecca Cavendish would say the same fucking thing if Roxy was a man, not a woman. And *shit*, they don't even like Roxy as she is."

"No," I said bitterly. "No, they don't. She doesn't, well, look the way they'd like. Or have a respectable job. Or a wealthy family my parents can milk for their societal connections."

"And you, Edward Christopher Cavendish, are willing to let *those two shit-heads* control your life. Who judge someone's value based on the way they look. Even though they've never been affectionate or loving or cared about you in any way. Even though I know you love that bloody hotel, but this city is filled to the brim with bloody hotels, and you could have any of them if you worked hard enough for it."

I rubbed a hand down my face, feeling the beard on my jaw from my lack of hygiene the past week. "Why do I want their love and approval so much?"

"Because, mate," he said. "You're the child, and they're the parent. You're set up to want that. But they should have given it. You don't have to *earn* it. And I think because of that, you royally fucked up with Roxy, and now you're miserable. So what does that say about living your life the way they want you to?"

"Goddammit," I said wearily, dropping my head into my hands. "You're right. Incredibly right. The most right a person can be, and I have no idea what to do about it."

The grin was back. "Well, that's where I have an idea."

49

ROXY

"All right, a little bit more to the left," Scarlett shouted up at Mack and I, balanced on two separate ladders and holding up our new sign. "No, the other left."

"Fuck, this is heavy boss," Mack grunted, hefting it with his shoulder. I had the power drill on my belt, bolts in my pocket.

"I know, I know. We just gotta line it up straight." I turned back to Scarlett. "How about now?"

"Um... I don't know. Maybe more to the right now?"

I glared down at my employee. "From up here, I don't know, it kind of sounds like you're fucking with us. You wouldn't be doing that, would you, Scar?"

"Oh no, boss," she said, grinning cheekily. "Just trying to help you two get it straight."

Ten minutes and a lot of grunting later, Mack and I had secured our new sign. I climbed down the ladder, looking up at it, shielding my eyes from the late afternoon sun.

"Well?" I said, turning to Mack and Scarlett. "What do you think?"

"It's glorious," Mack said with a nod. Per the business and

marketing plan that Edward and I had finalized two weeks ago —right before he broke my heart—I replaced my old, busted sign with a vintage sign that said 'TATTOOS' and lit up with glowing bulbs. It looked funky and old and managed to both blend in with our older block and stand out at the same time. Across the front of my shop, on the glass, was painted "Roxy's: No Crying Allowed."

"Yeah," I said, feeling slightly disgusted that Edward's suggestion was panning out so well. "It's hard to admit, but I like it too. A lot actually."

Scarlett squeezed my shoulder. "We're entering a new era, but it doesn't mean we have to change everything." She reached down, picking up the old sign. "Let's keep this and hang it up in the shop, what do you think? Like a tribute to our past."

"Love it," I said. "And Mack, can I talk with you in the back for a second? Scarlett, just give us a call if our new signage causes a surge of walk-ins." She winked at me before giving a cheeky salute.

I led Mack to the back, his giant bulk taking up most of the tiny room. I had a brief memory of Edward walking back here and pulling me onto his lap. Kissing me fervently, surrounded by financial reports and highlighters.

"Are you firing me?" Mack asked warily, hands folded across his stomach. "Because I'll straight-up cry."

I smiled. "No, the opposite. I already talked with Scarlett about this yesterday, but I just want to... check in. See how you're doing with working here. I really value you, Mack, but a lot of times I just let you and Scar run off and do your thing because I trust you. But as your supervisor," I paused, attempting to remember the script that Edward had helped me craft weeks ago, "as your supervisor, I want to make sure you're happy. Satisfied."

Mack's eyebrows shot up on his round head. "*Satisfied?* Aw, Roc. This is my favorite place to be, even if it is a bit of a shithole."

I grimaced. "I know. And I'm working on that. Hopefully with your and Scarlett's help. And I just want you to know that, you know, even with our financial woes, keeping you and Scarlett on as staff is my priority. You're my priority."

Mack grinned, squeezing my hand quickly. "Thanks, boss. We'll help anyway we can. Especially since Sir Edward is out of the picture now."

I opened my mouth, about to disagree except that it was true. I'd successfully ignored all of Edward's pleading calls and messages, which meant he *was* out of the picture.

My stomach twisted, since I had to deliver my presentation, filled with *Edward's* ideas, in two days and have then one final sit down with Professor Stevens. But then, after that, I would finally be free of that smug, corporate asshole.

"Yeah," I said, swallowing past a sudden lump in my throat. "It's just us now. And Edward's ideas are good, but they're just the beginning. Do you want to take the lead on our street fair next month?"

"Fuck yeah," he said, fist-bumping me. "I'm on it. Thanks for not firing me."

"Thanks for being so wonderful," I said, giving him a watery smile. Scarlett and Mack's total support for me and this business was more than I ever could have asked for.

Edward was right. Check-ins were good.

Another twist of my stomach, but it was replaced by a surge of happiness because, as Mack and I walked back out, Scarlett was chatting with two younger men who were animatedly pointing at some of my pieces hanging on the wall.

"Oh, hey, guys," Scarlett beckoned. "Come meet Roxy. She's our owner and the artist of those drawings."

"Nice to meet you," I said, shaking their hands. "What are you two looking for today?"

They shrugged before one gave me a shy grin. "I love sailor tattoos and always wanted one. Like my grandfather has. And, uh, we were out today and thought we'd stop in. We saw your sign."

Behind me, Mack and Scarlett were doing a little dance. I bit my lip, hiding a smile. "That so?"

"Yeah," he said. "It was fucking rad."

Fucking rad indeed.

50

EDWARD

*E*lliott and I were sitting in his executive office at The Logan, the hotel he'd run for almost the same amount of time I'd run The Cartwright. Where my hotel was older and elegant, The Logan was all modern. Different from The Cartwright, but I found myself oddly fascinated with the design as we sat there. It felt geometric, urban—futuristic in a way that piqued my interests.

"Are you finally going to fill me in on your Mystery Plan?" I asked, cradling the latte one of his assistants had pressed into my hand. It'd been nothing but sleepless nights the past two weeks.

"Yes. But I need you to prepare yourself because it's going to be some big changes," he said. "Dante and I are leaving New York City for a while."

"What?" I asked with concern, leaning forward. "Whatever for?"

Elliott grinned, sitting back in his chair. "Because I've done nothing but work my arse off for a decade, and I'm *tired*. The last time I took a vacation was *never*. And neither has Dante.

We're two workaholics, passionately in love, with no sense of how to actually *live*."

I crossed my legs. "So you're leaving The Logan? And Dante is quitting on me?"

"Yes," he said. "We'll both be done by the end of this month, and then we're packing up a bag and flying to Bali."

"*Bali*?" I exclaimed. "For how long?"

Elliott shrugged. "However long we want. Until we decide to travel someplace else. Or maybe we'll just live there forever, who knows?"

I knew I looked completely daft with my jaw hanging open and eyes wide. But I couldn't have been more stunned if an elephant strode into the room and started talking about profit margins.

"This is... surprising to say the least," I finally managed.

"And I haven't even gotten to the part that involves you," Elliott said. "Because I want you to take my place at The Logan. Here. As president, but *true* president. Not in name only like it's set up now with your parents. You'd still have a Board and stakeholders you'd report to. But it'd be your hotel, truly, and you could do whatever you wanted and make your own decisions, and you wouldn't have to be reliant on your parents for one bloody cent."

My best friend crossed his arms smugly, impressed with his Mystery Plan.

"I'm absolutely boggled over here," I admitted. "Can we start from the beginning?"

"Edward," Elliott started. "One thing I know to be very true about you. You love your job."

"I do," I said. "I love hospitality. I love hotels. I love The Cartwright. Or rather... I'm not sure anymore."

"Because you're only allowed The Cartwright if you play nice with your parents and do everything they say, which, as we talked about last week, is a crock of utter and complete shit."

I nodded. "I haven't seen them since that day in Central Park, although I've been dodging their calls as much as Roxy has been dodging mine, holed up in my office. All the final work for the charity ball I've been doing via email." I paused for a moment. "I don't miss them, Elliott."

"And that's who you gave up Roxy for," Elliott said gently, and my chest tightened painfully.

"So, I've been thinking. You love hotels. You don't like your parents. You love The Cartwright, but that means you're beholden to your parents and their bullshit marriage clause. What if you ran *this* hotel instead?"

His words were starting to sink in fully, clashing with the concept of my future I'd had for ten years. Marrying someone like Emily and starting a family. Taking over full ownership of The Cartwright. Finally having my father look me in the eye and say 'Good job, son,' which is our family's equivalent of *I love you*.

But then, well...

Then I walked into Roxy Quinn's tattoo parlor, and she'd smashed that future to absolute bits.

"I haven't been that invested the past two years, mate," Elliott said. "I'm not sure this business is for me, quite frankly. Or it was, but now I want to do something different. But you live and breathe this industry, and The Logan is on the cusp of some big, scary new changes."

"Oh, like what?" I asked, immediately perking up.

"Can't tell you, I'm afraid," Elliott said. "That's something our new president would be discussing with the Board."

"Cheeky bastard," I grinned. "Is this nepotism though? Shouldn't I go through an interview process? And fuck, my parents are going to kill me, and *fuck* what am I going to do?" I ran my hands down my face, an exhilarating combination of sheer excitement and spiky terror.

"First, let's not rush it. Spend a few days with me here, see what it's like. Meet the staff. Then, if you like it, let's set up an interview, get you some meetings with the Board. *Then* if they want to hire you, give notice at The Cartwright, help them find your replacement, and then tell your parents to bugger off because, remember, you don't care about their opinions anymore."

"God, it's like re-learning how to walk," I admitted, the thought of doing something against their wishes ingrained in my brain to feel terrible.

But it didn't have to feel terrible. Being with Roxy felt *glorious*, and if I could feel that way again, even just an iota, it'd be worth it.

"It is. And the days after I essentially told my parents to do the same thing, I felt like shit. Unloved. Unwanted. But then Dante came over and I remembered that's not true. And our family doesn't have to be our *family*. You're my family, Edward. My brother."

I nodded. "True. You're more a brother to me than George is. I'd do anything for you."

"And I'd do anything for you, mate," he said. "Like give you my hotel."

"Holy shit," I said again, falling back against the chair. "What is *happening*?"

"Whiskey," Elliott said, snapping his fingers. "Let me just call in some whiskey."

～

LATER, I opted for walking home instead of calling a driver. There was a phone call I needed to make—not Roxy this time.

Phoebe.

She felt like an innocent victim in all of this, and if I was going to take the right steps to shift my course in life, I knew I'd regret not telling her the truth.

She was surprised, of course, when I called.

"Your parents and my parents are quite furious with you, Edward," she said, but there was mirth in her voice.

"I'm well aware," I said dryly. "And I'm used to it. But I'm calling to say I'm sorry, well, for a lot of things, but I'm sorry if any of this is blowing back on you."

"It's really okay," Phoebe said. "And to be honest... I've met someone. Someone lovely."

"Really?" I said, voice brightening. "I'm happy for you."

"I'm happy for me too," she said. "I think our parents will have to give up the idea that you and I will be married and have tons of little babies."

I smiled into the phone. "Yes, they will. And Phoebe... I apologize for not being honest with you after our date about my intentions. It's a problem in my life I'm attempting to rectify. Attempting to be a more... authentic person."

"I appreciate that," she said. "And thank you."

We didn't chat for long after that—since we'd barely known each other—but she represented a piece of my old life I wanted settled.

I wasn't entirely sure I deserved Roxy taking me back. But I at least wanted to be my true self when I apologized.

51

EDWARD

One week later

My resignation letter burned a hole in my tuxedo pocket for the entirety of The Kenley Collection Charity Ball.

Through sheer force of will, I'd somehow managed to stay focused on the event the past few weeks, even as I'd been miserable, throwing myself into the smallest details. Oddly, knowing that I was leaving this place made my parents' endless, incessant criticism roll off my back like water.

The event, as usual, went off without a hitch. My brilliant staff transformed our ballroom into an elegant art gallery, and as I greeted friends of my parents and other big corporate donors, I could practically taste my freedom.

And I knew, after the event ended, I'd find my parents up in their suite, drinking a celebratory gin and tonic, as was their tradition. In years past I'd joined them, although I'd never once enjoyed it.

"You're still awake, I see?" I said, letting myself into their magnificent kitchen area. They were only supposed to be in New York for another two weeks before flying back to London.

"Just about," my mother said. "You know I always struggle to sleep after the bloody thing is over."

"It met your expectations, I presume?" I asked, already knowing the answer.

"Of course not," my father scoffed. "But there's always next year for improvements."

I slid my hands in my pocket, grasped the letter. "I won't be here next year to implement those improvements, I'm afraid." I slid the envelope across the table, directly between their half-filled glasses.

"And what is this?" my father asked, sliding the sheet of paper out.

"My resignation as the manager of The Cartwright Hotel," I said on a long exhale. I kept my back straight, chin lifted, imagining Roxy standing next to me. "I've taken a new job. Elliott is leaving The Logan, and I've been hired on to take his place as President."

My parents looked up sharply—and I felt not an ounce of regret.

"Ludicrous," my father said. "You are a Cavendish, Edward. You work for us."

"Not anymore, actually," I said. "I start with The Logan on Monday. I've set everything up for my successor, whoever that might be, but tomorrow is my last day here at The Cartwright. And actually, father, there isn't a damn thing you can do to stop me."

Which was the brutal truth—one I'd had to admit to myself in the darkest hours of each early morning, lying awake in my bed. The control my parents wielded over my life and decisions was emotional and manipulative—but it wasn't, ultimately, *real*. Or it was as real as I chose to believe it to be, which I had. For thirty-five long years.

"If this is about that Roxy woman—" my mother started.

I cut her off.

"It is about Roxy," I said. "But it's also about *me*. For my entire life, I made decisions that would fulfill your legacy, even when it made me distinctly *unhappy*. I loved this hotel," I said, surprised when my throat tightened. "I loved this hotel and gave it everything I had for ten years. You could have given me ownership at any time regardless of that bloody marriage clause. You could have given it to me because I am *good* at my job. And because I am your son."

I had never seen my parents exhibit such shock in their entire lives. Shock, betrayal, but still—just as Elliott had predicted—not a bit of understanding.

"Roxy and I are no longer dating, although I'm pretty sure she was my soulmate," I said, and the fury was back, seething in my chest. "And that is because of a massive mistake that I made. A mistake I won't ever make again. Living my life for myself means breaking free from this legacy. Creating my own." My voice shook with passion, but I wasn't scared. I wasn't nervous. I felt *liberation*.

"This is our family's *responsibility*," my father snapped, slapping his palm down on the table. He was trying to manipulate me again. Scare me.

But I wasn't having it.

I leaned forward, making sure my parents could *feel* how serious I was. Locked eyes with them both as they gazed back at me with anger and disappointment.

I thought about Roxy. About the woman I had lost.

Never again.

"And this is my fucking *life*," I said, before turning on my heel and striding out of the room.

52

ROXY

I took a deep breath, steadying my nerves, heart galloping.

I could do this.

Of course I could do this. I'd known nothing about running a business before I'd started this program. Nothing about marketing or strategy or building a customer base. I'd sat in classes filled with people I was pretty sure were smarter and more talented than I was, but I'd stayed. Finished everything.

And as long as I passed this presentation, I would graduate.

You're an incredibly savvy businesswoman, Roxy Quinn.

I looked down at the floor, willing Edward's voice out of my head. He'd said he'd be here for my presentation, but that was almost a month ago. When we'd been dating. Before he'd denied my existence.

Plus, I wasn't sure I'd be able to give this presentation, talk about our ideas, while looking at his refined, handsome face.

I'd burst into tears.

So instead I stared out into the dark auditorium, hearing the gentle rustle of the audience, and picked up my notes.

"Good afternoon," I said, clearing my throat. "My name is Roxy Quinn, and I am the owner of a small tattoo parlor called Roxy's in Washington Heights. I assumed ownership from a previous owner who had not invested in marketing, branding, or customer outreach in more than a decade. And to complicate matters, the neighborhood we operate in is changing. Becoming trendier and attracting a different kind of audience—a younger audience, which seems to not identify with the older, more traditional style of my shop. The profit we generate from walk-in appointments is down 30% from five years ago, and appointments are down 7%. Overall, our customer retention is good," I said, flipping through a few pie slides that showed various pie charts, "but we lack in awareness and branding."

I looked out into the audience again, but it was so dark I couldn't really see.

Not that I wanted to see Edward.

"My mentor, Edward Cavendish," I continued, surprised that I'd managed to say his name without tears, "is the manager of The Cartwright Hotel and has a decade's worth of business experience. With his guidance, we crafted a branding strategy that positions Roxy's as the tattoo parlor your punk-rock grandfather used to go to." I switched to a slide that showed the difference in my store fronts—the first one, taken by Edward when we'd started, showed my formerly grimy window with a peeling sign that looked decidedly *unwelcoming*. Our new store front, with the vintage flashing lights, looked cheerful but still trendy. And the painted sign on the window: *Roxy's: No Crying Allowed.*

Laughter rippled through the audience, and I smiled. Seeing the two storefronts side by side as I'd put this together had been illuminating. Edward had been right again, *goddammit*: it was often hard to see the changes you needed to make because you were too close. You need outside eyes. Like a mentor.

A sexy, funny, kind, silly, growly, bitey mentor with a smile that made your heart race faster.

"Anyway," I said, more to myself than to the audience. "Edward and I decided that what made Roxy's special was that we *weren't* going to be a trendy, hipster paradise for tattoo lovers. This shop has been around since 1975," I said. "We were tattooing people when it was illegal. We were tattooing people when society considered ink to be something prisoners and terrifying gang members had. When the act of having a tattoo was subversive and strange." I clicked through a few more slides, showing the changes we'd made in the shop. They were subtle but made a difference. "So moving forward, our branding will reflect that: the slight danger, the counter-culture energy of tattoo parlors. And to launch all of this, we'll be hitting the tattoo convention scene in New York, New Jersey, and Pennsylvania pretty hard, wanting to drum up shop awareness and gain some new customers. And we'll be hosting a street fair in a month, coordinated with the other small businesses in a three-block radius. Music, games, face-painting, and ink," I said, ticking them off on my fingers.

I flipped through a few more slides: profit margins. Financial comparisons from last year to this year. A few highlighted sections from my business plan. I felt oddly confident up there, putting the mistakes I'd made out in the open. Welcoming the feedback—both positive and negative—that Edward had given me. Recognizing the bigger picture: that running a business can be a lonely, isolating act. And only by welcoming other businesspeople into your life, and trusting their guidance, can you gain *support*.

I thought about my first real mentor meeting with Edward when I'd all but thrown him out of the parlor in the first ten minutes.

And now, of course, I was angry with him for an entirely different reason.

"Thank you again for listening," I added at the end, surprised that twenty minutes could fly by so quickly. "I was looking forward to this Capstone Experience, and in fact chose this program specifically to participate in this." *You can do it—so close!* "I... want to thank my mentor, Edward, for his thoughtful and creative wisdom and guidance. The hands-on learning, the job shadowing—all of it contributed to the presentation you see before you, and I truly believe that 'Roxy's' will have a stronger future because of it."

I sat down quickly to applause, pressing a hand against my chest where a churning emotion was gathering there, as violent as a storm. The next student was already setting up, and it was dark, so no one could see the tears I wiped quickly away.

An hour later, and I walked into Professor Stevens' office to find Edward sitting elegantly in a chair, long legs crossed, dapper in a dark blue suit and a yellow tie. He was typing away on his phone, and my professor wasn't there.

"Oh," I said, stopping up short, even though this was our last check-in meeting and technically, regardless of our relationship, he was supposed to be here. But the shock of seeing him was like a swift bolt of lightning to all of my senses. Edward looked up, and a smile burst across his features. A real smile. A just-for-Roxy smile.

"Roxy," he said. "It's good to see you."

I settled gingerly in the chair across from him, heart racing faster than when I'd given my fucking presentation. "Can't say the same."

He grimaced. "Well deserved." He turned around in his chair, shuffling for a moment before pulling out a small bouquet of pink daisies. "Before our meeting started, I just wanted to congratulate you on your presentation." He pressed the daisies into my hand, tips of our fingers barely brushing together. "I was in the back, a bit incognito, I'm afraid. I wanted to be there, to support you, but given what..." he trailed off, looking at the open door, "... well, today is about you and your accomplishments. If my presence was going to be an angering distraction, I didn't want to draw attention to it."

The daisies bobbed their heads cheerfully as those same stupid tears threatened to come spilling back over. "I thought you hadn't come." And I wanted to shove those vulnerable-sounding words right back into my mouth.

Edward shook his head. "Oh, Roxy... I'm sorry. Of course I was there. I wanted to be there. And your presentation was absolutely smashing."

"Smashing?" I repeated, my lips quirking up. Traitors.

He opened his mouth to respond, but then Professor Stevens walked in wearing a harried expression and leaving a trail of papers behind her.

"Edward! Roxy!" she exclaimed. "So happy to see you both." She collapsed into her office chair. "Roxy, well *done* on your presentation. Truly wonderful. Well-researched and strategized." She leaned forward. "Obviously, we'll be final-izing grades by the end of the week, but I don't want you to worry. You'll be donning a graduation gown two weeks from now."

Relief coursed through me, and I took a big, satisfying

breath. "That makes me incredibly happy to hear, thank you. I worked hard for it."

"That you did," Professor Stevens agreed. "And it seems like this pairing worked out, which I thought it would. I know your industries are pretty markedly different, but I had a feeling the two of you belonged together."

I almost fainted, and Edward coughed awkwardly for about a minute.

"Sorry," I said, apologizing for us both. "Yes, Edward and I worked very well together, and I'll be implementing his ideas in the future for sure."

I glanced at him out of the corner of my eye, and he was smiling warmly at me. My fingers itched to reach over and hold his hand.

"Wonderful," Professor Stevens said. "And as of," she glanced at her watch, "right now, your formal mentoring program is now over. Although I encourage you to stay in touch, continue to support each other. I know Edward has friendships with many of his mentees."

"That's right," he said, eyes on mine. "I take my relationships very seriously."

Except when you're denying them, I wanted to say.

"Okay," I said noncommittally. "Well, I look forward to receiving news of my grade. And thank you for all that you've done for me. Both of you," I said, standing up to shake her hand.

"My pleasure. You're a natural businesswoman, Roxy," she said. "And I'm happy to see that Edward helped you find your confidence."

"Yeah," was all I could manage because Edward had helped me find a lot of things.

"And correct me if I'm wrong, but did I read in the paper

that you're leaving The Cartwright?" Professor Stevens continued.

I was half out of the door, bag slung over my shoulder, but I paused and turned to see Edward, hands in his pockets.

"You're correct, actually," he replied. "It was a hard decision because, as you know, I work with my family members. Who are *not* happy about this, but I've been assured by other, rational people in my life that they will somehow find the will to go on."

Professor Stevens laughed, and I tried to take in this new information. Edward wasn't at The Cartwright anymore? So did that mean... he was out from under their thumb?

"Well, The Logan is lucky to have you," she replied. "And I know that working with family can certainly have its drawbacks."

I slid out the door, thoughts racing, as they continued their conversation. I didn't care if Professor Stevens thought it was odd—everything was done. School, presentation, working with Edward.

I was a free woman technically, in more ways than one. And nothing could have prepared me for the emotional turmoil I felt at that recognition, so different from the calm happiness I'd expected.

I shoved open the back door, taking in deep, gulping breaths in the twilight of the parking lot, clutching the daisies. For the first time in a year, I wasn't sure what to do next; I had no schoolwork, no class. No mentoring meetings with Edward. The shop was closed for the day.

A peculiar emptiness slid through me, and I could feel tears building swiftly again.

"You can't avoid me forever, Roxy darling," Edward said behind me. I ignored him for a moment, striding quickly toward the subway station.

"Watch me try," I bit back, turning to find Edward too close —too alluring, too tempting. I took a step back, scowling. Arms over my chest.

"Thank you for coming. And for the flowers. And for the mentoring. I truly appreciate it," I said. "But the rest of our friendship and... and relationship is over, so I don't see the point of continuing to talk to each other."

His blue eyes burned like bright stars in the dim light. "Can I at least apologize to you in person? Apologies over the phone are rubbish, in my opinion."

Fiona's advice danced through my subconscious, but I shook my head. "Not necessary. I'm sure you are sorry. But it won't change anything." I tapped my wrist, my tattoo. "Never Again, remember?"

"Roxy, I'm so incredibly sorry about the park—"

"Stop," I snapped, silencing his apology. Anger rippled across his handsome features.

"So it's one strike and you're out?" Edward asked, bright eyes narrowed now.

I shrugged. "My rule. Doesn't matter if the finality of it makes you uncomfortable."

Edward took a step closer so that I had to crane my neck to look up at him. "I'm not *uncomfortable*, love. I'm bloody miserable."

"Yeah, well, so am I," I snapped, heading quickly down the subway steps, refusing to turn back and look at him.

53

EDWARD

*I*t was well past midnight as I skulked along quietly with my dog, feeling utterly broken hearted.

It'd been harder than I thought seeing Roxy today.

Watching her shine at a presentation I knew she'd personally spent months fretting over.

I loved the proud tilt of her chin, the strong glint in her eye. The way she'd let herself change and grow over the time of our mentorship. I was so proud of her it physically hurt, and instead of spending this day licking champagne from her gorgeous skin (my original plan), we were apart. Broken up. Alone.

I wouldn't be surprised if she'd burned those pink daisies back at her apartment. The fury that radiated from her skin had been white-hot and dangerous. I hadn't wanted to apologize to her in a *parking lot,* but I was desperate for her to hear my words. And I'd been furious when she stopped me.

Because if she wouldn't even let me apologize, then there was no hope, was there?

I sank down onto a bench, staring up at a few barely there stars, and Matilda climbed up next to me.

"You still like me, right?" I asked her big, dopey face. She responded by licking my cheek for a full minute. There was a buzzing against my thigh, and as I pulled out my mobile, my heart stopped.

A message from Roxy.

Which could be a photo of her giving me the middle finger. Or burning a tie I'd left at her place. But still, I opened it with trembling fingers and shaky breath.

Are you really not working for your parents anymore?

I stared at it, utterly stunned.

I hit 'dial,' fully aware this was a risky bet. And when her midnight voice came over the line, I was already smiling like a bloody fool.

"A little late, Dilbert," she replied, and I wondered if it meant anything that she wasn't sleeping either.

"Well, you texted me, remember?" I said. I pictured her scowling and missed her terribly.

"I was just surprised when I overheard you tell Professor Stevens that you don't work for The Cartwright anymore."

"So were my parents," I said wryly. "Although 'surprised' isn't quite the word. I think it might be... horrified? I believe they're drawing up the papers for me to be disowned as we speak."

There was silence on the other end. "You're joking," she finally said.

"Not really," I admitted. "Although I guess 'disown' is a bit dramatic since nothing legal is happening. We're still biologically related, and they promised to coldly welcome me at all family functions both here in America and in England. But I no longer have any rights or claims to the Cartwright empire and legacy, and I, well, can't change my mind. They want nothing to do with me when it comes to that hotel."

Another longer silence, this one laden with feeling.

"You loved that hotel," she said, and she sounded truly sad. My heart twisted but not because of some bloody hotel.

Because I was hopelessly in love with *Roxy*.

"I did," I said, choosing my words carefully. "I loved it very much. And it was very, very cruel of them to keep it from my reach for so long. To make my happiness contingent upon their endorsement—marrying someone only *they* approved of. A business obligation, not love." The words rushed out of me, and there was real anger there. These past weeks, Elliott had shaken me from my complacency. His bold choices and bravery made me realize that it was my life, mine to live fully. To embrace and make mistakes and laugh and fuck up and a million other things.

"You would never have made them happy, Edward," Roxy said. "They would have withheld their affection for your entire life. Regardless of who you married or how well the hotel did. You'd have been angling for their love until they died."

"And then they'd haunt me from the grave, passive-aggressively pointing out my mistakes and undermining my authority," I replied. "My only real regret is letting it happen for so long."

"That's your only regret?" she asked.

I sighed. "No. That's not my only regret." The memory of that day in the park tangled between us like a web. "Can I come over? To talk with you?"

"We're talking now," she said, and I heard those walls come roaring back up.

Fuck fuck fuck.

"I can't... Roxy, I need to talk with you in person. About what happened in the park with my parents. Not over the phone. Please."

"No," she said firmly. "You cannot. I've satisfied my morbid curiosity, so it's probably good if we stop talking now."

"No, don't—" I begged, but she'd already hung up the phone.

~

THE NEXT DAY, after some casual online digging, I sat in the reception area for the law offices of Cooper Peterson Stackhouse, holding a giant latte. When Fiona strode out to see her mystery appointment, she stopped dead in her tracks.

"Does that have caffeine in it?" she said, pointing one long, manicured finger.

"Of course. I'm not a total monster," I shrugged.

"Come on, Sir Edward," she said, and I followed her dutifully into her offices. "And I'll take that, *thank you very much*."

She perched on the edge of her desk, and when I went to sit in a chair, she shook her head.

"Cowards don't get to sit, even ones I happen to like."

"You still like me?" I asked, incredulous.

She held out her thumb and index finger, squeezed them a centimeter apart. "Just this much," she said. "And I'll say I currently like you a whole hell of a lot more than my parents do."

"Well, I would have gone to them first, but I was pretty sure they'd put my head on a pike. As a warning to all the other wealthy businessmen who might try and date their daughter."

"Fair assessment," she nodded. "So, let me guess. You're trying to get back into Roxy's good graces because you're in love with her?"

I rubbed a hand down my face. "Fiona, I'm losing my mind. Between the wracking guilt and the fact that I think my heart is actually, physically broken, I'm a mess. And yes, I want to get back into her good graces, and if she was magnanimous enough to take me back, it'd make me the luckiest man in the world. Truly. But right now, I only want to apologize to her face-to-face. She deserves that. Even if that's all I get to do I'll be grateful. Because right now, we can't even become friends with this hanging between us." I paused. "And yes, in case it's not abundantly clear, I am in love with her."

Fiona tilted her head. "Roxy doesn't forgive easily. It's one of her most endearing qualities."

"I'm well aware," I said dryly. "Do you have any ideas? Anything that could help?"

Fiona tapped her lip. Took a long sip of coffee. Let me wait, standing in her office like a penitent. "How do you think Roxy felt that day in the park? When you weren't honest about who she was to you?"

"Embarrassed," I said, wincing at the memory. "I'm sure she also felt dismissed. Diminished. Small."

Fiona nodded. "Is there anything in your life that gives you those same feelings?"

"Well, it used to be my parents," I said, and she smirked. "But now... I guess I'm still terrified of public speaking. Hate it more than anything on this earth."

Fiona snapped her fingers. "That's right! Roxy told me that." She bounced on her stilettos. "I have the best idea, and you're going to hate it."

I smiled. "Can't be worse than the past few weeks."

"It might be," she said. "And good thing you came to me first. Because you're going to need an emissary."

54

ROXY

e were only an hour into my graduation party, and I'd already reached my embarrassment quota. My parents had decorated the house with giant pictures of me from the time I was in diapers until just recently. In our small backyard, they'd hung poster board with more photos, had printed copies of my business plan for guests to read. It felt like every person I knew was crammed into our backyard—and since this was Queens, neighbors streamed in when they heard the music. And stayed for the cheap beer and taco bar.

The Hand Grenades were well into their set, and as Fiona and I danced to my parents covering 'Heart of Glass' by Blondie, I tried to lose myself in this moment of accomplishment.

Because I'd *done it*.

Gotten accepted into an MBA program. Completed it in a single year all while working full-time. Had done something I thought was *impossible*. Had a plan and a strategy for the future, and even though owning a business was still stressful, I no longer felt as overwhelmed.

I'd been looking forward to this day for a *year*.

And I missed Edward. Terribly.

"You miss Edward," Fiona smirked over the music, blonde hair flying around her face. My only request for my graduation party was that she come *not* in a business suit. So she'd dressed in a long pink dress that essentially made her the most beautiful person here.

"Lies, all lies," I shot back, wondering how on Earth it was possible that *certain sneaky siblings* could know your thoughts before you'd even voiced them.

"You can miss him. It's okay," she said, throwing her arms up in a cheer. "It doesn't diminish your accomplishments. You're only *human*."

I rolled my eyes. "I never think about Edward, so I have no idea what you're talking about."

"Lies, all lies," she mimicked, and I scowled.

"I'm dancing over here," I said, shimmying over to Mack and his wife, Rita, who were doing some kind of jig. "Mack and Rita won't say anything."

"Oh, is Fiona talking about how you miss Edward and all you do is moan about how much you miss him?" Mack asked, twinkle in his eyes.

Fiona and Rita laughed as I propped my hands on my hips.

"I am your *boss*," I said, but it lacked heat, and moments later, I burst into laughter. I was still laughing when the band stopped playing, exiting the small stage, although my parents stayed at the microphone.

"Is everyone enjoying Roxy's *motherfucking graduation party?*" My dad yelled into the mic, and a raucous cheer went up. Someone handed me a cup of cold beer, and I sipped it gratefully. It was only the end of May, but the sun was beating down, soaking our backyard in sultry, late-spring heat.

"We wanted to take a moment, before the party *really* got going, and say how proud we are of Roxy for this amazing accomplishment," my mom chimed in. Fiona reached over and held my hand. "I have to say, Sandy and I don't entirely understand 'business' or 'business school' or even 'business plans.' But what we do understand is Roxy's drive and passion to create a better life for herself. To lift up her tattoo parlor and make it something that will last."

I wiped my eyes.

"So thank you for being here and supporting Roxy on her journey. And before we get back to the music, there is one person here tonight who had a special message he wanted to share with Roxy."

I assumed it was Mack, but he was shrugging in confusion. Fiona let go of my hand, and when I turned, she was beet red, nervously biting her lip.

I narrowed my eyes. "Fiona..." I said slowly. And then I heard a nervous sound, someone coughing into the mic, and a crisp English accent.

"Um... hello everyone."

Up on the stage, in a cream linen suit, was Edward.

IT WAS NOT an easy crowd for anyone—but especially not for someone like Edward who struggled with public speaking so much he once told me he had regular nightmares about it. Would wake up in a cold sweat, heart racing.

This was an audience comprised almost entirely with punk rock fans, tattooed clients and fiercely loyal family members.

If anyone was going to get egged on stage tonight, it was going to be Edward.

And it was obvious he was well aware of that: face red, hands shaking, voice unsteady.

"My name is Edward Cavendish, and I am, or rather *was*, Roxy's mentor in her MBA program. I was also her boyfriend, although she has since broken up with me for very valid reasons." He said this in a rush, and it shocked me to my core.

The audience seemed similarly stunned.

"I don't enjoy public speaking particularly, or ever, or at all, and if I faint up here, just, um, leave me. But before I faint, I wanted to apologize to you Roxy."

Holy shit.

"You see, I did something absolutely awful. I denied who Roxy was to me, what she meant to me. A woman I was, and still am, absolutely, positively, and completely in love with."

His voice trembled. Someone *boo*ed him, and he looked moments away from passing out.

Fiona took my hand again, squeezing it. My jaw hung completely open.

"And I have no excuse for what I did, nor should I. No reasoning beyond utter cowardice. I'm ashamed of my actions, and the only reason I'm here today is not to beg for you to take me back because I'm not sure I deserve that. But you deserve a true apology."

Edward's eyes met mine, blazing blue with regret and pain. My heart was trying to climb out of my mouth through my throat.

"I'm sorry, Roxy. For everything. No forgiveness required; I just needed you to hear those words. And to tell you again how proud I am of you and what you're going to accomplish with your life. Over the past three months, I've watched you blossom into a savvy businesswoman. Watched you take on your role wholeheartedly, embrace all the terrifying change that comes from being in charge." He slid one trembling hand into his pocket as he gripped the mic with the other. "You care deeply for your staff. Deeply for your clients. And deeply for the art form that you create every day. And those attributes—more than any business plan or mentor—will make you successful. Thank you for letting me be a very small part of that."

He coughed nervously again, gave a shaking smile. Gave me a small nod and then exited the stage. There was a smattering of applause, another *boooo*, and then someone chanted "*Bring back The Hand Grenades.*" Edward disappeared behind the house quietly, without glancing back, as my parents came back up.

Meanwhile I stood stock-still, emotions in shreds, mouth hanging open.

"Well, that was Edward," my mother said, arching an eyebrow at me with a coy smile. "A lovely young man. And I think that was such a nice message about forgiveness. Opening up our hearts and letting in the people who may have hurt us, ever-so-briefly."

I gave a massive eye-roll, but Fiona tugged on my hand.

"Listen," she pleaded.

"Because all of us are stupid sometimes, isn't that right?" she said, and the audience, predictably, cheered in response. "And all of us deserve a second chance."

She said that right to me, with a calm smile, an *approving* smile, and I knew what she and my father were trying to convey.

"Now let's fucking *party!*" she wailed, and The Hand Grenades kicked off a new song. Fiona tugged me to the edge of the crowd.

"I'm going to guess Edward's probably out in the street, dry-heaving into our bushes," Fiona said. "And *no,* I'm not going to apologize for coordinating his public apology and also a nice little moment between Mom and Dad earlier today."

"He spoke with them?" I hissed. "About what?"

"We wanted them to know what he was going to do, and he wanted to make sure they didn't think it was a cheap ploy to get into your pants or whatever. And they gave him a little bit of a hard time about what he did, and then they forgave him."

A long pause hung between us, heavy with meaning.

"I think finding the kind of love, the kind of *connection,* that you and Edward have is rare. It doesn't happen every day. And he has certainly suffered these past couple weeks, Roc. He's a wreck. But *so are you.*"

"So?" I huffed.

"Think about after Jimmy cheated on you," Fiona said, exasperated. "Remember? You were pissed at him, furious, embarrassed. Hurt for a long time. But you weren't still in love with him, were you?"

I exhaled, bit my lip. Suddenly I felt ready to cry *again.* "No, I wasn't."

"Why are you crying right now?" Fiona asked, smoothing a palm over my hair. "My big sister doesn't cry over anyone."

"Because every time I think about Edward and how we're no longer together, I cry and cry," I said, leaning into Fiona's shoulder as she wrapped her arms around me. Held me for a minute as I processed whatever-the-fuck just happened. The emotional bomb that exploded in the middle of our backyard.

"Go talk to him, Roc," she said.

I pulled back, and when I didn't move immediately, she gave me a tiny shove.

"Do I look snotty and gross?" I asked.

But she only shook her head. "You look like a woman in love."

55

EDWARD

I was pretty sure I had actually physically died on that stage and was now a ghost, wandering around this street outside of the Quinn family bungalow in Queens. I half-expected one of the more terrifying-looking audience members to come out and beat my face in.

What I *didn't* expect was Roxy, looking like a punk-rock angel, to come striding up like a woman on a mission. I held up my palms, expecting her to toss a drink in my face. But instead she curled her fingers in the lapels of my suit jacket and yanked our lips together.

For a moment, I was too surprised to respond—but then my body recognized *Roxy,* and my arousal was so swift it hurt. I threaded my fingers through her long blonde tresses, holding her in place as I ravaged her mouth. Tasted her lips, licked inside with my tongue, allowed a storm of sensation to flow through us.

"I really missed you," Roxy said when she finally let us come up for air. She was panting slightly, hair mussed.

"Roxy," I started, palm stroking her cheek. "I... to be honest, I thought I'd never see you again after today. And I've missed you so fucking much. That day in the park was pure cowardice; I was so bloody caught up in their expectations and the pressure and all those years of living my life for *them*. And as you were walking away, it was like..." I searched for the right words, "it was like having a bucket of ice-cold water dumped on my head. This realization that *all* of that meant nothing."

"I want you to live the life that you want," she said. "Free from their expectations and judgments." She bit her lip, worrying it between her teeth. "And... I'm sorry too. I'm not really the forgive-and-forget type, and I wished we had talked later. About what had happened. I know you tried to reach out to me—"

"I'm pretty sure I deserved to marinate in that horrible, guilt-ridden, angsty limbo, love," I said.

"You did," she said with a particularly sly smile. "But I don't want you in that limbo anymore. I don't want *us* in that anymore, okay?"

I smoothed a hand down her back, bringing her flush against my body. "Okay. Tell me what you want."

"To be your girlfriend again. And for you to spend an entire week with your head between my legs as penance."

"That's not a penance, love," I said. "That's my idea of heaven. And do you think your party-goers will miss you for an hour? I have an idea."

She licked her lips. Tipped up on her toes and brushed her mouth against mine.

"What did you have in mind, Dilbert?"

I winked at her. "Not quite that."

～

AFTER A TAXI RIDE in which Roxy and I barely kept our hands off each other, we pulled up in front of the Greenspring Country Club, the most exclusive club in Manhattan. My parents and I were members, as were the majority of the inner circle the Cavendishes navigated through. As we stepped out, Roxy tugged down her plaid skirt and ripped fishnet stockings.

"Um... not quite dressed for the *club*," she said dryly, looking up at the stretch of manicured green lawn in front of us.

"I don't bloody care," I said. "Yesterday was my last day at The Cartwright, and when I went to go say goodbye to my parents, they were snobby and obnoxious about it. They're furious that I'm moving to The Logan because they think it's essentially a trash hotel and doesn't have the elegant reputation of The Cartwright."

Roxy snorted. "I'm sorry, but your parents are fucking ridiculous."

We strode inside, the front desk staff giving Roxy an open-mouthed look, but I was a Cavendish, and they knew not to bother me. "That they are, love. That they are. And I really *don't* care what they think about me anymore, I promise, but I feel like, to truly make amends..."

I pushed open a heavy white door that led to a small garden area where my parents were sitting around a table with glasses of chilled white wine.

"Edward?" my mother said, hand pressed to her chest in shock. "What are you doing here?" There was no outward affection there or concern—more like annoyance.

"Mother, Father," I said. "How are you?"

"Annoyed at this interruption," my father snapped.

"Ah well, fear not. This will only take a moment," I said, holding Roxy's hand. Her face was a wonder of amusement and complete bafflement, but her back was straight and chin tilted high.

"This magnificent woman right here," I started, "is Roxy Quinn. My girlfriend. And I quite hope in the future she'll be more than just that." Roxy squeezed my fingers. "I fell in love with her fairly immediately—she's hard not to love—but then that day in the park, when we saw you, I denied that. To her, to you, and to myself. I think I've learned these past weeks that denying who you love is utterly painful and heart-breaking."

I waited for my parents to smile or nod or show some kind of mild human compassion, but they looked quietly furious. "And I know that I've not lived up to your expectations, especially as compared to Jane and George. And I'm okay with that."

My father bristled in his chair, but I mustered on. "Elliott's found love too. With my former employee Dante. And they're running off to Bali together to live their lives. And you know why? Because life's too bloody short not to be in love with yourself, your choices, your job, your soulmate." I looked at Roxy whose eyes were shining. "I'm in love with Roxy, and I have a sneaking suspicion she might feel the same way about me."

Roxy shrugged with a wry grin.

"If we're invited to family events, and she wants to come, I will bring her. She will be with me. We will be *together*. And I don't give a *fuck* if you care or not. If you approve or not." I swallowed roughly. "I've spent the entirety of my life desperate for your love and approval."

A strange look passed over my mother's face.

"And I refuse to work for it anymore." I walked over and shook my father's hand, kissed my mother's cheek. "Have a safe journey home. If you want to talk about this, you know how to reach me. And when you're next in the States, I hope you come by to say hello to Roxy and me."

I looked at Roxy, seeking some sense that she could really see how unafraid I was. She was grinning broadly, hands entwined in mine like she'd never let go.

"It was nice to see you again," Roxy said with a nod toward my parents. "Edward and I are off to have some pretty kinky sex."

I laughed, tugging Roxy through the door, wrapping my arm around her shoulders.

"How was that?" I asked as we strode through the doors and down the lush hallway. Gold was everywhere, carved into the filigree and chandeliers hung heavy with crystals.

"I'd say that moment was truly, authentically *you*," Roxy said, eyes bright. "And uh... your mother's behind us."

"What—" I started, turning around, and came face-to-face with my mother. Who didn't look in tears but looked... *something*.

"Edward," she said. "And... Roxy, yes?"

"You got it," Roxy said, eyebrow raised.

"I..." she looked away. "I just wanted to say that perhaps, when we're in the States next spring, the two of you could have tea with me. At the club. Or... at your new job."

She said *new job* the way one might say *barrel filled with poisonous snakes,* but it was a start.

"Um... sure," I said. "I think Roxy and I could do that."

My mother tilted her chin. "Do you own anything that is not essentially ripped in two, dear?"

I worried briefly for my mother's safety, but Roxy smiled sweetly.

"No," she said. "I do not. But I'm sure I can find something club-appropriate."

My mother actually *smiled*. "Yes, well, when I was your age

377

I used to sneak out to this ghastly pub down the street wearing the most ludicrous outfits." She sniffed. "I see the appeal of these stockings."

We all looked at Roxy's torn fishnets, and I wondered if I'd fallen into a wormhole.

"Oh they're super comfy," Roxy said, twisting her legs to show them off. "I can bring you a pair if you want?" Her voice was light, absent of any sarcasm.

My mother's face reddened. "Oh, that... that won't be necessary. Just bring yourself. If you would like." My mother looked at me. *Really* looked at me. And I knew in that moment we'd never have the relationship that Roxy had with her parents. I'd never receive the love and approval I craved from them.

But. We were probably going to be... okay. And okay I was fine with.

"Well, I must carry on. I will call you when we land in Heathrow."

"I'd like that," I said and kissed her cheek again. And then she scurried off, flouncy hat in tow.

"Huh," Roxy said. "That was unexpected."

"It was but... I think it was good, yeah?"

"Yes it was," Roxy agreed. "And should we have that kinky sex now?"

I gave her a small nip on her jaw, and she curled her body into mine. "I plan to have kinky sex with you all night long, love," I said. "But first we should go back to your graduation party."

56

ROXY

One month later

$\mathcal{T}$he street fair raged all around us.

Out front, my parents crooned into microphones as people danced around them. Mack and Scarlett were happily doing flash tattoos for fifty dollars, and there'd been a steady line all day. My fingers ached, and my neck was cramped from helping, but I was finally taking a quick break to greet my boyfriend who'd arrived in an expensive three-piece suit.

"Dilbert," I said, head tilted.

"Roxy darling," he replied, lips tilted in a smile. I reached forward, grabbed his tie, and pulled him in for a hungry kiss. "Quite the street fair you've got going on."

"It's been a success so far," I agreed. "Tons of new customers, and people are really liking our rebrand."

His lips lifted gracefully. "Hm. That new sign seems to be working wonders."

"Yes, although we all know the *original* sign was really the best."

"Do we now?" he mused, cupping his chin. "Or are all of these ideas the stupendous, magnificent workings of your *mentor*?"

I brought him toward one of the black leather chairs where I'd already gotten everything prepped. "Maybe," I hedged. "Although I might have to be convinced later."

I kissed his cheek, pausing to bite his earlobe. His fingers flexed against my lower back. "I'm happy to convince you," he rasped. "Just say the word, love."

"In all seriousness," I said, snapping on black latex gloves. "The street fair is a huge success. Huge. I think next week, we'll finally start seeing walk-ins again. Maybe even make *more money* than we spend this month."

"Always a sign of progress," he said. "And I led my first shareholders meeting at The Logan this morning and *didn't* pass out. It was by no means my favorite thing to do, but after apologizing to you in front of a group of people carrying knives and then declaring my kinky sex life in front of my parents at a country club, going over financial reports with a handful of rich people doesn't seem so bad."

"Happy to hear I could help," I said. "And strip. Shirt, tie, jacket."

Edward gave me a fairly indecent look and then slowly removed the requested items of clothing: shrugging off his jacket. Sliding his tie loose. Unbuttoning his shirt one by one. As usual, I admired the way the clothing clung to his broad shoulders, his lean muscles, all the alluring things we might do with that tie later.

"Check out Sir Edward," Mack called back, and Scarlett wolf-whistled. "Who knew you were such a babe under all those fancy suits?"

Edward blushed adorably, crossing his arms over his chest. Quite a few customers peered *extra* closely.

"Don't be embarrassed to be so handsome," I teased, holding up the stencil. "And this is what I came up with. What do you think?"

He took it from me with an admiring glance. "Perfect. Absolutely perfect. And it'll fit here, on my side?"

I lifted his arm, pressing the stencil to his ribs. "It looks great to me, but let me get it set, and then we'll look in the mirror."

I quietly worked, feeling the burn of my own new ink along my rib cage. A surprise.

"What do you think?" I asked, nodding toward the mirror. Edward lifted his arm. When his eyes met mine, they were predatory.

"Do it," he said, voice rough as sandpaper. I shivered at the command. Laid him on his side on the chair, arm lifted.

"If you need me to stop, just let me know," I said, stroking his skin. "And you're sure about this, right? Because if you're not—"

"Never been more sure in my life, love," he said, stretching up to give me a sloppy kiss. "And you know I don't mind a bit of pain."

Biting my lip, I shoved him down roughly. "Okay then," I said lightly. "Here we go."

It wasn't a large tattoo, so I was done in thirty minutes. And in that time, I was pulled into the texture of Edward's skin —all the minute perfections and imperfections. The feel of his breath beneath my fingers, his deep breathing. The way goosebumps worked their way from his hipbones to his chest. I chatted with him about his work day, kept him focused on my voice instead of the needle stabbing across his tender bones.

Tried to ignore his obvious erection, even as the thought of arousing Edward through this tattoo made me squeeze my thighs together, attempting to dull the ache.

"Stay right there while I wipe this," I said, stepping back to admire my handiwork. As I wiped away blood and black ink, the tattoo revealed itself in its crisp glory. My heart sped up at the message there, the meaning, my own feeling hot against my skin.

"Why don't you go look?" I said, motioning toward the mirror. Edward looked a bit dazed, common after a tattoo, but slowly sat up. Gave me a rueful look. Strode over half-naked to the mirror to see what was written there.

All Hail Queen Roxy.

Beneath the clean text was a simple crown.

"I love it," he said, eyes on mine in the mirror. He looked even more turned on than earlier, and I could feel my nipples hardening through my shirt.

He definitely noticed.

"Let me get this bandaged," I said, voice shaking. "So hold still." I spread an anti-bacterial cream across the ink, and he hissed in a breath. Placed a clean wrap and taped it to his skin.

"I have a surprise for you," I said, avoiding his gaze as I laid down my tattoo gun and materials. If I looked at Edward now, I'd drop to my knees in front of everyone in this tattoo parlor, let him use my mouth for whatever he needed.

"What's that, darling?" he asked, voice silky with desire.

Walking over to the mirror, I lifted up my tank-top, turning until my left ribcage faced the mirror. I had two larger pieces that intersected over my rib-cage: a vine of blood-red roses and a large anchor. But there was about eight inches of bare skin that I'd had Mack ink this morning.

All Hail King Edward.

It wasn't so much a conscious decision as a *compulsion* that sent Edward and I walking boldly into the back room and locking the door. My king had me up on the desk, stockings ripped in half, and his fingers between my legs in a second.

"You got that for me, darling?" Edward demanded, fingers stroking deep inside of me. Curling right against the spot that made my vision dance.

"*Yes*," I panted, legs around his waist, clutching at his bare shoulders. He was so handsome in just his suit pants, fingering me to orgasm in this back room with hundreds of people right outside. "I did it... this morning. Wanted us to have matching ones, *oh God*."

Edward tipped my face up so he could crush our lips together, stroking and teasing and building me to climax, the only sounds in the room my soft moans and his wet fingers sliding inside me.

"And why is that?" he commanded, unzipping his pants and taking out his cock. Gliding it along my clit as I hissed in pleasure.

"Because I love you," I said and was rewarded with a hard thrust of his length. So deep I saw galaxies. "Because I love you more than anything on this earth. And I want to... I want to..."

Edward was fucking me in slow, tantalizing thrusts, driving me wild. "What do you want, love? Tell me."

"Worship you," I gasped. "Like a king. My king."

"Oh, Roxy," he said, speeding up his movements. Shaking the table as he fucked me. "That's my job. To worship you as my queen. My beautiful, scowling, passionate, fierce queen."

"Pretty sure that's what you're doing right now," I managed to say before giving in to the sensation of Edward's cock moving inside me, the beauty of our bodies coming together. The electric heat that seemed to dance to life whenever we were in the same room together. I'd never wanted someone more. Laughed with someone more. Loved someone more than Edward.

My climax struck like a bolt of lightning, and Edward kept me quiet by kissing me senseless, swallowing my cries and murmuring '*I love you, I love you*' over and over. Until we were both spent, panting and laughing, in the tattoo parlor that had somehow unexpectedly brought us together. Intersected our destiny.

A queen and her king.

EPILOGUE

EDWARD

One year later

*J*t was nearing midnight as I walked toward Roxy's no-longer-dodgy tattoo parlor. Or rather, dodgy in a *nice* way. Her vintage sign blinked cheerfully as I neared the front, grinning at her glass storefront.

Roxy's: No Crying Allowed.

That was my girl.

Or my queen, rather, and I knew as I soon as I strode inside she'd sense my nervousness. The trepidation. My left pocket felt slightly heavier than my right, even though that couldn't technically be possible.

Roxy had closed the shop early so we could stage this sexy interlude, but for a moment, I simply watched her through the doorway. Engrossed in a sketch, music playing (it sounded like The Hand Grenades, but I couldn't be certain), white blonde hair falling long over one shoulder. I'd helped her re-shave the sides this morning, laughing in our bathroom, and there'd been something beautifully intimate about the entire thing.

Our bathroom, as in our *home*. A bright and airy apartment in Washington Heights with a large deck that overlooked the Hudson River. Quite frequently, Roxy and I ended our nights there: reclining on chairs, hands entwined, Matilda and Busy Bee curled up at our feet. Apple and Cucumber had quite taken to the new space, and the dogs had already destroyed half of it.

Roxy spent a lot of time trying to convince me to adopt a third dog from the shelter.

But I didn't need much convincing. I'd already called and asked if we could come by next week. There was an old, graying mutt named Lulu they'd found abandoned, in need of a good home to live out her remaining years peacefully.

I thought she'd get along beautifully with our little punk-rock-English family.

We were busy but not *too* busy. Happy busy. The Logan was slowly becoming the hotel of my dreams, and even though I felt a pang every time I walked past The Cartwright (which was every day), to sit at the helm of my own hotel and make decisions without fear of my parents destroying them was fucking *liberating*. Elliott and Dante had moved along to Belize but still had no plans to come home. Roxy and I video-chatted with them frequently, Elliott and I both expressing the sheer delight of finally living our lives out from under our parents' thumbs.

Roxy and I had had tea with my mother at the Club just a few weeks ago. She had worn her *Eat the Rich* blazer, but her stockings were hole-free. It was awkward, and stilted—we had an ocean of distrust and miscommunication to cross. It would take time, and it would never, ever be the kind of family I yearned for.

But Roxy did make my mother laugh—once—and that I considered a *win*.

And of course Roxy's shop was slowly, carefully re-gaining its footing. We'd spent the past year implementing every step of her business plan—fighting and fucking along the way—and Roxy discovered that she'd had the knowledge and the strength all along.

She even had a tiny wait-list now for her services.

Small steps.

But our lives were growing forward, growing together.

I pushed open the door finally, the bell chiming. Just like that night. The night we'd met.

"We're closed," Roxy smirked, eyes still on her sketch, but I could sense every part of her body aware of my eyes.

"Please don't be closed," I fake-sighed. She finally looked up, eyes bright with mischief.

"We're definitely closed. And you've got the wrong place anyway." She popped her hand on her luscious hips, and the hot, vibrant memory of that night—the night we were now role-playing—had me hard in a second. So hard I almost forgot the *real* reason I'd suggested we do this tonight.

"And why is that, love?" I taunted, strolling slowly her way. She was leaning way over her desk, ass in the air, breasts pushed together.

"Because the bank is that way," she purred. "Corporate asshole."

Roxy reached forward, wrapping her fingers in my tie, slowly pulling our lips together. No kiss, not yet, but I had to fight to remain focused. "I come from a long line of corporate assholes, actually."

"Is that so, Dilbert?" Her lips grazed mine.

I slid my hand into my pocket, anchoring myself. Allowed myself a brief, hard kiss of good luck and courage. Then I untangled her fingers from my tie. She pouted, but her eyes were bright with desire.

"Roxy," I started, and my voice was already shaking, "I don't just think about this night because we spent it having quite possibly the hottest sex anyone has ever had." I started walking around the desk toward her. She smiled at me, thankfully still oblivious.

"What else do you think about?" she asked.

"My world, ending," I said. "Walking toward your old, broken sign, I thought my world was shrinking. Growing smaller. Destroyed. That was also the four drinks talking," I said. "But without Emily, I wasn't getting married. And without marriage, I wasn't going to inherit The Cartwright. And without *that*, I had no idea who I was. Inside. I was a... a shell."

Roxy had stilled now, aware that this was outside of our role-playing script for the evening.

"But something else happened instead."

I dropped to one knee.

The ocean of feeling that moved across Roxy's face was extraordinary. A sea-burst of surprise and then a wave of joy.

"What was that?" she asked, voice starting to tremble.

"My world began," I said. "You, Roxy Ramone Quinn, showed me a different world that night—and it went beyond exploring the kinky sex we both enjoy. You showed me that my thoughts, my desires, my needs mattered. My life was *mine* to do with as I pleased. Not controlled by someone else."

I took her hand, rubbing my thumb over her left ring finger.

"And the first thing I discovered that I truly wanted, truly *needed*... was you." I swallowed hard. "Roxy, the day I walked into that classroom and saw you there—" my voice broke slightly, but I regained control. "Darling, it just made sense to me. *Of course* we'd be brought back together. Because we're meant to be, you and I."

"Soul mates," Roxy said, and two glistening tears streaked down her cheek.

"Soul mates," I repeated, her hand pressing against my face. I nuzzled against it briefly. "And I have spent the last year continuing to fall deeply in love with you, Roxy. My queen. My *everything*. I want to spend the rest of our lives together surrounded by dogs and cats and babies and tattoos."

Roxy was truly crying now, so beautiful I willed myself to imprint this memory on my brain. To remember the night our love fused together, becoming greater and more magnificent than we'd ever imagined.

A king and his queen.

I reached into my pocket and took out the small black box. Popped it open to reveal a white ring with a skull etched into it, rubies for its eyes. It matched Roxy's aesthetic perfectly.

Roxy laughed and cried when she saw it.

"Roxy Ramone Quinn," I said, taking her hand. "Will you do me the honor of becoming my wife?"

"Fuck *yes*," she cheered before launching herself at me, knocking us both to the ground. I wasn't even able to slide the engagement ring onto her finger until an hour later after she'd torn off her clothes. Torn off my suit. And made sweet, passionate love to me on the floor of her not-so-dodgy tattoo parlor.

And later, just like I'd originally wanted to, on that serendipitous night of our meeting, I *did* take Roxy out for breakfast at the diner down the street. And we spent the morning enraptured with each other, discussing wedding plans and engagement parties and bickering mildly over whether Matilda or Busy Bee would be the ring-bearer.

Roxy, my queen. My punk-rock goddess. My future wife.

The woman who set me free.

And my world became even brighter.

BONUS EPILOGUE

ROXY

Amelia Elizabeth Quinn-Cavendish was ready to take her first steps.

Our boisterous, silly, headstrong baby girl had been trying for *weeks* with Edward and I rooting for her like cheerleaders at a football game. Even Matilda and Busy Bee, both gray and dignified in their older age, perked up to watch their human sibling closely.

"It's time," I'd said into the phone, calling Edward as he was wrapping up a board meeting.

"You're sure?" he'd said, voice tight with excitement. "How do you know?"

"Well she just looked at me and said *I'm ready to fucking walk now, Mom.* It was incredible."

There was a scuffle, and I imagined him heading into the corner of the room. "That mouth is going to get you into trouble one of these days, Roxy darling." His English accent couldn't suppress the sex and longing inherent in that promise.

I smirked. "Do you have any ideas for that, Mr. Cavendish?"

"I might," he said. "But first let me make up an excuse to leave... oh wait, I'm in charge of this bloody hotel." Another scuffle. Then, I heard him say, "Right, so my amazing daughter is about to achieve walking greatness any moment. I'm off to see it, so don't call me unless the entire building is burning down, yeah?" Another scuffle and then: "Get the video camera ready, love. I'll be home soon."

For the next twenty minutes, I was stuck thwarting my daughter's attempts to put one foot in front of the other. Every time she stood up, I'd scoop her into my arms and distract her with Cheerios, trying to remember that only nine months earlier a slightly harried doctor had placed Amelia in my arms as I wept from happiness against Edward's shoulder.

My parents had brought her a onesie that said *Baby Anarchist* and a mix-tape of punk songs they swore used to put me to sleep as a baby. Mack, Rita, and Scarlett had stayed for hours, cracking jokes and filling the room with inappropriate balloons. Elliott and Dante had rushed in, jet-lagged, and I'd cried again when Elliott and Edward hugged each other for a long, long time.

Even Rebecca and Edward Cavendish, resplendent in furs, had managed to fly to New York City, declaring their grand-daughter to be "quite presentable."

For the past nine months, the busy, happy life Edward and I had created with each other was rocked to its core in the best way. I'd thought I'd known intimacy with Edward, but I discovered that stepping out of my first shower in ten days to find my infant daughter fast asleep on the bare chest of my handsome husband (also asleep) was like nothing I'd ever known.

And now, Amelia was ready to walk.

"I gave my cab driver the express directions to drive like he was an extra in those god-awful *Fast and the Furious* movies and we *might* have run over some things, but I feel like it was the right decision." Edward said as he burst through the door, shedding his tie and jacket, dropping to one knee to hug Matilda. Her tail thumped against the floor.

"Absolutely," I agreed. "This is *Amelia*. The World's Greatest Baby. How could you miss her first steps?"

"Never, my darling," he said, grabbing my face and giving me quite the passionate kiss for two sleep-deprived parents. He picked up Amelia from my arms, dancing her about as she laughed.

"Now let's see what you got," he said, dropping gracefully to the floor as she wiggled her tiny, fat legs.

"If she walks today," I said, sitting cross-legged on the floor a few feet from them. "I'm buying her baby combat boots. Immediately."

"I like this plan," he agreed. Edward held her arms out as her legs found the floor. "Now walk to Mommy, my sweets."

I smiled, eyes meeting Edward's, and a million memories hung between us. To go from that singular evening, when he'd drunkenly stumbled into my shop, to *now* seemed almost... impossible.

"Oh fuck!" I said, standing suddenly. "The video camera. Wait, wait..." I trailed off, running for the device we'd used non-stop since she was born. Edward was murmuring to our daughter, something like "your mother grew up using the word *fuck* as a child, and she turned out... quasi-normal. So I'm sure you will as well."

"I'll have her in the mosh pit by ten," I called over my shoulder, setting up the camera. Edward and Amelia came into frame as Matilda and Busy Bee watched on.

"Okay," I said, scurrying back to my seat. I leaned forward, kissing Amelia. Kissing Edward. Unable to stop the contagious joy of this moment. "I'm ready."

Amelia gave us a look that could only be translated as *I've been ready this whole goddamn time.* And then, with barely a tremble, my daughter took her first full steps from Edward's arms into mine.

"That's my *girl*," I squealed, wrapping her in a hug as she giggled against my chest. She was proud of herself. And when I looked up at Edward, his eyes were shining.

"I think that might have been the most astonishing thing I've ever seen, love," he said softly, hand over his heart. I nodded, throat tight, and then I turned Amelia around and watched her take three more confident steps toward her father.

Again and again she did it, the three of us laughing, until Amelia finally fell asleep against Edward's chest, snoring softly.

An hour later and Edward gently pulled me toward our giant shower, letting me sigh against his body as the hot water steamed around us. Washed my hair, untangling the strands. Washed every inch of my body, fingers everywhere. Dropped to his knees and lazily explored my pussy with his tongue before fucking me with finesse against the shower wall. I climaxed in slow, rolling waves as Edward trembled with his orgasm, and I made a mental note to remember *this day*. A day of sun and light and joy—the steps of our daughter, her bright laughter. Edward's fingers in my hair and my legs around his waist. A day of momentous feeling.

Our life, together.

A NOTE FROM THE AUTHOR

The week of Thanksgiving 2017 my husband and I were five months into our epic road trip across the country, staying with some family outside of Houston. Everyone else was asleep (I'm an early morning writer) but I had an idea for a Sexy Short – these short pieces of erotica I write for my Facebook group, The Hippie Chicks.

I have the notebook page in front of me right now. I'd written: "suited-up corporate guy comes in for a tattoo and he's heart-broken. Roxy, tattoo artist, tells him he's not her type."

And thus...the beginning of The Suit, which was originally conceived of as a one-off Sexy Short but ended up being a weekly serial I posted in my group until January. Edward, the corporate guy, and Roxy, the scowling tattoo artist, were flirtatious, chatty, teasing, interesting and supremely sexy. Their story ended, sort of, but Edward and Roxy continued to talk to me, pull at me, whisper all of their hopes, dreams and fears in my ear.

They needed a book – a *full* novel – and that is STRICTLY PROFESSIONAL. Writing Edward and Roxy's full story felt like a fever dream to me, with every scene a beautiful discovery of who they *really* are. More than archetypes – real people. Their love story is one of the steamiest I've ever written (prepare yourselves) but also the most tender.

Enjoy Edward and Roxy – I hope they steal your heart like they stole mine.

~Kathryn

ACKNOWLEDGMENTS

An abundance of gratitude goes out to the amazing support system that makes every single book possible – including Edward and Roxy's story.

For Faith: my best friend, roommate, Editor Extraordinaire, beta-reader, soon-to-be-famous author. Let's never stop writing or being best friends, ever.

For Jodi, Julia, Lucy and Lynsey, who shaped this story with their finely-honed beta reading skills and enthusiasm. This book would not be the same without your notes, suggestions, ideas and feedback.

Always for Joyce, Julia and Jodi, who (among many other things), help me every day, in so many ways, with their hard work, humor, support and friendship. Best admins around, I swear.

For Tammy, who might love Edward even more than I do! And who's cheerleading of this book was deeply appreciated. Also superior graphic-making skills...

For Bronwyn, who did not necessarily have a specific role in this book-writing process, but who made me laugh every day and *that* made this process even more joyful.

THE HIPPIE CHICKS: the original Suit-lovers! You've been along for this ride since November, so I thank you sincerely. Your love for Edward and Roxy makes my heart so happy!

And finally for Rob: thank you for being my real life romance novel hero.

HANG OUT WITH KATHRYN!

Sign up for my newsletter and receive exclusive content, bonus scenes and more!

I've got a reader group on Facebook called **Kathryn Nolan's Hippie Chicks.** We're all about motivation, girl power, sexy short stories and empowerment! Come join us.

Let's be friends on
Website: authorkathrynnolan.com
Instagram at: kathrynnolanromance
Facebook at: KatNolanRomance
Follow me on BookBub
Follow me on Amazon

ABOUT KATHRYN

I'm an adventurous hippie chick that loves to write steamy romance. My specialty is slow-burn sexual tension with plenty of witty dialogue and tons of heart.

I started my writing career in elementary school, writing about *Star Wars* and *Harry Potter* and inventing love stories in my journals. And I blame my obsession with slow-burn on my similar obsession for The *X-Files*.

I'm a born-and-raised Philly girl, but left for Northern California right after college, where I met my adorably-bearded husband. After living there for eight years, we decided to embark on an epic, six-month road trip, traveling across the country with our little van, Van Morrison. Eighteen states and 17,000 miles later, we're back in my hometown of Philadelphia for a bit... but I know the next adventure is just around the corner.

When I'm not spending the (early) mornings writing steamy love scenes with a strong cup of coffee, you can find me outdoors -- hiking, camping, traveling, yoga-ing.

BOOKS BY KATHRYN

BOHEMIAN

LANDSLIDE

RIPTIDE

STRICTLY PROFESSIONAL

NOT THE MARRYING KIND

SEXY SHORTS

BEHIND THE VEIL

UNDER THE ROSE

IN THE CLEAR

WILD OPEN HEARTS